DYING
of the
LIGHT

Joe Regenbogen

ARS METAPHYSICA

an imprint of Sunbury Press, Inc.
Mechanicsburg, PA USA

ARS METAPHYSICA

an imprint of Sunbury Press, Inc.
Mechanicsburg, PA USA

For information about special discounts for bulk purchases, please contact Sunbury Press Orders Dept. at (855) 338-8359 or orders@sunburypress.com.

To request one of our authors for speaking engagements or book signings, please contact Sunbury Press Publicity Dept. at publicity@sunburypress.com.

FIRST ARS METAPHYSICA EDITION: December 2023

Set in Adobe Garamond | Interior design by Crystal Devine | Cover by Lawrence Knorr | Edited by Lawrence Knorr.

Publisher's Cataloging-in-Publication Data
Names: Regenbogen, Joe, author.
Title: Dying of the light / Joe Regenbogen.
Description: First trade paperback edition. | Mechanicsburg, PA : Ars Metaphysica, 2023.
Summary: When his wife of forty years passes away, Ethan realizes he has lost the guiding light of his life. He is also haunted by the specter of a decision he made years earlier. During a road trip to the West Coast, Ethan learns about the opportunity to right this wrong and, at the same time, find the redemption that will enable him to rage against the dying of the light.
Identifiers: ISBN : 979-8-88819-175-0 (paperback).
Subjects: FICTION / Family Life / Marriage & Divorce | FICTION / Friendship | FICTION / Crime | FICTION / Legal.

Product of the United States of America
0 1 1 2 3 5 8 13 21 34 55

For the Love of Books!

To Ava and Delaney, who have made it fun to grow old.

Do not go gentle into that
good night,
Old age should burn and rave
at close of day;
Rage, rage against the dying
of the light.

—Dylan Thomas

PART I

chapter

1

Ethan Marshall gazed hypnotically into the distance. Then, finally, a gust of cold air broke the spell, bringing him back to a state of consciousness he would have preferred to avoid. A curtain of gray was draped over the lake's icy surface like the backdrop of a stage, with misty clouds shrouding the horizon. The lengthening shadows over Creve Coeur Lake this late Sunday afternoon perfectly matched his current state of mind.

Ethan arose from his perch on the park bench and strolled towards the bronzed sand of the beach. He shook his head at the thought of calling this stretch of sand in a suburban county park a beach, but Ethan knew this had been one of Sarah's favorite places. Except for those burly winter days that forced even the hardiest of souls in St. Louis to remain indoors, Sarah could be seen marching on the path around the lake every morning. It had become more than exercise. He knew this was where his wife started each day, organizing her schedule and meditating on her good fortune.

Ethan stood at the water's edge, where the pulse of waves lapped at his feet. He was wearing the galoshes Sarah had bought him for those snowy days when he walked to his law office on a busy stretch of Olive Boulevard that served as a feeble excuse for Creve Coeur's downtown. Ethan had worn them today so he could later step far enough into the gentle surf to empty her remains from the urn.

Ethan had purposefully arrived early to gather his thoughts. The setup had been simple. He wanted to keep the ceremony brief since it was a chilly, overcast day in mid-April. Ethan didn't bother to set up any chairs, planning instead to use the tables inside the nearby picnic shelter. He placed the small urn in the middle of one of those tables.

Ethan thought about the biblical quote, "All are from the dust, and dust all return." He had never been religious but, for some reason, was familiar with this line from Ecclesiastes. Never had it made more sense than today. So strange that one moment, Sarah was lying in their bed, feebly attempting to laugh at one of his lame jokes, and a week later, her remains would vanish into the depths of this small lake.

Images flashed through Ethan's mind as though arranged on a time-line. He could visualize pictures of Sarah as an infant standing in her crib, as a young girl on her first day of kindergarten, as a teenager posing next to her prom date, and as a bride at their wedding that had taken place more than forty years ago. Always the same alluring smile. Sarah had been Ethan's rock, never changing, always providing a sturdy foundation. Ethan could sometimes be moody, wavering between kinetic energy and bleak sullenness. But Sarah was always there with patience and compassion to smooth out his ups and downs.

Even after her leukemia diagnosis six months earlier, Sarah had been unflappable. Since entering her sixties, a few crow's feet had sprung around her soft brown eyes, and some gray had invaded her dark hair, but her smile never quit. When he closed his eyes, Ethan could see additional images of his wife. There were pictures of her driving on their first road trip out West, cutting the cake at their children's birthday parties, riding the donkey from the cruise ship up to the heights of Santorini, and attending their kid's graduation ceremonies from college. Visions of Sarah's progression from infancy to becoming the matriarchal centerpiece of their family sailed through Ethan's mind, flowing together like a biographical film.

Twenty minutes later, Ethan was part of a flock of about twenty people congregating inside the shelter. In addition to a few close friends, Ethan's son and daughter, Noah and Jenny, had attended with their spouses. Jenny's apartment was in Kirkwood, another community that formed part of the suburban quilt encircling St. Louis, but Noah and his wife had flown in from Portland, Oregon.

Noah took the lead, calling everyone to gather around the table with the urn. He said Sarah's wish was that this ceremony be kept short, simple, and informal. Therefore, he requested that anyone who could share stories about his mother. After a brief moment of awkward silence, several hands simultaneously rocketed into the air.

A couple of friends spoke first, reminiscing how they met in a play-group when their children were young. Next, a childhood friend returned to stories from their idyllic days in elementary school. Then Jenny's tale about her mother's uncontrollable bawling at her wedding put smiles and tears on several faces. Noah then related how his mother behaved similarly at the start of his medical school graduation. The common thread running through each story was Sarah's uncommon compassion.

After everyone who wanted to speak had had their turn, Noah pivoted to his dad. Ethan stood, cleared his throat, and glanced at the attentive faces. He had been married to Sarah for over four decades. They were only 22 when they exchanged vows, so there were unlimited memories, anecdotes, and reflections from which to choose. However, now that the time had come, none would effectually communicate what he wanted to say. Instead, Ethan hoped inspiration would come to him, and the words would naturally flow. This approach usually worked during the informal negotiations of his daily job.

Ethan also did not consider the swirl of emotions he would feel at this moment. He froze. He glanced over the heads of his audience at the trickle dripping down the modest waterfall. Ethan thought about the legend of the Indian maiden who had supposedly leaped to her death at this spot when a French fur trapper had not returned her love, thereby changing the shape of the lake into a broken heart, a Crevecoeur. He frantically tried to refocus on those images from Sarah's life, but there were still no words. Ethan had spent a career arguing cases in court, but he was speechless for the first time in his life.

The silence dragged on until some of his listeners began exchanging worried glances. Ethan clenched his lips together and inhaled an enormous breath. Then, after a moment that seemed more like an hour, he shook his head and stared down at the urn. Ethan looked up one more time with moist eyes.

Noah and Jenny finally jumped to his rescue. They each stood to embrace him, forming a small huddle. Finally, Ethan gently broke away and stepped towards the urn. Picking it up, he glanced at his children, who both nodded. Ethan pulled off the urn's lid and drew out a clear plastic bag filled with their mother's remains. Flanked by Noah and Jenny on each side, they walked towards the shoreline, followed solemnly by the small crowd. Ethan entered the shallow surf and slowly emptied the gray contents of the bag.

Shortly afterward, the assembly broke up to return to the warmth of Ethan's ranch-style home a few miles away. Refreshments were waiting to help lighten the mood. Jenny left with the first group to play host, and Noah was among the last to depart. Looking around, he realized his father was still sitting alone on a bench. Noah ambled over and sat next to his dad.

"Can I join you?"

Ethan nodded but continued to gaze at the far shore of the lake.

"That was pretty rough, huh?" Noah waited for a response, but none was forthcoming.

"Dad, Jenny and I have been talking some things over." Noah paused, but when Ethan continued his silent vigil, he continued with remarks that had obviously been prepared.

"Look, Dad, we understand your marriage to Mom was *really* special. I mean, in many ways, she was your whole life."

Ethan glanced at his son but then returned his attention to the lake.

"To be frank, we're a little worried about you. Amy and I have a flight back to Portland tonight, and Jenny needs to get back to work tomorrow. We know you've scheduled some time off, but what are you planning to do with your time?"

Ethan let out a massive sigh and then turned to face his son.

"I appreciate your concern, Noah, but I'll be alright. I'm a big boy."

"We know, Dad, but this isn't a good time for you to be alone. That's why Jenny and I think you should take off even more time and come out to Portland for a while."

"What about *your* work?"

"I've got some vacation time built up. Amy often complains that I'm married to the hospital, so if you come out, maybe the three of us can enjoy some downtime. There's a lot we can do. How about some backpacking around Mount Hood? Or maybe we can spend some time down at the coast? It could be like one of those trips we used to take out West when I was a kid."

For a brief moment, a slight smile cracked Ethan's stone expression. Then, as he pivoted to return his gaze westward across the lake, he noticed the setting sun had escaped from beneath a steely stratus cloud. Framed by an iridescent orange glow, the western sky almost seemed an omen. Staring intently at the glowing horizon, Ethan mumbled, "I'll think about it." Then, turning again to face his son, he added, "Either way, it's a sweet offer."

Noah waited to see if there was any more to the answer. Then, after a few seconds of silence, he stood.

"That sounds good, Dad. Should we get going?" He offered his hand to help his father up.

Ethan looked at Noah's hand but didn't rise. Upon hearing the slamming of a car door, he instinctively turned back toward the parking lot and saw that Helen, one of Sarah's close friends, had just entered her aging Toyota.

Ignoring the noise behind them, Noah asked, "Dad? You okay?"

Ethan forced a smile. "I just need a few minutes. You go on ahead. In fact, why don't you leave me the car and catch a ride with Helen? I'll be home in a little while."

Noah thought briefly about challenging the idea but decided to give his dad a little privacy might be better. Besides, he could not think of anything else to say. So Noah turned towards the parking lot, waved to Helen, who had just started the engine and jogged over to the passenger side of her blue Corolla. He disappeared inside the car, and they promptly drove off. Ethan was now completely alone.

He remained on the bench for almost an hour, impervious to the bone-chilling breeze. Then, finally, since no one was left in the park to bear witness, he buried his face in his palms, thinking this would be an excellent time to let the tears flow. He felt like a volcano had been churning inside for a long time. Maybe this was the time to let it explode.

There was nothing. Tears simply wouldn't flow. Ethan hoped a cathartic cry would release some of the demons, enabling him to feel a little better, the same way heaving brings relief to a roiling stomach. After finally acknowledging you cannot force a "good cry," Ethan decided to take instead this opportunity to clear his mind and think.

There was an obvious question—What comes next? What would life be like in a world without Sarah? But, try as hard as he could, there was no answer. It was like peering into a tunnel and seeing nothing but darkness. Ethan was confident he could care for himself since he had looked after Sarah for the last several months. He had grown comfortable doing the laundry, shopping, cooking, cleaning, and other household chores.

Ethan also had confidence he could continue with his legal practice. He and a partner had built a small firm based primarily on criminal defense work. Over the years, it had generated a comfortable income despite Ethan's pro-bono work on the side. There was no question Ethan *could* continue his life without Sarah from one day to the next. The question boiled down to *why*? Why should he want to climb out of bed every morning?

Ethan tried to visualize what life would be like in the future. It was easier if he focused on a single day, from reading the morning newspaper to watching the 10 o'clock news. The problem was trying to bring focus to the bigger picture. What would his life look like in five years? Would he be retired? Would he be a grandfather? Could someone else step into his life to replace Sarah?

After practicing law for almost four decades, Ethan had to admit the work had grown stale. But how would he fill his time if he retired? And his family? Both kids were married and might soon have children of their own, but as much as he hated to admit it, the thought of grandkids did not hold much appeal. He had relished being a father, but reliving this experience would be like watching a terrific film for the second time. Besides, he and Sarah had purposefully raised Noah and Jenny to be self-sufficient; now that they were, neither seemed to need him.

As for a second wife, Ethan grew queasy just thinking about it. Sarah had been his one true companion, and no one could ever replace her. Ethan and Sarah both understood that what they had was extremely rare.

Most people fall in love, but it does not last for many. The marriages that survive often do so only because both people learn to tolerate each other. Ethan and Sarah knew their relationship was different. They had instantly become best friends and, from the start, spent every free moment together. For more than forty years, Ethan began every day marveling at his good fortune in meeting Sarah.

Ethan noticed how the remaining shadows had vaporized when the sun dipped below the skyline. It was getting colder, and soon it would be completely dark. Ethan could spend all evening on this bench and probably never come up with a good answer to his question. His best days were behind him, and anything coming in the future would be anticlimactic. For now, though, it was time to go home.

When Ethan turned onto his street, he immediately saw a couple of cars parked in his driveway, so he pulled up alongside the curb in front of a neighbor's house. The road was dark, so the street lights had come on. When Ethan entered the front foyer, most guests were putting on their coats and preparing to leave. He nodded and forced some doleful smiles at their final expressions of condolence, but it was clear he did not want to make conversation.

Noah and his wife, Amy, were the next to depart. They each fervently hugged Ethan and exchanged worried expressions on their way through the front door. Since their flight back to Portland left in a couple of hours, they did not have the luxury of huddling with the family any longer to grieve and console. As he walked onto the front porch, Noah reminded Ethan about the idea of coming to Portland.

Once they drove off, Jenny and her husband, Matt, were the only ones left standing with Ethan on the front porch. Jenny shivered a little. Seeing this, Matt threw an arm around her.

"Dad, should we hang around?"

"No," Ethan replied. "I'm really beat." Then, seeing the concern on their faces, he added, "You don't need to worry; I'll be okay. It's been a long day, and you guys have work tomorrow. So you should grab your coats and get going." With another forced smile, he accented the final point and gently nudged Jenny toward the open door.

Once inside, Jenny grabbed her handbag and placed it on the couch while Matt helped with her jacket. After he zipped up his coat, the young couple turned to face each other and simultaneously sighed. Each knew what the other was thinking. Stepping back onto the porch, Jenny swiveled around to face her father.

"You sure, Dad? You know, we were all worried when you stayed so long at the lake." She paused and glanced over at Matt. Then she added, "Frankly, we're still a little worried. But, you know, maybe we could spend the night? We could sleep in my old room. Maybe make it a little pajama party or something?"

"*No*, don't be silly. You guys both have work tomorrow. But, as I said, I'll be *fine*."

Jenny knew how stubborn her dad could be, especially when she saw this determined expression on his face. She turned around and began to walk with Matt toward the driveway. After she had taken a few steps, Ethan called to her.

"Hey, thanks again for playing host this evening." Jenny turned and smiled to acknowledge her father's gratitude.

"And guys," After a pause, Ethan added, "I love you."

"Love you too, Dad. We'll give you a call tomorrow."

Ethan stood on the front porch momentarily and watched as Jenny and Matt pulled out of the driveway and drove off. Then, he calmly strode with a steady deliberation to the street where he had parked his car. Wearing a placid expression, Ethan climbed into the SUV, pressed the ignition button, touched another bar on a remote to open the garage door, and then smoothly glided into his usual spot.

Once inside the garage, Ethan pressed the bar on the remote again to close the automated door. Finally, with the same serene smile, like that of the Mona Lisa, and with the engine still running, Ethan put the car into park, reclined back in his seat, and closed his eyes.

chapter

2

Jenny instinctively knew something was missing. She always kept her purse on the floor between her legs when she rode in the front passenger seat of a car. But, of course, recent events had thrown off her equilibrium. Having no memory of placing her handbag in its usual place, she squeezed her feet together in the darkness and came up empty.

"Shit!" she uttered.

"Forget something?" Matt replied. He recognized the irritation in her voice.

"My purse. We need to go back to my parents' house. It's only been a few minutes. I'm sure Dad's still awake."

Without uttering another word, Matt veered right and cut hard to the left to make a tight U-turn. Two minutes later, he pulled into the driveway in front of his in-laws' house.

"You wait here," Jenny said, "I'll be back in a minute."

She jumped out of the car and jogged up the front porch. As she approached the door, Jenny realized the key to her parent's house was in her purse. She hoped to quietly let herself in, grab the bag, and head out without disturbing her dad, but now she would probably have to ring the doorbell. Checking the doorknob, though, she was pleasantly surprised when it turned.

Lights were still on throughout the house, but everything was eerily quiet. Her purse was still on the couch, where she had left it. Jenny grabbed the handbag and spun around to go, thinking she had accomplished her mission without disturbing her father. Then she froze. Something was not right.

"Dad?"

After hearing no reply, she called out again. "Dad? Are you okay?"

The silence was unnerving. Jenny felt like she had stepped into a horror film. Nevertheless, she rapidly began to explore the house, continuing to call out to her father. The quiet slowly gave way to a low humming noise when she entered the kitchen. What was that sound? As she crossed through the kitchen, the droning grew louder.

The garage! It was coming from inside the garage. The unmistakable smell of exhaust fumes greeted her when Jenny opened the door. The garage was dark except for the illumination from the kitchen light behind her. Jenny reached over and slammed hard on the garage door button. Immediately, a light above the cars flickered on, and the bulky door began to rumble open. The engine of her father's SUV was running. Had he forgotten to turn off the ignition?

As Jenny circled her mom's Honda Accord, the driver's door of her father's SUV suddenly flung open. The growling noise and the light had revived Ethan, who stumbled out of the vehicle, evincing a confused look. For a moment, father and daughter gaped at each other. Ethan had fallen asleep and needed a few seconds to recall why he was standing next to his car in the garage. On the other hand, though, Jenny figured it out immediately.

"Dad! Dad, what are you *doing*?"

Matt darted past her before she could say more, grabbed Ethan's shoulders, and yanked him out to the driveway. Then, after checking to see if he was fully conscious, Matt sprinted back into the garage, stepped into Ethan's car, and shut off the engine. Finally, he gently nudged his wife, now in a state of paralysis, out of the garage and towards her father. The two stood like zombies beside Matt's black Mazda in the driveway.

Finally, regaining her composure, Jenny angled toward her husband and whispered, "Matt, should we call 911?"

"No, please don't do that," Ethan muttered. "I'm fine. *Really*, it's not necessary."

Matt and Jenny exchanged anxious glances. Before either could respond, Ethan continued, "Let's go inside. We need to talk."

Matt and Jenny filed in behind Ethan. As they passed through the garage and the kitchen, Ethan looked over his shoulder and added, "We'll leave the garage door open to air things out."

When the threesome arrived in the den, Matt and Jenny sat on the couch directly across from Ethan, who tumbled into his favorite leather recliner. For a moment, the only sound was the ticking clock on the fireplace mantel. Then, finally, Jenny ended the silence.

"Are you sure we shouldn't take you to the hospital, Dad?"

"No," Ethan responded, "that'd be a waste of time." Then he added, "I was only asleep for a minute or two. I guess the fumes hadn't made it into the car yet." Then, seeing lingering doubt on their faces, Ethan added, "Let's put it this way: When I woke up, I wasn't even coughing, was I?"

"That's true," Matt answered. Then, spinning toward Jenny, he inquired, "So, what do you want to do?" Although Matt did not speak the words, his tone conveyed, "It's your call; he's your father."

For a minute, Jenny gazed at the ticking clock like it was about to explode. Matt understood this behavior. To others, it might appear someone hypnotized his wife, but Matt could almost see the wheels spinning inside her brain. Jenny was constructing a plan.

"I think," Jenny stated, speaking slowly and choosing her words carefully, "We should all stay up for a while and talk about what just happened. And then," Jenny added, turning toward Matt, "You should go home and get some sleep. I want to spend the night here. In the morning, I'll call in sick."

Matt slowly nodded in agreement. Ethan grimaced and then, after a moment, responded, "Under the circumstances, Jenny, I understand why you'd want to spend the night."

"Okay," Jenny replied, "Then if that's settled, let's cut right to the chase. Dad, we all know you're depressed about Mom, but how do you think she'd feel about what you just tried to do?"

"She wouldn't be happy," Ethan answered hesitantly. "But she's not here anymore. That's the whole point. And frankly, I'm not sure how well she would've held up if I'd gone before her."

"So you mean to say," Jenny argued, "That you have *no* reason to go on without Mom?"

This time, Ethan paused. He glanced out the sliding glass door leading to a darkened deck. Finally, Ethan leaned forward, rested his forearms on his thighs, and firmly locked his fingers together.

"Look, Sweetheart, your mom and I raised you and your brother to be independent, and I think we succeeded, don't you?" Not waiting for a reply, Ethan continued. "You guys have to live your own lives. You don't need me getting in the way. Believe it or not, I gave this decision a lot of thought. It wasn't as rash as it probably appeared."

Ethan looked up from his clenched hands and stared directly into his daughter's eyes. He swallowed hard before continuing.

"Look, I knew it would be tough for you and your brother to lose both parents so close together, but eventually, you would get over it and could get on with the rest of your lives."

"That is *so* untrue," Jenny countered. "Every word you just said is bullshit. Noah and I would not "'get over it.'" She paused to regain her bearing. "There was no way to avoid Mom's death. It's still going to take a long time to come to terms with why leukemia took her at such a young age, but at least we never felt like she was *deserting* us."

Ethan leaned back in his recliner, clasped his hands behind his head, and loudly exhaled. He had to acknowledge that Jenny had made a good point. For a moment, he wondered if she had ever regretted leaving law school to pursue a career in education.

"Okay, Jenny, I get it," responded Ethan. "I know suicide's a selfish act. But I'd convinced myself that whatever pain I caused you and Noah would be far less than what I felt."

Moisture gathered around Ethan's eyes. He grabbed a Kleenex, blew his nose, and then continued.

"Jenny, you asked if I had a reason to go on without Mom. The short answer is, *no*, I don't. I've already experienced my best years in the courtroom. You and Noah will be okay without me, and I just didn't want to face an empty house at the end of the day."

Ethan observed how Jenny and Matt simultaneously raised their eyebrows in alarm at hearing this last statement. Still, he smiled slightly at the thought that their marriage was so reminiscent of his own. Then, he cleared his throat and continued.

"Look, you two have an amazing relationship, but you haven't been married long enough to fully appreciate what your mom meant to me."

Jenny glanced at Matt and grinned. Ethan noticed how he subtly winked back at her.

"Then *tell* us, Dad." Sensing it might help if her father openly talked about her mother, Jenny asked a more pointed question. "How did it start? Tell us about your first date with Mom."

She looked over at Matt again, and he nodded his approval. If nothing else, Jenny figured this tact would help settle things down. Ethan inhaled deeply, wiped his nose with a tissue, and clenched his hands together. As he stared down at his lap, a smile puckered his face.

"You know," Ethan said while glancing up, "I'm going to make a bold statement."

"Yeah?" replied Matt.

"*Yeah*. My first date with Sarah was arguably one of the most romantic of all time."

"Then we've got to hear this," Jenny responded, once again smiling at Matt.

Sarah and I met during our senior year at Washington University while volunteering at the ACLU. The director had asked us to do some background research on a community in danger of exploding. Since we had been burying our heads in file cabinets for the last several weeks, we both welcomed the chance to do something different. In addition, we felt honored to help with a case that could have national implications.

The American Nazi Party in Chicago had just won a case before the Supreme Court, giving them the right to protest in the predominantly Jewish suburb of Skokie. Although this was controversial, ACLU lawyers had defended the Nazis' First Amendment rights. So when a group of thugs in the North County suburb of Breckenridge Hills wanted to parade their swastikas here in St. Louis, it began to look like chapter two of the Chicago freakshow. Sarah and I agreed the ACLU had been right to defend the Nazis, but we'd hoped those idiots would disappear once they had proven they had the right to march.

Our task was simple. The director wanted us to spend time in Breckinridge Hills to understand the political climate better. You know, I guess it was a little undercover work. For safety reasons, she wanted two people going in together. The director told us to pretend to be a young couple recently moving into a local apartment complex. We were to shop in the stores, get haircuts at barbershops and beauty salons, and hang out in local taverns. Years later, we've often wondered if the director was trying to play matchmaker when she sent us on this mission. She claimed credit for this at our wedding reception, but who knows if she was kidding.

As it turned out, the expedition into this mostly blue-collar community became our first date. Breckenridge Hills at the time was populated mainly by Whites attempting to resist integration from African Americans moving in from the north side of St. Louis. Its main drag was a busy thoroughfare called St. Charles Rock Road, lined with fast food outlets, car dealerships, and mom-and-pop businesses. It was not exactly an area where the tourists tended to flock when visiting St. Louis.

Our day started with lunch at Taco Bell, followed by haircuts and local shopping. Sarah and I didn't pay much attention to each other for the first few hours since we mostly tried to engage others in conversation. After leaving each site, we scribbled down some notes of what we had just learned.

We quickly discovered that the best word to describe the political culture in Breckenridge Hills was apathy. Most of these people did not care if a band of Nazis paraded up their streets. There would never be an ordinance keeping them out as there had been in Skokie. This news made our director happy since if there were no local laws to challenge in court, there would be no publicity spotlighting our local fascists.

Sarah and I decided to cap off our day by having dinner at a local dive called OT's Bar and Tavern, also on St. Charles Rock Road. There was a parking lot badly needing asphalt in front of the crumbling facade, but the inside was surprisingly charming. A string of green lamps illuminated a bar on one side of the room. Pool tables dominated the middle, and to the left was a dining section where each table sported a red plaid tablecloth.

Since the dive was empty when we first entered, we grabbed a table in the corner and began to look through our notes from the day. While

I worked on an outline summarizing the main points, Sarah went up to the bar, turned on the charm, and engaged the bartender in a lively conversation. This plan worked to perfection. Bartenders are a wealth of knowledge if you want to learn local gossip, and this aging hippie was no exception. Your mom could hardly keep up with his banter once he began talking about the community.

After a while, Sarah and I decided to take a break. We ordered a pitcher of beer and a couple of burgers. A few other diners entered and were seated on the other side of the room, but the bar remained empty. Seeing a chance to work a bit of romantic magic, or maybe just out of boredom, the bartender switched the radio station from Country to a more mellow Rock and Roll, lowered the lights, and then placed a lit candle on our table. Standing behind Sarah, he smiled in my direction and even gave me a thumbs-up.

Looking to rotate the conversation away from the racial climate in Breckenridge Hills, I commented to Sarah that the two of us made an exceptional team. A gorgeous smile, highlighted by the candle's dancing flame, erupted across her face. Sarah was *stunning*. Her long dark hair curled around her shoulders and big brown eyes reminded me of a young Shirley Temple or an older Natalie Wood. I had a little crush on Sarah from the moment we first met, but when she flashed that smile at me that night in OTs, of all places, I fell hopelessly in love.

Sarah and I shared our life stories and talked about our favorite books, music, and movies for the next two hours. It was amazing how similar our tastes were. The turning point of the evening came when we simultaneously blurted out that *To Kill a Mockingbird* was our favorite book of all time. As it turned out, it was Atticus Finch who inspired us to volunteer at the ACLU. I reached across the table without thinking, and she instinctively took my hand.

An hour later, we were making out on the couch in Sarah's efficiency apartment, but you probably don't want to hear this part. I'll just say that your Mom would not let me spend the night. She always maintained the highest standards. But, since it was getting late, and we both had eight o'clock classes the following day, I suggested that maybe I should go. Then came an inspiration that changed our lives.

"Sarah, I have a proposal."

"Already?" she giggled, her face still half-buried in my chest.

I pulled back a little to face her directly. "No, I'm *serious*. Look, would you call this a date? I mean, I never even asked you out."

"I'd say it *became* a date."

"To my way of thinking," I added, "It became a *lot* more. Today was the best date I've ever been on."

Parting her lips into a smile, Sarah nodded in agreement. "Me too," she whispered.

"Before I go, though, we should probably talk a little about the future. "

Sarah sat up but remained silent. I decided to continue.

"Look, we'll both graduate in a couple of months, and then you're planning to go back to Chicago to look for a teaching job, right?" Sarah nodded.

"Therefore, this isn't a good time to start a new relationship, is it?"

A look of concern erased Sarah's glowing smile.

"When I awoke this morning, I never dreamed my day would end like this. And I'll admit I'm a bit confused right now." Then, after pausing briefly to gather my thoughts, I added, "But there's one thing I know for certain, Sarah. I could go the rest of my life and never meet someone else like you."

She gazed at me eagerly, anticipating my next words. A desk lamp in the corner was the only light source in the room; its rays cast fire into her eyes.

"I think we have two options. First, we remain working buddies at the ACLU and then go our separate ways after graduation."

"And the second?" she asked with a hint of concern.

"And second, we spend as much time together as possible and see where things stand by the time we graduate."

A dreamy smile returned to her face. It was like she was staring at a fireworks display.

"I vote for option two," she emphatically stated. Then she reached for the back of my head and pulled me in for another kiss. For the next several minutes, the only sound was Cat Stevens singing "Don't Be Shy" through the speakers of Sarah's ancient record player.

Sure enough, Sarah and I saw each other daily for three months. Then, in late May, I made it official by taking your Mom out for a nice dinner that ended with me on one knee and an engagement ring on her finger. She soon found a teaching position at Ritenour High School, ironically teaching kids from Breckenridge Hills. We found a nice little place to live just south of the Delmar Loop and married in late July. Only about 25 people were at the wedding, but it was a lovely little ceremony followed by one hell of a celebration. Throughout the day, I thought your Mom looked like an angel. She was so *beautiful*. After the wedding, we spent a week in Maui and then returned to St. Louis to start our new lives.

I've always been astonished that such an enchanting person could fall for a shlub like myself. Nevertheless, from that day in Breckenridge Hills right up to her passing, your Mom and I have been joined at the hip. Sarah became the epicenter of my life. What you witnessed in the garage was admittedly wrong and stupid, but I still don't know how to make it without your mother.

A thousand-mile stare slowly displaced the lively expression Ethan had been wearing while talking about his first date with Sarah. Finally, he looked down at his hands clasped together in his lap.

"Wow!" exclaimed Matt, attempting to lighten the mood. "You weren't kidding, Ethan. That *was* quite a date!"

Ethan looked up and forced a weak smile. "Yeah? You think so?"

Then he glanced at his daughter. After aiming a scowl at Matt and rolling her eyes, Jenny turned back to confront Ethan. Worry was painted across her face. Ethan remembered some of the more challenging times he and Sarah had dealt with when they were younger. At that moment, Jenny looked just like her mother.

chapter

3

For almost two hours, Ethan tossed and turned in his queen-sized bed. He could not sleep. It had been nearly two weeks since Ethan had last shared the bed with Sarah, and he still was not used to sleeping alone. Plus, Ethan was a creature of habit. Usually, when he laid his head down on the pillow between 10:30 and 11:00, Ethan was unconscious within a few minutes. If he stayed up past this time, though, sleep became elusive. Since Ethan had talked with Jenny and Matt well past midnight, his eyes kept popping open, even though he was fighting for some rest.

If tomorrow were a typical workday, this would be a problem. Ethan did not function well on less than six hours of sleep. Since he had no plans for this week except for taking time off to grieve, there was no point in adding more stress to his insomnia. Glancing at the digital numbers glowing on his night table, Ethan saw it was approaching 2:30. He reached over, turned on the lamp, and propped himself up on his pillow. There was no point in fighting this battle anymore. Since his mind was surprisingly alert, he might as well use the time to think.

Ethan purposefully allowed his mind to wander. Glancing over at the emptiness on the other side of the bed, he conjured up recent images of his wife. Since her diagnosis six months earlier, Sarah had been remarkably resilient. When it finally came about two weeks ago, her decline had been precipitous. Sarah spent the final week of her life in the hospice section of St. Luke's Hospital. Morphine had kept her unconscious most of the time, sparing her the suffering they both had dreaded.

In one respect, Sarah's passing was a bit of a relief. Over the last several months, there had been nursing care when Ethan went to work, but Sarah became his responsibility in the evenings and on weekends. Physically, this was not hard since, up to her hospitalization, she had maintained a high level of vigor. Sarah could still eat, drink and go to the bathroom independently. The only adjustment was that Ethan inherited Sarah's household chores. After retiring from teaching, Sarah had assumed most of the cooking, cleaning, and laundry duties, and now Ethan insisted on doing these errands himself. Of course, despite Ethan's objections, Jenny and Matt also came over frequently to lend a hand.

Psychologically, however, the last six months had been like a bad dream in slow motion. Since Sarah had been diagnosed with the most advanced stage of cancer, the doctors offered little hope. Her prognosis was essentially a death sentence. They never provided a specific execution date, but Sarah and Ethan knew their time was limited.

Ethan offered to take off from work so they could cruise around the world or do whatever Sarah wanted with her remaining time. She adamantly refused. Sarah made it clear that what she wanted more than anything else was normalcy. This pronouncement primarily meant spending time with books, puttering around her garden, and visiting with friends. For Ethan, the effort required to act like everything was okay while waiting for a hand to shove him off the edge of a cliff proved emotionally draining. It was not much consolation, but whatever he decided about the remainder of his life would at least not include this burden.

Ethan suddenly felt a surge of guilt for even harboring this thought. Was Sarah's ghost reading his mind at this moment? Ethan had spent his entire life convinced there was no afterlife. When we die, we return to that state of nonexistence we occupied before our birth or conception, or so he thought. But was he certain? On the off chance that most of the population was right about life beyond death, Ethan glanced over at the tiny vessel on his nightstand that still contained some of Sarah's ashes. He softly whispered an apology.

Thinking he heard a noise, Ethan turned to face the hallway. Was that Jenny? After a moment of silence, Ethan redirected his thoughts toward his daughter. Jenny had always been such a great kid. She was loving, compassionate, and unswervingly empathetic to the needs of others. Jenny was like her mother in many ways but was even more sensitive. Ethan pictured the distressed look on his daughter's face in the garage. He had seen a similar expression the few times he had raised his voice to her when she was a little girl.

Ethan admitted he had not sufficiently thought through the decision to take his life. And seeing the anguished look on Jenny's face also reinforced the notion it had been selfish. But what if the best part of his life *was* behind him? Why should he try to forge ahead without Sarah? We all die; the only question is when. Should Ethan enter his senior years solely to maintain the happiness of his children? The future looked barren. Additional wrinkles, grayer hair, and, eventually, the use of a walker would soon accompany his loneliness and despair.

Ethan understood he had come to the proverbial fork in the road. He knew that in the morning, Jenny would call Noah out of concern for her father and tell him about last night. They would be rightfully concerned, and who knows what they might do if Ethan could not alleviate their worries. What would he say to his children? Should Ethan consider ending his life before they could take measures to stop him? Was he sure suicide was the answer?

Throughout Ethan's life, he usually relied upon his instincts for inspiration whenever he faced a challenge. After a moment, a smile broke across his face. Ethan reached over to his nightstand, opened the drawer, and pulled out a legal pad and a pen. For the next hour or so, he scribbled down notes summarizing the details of his plan.

When he finally finished, Ethan noticed the pale light stealing through the vertical window blinds. It was almost dawn. Then he heard a muffled sound again. When he glanced towards the hallway, his bedroom door slowly swung open, revealing Jenny's troubled face.

"Dad, have you been awake *all* night?"

"Yeah, I guess so," Ethan responded. "I couldn't sleep."

"Me either," Jenny confided. "I'm still worried. I kept getting up to check on you. I noticed you turned on a light a couple of hours ago."

"So that's what I was hearing." Ethan glanced down at the legal pad in his lap and smiled. Then he added, "Sweetheart, I greatly appreciate your concern and everything you've done, but you *really* don't need to worry."

"I wish I could believe that," Jenny replied. Then, after a pause, she added, "You know, Dad, after I call in sick this morning, I need to call Noah and tell him about last night. After that, he'll probably want a FaceTime call with us to figure out what to do next."

Ethan grimaced and then shook his head to show he understood. For a moment, father and daughter held each other's gaze. Then, finally, Ethan remembered the notes he had been composing for the past couple of hours.

"Come on in and have a seat, Sweetheart. I'd like to talk to you."

Jenny ambled over and lay back on her mother's side of the bed with her head propped up on a pillow. She was still wearing the same clothes from the day before, although they appeared more wrinkled.

"Do you ever think about those road trips we took when you were a kid?"

Jenny smiled. "Of course. Thanks to you and Mom, we've been to every state west of the Mississippi and probably most of the national parks."

"Those were great times," Ethan added nostalgically. "You know, I truly believe it's different out West. The skies are more open, the air's drier, and there're fewer people except for a handful of cities."

"You should be writing TV commercials for states like Colorado or Montana," Jenny teased.

Ethan smiled but quickly reverted to his original train of thought. "Seriously, it *really* is different out West. At least, that's been my experience."

He thought about a book he had read many years ago in college. One of his favorite lines from the book came back to him now. "Beyond the glittering street was darkness, and beyond the darkness the West. I had to go."

"What's that from?" asked Jenny. "It sounds familiar."

"*On the Road* by Jack Kerouac," responded Ethan. "It used to be one of my favorites."

"So, Dad, why are you bringing this up now?"

"I couldn't sleep last night," Ethan answered. "Finally, after hours of staring at the blank TV screen, I came up with an idea. If I could spend some time out West, Jenny, possibly on a road trip, I think it would help me figure out some things about my future."

A smile crossed Ethan's face. Even though heavy bags sagged beneath them, a flame was burning in his eyes. Jenny had seen this look before.

"I've been working out some of the details," Ethan continued, pointing to the legal pad on his lap. "For starters, I should tell you I'm glad your mom won an argument with me years ago about money."

"Oh yeah," Jenny replied. "What was that?"

"When I made partner 20 years ago, and they gave me a big pay raise, I came home excited about moving to a fancier house in Des Peres or Chesterfield. I also suggested we should upgrade our cars to something like Mercedes or BMW. But, rather forcefully, your Mom argued we could be just as happy remaining in our current home, especially since we'd soon be facing an empty nest. And she laughed at the idea of shopping for new vehicles, saying the only thing that mattered was reliable transportation. She said saving for our senior years was far more prudent."

Jenny nodded for her dad to continue.

"With the help of a financial advisor, we developed a *considerable* savings and investment plan." Ethan repeated the word "considerable," clearly proud of this accomplishment.

"Jenny, while I'm counting on this money to supplement my retirement income, there should still be enough, I believe, to pay for this trip and for me to take an extended, unpaid leave of absence from work. If I'm frugal, there's no reason why it couldn't last for a year, maybe more." Then, looking straight up toward the ceiling, Ethan added with a slight grin, "Thank you, Sarah."

"What about your clients? Will Keith support this idea?"

"I think so," replied Ethan. "Since my absence will be unpaid, Keith can afford to bring on a young associate for a third of my salary. Besides," he added, "I don't intend to give him a choice."

"What about the house?" Jenny inquired.

"Well, that's where you and Matt come in. Why don't the two of you move in and take care of this place while I'm gone? You can live here rent-free, save some money, and then I'll help you find a place to purchase when I get back."

Jenny smiled. She liked everything she had heard so far. Then she thought of another concern.

"What about Grandpa?"

"Yes, that's a problem," Ethan responded. "I've been trying to figure out what to do about your grandfather, and he may be the reason why this plan won't work."

Jenny looked directly at her father and bit down on her lower lip. By this point, she believed the road trip was in her dad's best interest.

After a moment, she finally responded. "Matt and I will look after him, Dad. You go on this trip. Grandpa will be fine."

Ethan glanced at his daughter but didn't reply. He knew that James, Sarah's 89-year-old father, was in the latter stages of Alzheimer's. He was receiving exceptional care at the Brookdale West County Senior Living Center. Sarah visited her dad every day until she could no longer, and then Ethan assumed the responsibility. However, he had recently reduced the visits to twice a week since James had become unresponsive.

"You know," Jenny added after not receiving a response, "Grandpa doesn't even know you're there, right?" Then, after Ethan nodded, she continued, "I know Mom would still want us to visit him, so I promise I'll get out there at least twice a week. Okay?"

Ethan exhaled loudly and, for a moment, stared at their muddy reflections on the television's empty screen. Then, he slowly began to nod and pressed his lips tightly together into a fragile smile.

"Jenny, you're amazing. Thank you *so* much."

Jenny returned his smile and then spun around to face her dad directly.

"Okay, then it's settled?" Ethan nodded. "Then I'll go over all this with Matt, but I'm sure he'll be on board." She pointed to the legal pad and added, "So what else is in those notes?"

"Oh, I started planning the trip's itinerary," Ethan responded with a chuckle. "But after an hour or so, I gave up on that idea. I remembered that, more than anything, I wanted to experience absolute freedom. That means *no* schedule. Instead, I want to buy a nice little camper, hitch it to the car, and start driving toward the West."

"No plan at all, huh?"

"Well, your brother invited me to spend some time with him in Portland, so that'll be my final destination. But . . ." Ethan paused, and his smile blossomed. "There's a *lot* of open country between here and Portland."

Ethan saw his excitement reflected in his daughter's face for a moment. Then the corners of her mouth turned downward, and wrinkles once again streaked her forehead.

"What?" asked Ethan. "Is there something I haven't thought of?"

Jenny turned to gaze directly at her father but remained silent.

"*Oh*," Ethan finally responded. "You're still worried about last night."

"Yes, Dad, I am. How do I know you won't do a 'Thelma and Louise' somewhere over the Grand Canyon?"

Ethan smiled at the Hollywood reference. He still recalled how the film's ending had disturbed his daughter when they watched the videotape together during her preteen years. Then, Ethan turned from Jenny for a moment and studied the view of the backyard through the bedroom blinds. The sun had risen enough to cast dancing shadows beneath the lofty elms.

"I guess you don't," Ethan finally responded. Then, twisting to face his daughter directly, he continued, "But I give you my word, Jenny, right here and now, that I won't do anything like that again, at least not while I'm on this trip. And you know I'm true to my word, right? I've never lied to you."

Jenny nodded but did not reply. Ethan then continued, "Besides, unless you and your brother find a way to have me committed and then placed in a straitjacket, you couldn't stop me from doing what I believe is in my best interest. But let's not talk about that anymore, alright? I've given you my word."

"Alright," Jenny agreed, "But . . ."

Knowing what she was about to say, Ethan interrupted, "And let's not tell your brother about last night, alright? At least for the time being. He's already got enough on his plate." Ethan paused momentarily and added, "I'll call Noah and tell him about my travel plans. He should be happy to know I'd like to take him up on his offer."

Jenny glanced down for a moment, and when she finally looked back up, the alarm had vanished from her face.

Ethan added, "I'll call Noah in a couple of hours." Then, glancing over at the alarm clock on his nightstand, he continued, "It's only 5:30 on the West Coast. In the meantime, there's something I want you to do, alright?"

"Sure, anything," Jenny responded. "Name it."

"I want you to *go home*," Ethan replied assertively.

When Jenny remained quiet, Ethan persisted, "I'll be *fine*, Sweetheart. You don't need to worry. I'll use today to start planning the trip. In the meantime, you go home, shower, and then crawl into bed."

Jenny reached out and took her father's hand. "I'll go home and grab a shower, Dad, but then I'm going to work. I still have time."

Jenny stood to leave. When she reached the bedroom door, she pivoted to face Ethan. He could see the apprehension had returned to her face.

"*Go*," Ethan commanded, "And for the *love of God*, stop worrying about me. I'll be fine."

For a moment, Jenny wobbled back and forth in hesitation. Then, she did her best to return her father's smile. Finally, without uttering another word, Jenny spun around, entered the hallway, and vanished.

chapter

4

Ethan heard the front door close and, a minute later, the rumble of Jenny's car as she backed out of the driveway. He rolled over, pulled the covers up to his neck, and closed his eyes, thinking he would catch up on the sleep that had alluded him the night before. Instead, ten minutes later, his eyes popped open, and Ethan found himself staring directly at the picture on Sarah's side of the bed. He and Sarah had taken this selfie during their Alaskan cruise. They were seated on the balcony of their stateroom while, in the background, aquamarine chunks of ice from a colossal glacier calved behind them. Ethan and Sarah were smiling like two teenagers posing for prom photos.

For a moment, Ethan could not move. Then, aware of the empty space on the other side of the bed, he felt himself again sliding into despair. Tears welled in his eyes as Ethan forced himself to think about his recently formulated travel plans. He knew himself well enough to realize the best antidote in the short term was to stay busy. The more Ethan focused on preparing for his trip, the less he would think about Sarah. Finally, Ethan leaped up, yanked the covers half-heartedly to make the bed, and then marched into the bathroom.

While brushing his teeth, Ethan made a mental checklist of what he needed to do over the next few days before hitting the road. Call Noah; drop by the office to arrange his extended absence; purchase and stock a camper; and pack everything he would need for an indefinite period on the road. Ethan also wanted to drop by Brookdale to check on James.

Although Sarah's dad would not be aware of his presence, Ethan still wanted to say goodbye since he was unsure when he would return. In addition, he also had a dozen domestic chores to do, such as cleaning the house, washing the laundry, and paying the bills. That was enough to keep Ethan from spending too much time in dark places.

The call with Noah went well enough. His son was delighted that his father wanted to spend time with him in Oregon, although he was a little uneasy when he could not pin Ethan down on an expected arrival date. To save time, Ethan made the call while driving to the office. Shortly after parking the Subaru SUV in his reserved parking spot, he ended the call.

When Ethan pushed open the front door, he immediately regretted the decision to arrive at the commencement of the workday. There was no avoiding the condolences from secretaries and paralegals. It felt even more awkward when one or two graciously inquired why he had returned to the office so soon after Sarah's passing. As quickly as he could, Ethan darted down the hallway. Upon reaching Ruth's station, which stood sentry in front of her boss' sizable office, Ethan smiled and pointed to inquire if Keith was inside. The bulldog secretary nodded but instinctively held a hand to check her boss's availability. Then, noticing the haggard look on Ethan's face, Ruth put down the phone receiver, forced a sympathetic smile, and waved him in.

Keith Robbins started the firm almost fifty years ago. Now in his mid-seventies, he still practiced law full-time. Keith was a tall man who stood surprisingly erect, like a soldier on guard duty. He had a full head of wavy gray hair accentuated by an equally gray goatee. Keith had never married, so the firm was his entire life. He had hired Ethan more than forty years ago as an intern while still in law school. Since then, the two men had become friends, although they seldom socialized outside the office. Their relationship was based more on mutual respect than a desire to hang out as drinking buddies while watching Cardinals games.

When Ethan gently opened the door and entered, Keith peered up from his laptop, displaying an expression like he was staring at a ghost. The Tiffany lamp on his mahogany desk illuminated only a corner of the room, making Ethan feel more like he was inside a shrine than a legal office. Quickly realizing this was not a social call, Keith motioned for Ethan to join him on the leather sofa across from his desk. A quick word to Alexa turned on two table lamps flanking the couch.

"Sorry to interrupt, Keith, but do you have a few minutes? There's something I'd like to discuss."

"Sure, no problem," responded Keith. "I know you're going through a tough time." Then, after a moment, he added, "I'll admit, though, I'm a little surprised to see you so soon after yesterday's service at the lake."

There was silence as the two men settled into the plush, worn leather. Keith placed one leg over the other, folded his hands in his lap, and patiently waited for Ethan to continue.

"Well, I appreciate that you gave up your Sunday to join us," Ethan responded. "And I wasn't planning to stop by today, but something's come up, and I need to ask you a question."

"Go on," Keith said, "I'm all ears."

"Alright, I'll cut right to the chase," stated Ethan. "I need to get away for a while. So I'm planning a road trip out West. I want to visit Noah in Portland, but I'm not sure how long it'll take to get there."

"I see," answered Keith. "So I assume we're talking about more than just the week you originally planned to take off?"

"That's correct," Ethan replied, pausing to gather his thoughts. "In fact, it may be several months, possibly more."

Seeing a deep furrow unfold across Keith's forehead, Ethan swiftly added, "Unpaid, of course."

"What about your clients?" Keith interjected.

"I've thought about that. You remember Ellen, the intern who worked here a few years ago?"

Keith nodded for Ethan to continue. "She was outstanding, but when we offered her a position, she declined because, at the time, she was moving to Dallas with her husband. Anyhow, she emailed me several days ago inquiring about a job. Ellen's going through an ugly divorce and wants to return to St. Louis immediately. So . . . , I thought you could hire her to take my cases for half of what you'd pay me. The only thing I'll need is for you to continue to provide health insurance. Otherwise, this plan works. It'll be a win-win for everyone."

Keith glanced down at the arms folded across his chest. Ethan could visualize the wheels spinning inside his partner's head. Before Keith could respond, Ethan added, "*Oh*, and once I return, I'd be happy to share clients and my current salary with Ellen. Therefore, this wouldn't have to be a temporary gig for her."

For a moment, silence once again permeated the office. The muted ticking of a pendulum swinging beneath the contemporary clock on the far wall provided the only sound. Then, finally, Keith looked up, still flashing the same furrowed brow.

"Win-win for everyone?" Keith inquired. "Ethan, if your leave is unpaid, how's it a win for you? What's more, your salary will be significantly lower after you return."

"It's a win for me because I'll be able to take my trip," Ethan countered. "I've got enough in savings to cover the lost salary. As for lower pay when I return, sharing clients with Ellen will give me a chance to semi-retire. You know, I could go part-time." After a brief pause, Ethan added, "Oh, and by the way, while I'm on the road, I'll still be available by cell phone to help Ellen whenever needed."

Keith scratched his head and then rotated his position to confront his partner squarely. A hush filled the expansive office as the two men momentarily gazed at each other. Ethan had always admired his partner's physicality, but even in the dim light, he observed new wrinkles, expanding age spots, and more gray hair.

"Look, Ethan, you know I'm a confirmed bachelor, so I can't pretend to understand what you've been going through." Keith stopped, and his voice had noticeably deepened when he started up again as though he was addressing a jury. "But I *did* know Sarah. I've known her almost as long as I've known you. She was a wonderful woman, Ethan. But, of course, you already know that."

"Yes, she was," replied Ethan, looking away to conceal moisture gathering in the corners of his eyes. He hesitated and finally added, "And I don't know what to do now that she's gone."

Like reflections in a mirror, the two partners simultaneously shifted to stare straight ahead, avoiding eye contact for the moment. When Ethan briefly closed his eyes, he heard a loud sigh coming from the other end of the couch. Ethan was technically an equal partner in the firm but would always be the protege in this relationship.

Finally, Keith turned to face his partner. He cleared his throat and waited for Ethan to reestablish eye contact.

"Alright, Ethan, I think you should go on this trip, and I want you to take as much time as you need. Say farewell to Sarah, and then figure out how to move on with the rest of your life. You're not the first man to become a widower, but that said, I know how much Sarah meant to you."

Ethan remained quiet, but a restrained smile slowly crept across his face.

"*However*," continued Keith. "I will not let the firm profit from the loss of your wife."

A look of bewilderment immediately replaced Ethan's smile. Seeing this, Keith added, "If we follow your plan, Ellen will do your work for what will probably be a *third* of your current salary, and the firm will pocket the difference."

"Then what do you think is fair?" Ethan inquired.

"Fair?" Keith asked. "Was it *fair* that you lost Sarah? Would it be fair, under these circumstances, for the firm to pocket the difference between your salary and Ellen's?"

Ethan did not respond since he immediately recognized Keith's standard practice of asking rhetorical questions. So, instead, he waited for his partner to continue.

"But as a practical matter," Keith added, "Here's what I propose. You stay available by cell phone to work with Ellen as much as she needs, and I'll deduct her salary from yours. Otherwise, you'll continue to draw a paycheck, including health benefits."

After another momentary interlude, Ethan finally responded, "Alright, Keith, that's being *more* than fair. But I've worked with you long enough to know when you're mind's made up, so I guess I have no choice but to accept your offer."

A smile erupted across Ethan's face like a fault line during an earthquake. Then, the two old friends stood and faced each other. Ethan offered his hand to shake on the deal, but to his astonishment, Keith ignored the hand, stepped forward, and reached out to embrace his partner. The two men shared a warm hug for the first time in their long relationship.

An hour later, Ethan pulled into the expansive parking lot in front of Camping World in Wentzville, a rapidly surging suburb on the western fringe of St. Louis. After describing his needs, Ethan soon signed documents to take possession of a five-year-old camper. Twenty-one feet long, it had an awning, air-conditioning, a shower, a kitchen, and enough room to sleep four. He used negotiation skills honed over decades as an attorney to knock $1500 off the sales price, plus he persuaded the salesman to throw in the free installation of a trailer hitch. Ethan was pleased with purchasing his home for an uncertain future. While waiting for Camping World to install the hitch, Ethan hiked to a nearby McDonald's for lunch.

An hour later, Ethan was home, backing the camper into the driveway. Then he returned to his SUV, filled its tank at a nearby QuikTrip, and drove twenty minutes to Brookdale for a final visit with James. So far, the brisk, non-stop approach had achieved its goal. Ethan had barely thought about the enormous crater in his life left by Sarah's passing. As he climbed out of the SUV and saw the wheelchairs curving around the pond's edge, Ethan felt his mood deflating like a punctured tire.

It was a lovely afternoon. The azure sky was cloudless, and a gentle breeze relaxed the heat, which had climbed into the low eighties. It was the perfect day for the assisted living to go outside for sunshine, fresh air, and a change of scenery. Ethan waved at a couple of familiar faces and then quickly scurried inside the lobby. While signing in, he noticed more residents in wheelchairs preparing for their turn to meditate on the exploding fountain at the center of the pond.

Moving with even greater haste, Ethan glided down the tiled hallway toward James' room. He once again noticed the discreet railings on each side of the hallway. Above the handrails was a series of vivid panoramic photographs depicting familiar landmarks in St. Louis. Ethan assumed these images of Forest Park, the Arch, the zoo, the Hill, the botanical gardens, and other local sites were ever-present to stimulate faltering memories and brighten gloomy moods.

When Ethan approached room 179, he saw the familiar images on the shelf outside James's room. Sarah had long ago decorated this area with a fake potted plant surrounded by family photographs. There were pictures of Noah and Jenny at different stages of their life. There was also a professionally-taken portrait of the family encircling a younger James. Sarah was donning the same smile that had first attracted Ethan's attention during their ACLU days.

After a gentle knock, Ethan heard a woman's voice beckon him to enter. Once inside, he took a moment to adjust to the dim light. Someone had drawn the shades for some reason, so the only illumination came from a floor lamp tucked away in the back corner and the television currently broadcasting an old *Jeopardy* episode. Ethan knew it was a repeat because Alex Trebek was still the host. Glancing around the room, he finally spotted Miriam's beaming smile as she adjusted her oversized glasses to see who had entered the room.

Miriam had been James' primary daytime caretaker for the past few years. In Ethan's mind, she was not much younger than James, but she was still sharp as a tack and seemed to relate well to her generation. James was seated next to her on his Archie Bunker-style recliner. His head was leaning toward the right, but Ethan could see his wide open, glassy eyes. They were hypnotically drawn toward the cable box beneath the television.

"Ethan, is that you?" Miriam inquired in her familiar, matronly voice.

"Yes," Ethan answered. "It's good to see you, Miriam. How's he doing today?"

Miriam glanced toward James and then patted the sofa, inviting Ethan to join her.

"Oh, you know, he's pretty much the same," Miriam replied. "I've had to cut back on the snacks lately since he'll eat everything in sight. Now, I only give him a small bowl of M&Ms rather than leaving out the whole bag. As you can see, he's gained some weight." After a pause, she added, "James is sleeping more than ever, but as you know, when he's awake, he still mostly just stares off into space."

"So, in other words," Ethan stated as he glided around the coffee table to sit on the worn couch, "There's been no change."

"Yes, that's pretty much it," Miriam snickered. Then, her smile vanished as she continued, "Hey, I'm so sorry to hear about Sarah. Ethan, you have my *deepest* condolences." Then, glancing toward James, she added, "You know, it was probably a blessing he didn't understand what was going on."

"Thank you," responded Ethan. Then, feeling the need to change the subject, he looked toward the television and asked, "Miriam, could you mute the TV for a moment? There's something I'd like to discuss."

"Sure," Miriam replied, "What's on your mind?"

"I'm planning a road trip, and I may be gone for a while."

"I see," responded Miriam.

"I just need to get away. I bought a camper today and plan to hit the road as early as tomorrow." Glancing toward James, Ethan continued, "I doubt he'll know I'm gone, but I'd still like to be able to FaceTime with him every few days. Will it be alright to call your cell phone?"

Without hesitation, Miriam smiled and nodded. "Of course, that's no problem."

"And if there are *any* concerns whatsoever, you guys can call me as well as Jenny, right?"

Miriam nodded again, "Yes, I have both of your numbers on my phone."

"*Great*," replied Ethan. "Hey, listen, Miriam, I appreciate everything you've done for James over the years. Sarah always felt you were the biggest reason it was a good decision to move him into Brookdale."

"Well, Ethan, he's not just my job." Then, glancing in James' direction, she added, "I have the highest respect for that man."

"Same here," Ethan replied. Then, after a brief pause, he added, "Do you know he once saved my life?"

"*Really?*"

"Years ago. I was at their house for Thanksgiving. Jenny was just a baby at the time and was seated on a high chair between Sarah and myself, gobbling down tiny bits of turkey. When she let out this baby fart and grinned from ear to ear, I laughed uncontrollably. Next thing you know, I was choking on turkey."

Miriam raised a hand to cover the smile unfurling across her face. "Oh my. What happened next?"

"James calmly stood up, walked around the table, grabbed me from behind, and used those powerful guns he once had to squeeze the turkey right out of my air pipe."

"Oh my," Miriam responded again. "James was an EMT as well as a fireman?"

"Yes," replied Ethan, "Good thing for me." Then, almost as an after-thought, he added, "James was also a *wonderful* father."

"I can imagine," Miriam replied.

"Sarah once told me that when Wash. U. accepted her, she was burst-ing with joy until she remembered the cost."

"Oh yes," Miriam interjected, "It's a fine school, but their tuition's a fortune."

"When Sarah broke the news to her parents," Ethan continued, "Her mother immediately brought up the money issue. This response, of course, wasn't the reaction Sarah had wanted, but then again, she wasn't surprised. Her mom told her that without a full scholarship, she'd have to go to Mizzou, her backup school."

"I see," responded Miriam.

"If she'd gone to Mizzou," Ethan added immediately, "We never would've met. Anyhow, Sarah told me that when she broke the news, her dad was standing behind her mom, beaming with pride. When Sarah told them that Wash. U. had only offered a partial scholarship, James placed his hands on his wife's shoulders, looked her squarely in the eye, and declared that Sarah *would* be attending Wash. U. He then added that they were going out for a nice dinner to celebrate."

"And that's what happened?" Miriam inquired. She glanced over at James and smiled.

"Yes," Ethan replied solemnly. "He took out a second mortgage on the house and sent his daughter to Wash. U., where three years later, she met me. He also took them to a nice steak dinner that night at Carmine's downtown."

Miriam and Ethan grinned at each other and then turned to face James. *Jeopardy* had just ended, but James continued to gaze at the open space beneath the television.

"Hey, isn't your shift about up," Ethan inquired, remembering *Jeop-ardy* ended at 4:00.

"Why, yes, you're right," Miriam answered. "Ben should be here any minute, although lately, he's been coming in about ten minutes late."

"Go on and go," Ethan suggested. "I've got this until Ben gets here. Besides, I wouldn't mind a few minutes alone with James. You know, to say goodbye and all."

Miriam stood up, grabbed her purse, and turned to leave. "You have a good trip, Ethan. And drive safely."

"Will do," Ethan replied. "I'll see you on my phone's screen in a few days."

Miriam nodded and left. Ethan then turned to face James. He leaned forward with his hands clasped between his knees, staring at his father-in-law while trying to gather his thoughts.

"I don't know if you can understand or even hear what I'm saying," Ethan finally stated. "But I want you to know, James, you've been like a father to me." Then, after pausing, Ethan added, "You also raised an *incredible* daughter. For that, I will be forever grateful."

Ethan paused again, and this time, a stillness filled the room. He studied his father-in-law's eyes, wide open but staring ahead, rarely blinking. The same wave of depression that had washed over him the night before suddenly struck again. A disheartening thought occurred to him. James had lived a rich life. He had led a successful career saving the lives of others, he had been a loving family man, and practically everyone he knew admired him. But look at him now. This condition is how it always seems to end for those who stubbornly cling to the light.

Ethan forced himself to go on. "James, I'm afraid we've lost your precious Sarah. But, who knows, maybe the two of you will be together again soon. Meanwhile, though, I'm here all alone."

Ethan glanced toward the front door, listening for Ben's approach. Hearing nothing, he returned to the one-sided conversation. "I'm lost, James, I'll admit it. I don't know how to go on without Sarah, especially since I *know* the best part of my life's behind me."

Ethan noticed some drool on James' chin. He grabbed a Kleenex and wiped it off, along with some more that had dripped onto his father-in-law's liver-spotted forearm.

"For now, all I can think to do is hit the road," continued Ethan after returning to the couch. "I'm planning to leave tomorrow on a trip that will eventually take me to see Noah in Portland. Between you and me, though, this is mostly just to satisfy your granddaughter." Then, looking away for a moment, Ethan whispered, "I think it's probably just a last hurrah before I confront the inevitable."

Ethan glanced down, paused, and pressed his lips tightly together. Then, finally, he realized it was time to wrap up his monologue. "Anyhow, James, I just wanted to say goodbye. I'll check up on you from the road, but it may be a while before we see each other again. You take care, my friend."

Ethan stood up to face James. He had known his father-in-law for over four decades, and they had always enjoyed a warm relationship based on mutual respect. Ethan made a concerted effort to look into the past for a moment. He visualized James as a vibrant young man in the prime of his life. There were images of a stout father playfully heaving his baby girl into the air. Another that came to mind was a robust firefighter with charcoal streaks on his forehead hoisting a pitcher of beer up to a table crowded with the crew that had just extinguished a downtown inferno. Finally, Ethan saw a bashful figure down on one knee offering an engagement ring he couldn't afford to the woman who would become Sarah's mother.

The magic abruptly ended when Ethan heard voices in the hallway. Suddenly, he was staring at a hulking figure slumped over in a recliner. Like many older men, James' cranium appeared too big for his body. A ring of wispy gray hair crowned his head, flanked by fleshy lobes spouting dark fuzz at the entrance to his ear canals. James' face was checkered with age spots and deeply rutted wrinkles. But this was just his physical appearance. The worst part was the advanced level of Alzheimer's that had devoured most of his identity.

Living like this was the only reward for achieving such an advanced age. It was a cruel irony. As the front door opened, Ethan whispered goodbye to James, nodded a forced smile toward Ben, and then quietly strode out of the room.

chapter

5

Ethan got off to a late start the following morning. He slept later because he had been up half the night packing for the trip. The first part of the evening had been spent taking Jenny and Matt out to dinner and then going over home maintenance details. They were planning to move their belongings in slowly since the lease on their apartment still ran until the end of the month, but Jenny assured Ethan they would be sleeping in his house by the start of the weekend.

After they left, Ethan began the tedious process of packing the camper. Since he had never done this before, it went slower than expected. He had to carry clothes to the camper's closet, food to the pantry, and books, family photos, and other items to various nooks and crannies scattered throughout the house trailer. It was after 2:00 am by the time Ethan went to bed, and even then, it took another hour to fall asleep. It was mid-morning when Ethan finally towed the camper out of his driveway.

The high ramp leading onto Interstate 70 immediately brought back memories. Ethan had steered over this ramp for countless years at the start of long road trips heading west. Most days, he drove around the Creve Coeur area, and if there was a more extended expedition to Busch Stadium for a Cards game or maybe to a nice restaurant in the city, it almost always involved motoring toward the east. Turning west onto I-70 was like opening a portal into Estes Park or Jackson Hole, two of Ethan and Sarah's favorite destinations.

As Ethan crossed the Blanchette Bridge into St Charles County, he reminisced about some of those trips. Over the years, he and Sarah had

perfected the balance between challenging hikes in the morning and re-
laxing activities in the afternoon. There had been trips to Europe and
the Far East, but for Ethan, the American West had been the source of
his best memories. Since Sarah was a teacher, the longer road trips had
always occurred during the summer. Jenny and Noah had spent some of
their best childhood moments out West on hiking trails, rafting expeditions, and on the backs of horses.

As amateur photographers, Sarah and Ethan had plastered the walls
of their house with enlarged pictures from these trips. Ethan had posted
photographs of the Eiffel Tower, the Taj Mahal, and the Great Wall of
China to placate Sarah. His favorites, though, were the Grand Canyon,
Yosemite Falls, and Longs Peak in the Colorado Rockies. While these
were reminders of magnificent memories, the problem was he had shared
them all with Sarah. Now that Ethan was preparing to create new memories, a hollow sadness struck like an unexpected rainstorm.

Reminiscing like this would not do. The whole point was to use this
trip as a distraction from the grieving that had almost ended everything
just a few days before in Ethan's garage. There was purposefully no itinerary to follow except to keep his vehicle pointed west. After all, Ethan was
hoping to maximize the excitement resulting from complete freedom.
Right away, though, it was apparent that too many hours by himself on
the open road was probably a mistake. He would be an emotional wreck
when he found a campground to spend the night somewhere in eastern
Nebraska.

Ethan needed to drive less on his first day, and even more important,
he wanted to find someone with whom he could spend the evening. He
also wanted to get off I-70. This section of highway running from St.
Louis to Kansas City was one of the first stretches constructed as part
of the interstate system that crisscrossed the nation. Unfortunately, the
state had never widened it despite the increasingly heavy traffic flow. The
18-wheelers, in particular, added to Ethan's stress as they frequently occupied both lanes for long stretches and created massive logjams behind
them. This 250-mile expanse had always been the dreariest part of the
trips out west.

Ethan pulled into a rest stop to collect his thoughts. Then, he con-
ceived an idea just as he climbed out of the SUV to use the men's room.

Tom Flaherty. During his first year of college, Tom had been his room-mate. It was a unique arrangement since Tom was a senior, but he happily took Ethan under his wing. By the holidays, the big brother/little brother relationship had evolved into a full-scale friendship. Since Tom was from Fort Scott, Kansas, he moved on to KU law school after graduating from Wash. U. After a brief stint with a large firm in Topeka, Tom moved back to his hometown, hung a shingle, and then finally, at the age of 42, married his high school sweetheart.

Ethan and Tom worked hard to maintain their friendship for many years. Both were attorneys and only lived a half day's drive from each other. However, when Tom married Alice about 25 years ago, Ethan and Tom began to drift apart. As Ethan observed on more than one occasion, marriage can change a person. About ten years ago, on a camping trip out west, Ethan and Tom spent most of an evening arguing about an up-coming election. It seemed that politics had also become a wedge in their relationship. After returning home, they communicated even less, and Ethan realized it had now been almost five years since they last spoke.

Should Ethan give Tom a call? They were now in different stages of their lives, so an evening spent catching up might be a pleasant experi-ence. If nothing else, it would help Ethan take his mind off Sarah.

The drive to Fort Scott meant that Ethan could exit I-70 in Fulton and drive the less crowded state highways through Jefferson City and the Lake of the Ozarks. In addition, Ethan was towing a camper, so he would not need to stay with Tom. He wanted to hang out with an old friend. It was short notice, but Ethan decided to give him a call.

Tom answered on the second ring. "Ethan, buddy! It's been a long time. How yah doing?"

"Not well," Ethan responded without hesitation. "I've got some bad news, Tom, and I apologize for not reaching out sooner." Ethan purpose-fully paused to give Tom a moment to process what he said. "Tom, I lost Sarah last week. It was leukemia."

Ethan heard a long sigh, like a balloon slowly deflating. "It went fast, Tom, and she didn't suffer."

"I see," Tom finally replied. "Ethan, I'm *so* sorry." Then, after a pause, he added, "Man, you guys were married forever. I remember going to your wedding, what was it? Forty years ago?"

What went unsaid was that Ethan had missed Tom's wedding 15 years later because he and Sarah had been on a road trip with the kids.

"Yeah," answered Ethan. For the moment, he couldn't think of anything to say.

"So how yah holding up?" Tom inquired.

"Not well. I took a leave of absence from the firm, bought myself a camper, and just started a road trip out west."

Ethan recognized the same echoing laugh he first heard in college. "That's the old Ethan I remember," Tom chuckled. "Horace Greeley must've had you in mind when he wrote 'Go West, young man!'" Then, before Ethan could respond, Tom asked, "Wait a minute, did you say you just *began* your trip? Where are you right now? You want to swing through Fort Scott?"

"I'm sitting at a rest stop just east of Columbia," Ethan replied. "And *yes*, I'd love to come through Fort Scott. That's kind of what I had in mind. You free tonight?"

"Well, let's see," Tom responded. "Let me check my social calendar. You know, of course, that I have formal plans in this thriving metropolis just about every evening."

Ethan forced a laugh but did not respond. "Nah, I'm just kidding," Tom continued, stating the obvious. "But I tell yah what, Ethan, why don't you stay with me for a couple of nights? I can take a day or two off, and believe it or not, there are things here worth seeing."

"I've already been to the DQ and the grain elevator," responded Ethan. "You mean there's more?"

"Yeah, alright, smart-ass," Tom replied. "Trust me. I can fill at least a day or two. So, when can I expect you?"

"Late afternoon," answered Ethan. "And while I appreciate the offer, I'm not going to stay with you overnight. I bought a camper, and I'm eager to try it out."

"Alright," Tom replied. "I've got some luxurious accommodations, but suit yourself."

"Maybe another time," said Ethan, "Meanwhile, can you recommend a good place where I can set up the camper for the night?"

"Yeah, there's a place called Crossroads just north of town. Use your GPS; it's easy enough to find. Text me once you're here, and I'll swing by to pick you up."

"Sounds good," Ethan responded. "I'll see you in a few hours. It'll be great to catch up."

"Sure will, buddy. See you soon."

Ethan felt a weight had been lifted from his shoulders. He grabbed a bag of pretzels from the camper and set off for the three-and-a-half-hour drive to Fort Scott. Except for filling the gas tank, Ethan motored nonstop until he parked the trailer in the empty campground.

Ethan had been to Fort Scott, but not for at least a decade. Located just west of the Missouri-Kansas border and about sixty miles south of Kansas City, this sleepy little hamlet of about 8,000 occupied a historically strategic area. The actual fort, named after General Winfield Scott and constructed along the frontier in 1842, was built to keep the peace between indigenous tribes and white settlers. The fort also played a crucial role in securing the area for Union forces during the Civil War.

After parking the camper and plugging it in for electrical power, Ethan walked to the campground's entrance to wait for Tom. It didn't take long. A silver Ford pickup truck that looked like it had just rolled off the assembly line soon pulled into the campground's parking lot. Of course, the F-150 model had been around forever. Leave it to Tom to drive such a traditionally American icon.

Ethan barely recognized the man who strained to climb out of the truck's cab. Tom had gained at least 75 pounds. His hair was thinner and entirely gray, and Ethan noticed a bald spot that resembled a fleshy yarmulke. Wrinkles creased his inflated forehead, and judging from the gray stubble, Ethan guessed a razor had not touched Tom's face in at least a week. The radiant smile was the only familiar feature. Tom waddled more than walked, but as he made his way toward Ethan, he extended his stubby arms, anticipating a hearty man hug.

"Hey, buddy!" Tom bellowed as he gripped Ethan's shoulders and vigorously slapped his back. "What a nice surprise. Man, you're still looking fit. I'm sorry, though, about the circumstances that led you to take this trip."

As the two men pulled back, Ethan observed that Tom was wearing khakis and an old sweater, not what he expected from a small-town lawyer in the middle of the week. Tom was now in his upper sixties, but as far as Ethan knew, he had never considered retiring.

"It's great to see you, too," Ethan echoed, acting like there had been no changes in Tom's appearance. "And I appreciate your flexibility. I certainly didn't give you much notice."

"No problem," replied Tom. "It's been another slow day." Then, slowly surveying the campground, Tom switched topics and asked, "So which is yours?"

Tom and Ethan grinned since there was only one camper in the lot. After all, this was a weekday afternoon in eastern Kansas before the start of summer vacation.

"You want a tour?" Ethan asked. "I've got a six-pack in the fridge."

Tom's eyes enlarged like those of a starved street mongrel looking at a leg of lamb. "Hell *yeah*, that sounds great."

After a "tour" that took only 30 seconds, Ethan grabbed the six-pack and a couple of folding chairs he had stowed for just such occasions. He noticed the flicker in Tom's eyes when he saw the Bud Light logo. As the two men stepped out of the camper, Ethan observed the sun had begun its descent toward the cloudless horizon. He unfurled the camper's striped awning, and once he had created the feel of a shady porch, Ethan unfolded the chairs, offered a beer to Tom, and popped one open for himself.

Ethan winced at the creaking sound he heard when Tom sluggishly sank into one of the chairs. The canvas sagged until it was only six inches above the gravel, but in the end, it held. Ethan sighed in relief and lowered the sunglasses above his forehead as he settled into his chair. The two old friends smiled and touched their beer cans in a silent toast.

"So," Tom said, "I was serious about some new places in town I wanted you to see."

While Ethan used one hand to sip his beer, he waved the other in a *comme ci, comme ca* motion. "I've been here before, Tom. I'm sure you remember. The old fort's a cool place, but I don't need to see it again. And while I always liked Gunn Park, it's okay if I don't see that again either."

Then, after pausing for another sip of beer and wiping his mouth with the back of his hand, Ethan added, "I mostly just wanted to see you."

"Yeah, I get it," Tom replied. "The flood of tourists who flock to this town every year feel the same way. They just want to hang out with ole Tom." After swallowing a giant gulp of beer, Tom came up grinning with a line of foam carpeting his upper lip.

"I'm serious," responded Ethan. "I wouldn't mind grabbing a bite to eat with you and Alice this evening and then maybe stopping by your place afterward to hang out for a little while. Otherwise, I'm good right here."

"At the very least, then," Tom countered, "Let me take you to this center tomorrow that recently opened in town. It's a museum dedicated to unsung heroes that some locals, mostly school kids, have researched."

"Nah," replied Ethan, "I'll take a raincheck. I'd like to hit the road early tomorrow."

Tom made little effort to mask his disappointment. He looked like a scolded puppy. Glancing westward toward the sinking sun without any shades, Tom finally lowered his gaze between his bulky thighs. He finished his beer in one long sip and then crushed the empty can like his fingers were a trash compactor. Then, finally, he looked up and smiled.

"Okay," Tom exclaimed with renewed energy. "How about we have dinner tonight in a place south of here called Chicken Mary's? I *know* you've never been there, and it's one of my favorite restaurants."

"Sure," responded Ethan. "That sounds good."

"There's one other thing, though," Tom added. "I don't have Alice anymore."

"*What?*" Ethan turned directly to face Tom. "What happened?"

"Ethan, man, I *love* this town, but Alice never felt the same way. And this town's been dying a slow death." When Tom reached for another beer, Ethan silently noted he would be the designated driver that evening.

"The hospital's gone," Tom continued. "A lot of businesses are boarded up. And my little practice has also been slowly dying. I have fewer and fewer clients every year, and I'm just too old to be chasing ambulances, you know what I mean?"

Ethan nodded sympathetically and waited for his friend to continue.

"I know some of it's my fault. For a while, I'd get on my political soapbox, and even though this is a fairly conservative community, I probably drove some people crazy." As Tom popped open his second beer, he added, "I guess one of those people was Alice."

For a moment, the only sounds were a gentle breeze whistling through the maples on the edge of the parking lot and the two friends swallowing their beer. Then, finally, Tom continued.

"You know, she was a good bit younger than me, right? So then, one day, out of nowhere, Alice just picked up and moved to Wichita. This town was always too small for her, and she'd finally had enough." Then, after a pause, he added, "Ah *hell*, I don't blame Alice. She's still got some life left to live, and this isn't where she wanted to live it."

Ethan glanced at Tom and thought about the syrupy life of a small, ailing town. Then, without bothering to activate his social filter, he blurted out, "Was there another man in the picture?"

"You know, that's the funny thing," Tom replied. "There wasn't, at least, I don't think there was. Besides, around here, it's pretty hard to conceal an affair. I just don't think Alice wanted this life anymore." He glanced at Ethan and added, "And I was a part of this life."

"Did you think about moving to Wichita with her?" Ethan inquired.

Top leaned back to chug the remaining suds of his beer like a determined pledge at a frat party. He wiped his mouth with the sleeve of his sweater, belched at full volume, and smiled sheepishly at Ethan.

"I did for a day or two," he finally answered. "In fact, I might've welcomed the change of scenery. But what would I do in Wichita? Besides, I don't think Alice was too hot for me to come along."

Ethan glanced over at his old college roommate. The look on Tom's face was heartbreaking, worse than the scolded puppy expression he had seen earlier. Ethan thought about Sarah and briefly wondered who had it worse. Then, he felt the need to steer the conversation in a different direction.

"You mentioned that your law practice is declining. Tell me more about that."

"It pretty much reflects the town's demise," Tom replied. "There simply aren't enough clients left to go around. And you probably noticed I'm not a spring chicken anymore." Tom glanced sideways at Ethan before continuing. "I just don't have the energy to keep up with kids right out of law school. And frankly, I don't have the desire." Finally, he turned to face Ethan squarely and added, "Maybe it's time to retire. The good thing is I've saved enough to comfortably spend my final years in that old house over on the west side."

Ethan drew in a deep breath, slowly shook his head, and then swallowed the last sip of his beer. He glanced toward Tom, who had withdrawn into a catatonic silence.

"And what would you do then?" Ethan finally asked.

Tom continued to stare absent-mindedly at the line separating the brilliant sunlight from the darkening shade, a border gradually drifting in their direction. Then, without shifting his gaze, the corners of his mouth lifted into a weak smile, and he slowly began to shake his head.

"I don't know," Tom finally snickered. "That's a *good* question. Gardening maybe? I've got a stack of books waiting to be read." Then, turning toward Ethan with a broad grin, he added, "Who knows? Maybe I'll buy myself a camper and take a road trip out West."

Ethan started to respond but realized there was nothing left to say. So, instead, he glanced at the sun falling into the skyline. There was now a hazy edge of gray above the horizon that might soon create one of those unique wine-colored prairie sunsets.

Ethan thought about his old college friend. They were only three years apart, but Tom looked much older. At this rate, he would be dead in less than a decade. Ethan and Tom had been roommates for only one year at Washington University and had then lived apart for the next forty years. Nevertheless, at this moment, Ethan felt a bond beyond mere sympathy. Both men were lawyers whose legal careers were largely behind them. And both were alone. Unlike Tom, Ethan had two children, but since they were adults living independently, he still feared the loneliness stalking his future.

Ethan quietly shook his head. His predicament was similar to Tom's, but he was *not* Tom. No matter the future, Ethan was confident about his inner strength. He would not allow himself to deteriorate slowly. Tom had been an inspiration in their youth, but their roles had flipped.

Ethan believed he possessed the free will to live on *his* terms, including deciding when to end his life. As long as he drew a breath, though, he was determined to be resilient.

Ethan glanced over at his friend, sagging in a chair that looked like it could collapse at any moment. He suddenly experienced a wave of compassion. Tom might be thrashing in quicksand, but his head was still high enough to breathe. He had been a friend for over forty years. You can always make new friends, but it is impossible to make old ones at this stage. Could Ethan just sit back and watch his friend sink into the swampy muck? Finally, he pivoted toward Tom and smiled.

"You know, I'm not in a rush," Ethan finally declared. "When I first thought of taking this trip a few days ago, I told myself *not* to follow an itinerary. The idea was to enjoy a freedom I've never experienced in my entire life." Then, after a brief pause, he added, "Tomorrow, let's check out that center you were talking about earlier. And while we're at it, I wouldn't mind seeing that park again. What's its name? Gunn Park?"

Tom silently nodded but kept his gaze fixed on the encroaching edge between light and darkness. Once again, though, Ethan observed the corners of his mouth turn upward.

chapter
6

As Ethan and Tom strolled along the quiet road winding through Gunn Park, they both enjoyed another luminous spring day with temperatures in the upper seventies. At first, the only sound came from a few robins fluttering in the upper brush, but they could soon hear the growl of an unseen waterfall. When the falls came into view, Ethan observed they were only a few feet high, but he could still make out the hint of a rainbow within their mist.

As Ethan observed the spray tumbling toward a distant pond, he realized Tom had fallen behind. His old roommate was seriously out of shape, and his breathing had begun to shrill like a blacksmith's bellows. So finally, spying picnic tables inside the shade of a shelter looming over the pond, Ethan led Tom in that direction to give his friend a badly needed breather.

Realizing it might be a minute or two before Tom could speak in complete sentences, Ethan decided this might be a good time to offer some reflections on the day.

"You were right, Tom. For its size, Fort Scott does have a lot to offer. I've always liked that area where downtown backs up to the old fort. The burgers and Suzie Q fries at the Nu Grille were delicious. But most of all, I *really* enjoyed checking out the Lowell Milken Center."

Tom wiped the moisture from his crimson forehead as he plopped down on the bench opposite Ethan. He nodded but remained quiet.

"What a cool idea," Ethan continued. "Tourists flock by the millions to those immense museums in cities like New York and Chicago, but right here, in your little community, you've got a place that'll inspire visitors with unknown heroes and their stories. And the best part is how it's local school kids who do the research."

"Yeah, it's pretty unique," Tom responded. Then, after pausing to gather his breath, he added, "What'd you think of Irene Sendler?"

"Maybe the best story of all," Ethan responded. "It's hard to believe I'd never heard of her before."

"If it hadn't been for some local high school kids and their research project," Tom replied, "You probably never would have." Tom wiped off more sweat and added, "You know, there's a decent little film about Irene Sendler. Hallmark made it, but without their usual schmaltz. You should check it out."

"There's no discounting the power of film," Ethan responded. "If it hadn't been for Steven Spielberg, who would've heard of Oscar Schindler? His story has become one of my favorite movies of all time."

"Good point," Tom responded. "But Irene Sendler's story is arguably even more compelling. After all, she saved the lives of nearly 2,500 kids in the Warsaw Ghetto. That's more than double the number on Schindler's list."

Ethan added, "What's more, she took considerably bigger risks. Of course, Schindler's story was portrayed in an Oscar-winning film, while Sendler only made it to where? Hallmark?"

Tom nodded in agreement but remained quiet. He then turned toward the pond and sighed. "You know, I've been coming here my whole life. It's always been a good place to think." Then, turning back to Ethan, he added reflectively, "Did you ever have any desire to become an unsung hero?"

Ethan chuckled. "What made you think of *that* question? Those stories this morning were inspiring, but that's still quite a leap."

Tom's breathing had finally settled, and the rosy color had drained from his face. "I don't know, Ethan, but as I said, this is a good place to think." Then, after a pause, he continued, "I mean, look at us. At best, we might have another couple of decades, and then it's all over. And let's face it, most of what's coming will be tougher because . . ."

"Everything'll get harder as we grow older," Ethan interjected.

"Both physically and mentally," Tom agreed. There was another pause as the two friends exchanged troubled glances and shook their heads. Then, finally, Tom added, "That's why I asked about being an unsung hero. So far, neither of us would qualify for a spot in the Lowell Milken Center, right? I *definitely* wouldn't. We'll both be dead pretty soon and then that'll be it. I don't know about you, but I don't believe any of that nonsense about heaven or hell. When we're dead, we'll simply cease to exist. We'll go back to how it was before our parents decided to have children."

"You come here to think?" Ethan asked, "Or to depress the *hell* out of me?"

"Well, we're not dead yet," responded Tom. "And it's not too late to do something that'll make a difference in someone else's life, right?"

"Why? What are you planning, Tom? I think it's too late to join the Peace Corps."

The scolded puppy look returned to Tom's face. "I don't know. I guess I was just thinking out loud."

"Okay," Ethan replied, "I think I've made a difference in the lives of some of my clients."

"Weren't most of them guilty?" Tom asked as though conducting a cross-examination.

"I suppose so," answered Ethan. "But that's not the point. They all had a constitutional right to a good defense. So, in theory, they were innocent until some prosecutor proved their guilt beyond a reasonable doubt. And my job was to make sure the prosecution did theirs."

"Granted, counselor," Tom conceded, "But you were their defense lawyer, not their social worker, correct? So, in the end, did you make that big a difference in their lives?"

"Is that *so* important?" Ethan asked rhetorically. "Making a difference in the lives of others?"

Tom suddenly bent down to pick up a flat pebble he spied beneath a neighboring picnic table. He stood, approached the railing above the pond, and skipped the rock sideways so it bounced along the calm surface of the water below. It left behind several circular ripples before disappearing out of sight.

"Is that act supposed to be metaphorical?" Ethan asked with a wide grin on his face.

"Maybe," Tom replied. Then, after a pause, he added more gravely, "I just think we're obligated to leave the world a better place than we found it. And so far," he pronounced desolately, "I've made few ripples. How about you?"

Ethan glanced at the quivering surface of the pond while trying to come up with a good response. Then, finally, he looked back at Tom and replied, "No, probably not. Until now, Sarah was the only unsung hero in our family."

"Yeah," responded Tom. "I suppose the best high school teachers are in the best position to become unsung heroes."

Ethan exhaled and bit down on his lower lip. Then, he finally turned to confront Tom face-to-face and asserted, "Sarah was one of the best. But I wasn't just thinking about her work in the classroom." Then, after a brief pause, Ethan asked, "Have I ever told you about Daryl?"

Tom shook his head but remained silent. "He was someone where Sarah and I could've made a big difference. Despite her best efforts, though, I was the one who screwed things up."

"Really?" Tom responded, sitting back down at the picnic table like a child preparing for storytime. "*Do* tell."

Sarah and I had been married less than a year. We had a two-bedroom flat in U-City, not far from the Loop. We only had one car back then, Sarah's little VW bug. She'd drive it to school each day, leaving me to walk to my law classes. Money was tight. We had Sarah's salary to support the two of us, but as you know, law school was expensive, and she was just a first-year teacher. You know how little they make, right? I later got a part-time position with a firm during my second and third years, which helped considerably, but that first year was quite a struggle.

Toward the end of that year, Sarah came up with an outrageous idea. Initially, I wasn't on board, but she made some compelling arguments. Sarah wanted to take in a foster kid. A teacher-friend at school had given her the idea. Sarah told me the state's only requirements were a clean record, being at least 21 years old, and the ability to provide a decent place to live. She said the kid could sleep in the second bedroom, which was mostly going unused for out-of-town guests. We would not have any trouble meeting those requirements.

Sarah made two points that won me over. First, since we were planning to start our own family in a few years, this would give us some good experience to prepare for that day. The second, as you can probably guess, is that it paid a salary. Not much, but enough to sufficiently supplement our income. I had already landed a clerking position for June and July, but Sarah was off for the summer, and she said this would give her something to do.

I'm sharing this story now because I believe Sarah also stated at the time that she wanted to make a positive difference in someone else's life. We're not exactly talking about Irene Sendler's efforts, but as quoted from the Talmud in *Schindler's List*, "whoever saves one life saves the world entire." You should know, though, that Sarah was the driving force behind this idea. From start to finish, I was simply going along for the ride.

After several days of heated discussion, I finally agreed to the plan under one condition. In most cases, taking in a foster child is a temporary arrangement since the long-term goal is to return the kid to the biological parents. Therefore, I agreed to take a child just for the summer. After that, we could negotiate an extension. I wanted to see how everything worked out before deciding on anything more permanent. By the end of August, we would continue as foster parents only if *both* of us agreed. That meant we each had a veto.

We made the final decision over dinner one Friday night in early May at Blueberry Hill. You remember that place, right? They still make those delicious burgers. We were sitting outside at one of their tables along the sidewalk. Sarah and I observed the sunset at one end of Delmar while a gentle breeze took the edge off the warm day. She brought up the idea again just as I finished my second beer. Sarah must have known I was feeling mellow and figured this would be the ideal time to make a decision. She had a little Machiavelli inside her, although it was always for a good cause.

The following day, Sarah filled out the applications, and within a week, the state completed its background check. Then, in early June, an eleven-year-old named Daryl Armstrong suddenly moved into our second bedroom. This development turned our world upside down. Daryl hardly spoke, but his presence was constant. I'd awake in the morning, and his blue eyes bore into me as I drank my coffee and tried to read the paper. When I staggered in from a long day of research at the firm, the first thing I saw was the back of his blond head watching cartoons. Every evening, Daryl would silently hug the other end of the couch while we watched TV shows like *MASH* and *Cheers*.

We constantly tried to engage Daryl in conversation, but his only responses were yes's and no's, and even those were difficult to hear. We did not know the details, but his mom was already a user long before Daryl was even born. I still can't imagine what it was like for that poor kid growing up. He never knew his dad, but his mom frequently entertained men for money, primarily to support her drug habit. If Daryl had grandparents, they were out of the picture. All he had was Brenda, his mother, who was far from reliable. After the cops arrested her one night, the state finally stepped in and put Daryl into the foster care maze. He was passed from one set of foster parents to another before finally ending up in our U-City apartment.

That summer, the state paid for Daryl to attend a camp for a few hours each day. Otherwise, he was Sarah's responsibility. She took to this task with a maternal instinct neither of us knew existed. Sarah filled our apartment with library books and spent hours each day tutoring Daryl. She spoke to him nonstop, even though the conversations were mostly one-sided. Sarah understood the only way to make up for years of Daryl's seclusion was to flood him with constant stimulation.

Sarah also took Daryl on field trips to places like Forest Park, the zoo, and the botanical gardens. I took a bus downtown each morning so she could have the car, and pretty soon, she was driving him to places like Six Flags, Cahokia Mounds, and Meramec Caverns. Sarah focused all her energy, usually expended on more than 120 high school students during the year, on this one child. What's more, she displayed unlimited patience. After several weeks, her efforts started to pay off. By mid-July, I noticed that Daryl was starting to ask questions and speak in complete sentences.

On an unusually cool Saturday morning in late July, Sarah suggested we picnic in Creve Coeur Park. I'd been joining them for excursions over the last few weekends but had mixed feelings. Don't get me wrong, Daryl was a sweet, harmless kid. I even bought him a baseball glove, and we played catch a few times. However, these weekend outings were biting into the time I wanted to spend with my wife. After all, we'd only been married for a year.

Sarah wanted to introduce Daryl to Creve Coeur Falls, where she had fond memories from her childhood. Afterward, she planned to spread a blanket on the leaden sand and maybe play a board game. I was not wild about this since it meant I would again have to share my beautiful wife with this little interloper. I also had doubts Daryl could play anything beyond Chutes and Ladders. But like I said before, the kid was harmless, and the weather promised to be ideal. I even brought along our baseball gloves.

The day didn't get off to a good start. One look at the falls, and Daryl made it clear he wanted to climb them like a monkey. Sarah and I had fallen into a good cop, bad cop routine, so I mechanically stepped into my role and firmly told him to stay off the slippery rocks. Daryl had recently begun to test our limits, and I wanted to provide consistent enforcement. The falls are not high, though, so despite the sign warning people to stay off, children climb them all the time. This decision was a judgment call, and although I think Sarah would have let Daryl scramble up the falls had I not been there, she deferred to my call. Daryl was visibly upset and quickly fell into a sullen mood.

After spreading a blanket, Daryl asked about wading into the lake. There were good reasons, however, why the county had posted signs to stay out of the water. The lake was a petri dish for waterborne bacteria and a watershed for every chemical sprayed on the surrounding suburban lawns. Once again, I told Daryl no, and once again, he pouted. Then Daryl retaliated by telling us no when we asked him to play a board game or throw a baseball. He only nodded to say yes when offered some drumsticks from the Colonel's bucket of chicken.

After lunch, Sarah took Daryl off to wander down the beach. Meanwhile, I relaxed by watching a couple of Sunfish sailboats take advantage of the gusty breeze to race each other from one end of the lake to the other. There were a few wispy clouds on the western horizon, but otherwise, it was the perfect day. In slow motion, I descended from sitting with my legs crossed to laying back propped up on my elbows to a full-blown nap.

A few minutes later, what appeared to be an eclipse blocked the sun and promptly woke me up. It turned out to be Sarah standing above me, dripping lake water from her clothes and hair. She was standing next to Daryl, and it was apparent he was also soaked from top to bottom. Despite the brilliant glare, I could see Sarah shaking her head and Daryl biting down on his lip.

"What happened," I inquired. "Why are you both wet?"

"I ran into Lizzy," Sarah replied. I could tell my question didn't have a simple answer.

"You remember her?" she added. "From my high school? While we were catching up, this one here decided to wander into the lake." Sarah nodded toward Daryl.

"It was getting hot," Daryl whined, suddenly finding the ability to chime into a conversation. "So I took a few steps into the water to cool off."

"Unfortunately," Sarah continued, taking back control, "He stepped into a drop-off and, for a moment, disappeared. I didn't even notice since my back was turned. Lizzy's the one who screamed. Next thing I know, we're pulling Daryl out of the lake like a couple of hillbillies noodling a catfish."

By this point, I was sitting up, trying to appear concerned, but I just about lost it when Sarah mentioned the catfish. "So, he's alright?" I manage to ask.

"Yeah, man, I'm fine," Daryl sneered, answering for himself. "I was only under for a second before she grabbed me. I would've gotten out on my own if she'd given me a chance."

I stood to face the two of them directly. Sarah's anger was starting to dissipate, but Daryl's annoyed expression was a mix of scorn and embarrassment. Then he glanced down, placed his hands behind him like they were handcuffed, and started to sway back and forth.

"Well, let's get going," I finally uttered. "The sooner you both shower, the better."

The rest of the weekend proved to be uneventful. By Sunday morning, Sarah and Daryl had forgotten their baptism from the day before. While watching the Cardinals clobber the Cubs that night, we brought in a pizza. After Daryl went to sleep, Sarah and I quarreled about what to do when the summer ended. I reminded her that everything would change once she returned to teaching. Daryl would attend school during the day, but in the evening, he would again be our responsibility. I told Sarah we wouldn't have the juice to look after a fifth-grader at the end of a full day of teaching and law school.

Before going to sleep that night, we decided to put the decision off for another week. Meanwhile, Sarah suggested we take a road trip out to Colorado. It was the start of August, and my summer internship had just ended, leaving us a couple of weeks before the start of Sarah's school. So, we reserved a small cabin on the Fall River near Estes Park. Sarah hoped that taking Daryl on vacation might persuade me not to exercise my veto.

Each day, we took Daryl on hikes in Rocky Mountain National Park. The kid had never seen a mountain before, but he took to hiking through them like a miniature Kit Carson. The hikes grew a little longer each day, and Daryl spoke a little more each night. We quickly learned how much he loved animals. Each day, we'd spot a different critter—beavers, bald eagles, pine martins, moose, big-horn sheep, and god knows how many elk. By the end of the week, Daryl was talking about growing up to be a park ranger. What's more, we were all starting to feel like a family.

This state of affairs made me increasingly anxious. Sarah was falling for this boy, and I was also starting to enjoy his company. On the other hand, though, I was just 23 years old and was staring at two more years of law school. As we drove east on I-70 for hundreds of miles, I kept peeking in the rearview mirror at Daryl in the backseat. While he was mesmerized by the fields of wheat and sunflowers encircling us in western Kansas, I was mulling over what to do with him once we got home. I also feared that if we became too attached to him, it would be even more painful to let him go once Brenda got her act together.

The first full day back in St. Louis was one I'll never forget. In the morning, I strolled to the Wash. U. campus to register for classes and purchase textbooks. As soon as I returned that afternoon, Sarah was waiting to pounce on me with some big news.

"We need to talk in private," she whispered excitedly. I noticed Daryl was planted in front of the television, watching a cartoon. Sarah had recently tried to wean him off the mindless garbage on TV, so allowing him to watch the *Transformers* made it clear how much she wanted to spring something on me. I can only imagine how much my blood pressure rose at that moment.

"Let's go into our bedroom." I followed her, and as soon as she closed the door, Sarah spun around and announced, "I got a call from Social Services this morning." She looked away and paused for a moment.

"Yeah? Go on," I replied.

Turning back to face me, she blurted out, "Brenda, Daryl's mom, has relapsed. She'd been clean for a long time and had made good progress. They were hoping to reunite her with Daryl sometime soon. It was much worse this time, though, so they decided that returning him to his natural mother was hopeless and to make Daryl available for permanent adoption. *Immediately.*"

There was a fire in Sarah's dark brown eyes, and her voice had taken on an urgency like we had to do something to keep a jetliner from going down. Her passion could sometimes be a little annoying, but overall, this was one of the things I loved the most about Sarah. Anyhow, she didn't need to say more. We gazed at each other, contemplating the ramifications of her last statement. Finally, she added, "So . . ."

I jumped in to finish the sentence. "So, the folks at Social Services want to know if we'd like to adopt Daryl." Sarah nodded as her lips parted into a hopeful smile. "Permanently," I added. Sarah's smile grew even broader.

"*Ethan,*" she asserted, "This is our chance to *really* make a difference. If we don't adopt Daryl now, no one else ever will. He's too old. If we don't keep him, Ethan, Daryl will get passed from one foster situation to another until he's a grown adult."

I knew adoption was always possible, but the more immediate issue had been whether to keep Daryl beyond the summer. The Daryl experiment was a success because it supplemented our summer income and convinced us that we'd be ready to parent our children when the time came. But despite the week in Colorado, I was still leaning towards exercising my veto. I'd decided that when law school started up again, and Sarah returned to her teaching, we should not continue to bear the burden of looking after an eleven-year-old kid. And I certainly wasn't looking to keep him forever.

Daryl was an agreeable kid, and we'd recently bonded in Colorado. There was also no question that Sarah had dramatically expanded his world. To be blunt, though, Daryl wasn't our kid. I am not opposed to adoption in theory, but if Sarah and I ever felt the need to adopt, I would want a newborn. Not only was Daryl the product of someone else's DNA, but someone else had molded and shaped him for most of his life. Except for one summer, we had nothing to do with the nature or the nurture that created this boy.

After Daryl went to bed that night, Sarah and I sat on our little balcony for hours, chewing over this dilemma. Much to Sarah's credit, the conversation never became hostile or contentious. I made a valiant effort to explain my position diplomatically, and Sarah was on board when we went to sleep. If nothing else, she respected the deal we had made at the start of the summer. Mostly.

Seeing we should sever our relationship with Daryl as quickly as possible, like ripping off a band-aid, I called Social Services the following day, and they promptly arranged a new placement. I reminded Sarah that Daryl had been through this many times before. Nevertheless, tears welled in his eyes when the caseworker came over the next day to tell Daryl about the new arrangement. It was the first time I had ever seen the kid cry. Sarah began to weep as well. She reached out, hugged Daryl for a long time, and then bolted from the apartment. I later learned that Sarah had walked for miles around the outer perimeter of Forest Park.

Meanwhile, I helped Daryl pack and then saw him off. I'll never forget his vacant stare as he mutely shuffled out of our apartment. He would not look me in the eye.

It took a while, but Sarah and I both moved on. The start of the school year proved to be a helpful distraction. Sarah cried a bit when she saw the Colorado pictures after we developed the film, but that was it.

Pretty soon, she mainly focused on the 120 high school kids who entered her English classroom daily. In time, Sarah's practical side finally suppressed her emotions. We would reminisce about Daryl occasionally, but he eventually faded from our consciousness.

For a moment, a gulf of silence separated Ethan and Tom. They both glanced downward, unable to speak for different reasons. Ethan concealed his sheepish expression, feeling embarrassed and maybe a little guilty. Tom did not know what to say. Finally, he sighed loudly and fumbled through a weak expression of sympathy. Ethan glanced at his watch and suggested they head back to town to think about a place for dinner.

An hour later, Ethan and Tom were downing margaritas and consuming Mexican fare at El Charro in downtown Fort Scott. Not surprisingly, Tom drank a little too much, and Ethan again assumed his role as the designated driver. Throughout the evening, the conversation wavered from pleasant ruminations over their college days to swapping tales about some of their most noteworthy clients. Ethan managed to steer clear of any talk about politics. As the night wore on, he realized how much he enjoyed Tom's company. That night, they were the last to leave the restaurant.

chapter

7

The following morning, Ethan struggled to climb out of bed. At first, he thought it was a hangover. Ethan had not had one since his drinking days back in college. Then he remembered he did not drink much the previous night. Ethan had dropped Tom off at a reasonable hour before retiring to the comforts of his new home on wheels. So, if it wasn't a hangover, what was the source of this morning's lethargy?

Ethan wanted to soon be on the road and, for one of the few times in his life, relish the freedom of going wherever he wanted. That thought alone should have been exhilarating. But instead, he felt battered and unmotivated. Something was weighing him down like he had gained a hundred pounds overnight. Then, turning toward the wall beside his bed, he caught a glimpse of Sarah. Before leaving St. Louis, Ethan had taped a photograph of her in front of the Waimea Canyon in Kauai.

Years ago, Ethan and Sarah had taken a three-week trip to Hawaii to celebrate their thirtieth anniversary. In Ethan's mind, they also took the trip as an antidote for Sarah's recent depression. Noah, her youngest, would soon be going to college, and she was facing the onset of the dreaded empty nest. One glance at Sarah's expression confirmed the trip had more than served its purpose.

In the picture, Sarah was wearing a bright red muumuu accented by a creamy yellow orchid in her hair. She was extending an arm toward Ethan while flourishing a sultry smile. Sarah's hair was dark and wavy, curling around her bare shoulders and unmarred by the streaks of gray that would appear years later. There was a sparkle in both eyes, and the Hawaiian sun had gently baked her skin into a smooth, olive sheen. Crow's feet flanked her eyes, but otherwise, Sarah looked like a woman in her thirties. She was beguiling. Ethan smiled at the memory of how they had spent so much time in bed. The trip had been like a second honeymoon.

While scrutinizing Sarah's picture, Ethan began to understand the source of his fatigue. It was simple depression. He may have been on an unfettered road trip, but Ethan was still mourning the loss of his beloved. Completing this journey toward Oregon would require a delicate balance. Ethan had promised Jenny he would use this time to plot out the remainder of his life, not to contemplate its premature end. Yet, at the same time, he had every right to grieve. The most challenging time would be days like today when he would be mindlessly cruising the open road.

Ethan knew his general direction would be to the northwest, which would probably mean spending the night at a KOA somewhere in eastern Wyoming. While journeying across the sweeping prairies, he dreaded the prospect that forty years of memories might haunt him over every open mile. Two thoughts persistently nagged Ethan: Sarah was gone forever, and the best part of his life was behind him. Is it any wonder he felt paralyzed? Ethan would brew some coffee, but that would not be enough.

Suddenly, his cell phone dinged. It was a text from Tom thanking him for their time together, and it ended with an offer that laid an appreciative smile across Ethan's face. Tom provided access information to his Audible account along with some simple directions. He had four credits available and told Ethan he could download whatever books he wanted. Tom ended the text by suggesting they would be good companions on the open road.

Ethan suddenly felt a surge of energy, like Popeye downing a can of spinach. After sending his old friend a thank you text, he quickly downloaded the app, signed into Tom's account, and began to explore its extensive library. What should he listen to first? Grisham's latest? Stephen King? Something a little more highbrow from the *New York Times* Best Sellers List? Considering where he was going, maybe a western would be in order.

Then he heard Sarah's voice. She taught everything from Shakespeare to the modern classics in her English class. Sarah had frequently urged Ethan to expand his literary interests, but he had always preferred historical or political nonfiction. Like most students, he had suffered through Homer, Tolstoy, and Melville. Ethan had enjoyed some of the classics by Dickens and Mark Twain, but overall, he still associated these older books with homework. They were assignments, not something pleasurable for a long road trip.

Glancing once again toward Sarah's photograph, Ethan briefly thought her lips moved. This image put another smile on his face. He recalled how Sarah looked forward to the spring semester each year when she had her students read John Steinbeck's *The Grapes of Wrath*. Sarah had always proclaimed this to be her favorite book, so in a recent moment of weakness, Ethan had promised to read it. Maybe this would be a good time? Ethan knew the book's main characters, the Joad family, were Okies traveling to California in search of a better life. So, *The Grapes of Wrath* suddenly took on a new meaning.

Ethan searched for the book and then downloaded it onto his phone. It would fill a large niche of his driving time at twenty-one hours. He began listening to the book's poignant reader even before pulling out of the campground. For the next twelve hours, as Ethan tooled across Nebraska and Wyoming on I-80, he was accompanied by Tom Joad and his family, who drove across New Mexico and Arizona on Route 66. They were good company and, for the most part, distracted Ethan from gloomier reflections.

After an uneventful night at a KOA just north of Laramie, Ethan continued listening to *The Grapes of Wrath* as he resumed his journey toward the Grand Tetons. A short time later, he observed that he was climbing in elevation. Ethan knew enough history to appreciate the significance of where he was currently driving. This stretch of highway reached through South Pass, the gateway through the impenetrable wall of the Rocky Mountains, where covered wagons once made their way to Utah, California, and Oregon. The climb was sometimes steep, even for his SUV towing a camper. What must this experience have been like for people in carts drawn by teams of oxen? And while Ethan would cross over the Continental Divide in a couple of hours, it took the wagon trains weeks to cover the same ground.

Ethan looked forward to exiting the interstate at Rawlins to angle toward Grand Tetons National Park. He had driven this route on more than one occasion and remembered how the scenery progressively improved as he paralleled the Wind River Range. This area was an untamed country, free from heavy traffic clogging the interstate. A cobalt sky crowned the white-crested peaks on both sides, unblemished by a single cloud.

As Ethan drove through the Wind River Indian Reservation, he recalled a conversation with Sarah about *The Grapes of Wrath*. One of the principal characters in the book is an itinerant preacher named Jim Casy. Sarah had said it was no accident that Casy bore the same initials as Jesus Christ since he was the moral spokesman of the story. Like Jesus, Casy had wandered into the wilderness seeking answers to unanswerable questions. One of these involved the nature of the human soul.

Once Sarah understood her cancer had become a ticking time bomb, she naturally took a renewed interest in this question about the human soul. Therefore, one evening, after attempting to eat a little dinner, she resurrected the conversation. Sarah informed Ethan that Steinbeck had espoused an intriguing thought on the human soul by using Jim Casy as his mouthpiece. She tried to explain his insights, but Ethan was tired that night and had trouble focusing.

Now, Ethan thought it might be providential that he had finished listening to the book with about an hour to go before reaching the park's entrance. Rather than start a new book, he would use this hour to discuss *The Grapes of Wrath* with Sarah inside his head.

"Sweetheart," Ethan stated aloud, "I know you're not physically here, but you're sitting right next to me in spirit. I've spent the last two days listening to your favorite book, *The Grapes of Wrath*, and I wanted to share some thoughts. Knowing you as I do, I think I can fill in your side of the conversation."

Ethan had just exited a speck on the map called Dubois, continuing west on Highway 26 toward Colter Bay Village in the heart of the national park. The road was surprisingly empty, the mountain scenery was intoxicating, and Ethan was anxious to dissect an epiphany he had just uncovered from *The Grapes of Wrath*. He paused, listening for Sarah's soothing voice, but heard only the growling of the SUV's engine straining to pull its heavy load through the winding mountain passes.

"At the risk of sounding like one of your students," Ethan continued, "I have a question about Jim Casy. I'm trying to make sense out of something he said."

Ethan understood he was engaging in a fantasy. Glancing around, though, he thought this was the ideal time and place to see where it led. Ethan believed he could supply Sarah's words inside his brain. He knew her so well this would not be difficult. Nevertheless, when her silky voice broke the silence, it was as though Sarah was sitting right next to him in her familiar spot, the passenger seat.

"Go on with your question, my love. What did Casy say?"

The voice was so natural that Ethan immediately pivoted to his right. The seat was empty, of course.

"Okay," Ethan finally uttered, "When Casy wandered into the wilderness to find his soul, he discovered that he didn't have one of his own."

Realizing he wanted his paraphrasing to be as precise as possible, Ethan paused to recall the passage better.

"Instead," he continued at last, "He discovered that within himself, he had just a little piece of a great big soul. He said that by itself, that little bit of soul wasn't much good. It only mattered when it joined with the rest of the *whole* soul."

Ethan paused again to gather his thoughts. Casy had expressed himself in a simple Okie vernacular, but his ideas were anything but simple.

"Now, thinking of you," Ethan continued. "I find this idea beguiling. Many years ago, I took a philosophy course in college, and I remember learning about a concept called the 'over soul' from Transcendentalism. It's the idea that all human souls are part of a larger soul. So is this what Casy was talking about?"

Without hesitation, the voice inside Ethan's head immediately answered. "Yes, my love, that's what Steinbeck intended."

Ethan smiled upon hearing Sarah's steady voice and how she kept referring to him as "my love." His imagination evidently had a romantic side. If someone observed this conversation, they might think him a bit deranged. After all, he was sitting inside his car, not just talking to himself but carrying on a complete conversation. On the other hand, people always speak to loved ones at gravesites. How was this any different? Regardless, hearing Sarah's voice at this moment was a soothing balm.

Suddenly, it was Sarah's turn to ask a question. "Ethan, can I assume you're raising this subject now because of my recent departure?"

From where was *this* coming? Until now, Ethan assumed he was in control of both sides of the conversation. Yes, after Sarah's cremation, Ethan had begun obsessing over what might have happened to her soul. He had overlooked this "over soul" concept until now. Maybe it sank into his subconscious. Nevertheless, what had begun as an effort to process *The Grapes of Wrath* had turned into a self-therapy help session.

"That wasn't my intent when I asked the question, at least on a conscious level," Ethan finally responded. "But yes, that might be why I find this idea from the book so intriguing.

Seeing a pull-out along the banks of the Buffalo Fork River, Ethan swerved over and came to a sudden stop. He would soon be at his campsite in the national park and wanted more time to continue this discussion. Besides, Ethan could not help but notice this was a strikingly picturesque spot. He climbed out of his Subaru, kicked off his sandals, and found a boulder where he could sit while sparkling water from the river playfully danced around his ankles. The chilly wetness was invigorating.

Ethan knew the water flowing over his toes would soon make its way down to the Snake River and, from there, into the Columbia, where it would eventually end up in the Pacific. Once the vast ocean absorbed these water molecules, some would evaporate into the atmosphere and then return as precipitation to this mountain tributary. Ethan smiled at the symbolic connection between this hydraulic principle and Casy's idea about each individual possessing a small piece of a soul that eventually reunites with a much larger entity.

"The idea of an 'over soul,'" Ethan finally continued, "is no more provable than the belief in a heaven or a hell, is it?"

"True," responded Sarah, "But you must admit there's more inside you than just muscles, bones, and blood, at least while we're alive. When I fell in love with you, it wasn't just with your gorgeous body." A slight smile flashed across Ethan's face, but he remained silent.

"There's something unique inside all of us," Sarah continued. "Do you think it just vanishes the moment our bodies stop working?"

"So then Casy got it right?" Ethan inquired. "Our souls *really* do join with a larger over soul?"

"I've always believed this to be true," answered Sarah. "There were times I wanted to explore this subject with you when I was alive, but you never showed much interest." Then, after a brief pause, she added sympathetically, "I understood why, my love. Until recently, you mostly focused on the here and now, your clients and your children."

"Okay, let's assume you're right," Ethan replied. "Let's assume that you, Casy, and all the Transcendentalists got it right." There was a pause because Ethan knew it might be challenging to speak the following words. "Sarah, when you died, this would mean your soul joined with the 'great big soul.' In that case, you've lost your unique identity. I find that depressing."

"It may be depressing *now*," Sarah stated, "But only until you pass away and your soul joins with mine. Meanwhile, a little piece of us returns every time a baby's born. That's not depressing, is it?"

Ethan pulled his feet out of the water and rested them on a nearby sandbar. A ray of sunshine suddenly peeked through the upper foliage to thaw them out and restore blood flow.

"*Oh*, Sarah," Ethan proclaimed, mindlessly gazing upstream where water cascaded over a branch between two boulders. "If I could only be certain you were right."

Then, an idea occurred to him. "In fact," Ethan added, "If I were sure our souls would be reunited, that would be just another good reason to quit this world."

Sarah again surprised him. This time, her voice took a different tone, the one he heard whenever she was annoyed. "No, Ethan! You're missing the point. Life is a precious gift, and you should make the most of each and every day. You'll be with me soon enough."

"But what if I don't want to continue?" Ethan countered like a petulant child. "I've lived a good life. I've had a rewarding career. Together, we raised two amazing children. I've done just about everything I wanted to do." Then he paused again. Finally, he added, "Sarah, your life ended *way* too early. Why should I get to go on with mine?"

"*Because*," Sarah answered, and this time, she hesitated. "Because there's another key point embedded in Jim Casy's vision. He wasn't just talking about an afterlife, was he? Ethan, if we all share a little piece of that same giant soul, what does that obligate us to do while we're *alive*?"

Ethan looked like a student who did not know the answer when called on in class. For a moment, he wore a blank expression. Then, suddenly, inspiration brightened his face.

"It *means*," Ethan answered, "We're connected. We're connected in life as well as in death. Therefore, we share an obligation to support each other whenever possible."

"Support just family members?" Sarah asked in her probing teacher voice.

"No, not just family members," Ethan affirmed confidently. "It's everyone. It's all of humanity. Casy's the teacher in *The Grapes of Wrath*, but it's the Joads who put his ideas into practice ."

"That's right," Sarah responded, sounding even more like a proud teacher.

"In fact," continued Ethan, "Steinbeck scattered moral dilemmas throughout his novel to test the Joad family and show their progress. Take Ma, for example. When she had to decide whether to share the family's food with the starving children in the Hooverville, she did it, even though it meant less food for her family."

"You've got it!" Sarah declared. Ethan could visualize the gratified teacher smile on his wife's face. "And if you think about it, there are several other examples of the Joad's transformation from self-preservation toward altruism."

"*Oh*," Ethan uttered as though struck by a bolt of lightning, "That might also explain the book's final scene."

"Yes, my love, it does," Sarah responded. "Although, as you might expect in a film released in 1940, that particular scene didn't make it into the Henry Fonda movie."

For a moment, Ethan joined Sarah in her laughter. Then, there was just silence. The only sound came from the river's gurgling waters. Then, finally, Ethan heard Sarah's voice, but this time, it was almost a whisper.

"So, Ethan, does that answer your question about *why* you should go on living?"

For a moment, Ethan was utterly perplexed. Did this insight come from the ghost of his wife, like a scene from *A Christmas Carol*? Or did it originate from somewhere in the deep recesses of his imagination? Ultimately, did it matter?

Ethan clenched his lips together and nodded. For now, at least, he understood.

chapter

8

For the tenth consecutive day, Ethan arose early. He had purposefully positioned the camper away from the towering pines so the sunlight would flood his cabin. Within minutes, he had dressed, brewed a pot of coffee, and prepared for his short hike around the eastern edge of Jackson Lake. Every morning, Ethan mindlessly adhered to the same routine. He zipped up his North Face jacket, positioned the red Cardinals cap atop his head, flung open the door, stepped down from the camper, and breathed in the magnificent scenery. Ethan could repeat this routine for many years, and this moment would still never fail to splash a smile upon his face.

Despite brilliant sunshine that would later bake the back of Ethan's neck, the day was starting out frosty. A steady breeze from deep within the Tetons glided across the lake, kicking up white-capped waves and arching the lodgepole pines. From experience, Ethan knew the only remedy for this biting chill was to hike briskly.

Ethan took less than a minute to reach the Colter Bay Lakeshore trailhead. This two-and-a-half-mile loop meandered around the outer perimeter of a peninsula jutting directly into the lake. The view of the saw-toothed mountains was striking, particularly on those rare windless mornings when the Tetons appeared inverted on the lake's mirrored surface. This morning, though, the surf was cascading through the boulders scattered along the curved shoreline.

Early morning was the ideal time to view wildlife. Since entering the park, Ethan had spotted a bull moose, several bison, a black bear with its cubs, a couple of bald eagles, and an incalculable number of elk. However, ten minutes into this morning's hike yielded a sighting Ethan had never before encountered. Marching around a bend in the trail, Ethan suddenly froze. A small, furry creature with pointed ears and beady black eyes was gazing directly at him. Its long, slender body rose vertically from a tripod of two hind legs and a bushy tail. Except for a white collar, its fur was a deep shade of chocolate brown.

Ethan and the furry beast eyed each other like nervous gunslingers in a western gunfight. While stealthily pulling out his phone to snap a picture, Ethan wracked his brain, trying to identify the little mammal he had engaged in a staring contest. It was too big to be a squirrel or prairie dog and too slender to be a marmot or beaver. Could this be a fox or even a wolverine? Ethan had seen those critters before, and none looked like this little fellow. Finally, after a few seconds, the small animal leaped up on a boulder, posed for one more photograph, and vanished into the surrounding brush.

Ethan studied the pictures he had just taken. The image in one reminded him of the adorable stuffed animals Jenny collected when she was a little girl. Ethan finally decided to send the pictures to Jenny and Noah. Besides asking for their help to identify the little fur ball, Ethan also thought it would be an excellent opportunity to let his kids know he was still alive and kicking. Immediately after touching the send button, Ethan was startled by the loud ringing and vibration in the palm of his hand. Ellen's name appeared on the screen of his cell phone.

"*Hello*, Ellen," proclaimed Ethan, hoping a chipper tone might ward off bad news.

"Hi Ethan," Ellen responded meekly, "I hope this isn't a bad time."

"No, I was just out for a short hike," Ethan replied. "What's up?"

"It's the Wallace file," Ellen replied. "His trial's coming up next week, and Stan called from the federal prosecutor's office with a deal." Ellen paused to give Ethan time to process this information from 1,300 miles away.

"I'd probably decline any deal," responded Ethan, faster than Ellen had anticipated, "But out of curiosity, let's hear it."

"Time served plus five years for a guilty plea."

"That'd be tempting with any *other* client," Ethan stated, "After all, the max for insider trading is twenty years."

"So why should I turn it down?"

"Because in *this* case," responded Ethan, "The evidence is relatively weak. We deposed several of Stan's witnesses, but only one, Murphy, had much to say, and there were serious questions about his credibility. In the end, it'll be Murphy's word against our client's, and since Henry Wallace will make a convincing witness in his own defense, it's no contest. Frankly, Ellen, of all the times I've defended Henry, this is the first where even I have questions about his guilt. It shouldn't be hard to create reasonable doubt."

"So, we should go to trial?" Ellen inquired, sounding apprehensive.

"Yes, if need be," responded Ethan. "But knowing Stan, he's probably bluffing. It's your call, Ellen, but I'd call his bluff if it were me. There's a chance he might even drop the charges."

"Alright, that's what I'll do," Ellen replied. "On a different note, how're you holding up out there?"

"I'm doing *terrific*," responded Ethan in a slightly exaggerated tone. "I'm currently in the Grand Tetons. I hike every morning and then relax every afternoon. Not a bad life."

"Sounds like fun," Ellen responded. "I'm envious. Okay then, I'll let you get back to your morning hike. I may call again in a few days if that's alright."

"Sure, it's no problem," replied Ethan. "I'm glad you were available to step in when you did. Take care, Ellen. I'll talk to you soon."

Immediately after hanging up, Ethan noticed a sour taste in his mouth. Over the years, he had developed this response to any off-putting experience. In this case, Ethan was sure the conversation about his former client had generated this bitter flavor. Wallace's brinkmanship as a stock broker tended to attract a lot of unwelcome attention from the Securities and Exchange Commission, so he had been a client for a long time. In Ethan's eyes, though, Wallace was a materialistic sociopath. Dueling with prosecutors like Stan Armstrong appealed to Ethan, but defending scum like Wallace was becoming increasingly challenging. No wonder there was a foul taste in his mouth.

Two minutes later, Ethan received two text messages back-to-back. The first was from Jenny, who did not recognize the little critter but promised to call her dad that evening "just to catch up." The second was from Noah. He delicately inquired when he might expect to see his father in Portland and then ended his text by stating the furry animal in the picture was a pine marten. Ethan immediately googled pine martens to compare their photographs with those he had just taken. Sure enough, Ethan had had a close encounter with a pine marten. This revelation raised a smile and helped to cleanse his palate.

An hour later, Ethan approached the East Boat Dock on the much smaller Jenny Lake, about twenty miles due south. Ever since he arrived in the national park, Ethan had left his camper behind while driving to trailheads scattered from Moose in the south to the Yellowstone National Park entrance in the north. Today was the next big test. Ethan wanted to see how far he could hike into Cascade Canyon before turning back. He was a day hiker who did not carry backpacking gear, but he wanted gradually to increase the number of miles he could traverse in a single day.

Ethan could have hiked around the southern edge of Jenny Lake, but the boat ride would save time, enabling him to probe deeper into the canyon. He also wanted to see the surrounding mountains from the water. Once off the boat, Ethan knew it would be a tough climb up to the canyon in the heart of the highest peaks, particularly Grand Teton in the south and Mount Moran to the north. The first miles would include stops at Inspiration Point and the iconic Hidden Falls.

Ethan climbed aboard the launch, pulled off his day-pack, and settled comfortably onto a bench near the boat's stern. Then he noticed a shadow had followed him. Peering up, Ethan saw the dark outline of a towering man toting an oversized backpack. The giant stepped over to an empty area across from Ethan and jerked off his pack with a huge groan. Then, after planting the enormous bundle on an empty bench in front of him, he slowly descended onto a seat of his own, let out a huge sigh, and finally relaxed by extending his feet into the middle aisle.

Ethan could not take his eyes off the giant. He had to be at least six and a half feet tall. Judging from his overflowing gray beard, he also appeared to be at least seventy years old. The aging titan, however, had the physique of a man half his age. His muscles bulged out of a tight-fitting tee shirt, and the space between his cargo shorts and dusty boots revealed thighs thicker than Ethan's waist. The backpack was equally impressive. From its size, Ethan figured this colossus would spend several weeks deep in the mountains.

"Looks like you're doing some serious backpacking," Ethan observed as the launch pushed away from the dock.

The man sluggishly turned toward Ethan and lifted his head to peer from beneath the brow of a dingy blue Dodgers cap. "What gave you *that* clue?" he asked gruffly.

There was a scowl on his face because someone had invaded his privacy. Ethan's eyes widened, and he automatically recoiled. Then Goliath's lips parted into a wide grin.

"Hey man, I'm just *kidding*," the giant snorted. "Yeah, I'm planning to hike the northern section of the Continental Divide Trail this summer. I've already done everything to the south, so my goal now is to go from the Tetons up to Glacier. Once that's accomplished, I will have walked from Mexico to Canada."

Ethan glanced down at his modest day-pack and then looked back with a sheepish grin. "I'm planning to hike at least five miles today into Cascade Canyon. Once that's accomplished, I will have . . ."

He paused, and both men chuckled. Then the giant leaned over, extended a massive hand, and stated, "My name's John. John Cassidy."

"It's nice to meet you, John," responded Ethan, reaching across the aisle to shake the big man's hand. "Ethan. Ethan Marshall. After plopping back to his bench, Ethan asked, "So, where you from, John?"

"L.A. originally, but I've moved around a lot. I currently live in a small cabin outside of Granby, Colorado. How about you?"

"St. Louis. Although my current home is a camper, I'm slowly hauling out to Portland." Ethan then added, "I've never tried backpacking before. In my younger days, I'd hike up to twenty miles, but never with my home on my back."

"Like everything in life, there're tradeoffs," responded John. "This pack weighs well over forty pounds, and it's no fun dragging it up steep inclines at elevations where it's hard to breathe. And sleeping in a tent when it's ten degrees outside isn't for everyone." He paused to look toward the boat's bow, which had just crossed into the murky shadows cast by the increasingly soaring mountains. "On the other hand," he continued, "I get to see places day hikers never reach. And the sky at night is *beyond* description."

Ethan followed John's gaze and then turned back to see the rapture in his eyes. "Hey John, if you don't mind me asking, how old are you?"

"I just turned seventy-two. You?"

"Sixty-five," responded Ethan.

The two men nodded, silently acknowledging their growing fellowship. Then, before either could say another word, the craft decelerated, preparing to dock on the west side of the lake. Other passengers stood and started to gather their belongings.

"Hey Ethan, would you like some company up to the point where you turn back? It's fine if you say no. I don't want to intrude if you're looking for solitude. But I'll be spending weeks alone, so I always look for good companionship when I can."

"Sure," Ethan replied without hesitation. "Your pack must outweigh mine by at least 35 pounds, so that should help me keep up."

Both men smiled and then stood, tossing their packs over their shoulders. As they shuffled toward the exit ramp on the boat's starboard side, John glanced down at Ethan, lining up in front of him.

"You carrying bear spray?" John inquired.

Smiling in embarrassment, Ethan glanced back and replied, "No. People keep telling me I should, but I've been too lazy to get some."

"Don't worry," replied John, "I've got plenty. And believe me, up here, we may need it."

The two men said little for half an hour as they labored up the switchbacks to Inspiration Point. This celebrated spot looked down on Jenny Lake and beyond toward Jackson Hole. Getting there, however, meant the equivalent of climbing a fifty-five-story building in less than a mile. Ethan allowed John to take the lead since he worried about slowing the big man down. Sure enough, he struggled to keep up.

Ethan had fallen back about twenty yards as they neared the viewpoint. John had already yanked off his pack and was seated on a boulder, taking in the panoramic vista. Other hikers had scattered about, resting and studying the bird's-eye view. Ethan noticed that sweat had drenched John's back. The big man nodded toward a nearby boulder as though he had been saving it for Ethan.

"It'll get easier from here," John proclaimed. "This is the gateway into the canyon, so the trail mostly levels off from this point."

Ethan was still winded, so he just nodded. When he peeled off his pack, Ethan felt dampness across his back. He smiled to himself, realizing that up here, this was a badge of honor. Both men were silent for a couple of minutes as they took in the scenery and sipped water from the tubes extending to the plastic bladders hidden inside their packs.

"Hey John," Ethan finally managed to utter, "You're in *fantastic* shape."

"You do something long enough, it gets easier," replied John.

Ethan glanced admirably at his new hiking partner. "So, how long have you been into backpacking?"

"Since I was a kid," John responded. "At least sixty years?" Then he added, "I've probably camped out under the stars thousands of times."

"*Really*," Ethan retorted. "What did you do for a job that gave you so much freedom?"

John glanced down at Ethan and grinned. "This *was* my job. For years, I led group tours into the mountains. People paid me to guide them on summer backpacking expeditions. Then, in the winter, I'd do cross-country ski trips."

"Around here?" Ethan inquired, pointing towards the glacier-fed lake lying hundreds of feet below.

"Nah," replied John. "This is new territory for me. I mostly did this on the West Coast. You know, in the Sierra Nevada's in California and the Cascades further north."

"*Hmmm*," Ethan responded. "Sounds like you're a good example of that old maxim. How's it go? 'If you find a job you love, you'll never work again.'"

"Yeah," John snorted, "I guess that's true." Then, after a brief pause, he added, "Right out of college, I worked a few years as a probation and parole officer for the city of Los Angeles. I spent every day dealing with drugs, crime, and poverty. You know, Ethan, you can find the worst side of humanity right there in our largest cities."

Ethan nodded. He considered reinforcing that last thought by telling John about some of his clients. But instead, he decided to remain quiet and let the big man continue.

"Finally," John stated, "One of my clients who'd been making progress, or so I thought, was gunned down in a bad drug deal. That was it, the final straw. I took my savings, bought a tiny cabin near Kings Canyon National Park where I'd camped as a kid, and went into business for myself."

For a few seconds, the two men were quiet. There were inaudible conversations around them, but the loudest sound came from a breeze whistling through nearby pines. Further, in the distance, thousands of disc-shaped leaves in a grove of quaking aspens trembled as if a giant underground hand was shaking their roots. Then, finally, Ethan broke the silence.

"You have any family?"

John sighed loudly but did not respond.

"I don't mean to pry," Ethan added. "I just wondered how you balanced a job like that with a family. It's a real struggle for most of us, right?"

"It was never a problem," John responded, "Because I didn't have a family."

Ethan couldn't tell from John's tone whether he was embarrassed or bragging. Maybe a bit of both. "No? Never married?"

"My one marriage lasted less than a year and ended the moment I decided to leave the big city," replied John. "Annie didn't want to trade our Santa Monica condo for a little cabin in the mountains. I don't blame her, but my spirit was dying in L.A.. She was a nice girl, though. It was all on me." After a pause, he added, "We're still friends after all these years."

John suddenly leaned forward and stood. "Should we get going?" he asked while heaving the giant bundle over his shoulder.

For the next hour, the two men ventured westward into Cascade Canyon without saying a word. Mountains and massive rock formations bookended both sides of the trail. The only noise came from the raging waters of Cascade Creek, which, at times, could be deafening. Shadows gradually evaporated as the sun crept to its apex. Finally, when the trail widened so the hikers could walk side-by-side, Ethan resumed their conversation as though there had been no interruption.

"Looking back, John, did you ever feel like you missed something by not having a family?"

John glanced over at his new friend and chuckled. "I thought *that* might be coming." He yanked off his hat and pulled out a bandana to wipe the sweat that had been building over his brow. "The short answer is no. I don't have any regrets. Like I said earlier, there're tradeoffs in everything. We all make choices as we go through life, and then we have to live with them."

Before Ethan could respond, John turned the table. "How about you, Ethan? You have a wife and kids?"

Ethan swallowed hard and glanced toward a distant mountain. "I *had* a wife," Ethan finally answered. "I'm a widower now." Then, looking back at John, he added, "You know, that's the first time I've used that word."

"Oh, I'm *sorry*," John proclaimed. "So then, you just recently lost your wife?"

"Yes, it was cancer," Ethan responded. "She went fast." Then he added, almost as an afterthought, "We had been married for over forty years."

John slowed to a halt and then turned to face Ethan directly. "Man, I'm *so* sorry. It sounds like she was a special lady."

"Thanks," Ethan responded. "Yes, to borrow a heavily used cliché, she was the love of my life." Then, after a pause, he continued. "When we first met in college, I wasn't even thinking about getting married. But after a few dates, it was like I'd tried on gloves that fit perfectly. I never wanted to take them off. It just felt so natural. From the start, we became extensions of each other, and the longer we were together, the more it seemed like we were one person."

"Man, you're one of the lucky few," John commented. "Most people go their entire lives and never find *that* kind of love."

"Yeah, I know," Ethan replied. "But my good fortune didn't end there. Sarah and I also had two wonderful kids. Today, my daughter Jenny is a grade-school teacher. She and her husband, Matt, live nearby in St. Louis. Noah, my son, is a doctor in Portland. He's the reason why that's my eventual destination."

John motioned toward some boulders along the creek's edge, indicating they should use them as park benches for a rest. Ethan followed him, shed his pack, and pulled out some trail mix and bison jerky to share for lunch. After they were comfortably situated, John resumed the conversation.

"Now, I'd like to quote you, Ethan, but with a twist. Looking back, did you ever feel like you missed something by *having* a family?"

Ethan smiled, recognizing this was the same question he had recently asked John, except for one word.

"No, absolutely none," Ethan answered without hesitation. "I understand your point about tradeoffs, and that probably would have resonated more with me before the kids were born."

Ethan paused, feeling a lump rising in his throat. Finally, he continued.

"When Jenny was little, maybe two or three, she slipped in the bathtub one night and split open her chin. Sarah and I rushed her to the emergency room for stitches. A nurse wanted to take her into the back area and told us to remain in the waiting room. I'm sure this was their usual procedure, but when they started leading her away, Jenny looked directly up at me with panic in her eyes and started to scream."

Ethan paused again and looked down between his hiking boots. "John, something kicked in at that moment. I told the nurse in no uncertain terms that my wife and I would be *joining* our daughter, and she didn't argue. While an E.R. doctor stitched up the underside of my daughter's chin, Jenny gripped my hand and looked up at me, doing her best to smile. I instantly knew there was a bond between the two of us that would last forever."

Ethan looked up at his new friend with moist eyes and added, "John, we cremated Sarah's body a couple of weeks ago. Physically, she's gone, but her spirit will live on within the memories of her two children. And one day, long after I'm gone, we'll still reside inside Jenny, Noah, and their offspring. You see, we deliberately created those two kids. Their entire existence is a byproduct of our DNA combined with the environment in which we raised them. So, in a sense, children grant us immortality."

Ethan suddenly realized he had probably gone too far. Recalling that John never had children, Ethan carefully considered his following words. Since he did not want to come across as a proselytizing missionary, he decided it might be best to give some ground to John's experience.

"You're right, John; life *is* filled with tradeoffs. And since I've always loved hiking in the mountains, a big part of me envies the life you've led." Ethan looked up at John with an understanding smile but noticed the big man was peering wistfully off into the distance.

The silence that ensued was abruptly interrupted by the screech of a bald eagle. John spotted him first and pointed downstream toward a nest high in a grove of pines. It looked like any bird's nest, except this one had been inflated to a monumental size. Ethan saw two gray feathery heads poking above the edge of a nest that had to be at least 12 feet high. Both men smiled. Then, out of the blue, John broke the silence.

"Ethan, are you a religious man?"

"Hmm," Ethan exclaimed, smiling and shaking his head, "Why do you ask?"

"Because I'm *not*, and I wanted to know if you were before sharing some pretty heavy thoughts." After a few seconds, he added, "Also, all that talk about immortality made me think that maybe you were religious."

"There may be a god," Ethan finally responded, "But I don't buy into any organized religion. So I guess that makes me some kind of agnostic."

"I get it," replied John. "But you see, I don't believe in God at all, and I certainly don't believe in any kind of afterlife. It took me decades to reach that conclusion, but I'm quite comfortable with it."

Ethan realized the conversation had moved in a metaphysical direction and instantly decided it might be fun to go along for the ride. He understood that he soon would part ways with John, and in all likelihood, they would never meet again. However, Ethan also knew from prior experience that these dialogues often proved to be the most thought-provoking.

"So," replied Ethan, "If there's no spiritual component to our lives, what's the point? Why should we place any value on living?"

John pivoted to face Ethan squarely. His expression turned somber, as though he was about to impart some priceless wisdom.

"There *is* no point, Ethan, none whatsoever." Then, turning even more solemn, he added, "You see, we all come into this world randomly, without any purpose. I know that line of thinking depresses the hell out of most people, which is why they invent all those ideas about God, religion, and heaven. But this shouldn't be depressing. On the contrary, it should be liberating."

Ethan cocked his head and looked puzzled. "How's it *liberating*?"

"Because," John replied, "The moment we're born, we begin a temporal journey. Of course, we have no say about how it starts. As you just pointed out, our admission into this world was a conscious choice made by our parents, not us."

"Most of the time," Ethan interjected with a grin.

John snickered before continuing. "We don't get to choose our parents. We have no say in what we genetically inherit from them. And in the first years of life, we have little control over the environment where we're raised. However, once we come of age, then we can map out our journey as we see fit."

Ethan nodded to indicate for John to continue.

"The problem, though, is that most people never think about this on a conscious level. Instead, they sleepwalk through life, and if they're religious, as most tend to be, they just assume the best part's still waiting for them after they die."

"Now you sound a little like Karl Marx," interrupted Ethan. "What did he call religion, the 'opiate of the people?'"

"Yeah, that's true," John responded, "And what's more, on that score, Marx was right. However, I'm not bringing this up to justify his revolution by the proletariat. My point is . . ."

Ethan glanced up in anticipation but said nothing.

"My point," John finally continued, "Is the best way to live life is to chart your journey *deliberately*. To achieve the ideal life, you must take careful measure every time you reach one of those inevitable forks in the road."

"Yes, this all makes sense," Ethan retorted, "But what about an overarching purpose? In the end, what is it that *really* matters?"

"In the end," John answered, "It's not about the final destination. We'll all die, and then we'll simply cease to exist. You can't take your money or possessions with you. And while deeds and accomplishments may live on in the memories of those you leave behind, including your *children*, you won't be around to hear their accolades."

John momentarily fell silent to determine how Ethan might react to the inclusion of the word "children" in his last statement. Ethan suddenly peered up but then quietly acknowledged John's comment with a smile and a nod denoting "touché." After that, John decided it was safe to resume.

"The only thing that *really* matters is what takes place during your journey. In the end, when you're lying on your deathbed at what hopefully was a long life, you want to be able to look back at your journey and smile."

Ethan was about to comment on the irony of discussing a "journey" metaphor while on a long hike but then thought to glance at his watch. Remembering the final shuttle of the day would depart the west side of the lake in a couple of hours, he suddenly rose, grabbed his day-pack, and flung it over his shoulder. He glanced down at the trail that had brought them to this spot, knowing he would soon be hiking it back alone.

"I hope all my philosophizing isn't driving you away," John uttered with a slight smile.

"No, to the contrary," Ethan replied earnestly. "You've filled my head with much to think about on the way back to Jenny Lake. I'd be happy to sit here and talk to you all day. But I've already gone further than planned, and I want to get back in time to catch the final launch. Otherwise, my *journey*, at least for today, will be even longer."

Both men smiled and simultaneously extended their hands.

"It's been a *genuine* pleasure," Ethan pronounced while noting the firmness in John's handshake. "I wish you well on *your* journey along the Continental Divide. You stay safe, my friend."

"You as well," John replied as he slid off his boulder and reached for his oversized backpack. "I've enjoyed the company. It's too bad, Ethan, you didn't come with a backpack. It would've been nice to spend more time with you. And again, I'm really sorry to hear about your wife's passing. You take care and make lots of noise to scare away the grizzlies."

Ethan started to turn away from the big man but then stopped. "You know," he added, "I *really* like that metaphor about the 'temporal journey.' Did you come up with that yourself?"

After John secured the straps of his backpack, he used both hands to adjust the grungy Dodgers' cap on his head. Then he gazed up and nodded at Ethan.

"It's taken most of my life, but yes, I did come up with that analogy. And it makes sense, doesn't it? Think about it: Your journey, Ethan, included Sarah, whom you loved dearly, and two remarkable children. On the other hand, mine involved a passion for the outdoors unfettered by the constraints of a family. Is one journey somehow better than the other? No, not at all, not if we're both smiling at the end."

With that, John gave a final salute and then strode off westward. Before turning back east, Ethan took a moment to admire the soaring silhouette steadily vanishing into a sun that had already begun to set.

chapter
9

Ethan quickened his pace. The sun still baked the back of his neck in the more open areas, but he observed that his shadow was steadily lengthening. Ethan had neglected to bring along a flashlight, and the specter of completing his hike in the dark was becoming a distinct possibility. Much depended on whether he could catch the final shuttle before it left the West Shore Boat Dock.

Missing the ferry would add two-and-a-half miles to his hike. This stretch circled the southern perimeter of Jenny Lake. While relatively level, its random twists and turns and the haphazard sprinkling of roots and rocks would turn the trail into a treacherous obstacle course with the dying of the light. Ethan knew the sun did not officially set until around 8:00 this time of year, but he also recognized that Jenny Lake would fall into the inky shadows of the Tetons long before then.

Nevertheless, it was increasingly a challenge for Ethan to race through this canyon. With every bend in the trail, the scenery became increasingly dramatic. The late afternoon sunlight turned each vista into a picture postcard. Try as he might, Ethan could not keep from continuously stopping to yank out his phone to snap another photo. The sun's rays had turned the splashing waters of Cascade Creek into a kaleidoscope of colors. Mountains loomed on both sides of the canyon to provide ideal framing. More than anything else, though, the palette of wildflowers captivated Ethan's interest.

For just a month or two each year, wildflowers exploded throughout the Tetons. Then, as summer temperatures increased, gilia, larkspur, and

Indian paintbrush bloomed in the lower valleys. At higher elevations, moss campion, alpine forget-me-not, and sky pilots created a multi-colored carpet since these flowers were smaller and grew closer to the ground. According to Sarah, though, the most striking flowers were in the midlevel forests, like those scattered throughout Cascade Canyon. This was the realm of the blue-violet petals of the columbine, the helmet-shaped purple buds of the monkshood, and especially the magenta bells of the ubiquitous fireweed.

More than any other flower, Sarah treasured the fireweed. She had explained to Ethan that while these wildflowers grew and scattered like weeds, they had earned their name because of their ability to colonize desolate areas burned by fires. In 1980, fireweeds were the first vegetation to bring life back to the ground incinerated by the Mount St. Helens eruption. Although known by a different name, they also brought color back to the grim landscape in London burned by the blitz in World War Two.

Sarah also taught Ethan that fireweeds were more than just pleasing to the eye. Their leaves could be used to brew tea. Since they were high in vitamins A and C, some consumed fireweed shoots as a tasty spring vegetable. In addition, their petals could produce copious nectar that yielded rich, spicy honey. Fireweed honey, jelly, and syrup were especially popular in places like Alaska, where the species grows in abundance. Finally, the multihued flowers of the fireweed, which can quickly dominate any area, are always sure to attract lots of attention from pollinators.

Sarah had grown obsessed with fireweeds during their many hikes in the Rockies. They were more than just her favorite flower; they had taken on a symbolic meaning that Ethan had never fully understood. As he attempted to scurry through Cascade Canyon, Ethan noticed the fireweeds were everywhere. In certain spots, they decorated both banks of the creek. Fireweeds also towered above him in areas where they virtually strangled the trail. Their pink and purple hues added a delightful splash of color, particularly in the afterglow of the late afternoon sunshine.

Finally, after making another stop to photograph a patch of fireweeds hugging a small cataract in the creek, Ethan decided this might be a good time and place to resume a conversation he had previously conducted with Sarah inside his head. She had never come to him as a ghost or apparition he could see. Instead, Ethan could only hear her voice. Conversing with Sarah was, at minimum, a pleasant way to pass the time. On most occasions, these conversations were as natural as the numerous talks they had shared when Sarah was still alive. And like many of those, Ethan often gained new insights.

"Alright, Sweetheart," Ethan teased under his breath, "Is all this fireweed your way of trying to gain my attention?"

Ethan knelt to inhale a deep breath from a stem of fireweed. He then glanced around, listening for a response. Finally, he heard one of his favorite sounds in the world, the familiar cadence of Sarah's laughter.

"No, Silly," replied Sarah, "It's purely coincidental. You thought about me when you saw the fireweeds, that's all." Then, after a pause, she added, "You're by yourself now, though, and you seem to be in a hurry. Maybe by continuing our talk, you'll ignore the other distractions and make better progress in your hike."

"Okay, that sounds good," responded Ethan. "Let me begin with a question. On our countless hikes out west, you taught me everything there is to know about fireweeds. But for you, these flowers became an obsession. So my question is, *why?*"

Ethan again heard Sarah's trademark giggle, punctuated by the endearing snort that occasionally accompanied her laughter.

"You'll think this is crazy," Sarah finally responded, "but I've always associated fireweeds with a hike we did up at Banff. You know, the one where we got lost?"

"*Really?*" Ethan countered, "Why?"

"Alright, let's go back more than thirty years," replied Sarah. "We'd just arrived in town after driving up from Glacier National Park. It was still too early to check into the hotel, so you suggested we do this short hike you'd read about that started at a ski resort. You said it would give us a bird's eye view of the entire area. Does this ring a bell?"

"Yes," responded Ethan, "I'd always bragged about my excellent sense of direction and how I never got lost. That day proved otherwise. It was not one of my finest moments." Then, after a brief pause, he added, "But I don't see why this made you laugh or how any of it relates to fireweeds."

"Oh, it wasn't funny at the time," Sarah replied. "It was downright scary."

"Go on," Ethan said with mounting trepidation.

"If you'll recall, the first part of the trail was just fine," Sarah commented. "We made it to the top of the mountain, and you were right; it gave us a panoramic view of the town of Banff, the Bow River, and the surrounding national park. But then we learned about the shortcomings of Canadian signage, or at least that's what you increasingly made the target of all your cursing."

"Well, it was *true*," Ethan replied, "There were no signs to tell us where to go. I'd read that the trail was a loop, so it didn't make sense to turn around and go back. But there were at least two other options, so I picked the one that looked the most heavily traveled. I believe you agreed at the time."

Sarah giggled again. "Don't start getting defensive. I wasn't blaming you. I'm just reviewing the background before getting to the point of this story." Then, her tone hardened. "However, you still didn't want to turn back when the trail started to descend abruptly and then all but disappeared."

"That's true," Ethan responded reluctantly, "Looking back, it was stupid. I should never have led you down that mountain."

"I'm not sure I'd use that adjective," replied Sarah in her English teacher voice. "It was just you being characteristically stubborn."

"Well, at that point," Ethan argued, "Turning around would've meant an almost impossible climb. There were spots where we had descended on our butts because the slope was so extreme, remember? So how could we have climbed back up?"

"You're correct; once we had descended that far, turning back wasn't a good option either," Sarah conceded. "But now I can get to the point of the story. I don't believe I've ever shared this with you."

Ethan felt a chill go up his spine. This little fantasy had been a fun way to pass the time, but he had always assumed the voice he heard came from previous conversations held when Sarah was still alive. How could she possibly share something new with him *now*? "Go on . . . ," Ethan replied with growing unease.

"We stopped at a small meadow to catch our breath," Sarah continued, "One of the few relatively level places on the side of the mountain.

And everywhere you looked were some of the most beautiful wildflowers I'd ever seen. I didn't know it then, but they were all fireweeds."

Sarah paused, and Ethan heard a slight sniffle. This was another one of his wife's charming qualities, one he greatly missed. It never took much for Sarah to get a little weepy.

"Anyhow," she finally continued, "This is where I witnessed an astonishing transformation within you. Until then, Ethan, you'd been a bewildered child, lost and confused one moment, vexed and annoyed the next. Then, suddenly, you became a grown man. I don't know what got into you. First, you drew a deep breath, looked around, and studied the landscape. Then you turned to me and, in a voice that would reassure even the most frightened youngster, said, 'We've got this.' Remember?"

"It's coming back," responded Ethan. He waited for Sarah to resume.

"You pointed toward a break in the trees, possibly a trail. But, more important, it descended in the direction of something you could hear: the sound of traffic. You said it had to be the Trans-Canadian Highway, just to the south, and that if we could make it there, the rest would be easy."

"Yeah, and the plan worked," Ethan replied, "At least, until we made it to the highway. Then, we encountered that high, chain-link fence. I guess the Canadians had built it to keep wildlife off the thoroughfare, but it also kept us off."

"Yes, that was a problem," Sarah recalled. "But you were still exuding confidence. I remember you glanced back at me with that same unruffled expression and calmly told me to follow in your footsteps. Then you turned and began marching through the grass up to our necks. Finally, we came to an overpass crossing the highway, and there was a break in the fence. I remember that spot distinctly because a forest of fireweeds was guarding the area."

"More fireweeds? *Really?* I didn't remember that detail."

Ethan paused, attempting to visualize the image of fireweeds adorning their escape portal back to civilization. Then, after a moment, he added, "And as I recall, we split up for a little while. I hitched a ride back up to the car while you walked into town. A few hours later, we found each other, checked into the hotel, and had a nice dinner to celebrate our survival."

"Yes, and we had survived," Sarah verified. "Ethan, I knew we'd be okay the moment you found your mojo. And what's more, you *never* lost it after that day. I knew that *any* man who could get us off that mountain with such composure could handle whatever else life might throw at him. Even now, when I think about that day, what I recall most wasn't our risky adventure. It was the look of certainty on your face in that meadow."

"That meadow surrounded by *fireweeds*?"

"You got it," Sarah replied. "Despite the miserable experience of getting lost, I'd never loved you more than I did that day."

Ethan only heard the gurgling sound of the creek and his muffled footsteps for a moment. Sarah seemed to be waiting for a response, but Ethan did not know what to say. He had only remembered the general outline of the story and never considered his wife's perception. Finally, Sarah ended the silence.

"Do you remember what happened later that night, Ethan?"

"Yes, that's when we made our big decision."

"That's right," Sarah affirmed. "After a tasty steak dinner, followed by ice cream at Cows, we walked up Banff Avenue to where it crosses the river. Then, finally, we sat on a bench to eat our cones. And that's where we made the decision that forever changed our lives."

Ethan swallowed hard and drew in a deep breath. He wanted to finish this story but needed a moment to collect himself. Then, finally, he pronounced, "We decided to have children. For six years, we'd convinced ourselves not to have kids, that they'd be a huge expense and would only get in the way of all the travel we wanted to do."

"And do you remember," Sarah inquired, "*How* we came to that decision?"

"Hmm. I remember the deal we made when we first decided to get married," replied Ethan. "Since neither of us *strongly* opposed having children, we agreed that if one of us changed our minds, the other would go along."

"Right," Sarah responded. "And that night, who had a change of heart?"

"It was you," Ethan swiftly replied. "Although, I never understood . . ."

After a pause, Ethan's face erupted into a broad grin.

"Now, you see?" Sarah asked. Ethan nodded and continued to smile.

"It'd hit me earlier that day on the mountain. I had already been thinking about kids. More and more, it just seemed like we needed more in our lives than just self-gratification. But seeing how you took charge that day was the final step. As they say in the movies, Ethan, you became a man that day. After that, I was ready to become a mom, and you were destined to be a dad." After a brief pause, Sarah added, "Any regrets?"

"*None*," Ethan proclaimed without equivocation. He could not hold back his tears. Ethan vigorously shook his head and finally managed to state, "No, none whatsoever. Bringing Jenny and Noah into our lives was the best thing we ever did. Nothing, and I mean *nothing*, has ever brought me greater joy. I am *so* proud of those kids."

"Same goes for me, my love," Sarah replied. "And, by the way, as I recall, our celebration that night didn't end along the banks of the Bow River, did it?"

Ethan smiled and shook his head. He remembered Sarah's suggestion that if they wanted to time the arrival of a baby with the start of her summer break, there was no time to waste. Within a few weeks, Sarah was pregnant. As it turned out, Jenny and Noah were accommodating with their arrival times into the world.

Ethan had become so lost in his conversation with Sarah that he barely noticed the progress he had made on his hike to the boat landing. Ethan had just passed Hidden Falls, and the trail was beginning its steep descent. Downhill requires little energy, but braking could be tough on certain muscles. There also was no guardrail to help him keep his balance.

Officially, the sun would not set for a couple of hours, but within the dark shadows of the canyon and beneath the dense canopy of the foliage, Ethan did not see a root jig-sawing its way across the trail as though it was a giant python. Suddenly, it felt like the root reached up to grab his right foot, so it was not there to catch the falling weight of his body.

Ethan began to tumble toward the edge of a bluff. His right hand landed hard on the trail. He attempted to use it to break his fall but only seized a fistful of gravel. For a second, Ethan glanced down into the deep ravine where he was about to fall. There were trees far below, but in between, there was nothing but a vertical wall of solid granite.

Ethan managed to twist his body so, at the last minute, his left hand might grab something, anything, that would keep him from free-falling into the dark void. Feeling something soft growing in the narrow strip between the trail and the edge of the cliff, he grabbed and squeezed it with all his strength. The result was that his body spun over the edge of the cliff feet-first. Ethan felt his knees crash into the hard rock, but for the moment, whatever he clenched in his left hand had halted his fall. He was dangling hundreds of feet above a certain death.

Ethan looked down. If he let go, he would probably bounce once or twice off the side of the cliff and then plunge onto an invisible rock surface. Or there was also a chance he might land on a section of the trail he would have encountered after a dozen switchbacks. The following day, some unfortunate hiker would then discover his mangled body.

For a second, he considered letting go. Why not? There would be the scariest three seconds of his life, followed by an instantaneous death. Since Sarah's diagnosis, he had contemplated this option many times, and this would be the perfect place to execute his decision. Jenny might later have her suspicions, but to most others, his death would appear to be an unfortunate accident.

Ethan's shattered body would spend the night on the mountain before its discovery and eventual cremation. His soul, however, or whatever it was that had defined him for the past sixty-five years, would flow into the same ocean containing Sarah's soul. In some way or other, they would finally be reunited.

Then Ethan saw Sarah's face. For some reason, he could no longer hear her voice, but her eyes blazed with terror. Sarah's lips formed a perfect O, like in Edvard Munch's painting, *The Scream*, and fear had paralyzed her mouth into silence. Tears, however, were streaming from her swollen eyes.

"*NO!*" Sarah finally commanded. Then, more words began to flow like the cascading water of the nearby falls. "This is *not* what I want. It's *not* your time. You've got many years left, Ethan, and much more to do. You have Jenny and Noah, and you'll soon have our grandkids. They'll *all* need you. We'll still be together when it's all said and done."

Ethan clenched his eyes shut, inhaled deeply, and then slowly swung from side to side. His left hand was growing weak, and whatever it was clinging to might rip at any time. Nevertheless, he needed to grab some-thing with his right hand to have any chance. Ethan kicked like a dervish with both feet, hoping one might find an outcropping to gain additional leverage. Finally, he felt something solid under one foot. Ethan used it to propel himself high enough so that his right hand could snag another soft clump similar to what he was grasping with his left.

Like doing a slow-motion pull-up, Ethan levitated his body in a sky-ward direction. When high enough, he swung first one elbow and then the other over the rim of a flat boulder. Then, with one final surge, Ethan thrust his body over the cliff's edge and rolled onto the trail. He lay on his back for a moment with his torso rising and sinking like a blacksmith's bellows. Ethan stared up through the limbs of lofty Douglas fir trees at a distant mountain still illuminated by the setting sun.

Finally, Ethan turned toward the cliff's edge to see what he had grabbed, what had saved his life. He suddenly smiled while tears began to stream from both eyes. Even in the bituminous shadows blackening the steeply sloped trail, he could make out the mangled stems and randomly strewn petals of fireweeds.

chapter
10

No matter how Ethan adjusted his driving position, the pain radiated throughout his shoulders and lower back. His brush with death the previous day had taken a toll. Since he was now in his midsixties, Ethan's body did not heal as rapidly as it once did. Nevertheless, he was determined to put miles behind him. Yesterday's marathon hike into Cascade Canyon had satisfied any urge to lose himself in the wilderness. Now, Ethan looked forward to pulling into Noah's driveway in less than a day and a half.

Instead of beginning a new Audible book, Ethan decided to use this time on the open road to process everything that had occurred the day before. A profoundly philosophical discussion with a mountain sage had highlighted the morning. Then, in the afternoon, Ethan recalled some life-changing memories with the help of Sarah's ghostly presence flickering inside his head. Finally, Ethan had almost died. More important, after briefly considering using the fall as an escape hatch, Ethan had struggled valiantly to hold onto his life.

The conversation with John yesterday morning, if nothing else, had convinced Ethan that a permanent state of solitude had zero appeal. John may have no regrets about the path he took in life, but as far as Ethan was concerned, the mountains were a vacation playground and nothing more. Since Ethan had chosen family as his life's epicenter, Jenny and Noah were now more paramount than ever. Despite the dazzling beauty of the Tetons, hiking their lonely trails was quickly getting old. Ethan was now ready to descend from the mountains to spend time with his son.

Still, John Cassidy had made some compelling points that were worth considering. He reminded Ethan that we have only one opportunity to grasp whatever life offers, and we should not take this for granted. He had proselytized that you should make the most of your journey and live every day to its fullest. Ethan especially liked the journey metaphor and that what mattered most was not its final destination. Nevertheless, it would profoundly upset John if he had known how close Ethan had recently come to ending his life. If he could only have one journey, deciding to end his life now made as much sense as pulling over in Twin Falls, the next town on I-84, and choosing to spend the rest of his life in that isolated Idaho community.

If Ethan still harbored thoughts about suicide after his conversation with John Cassidy, they were flushed away entirely during his exchange with Sarah later in the afternoon. Remembering that day in Banff, regardless of where the memory had originated, reminded Ethan of a time when he was ready to grab life by the horns. And as Sarah recollected, if he had indeed become a man that day, why would he want to end it now? The final result of that day was the conception of a new life. What Ethan had attempted in his garage a few weeks earlier was antithetical to the spirit of that day.

Finally, there was the vision of Sarah's horror-struck face when Ethan was dangling from the ledge above Cascade Creek. What had she said? "You've got many years left, Ethan, and much more to do." And her point about being there for his grandchildren also touched a nerve. "They'll *all* need you," she had screamed. But more than anything, Ethan pondered Sarah's final words. "We'll still be together when it's all said and done." Ethan needed to be patient. If a reunion of sorts was possible with Sarah, it could happen just as certainly in 30 years.

When Ethan pulled into a rest stop for lunch, ironically near Twin Falls, he had adamantly convinced himself that ending life now was *not* an option. While eating his sandwich at a picnic table, watching the parade of SUVs, pickup trucks, and 18-wheelers whiz by on the interstate, Ethan made a personal pledge to himself to forever banish any thoughts of suicide. But while this thought wrapped a broad grin across his face, the smile immediately vanished when another question pierced Ethan's consciousness—What should come next?

What could Ethan see in his future? Returning to the malaise of his current legal practice was not an option; of that, he was sure. Ethan always enjoyed the gamesmanship of the courtroom, but looking back, who had benefitted the most from his efforts? Ethan had turned his back on a career as a public defender, primarily because it paid so little. How could he support a family on such a meager salary? But that meant Ethan only defended the clients who could pay. And because of his efforts, many of Ethan's wealthy clients grew even richer. As Ethan neared the end of his career, he had increasingly begun to detest his reflection in the mirror.

And on a more personal level, what about his relationships with others? Ethan had numerous friendships, but most were somewhat superficial. Sarah had always been his best friend, and her death left an unfillable hole in his life. Still, Ethan understood the importance of maintaining significant human connections. But with whom? His kids had their own lives to lead. Ethan did not want to be one of those sad older men who spent their remaining years trying to carve a life from those of his adult children. And while Ethan acknowledged anything might happen down the distant road, for now, he could never visualize dating again.

As Ethan climbed into the cabin of his SUV to resume a journey paralleling the Oregon Trail, he conceded that yesterday's epiphany may have been the easiest part. Yes, he would embrace life over death, but what was the best way to live that life? That question would be much more challenging to answer. Meanwhile, some time with Noah in Oregon might bring his predicament into a sharper focus.

In the short term, Ethan knew he craved spending some quality time with his son. Even during his rebellious teenage years, Ethan and Noah maintained a close relationship. Whether it was the Cardinals, chess, books, politics, or philosophy, Ethan and Noah had always possessed a rich cornucopia of discussion topics. Since neither Sarah nor Jenny was willing to rough it in primitive cabins, father and son had taken those road trips on their own. Ethan understood Noah possessed a private side and that some questions were probably better left unasked. Otherwise, though, Ethan and Noah had built a genuine friendship.

That is, until Noah went off to college. Ethan and Noah still embraced many rich conversations over the next several years, but since these mostly took place during holiday trips or long-distance phone calls, they became fewer and shorter. What's more, Ethan had to share these moments with Sarah, who also intensely missed her son. By this point, Ethan fully understood that one of the hallmark traits of good parenting was the ability to let go. He and Sarah had undergone this process twice, although it proved easier with Jenny since she soon agreed to move back to St. Louis. On the other hand, Noah ended up 2000 miles away, and sometimes, this distance felt more like he had moved to a far-flung planet.

By late afternoon, Ethan decided to pull into a campground outside Boardman, a small hamlet on the Oregon side of the Columbia River. His back was progressively getting stiffer, and there was no point in rolling into Noah's driveway late at night in a physical state of exhaustion. Besides, the short sprint to Portland the following morning would be on a route that would pierce through the Columbia River Gorge, so Ethan might as well enjoy the scenery in the bright morning daylight. He would even make a brief stop at Multnomah Falls if he felt up to it. Ethan had visited this iconic waterfall with Sarah many years earlier. However, since it was easily accessible from the highway, it might still be worth pulling over to snap a few pictures.

Before setting out the following morning, Ethan created an Audible account of his own. The prospect of seeing Noah inspired him to download *Shoeless Joe* by W.P. Kinsella. He had seen the movie *Field of Dreams* based on that novel at least a dozen times, and the father and son "you want to have a catch?" scene never failed to make him cry like a newborn. Sometimes, Sarah walked into the den, caught her husband watching *Field of Dreams*, and handed him a box of Kleenex without saying a word. Then, when Noah was old enough to play Little League Baseball, Ethan had driven him up to Dyersville, Iowa, just so father and son could toss a baseball on the field where the Major League ghosts had evaporated into the adjacent cornfield.

Like many other fathers and sons, baseball had been the glue that sealed the bond between Ethan and Noah. They had been to countless Cardinals games together at Busch Stadium and watched even more on television. Then, in 2006, Ethan managed to secure tickets for every World Series home game when the Cards finished the inaugural season in their new stadium by winning another championship.

Ethan had not followed baseball much as a kid, and his wife and daughter only took a mild interest, primarily during the playoff season. When Noah, as a preschooler, joined a T-ball team, however, Ethan immediately appreciated the value of sharing baseball with his son. At their first Cardinals game together, Noah was so little Ethan could hold him with one hand while catching a foul ball with the other. By the time Ethan took a teenage Noah to the Baseball Hall of Fame in Cooperstown, both had become life-long baseball addicts.

When he pulled over the night before, Ethan excitedly sent a text to Noah with the details about his arrival the following day. Noah's reply was brief, maybe even a little curt, but Ethan chalked that up to the lateness of the evening. He knew his son put in long hours in the emergency room at University Hospital. Still, Ethan went to sleep with a pit in his stomach. In recent conversations, Noah had played up how much he was looking forward to taking his dad to hike in some of the state parks along the Oregon coast. Noah's latest text, however, was like the final piece of a puzzle that did not quite fit.

The following morning, Ethan took several stunning pictures of the falls, but the experience proved to be anticlimactic. Maybe it was because Sarah was not with him this time. Still, Ethan suspected his growing trepidation stemmed primarily from Noah's text message the night before—"You're coming in a little earlier than expected, Dad, but I'll try to be home shortly after your arrival. Looking forward to seeing you."

The drive into Portland was a random patchwork of experiences and emotions. Upon leaving the falls, Ethan realized he had grown weary of sightseeing, at least on his own. But the more he tried to envision his upcoming reunion with Noah, the more anxious he felt. In his gut, Ethan instinctively knew something was not quite right. And what should have been just two and half hours of driving was significantly longer due to a

multi-car accident on I-84 that backed traffic up for miles. By the time
Ethan crossed the Willamette River into Portland, he felt like he had just
completed a flight with nonstop turbulence.

When Ethan finally pulled into the driveway of his son's modest
ranch-style home in Beaverton, a bedroom community on Portland's
western fringe, it was Amy, not Noah, who came out to greet him. Ethan
enthusiastically climbed out of the SUV and unfurled his arms, anticipating a traditional family bear hug. Amy's embrace was tepid at best,
though, and when she pulled back and brushed aside a strand of wavy
chestnut hair, her faint smile appeared forced. Ethan glanced over her
shoulder at the empty porch.

"Noah's not home yet," Amy pronounced stoically, "He's dealing with
a last-minute shooting victim and couldn't get away. He texted it should
only delay him an hour or two." Amy bit down on her lip, swallowed
hard, and added, "My shift's not till eight, so I'm around until then. Are
you hungry? Would you like something to eat?"

Ethan still did not know Amy well since they had never lived together in the same city. Nevertheless, he held his daughter-in-law in high
regard. Amy was a hospice nurse employed in the same building as her
husband. They had met at University Hospital in the final year of Noah's
residency. Amy and Noah had been married for four years and, from all
outward appearances, were following a path similar to the one he and
Sarah had traveled.

"Sure," Ethan replied, "I'm starving." Then, after a brief pause, he
added, "It'll be nice to catch up. We haven't had much time to talk. You
know, just the two of us."

Amy nodded and forced another smile. Then she spun around, beckoning Ethan to follow. Once seated at the kitchen table, Ethan glanced
around and observed the photographs on the wall. Since the house followed an open format, he could see additional pictures adorning walls
that reached around to enfold a large brick fireplace. Amy had her back
turned to Ethan as she mixed a salad.

"BLT's okay?" Amy inquired over her shoulder.

"Sure, that sounds great," replied Ethan. "Anything I can do?"

"Yeah, would you get out the salad dressing from the fridge? Also, there's a pitcher of iced tea. Will that be okay? If so, grab the tea and some glasses."

As Ethan stood to do as instructed, he inquired, "Who took all these pictures? They're *gorgeous*."

Ethan noticed a smirk on Amy's face when she turned to face him. "Who do you think?"

"Noah?"

From her silence, Ethan assumed he was correct. After a pause, he continued, "It's just, if you don't mind me saying, there are no *people* in any of these pictures. I recognize some of them. Mount Hood? Crater Lake? And that's what's left of Mount St. Helens, right?"

"You know the area quite well," Amy commented while placing two plates on the table.

Amy glanced around and then drifted over to join Ethan. She studied the condiments at the center of the table while pulling out her chair, sitting down, and picking up her sandwich. The hush continued as she took her first bite and began to chew. Ethan attempted to make eye contact but without success. Finally, he broke the awkward silence.

"I don't mean to be nosy," Ethan asserted, "But clearly, something's not right. I get that impression from you and from my last text with Noah. Would you be willing to tell me what's going on?"

Amy snapped out of her trance and glanced up with moisture beneath her almond-shaped eyes. She swallowed her first bite, nodded, and then glanced at Ethan. For a moment, they locked eyes, almost like they were engaged in a staring contest. Ethan could tell Amy was mulling over what to say to a father-in-law she only knew superficially. After a moment, she finally shook her head and uttered, "Maybe it's best if you hear it from Noah."

Before Ethan could respond, though, the door from the garage burst open, and Noah stepped into the kitchen. He was still wearing blue scrubs highlighted with a red streak.

"Hey, Dad, it's *great* to see you," Noah declared. He moved forward for a hug and then, remembering what he was wearing, held up a finger and stepped back. "Let me go change first."

As Noah maneuvered towards the back hallway, Ethan slunk back into his chair. He exchanged glances with Amy, observing how she inhaled deeply, then raised her eyebrows in resignation. Ethan and Amy took large bites from their sandwiches and chewed silently.

When Noah returned, he was sporting cargo shorts, a Cardinals tee shirt, and a faux grin.

For the remainder of the late afternoon, their talk mostly centered around Ethan's trip, Noah's job, and the current political climate. For the most part, Amy was a silent observer.

Later that evening, after returning from a tasty dinner at a local steakhouse, Amy excused herself and said she needed to get ready for work. Noah grabbed two cans of Bud Lite from the refrigerator, handed one to his father, and then fell back onto the couch. For a moment, they turned toward each other and grinned. The moment proved fleeting. Noah's smile quickly melted as he turned toward the opaque screen of the television. He reached for the remote, pressed the power button, and punched in three digits.

"I think the Cards are on tonight," Noah muttered, feigning enthusiasm. "They're starting a weekend series at the Giants."

Ethan ignored the TV and stared at his son. "That sounds good, Noah, but let's watch with the sound muted. Then, it'll be easier to talk."

Noah's chest swelled as he drew in a deep breath. He muted the television sound but continued staring at the screen. The fact that the Cards were already losing six to one in the third inning did nothing to brighten his mood. It had been several years, but Ethan recalled seeing similar petulance during his son's teenage years. He ignored the TV and continued to gaze at Noah, who had closed his eyes. Ethan observed the twitching of his son's facial muscles.

Finally, Noah's eyes sprang open, and he turned to face his father. He had plainly formulated a plan to get through the rest of the evening.

"Look, Dad," Noah pronounced, "There's something I'd like to talk about, but not now. Today was a long day, and I'm *really* beat. Plus, like you, I've been dealing with Mom's loss. So, let's just watch the game, pray for a miracle comeback, and keep things light. Then, tomorrow, we can delve into the more serious stuff. Who knows, I might even want some of your patented fatherly advice."

Ethan noticed the corners of Noah's mouth turn upward as though he had successfully managed to lighten the mood. Silence then ensued as Ethan waited to see if there was more. Finally, just as he was about to speak, Noah interrupted.

"Here's an idea. I can take a few days off. Why don't we drive your car and the camper to Ecola State Park tomorrow morning? It's just north of Cannon Beach, about an hour and a half from here. The park has great hiking trails above the most beautiful beaches ever. And the town of Cannon Beach is delightful. "

Ethan smiled. "And sometime on our trip, you'll share whatever's been troubling you?"

"I hate to add to what you're going through," Noah replied. "But yes, I'll give you the full story."

"And what about Amy?" Ethan asked.

"I think it's best if she stayed here," Noah replied. Then, he hesitated and added, "She's a big part of the dilemma." After chugging the final swills of his beer, Noah stood, belched loudly, and then pivoted to face his father. "If you don't mind, Dad, I'm going to desert you and go to bed. I'll text our plans to Amy. Let's plan to hit the road by eight o'clock or so, alright?" Then he added, "I promise I'll be a different man tomorrow."

As Noah turned toward his bedroom, he suddenly pivoted back and inquired, "Oh, I almost forgot, Dad, where would you like to sleep to-night? Would you like the guest room, or are you more comfortable in your camper?"

"All my stuff's out there," Ethan responded, "And if I'm only here for one night, I might as well spend it out there."

Ethan then sluggishly rose with a groan and spread out his arms. Father and son embraced, and when they pulled back, both reflected the same affectionate expression.

"I'm delighted you're here," Noah avowed. "I've been worried about you."

For a moment, Ethan wondered whether Jenny had shared information with her brother about his recent garage "incident." Ethan waited to see if Noah would elaborate, but when nothing was forthcoming, he relaxed and smiled.

"No need to worry," Ethan intoned. "I'll be alright." Then, after a brief pause, he added, "I may even have a story to share with you."

Noah remained quiet but nodded and continued to smile warmly.

"Goodnight, Son. I love you."

"Love you too, Dad. I'll see you in the morning."

chapter

11

Eight hours later, sunlight exploded into the camper. Ethan reached over for Sarah, but as his eyes sprung open, he remembered she was gone. Recalling today's plans, however, instantly injected a shot of adrenaline. Ethan briskly climbed out of bed, took a shower in the camper's cramped bathroom, and then sipped coffee while pouring over a virtual copy of Friday's *Post-Dispatch* on his iPad.

An hour later, he heard a light knock on the camper's door. Noah greeted him with a stuffed backpack slung over one shoulder. The two men smiled, neither saying a word. The routine of father-son travel had instinctively returned to them both, like remembering how to ride a bike. When they climbed into the SUV, Noah instantly commandeered the car radio, something he had begun doing in his early teenage years. He set it to a classic rock station, and then, as in the past, they competed to see who could be the first to name the band and song.

Ethan was anxious to hear about the issue troubling Noah and his wife, but he thought it best to wait. He knew from experience that his son would share when he was good and ready. Premature pressure would only drive Noah to withdraw inward, like a turtle pulling inside its shell. For most of the drive, Ethan responded to his son's interview questions regarding his recent road trip. Noah surprisingly showed the most interest in his father's recent reconciliation with his old college roommate.

Two hours later, they unhitched the camper at a site in the state park and then drove to a nearby trailhead. Throughout the day, Ethan and Noah hiked in the footsteps of William Clark, who had led twelve members of the Corps of Discovery in searching for a beached whale back in 1806. They wandered on a trail that rose and fell like a roller coaster, taking them up to cliffside viewpoints, down to secluded coves, and even out to a long abandoned lighthouse. Then, like young boys, they frolicked on a windswept beach, exploring tidal pools in search of sea anemones and starfish.

In the late afternoon, Ethan and Noah returned to the camper, cleaned up, and drove into town. After devouring hot Dungeness crab sandwiches at the Wayfarer Restaurant in the heart of Cannon Beach, they headed down to the seashore. The public beach stretched from one end of town to the other but was dominated at its center by the 235-foot-high Haystack Rock. One of the state's most recognizable landmarks, this iconic monolith was home to multi-hued tidepools and assorted birdlife. Without saying a word, father and son automatically set a course for the massive sea stack.

From the morning rap on his camper door to this moment, Ethan noted there had been no conversation about either Sarah's passing or Noah's other concerns. Throughout the day, they skirted around these subjects by discussing sports, politics, and other current events. The day's best moments occurred when they reminisced over distant memories, especially their summer road trips. Noah had also delighted in sharing stories about Jenny and himself in high school, antidotes he knew he could now safely divulge.

Ethan noted that when Sarah's name came up, Noah oddly spoke about her as though she had been gone for years. He also recalled that at her service a few weeks earlier along the dusky shores of Creve Coeur Lake, Noah had not cried. His son always took great pride in maintaining a stoic demeanor, a character trait that served him well in the emergency room. But Ethan also knew Noah worshipped his mother. It did not take a background in psychology to realize his son's handling of Sarah's death was a confluence of avoidance and repression.

Ethan observed the sun was starting to sink into the western horizon, casting a vivid reflection on the surf like the interior of a kaleidoscope. He slowed their pace, noting the gliding seagulls, the dive-bombing pelicans, and the soaring ospreys. As they neared Haystack Rock, he could hear a chorus of windborne sounds from thousands of cormorants, gulls, and puffins. Resisting the temptation to pull out his phone and snap photographs, Ethan nodded towards a polished driftwood log that could serve as a restful bench.

Noah took the cue and led the way. After securing their seats, they looked up to study the skyline. From their vantage, Ethan observed how remnants of sunlight played a game of hide-and-seek behind the shadowy haystack that towered above them. For a moment, father and son quietly absorbed the scenery. Then, finally, Noah broke the silence without taking his eyes off the hazy image of the rock reflected in the golden surf.

"I *really* miss Mom. I can't stop thinking about her."

Ethan slid closer toward his son and gently placed a hand on his back. He remained quiet, waiting for Noah to continue. Finally, after wiping his nose with the sleeve of an ageless sweatshirt, Noah pressed on. Without looking directly at his father, he sounded like someone who had just stepped into a confessional.

"Since her death, I've felt like a fraud. On the exterior, I go about each day acting like an adult. I drive to work, treat patients, and, on rare occasions, possibly even save a life. But inside, I feel like a little boy missing his mom. This isn't normal, is it?" Noah looked up, and Ethan could see the little boy.

Ethan slid closer, wrapped one arm around Noah's shoulders, and placed the other behind his son's neck. Noah twisted toward Ethan and placed a hand reciprocally on his dad's shoulder.

Within their little huddle, Ethan whispered, "What isn't normal, Noah, is keeping everything locked up. You're not in the emergency room now, and you don't have to be so brave." Then, after a brief pause, he added, "Your mom was always so open with her feelings. I think she'd want the same for you."

Impulsively, Ethan reached out to embrace his son. When they finally pulled back, Ethan's face resembled a Greek tragedy mask. Tears had quietly streamed down both cheeks, leaving behind a film as though two slugs had slithered down his face. For a moment, Noah gazed directly at his father. His eyes were searching while his mouth began to tremble.

Then, suddenly, like a volcanic explosion, Noah buried his face inside his dad's chest and began to bawl. He placed a hand over his forehead and attempted to smother the sobs within his father's silky sweater, but Ethan could still feel his son's body quaking. For a minute, they firmly maintained this posture. Then, looking down at Noah, a satiated smile crept across Ethan's face. Some of his joy hailed from the nostalgia of recalling his early days as a father. But he also appreciated the healing that was hopefully taking place.

Ethan glanced up and noted the sun had vanished entirely, leaving behind a peach glow. Higher up, wispy clouds radiated shades of pink and blue. The tears beneath Ethan's eyes had begun to dry in the billowing ocean breeze. For a moment, he remembered consoling Noah as a little boy after his pet goldfish had died. His son might now be a grown man and a skilled physician, but some things never changed.

When Noah finally pulled back, both cheeks were wet enough to reflect the remnants of light radiating from the ocean. He inhaled deeply and smiled in embarrassment. Then he started to laugh. Before long, as Ethan and Noah resumed their parallel positions on the driftwood log, they were cackling as though they had just shared a sidesplitting joke.

"*God*, that felt good," Noah finally declared. "You know, Dad, for some reason, I couldn't do that until now." He pulled back further, using both sleeves like a beach towel to wipe his face.

"No?" replied Ethan. "Not even when you were alone? How about with Amy?"

Noah glanced down but did not respond. Then, after a moment of silence, he looked up and announced, "She's tried to help, Dad; she *really* has. Amy's been *so* patient with me. It hasn't been her fault, even though I've sometimes acted like it was. It's all on me. I'm not just talking about getting over Mom, either; there's been something else."

Ethan noted how his son's posture stiffened as he prepared for the shift in their conversation. Noah locked his lips together and inhaled deeply. Ethan observed how much his son had inherited his mother's high cheekbones, giving him classically sculpted features. Noah was striking, like Willem Dafoe or a young Gregory Peck. Still, Ethan fretted over what his son was about to admit.

"What do you mean?" Ethan inquired. "What else has been going on?"

Inside, Ethan prayed Noah's words would not mention anything that sounded like infidelity. That would be wholly antithetical to the image he held of his son.

"Do you realize that when Mom died," Noah responded, "I was *exactly* half her age?"

"Yeah?" Ethan responded quizzically.

"Well, Mom's passing has made me question how I should live the rest of *my* life.

Ethan quietly mused over the similarity between Noah's reaction to his mother's death and his own thoughts since hitting the road. Sarah's passing had left a massive hole in both of their lives. Ethan knew that thousands died worldwide every day, but now he grasped how each death was like a bowling ball scattering millions of pins in every direction.

"Meanwhile," Noah continued, "I recently received an intriguing phone call. Out of the blue, a friend from medical school contacted me. She wants to open a clinic in Port-au-Prince and said she needs a partner."

Noah's verbal torrent washed over Ethan so fast that he did not know where to start. With his son's desire to change jobs? With Noah moving to the poorest nation in the Western Hemisphere? Or possibly with the undercurrents beneath his medical school friend's gender.

"Port-au-Prince?" Ethan asked insolently. "In Haiti? *That* Port-au-Prince"

"Yes, *that* one," responded Noah, without even trying to conceal an incredulous smile. "She's secured a sizable grant for a building in the heart of the city. There's also enough money to cover all the necessary equipment and staff. Dad, we could *really* make a difference down there."

"You mean, make a difference in one of the world's most violent, dysfunctional societies?" Ethan demanded, instantly regretting the words that leaped out of his mouth. He had momentarily disengaged his filter, making no effort to process what his son was saying. In addition, he squirmed a little at the unfair assault he had just unleashed on the poor Haitians.

"Isn't that what you and Mom taught me?" Noah snapped. "To always look for where I could make the *biggest* difference?"

Make a difference? For a moment, Ethan conjured up the image of Neil, who used to be his neighbor across the street. Neil had recently purchased a million-dollar mansion in Ladue after selling his Mercedes dealership for a hefty profit. Ethan wondered if Neil cared about the difference he had made.

"Portland's not *big* enough?" rebutted Ethan. "And what about your wife? I know Amy also wants to make a difference. Is she on board with this idea?"

"Portland?" replied Noah, "There are more than enough doctors happy to work in Portland. It's demanding work, sure, but plenty of professionals move to this city every day. That's not the case in Haiti. And yes, it may be violent, but that's just one more reason why they need good doctors."

"And what about Amy?" Ethan asked for a second time.

"Yeah, that's the rub," replied Noah, his passion noticeably deflated. "She's *not* on board. Her head's in a completely different place. Lately, all she talks about is wanting to start a family." Noah paused and glanced toward the lustrous surf that was now lapping closer to their bare feet. "And Amy adamantly refuses to raise children in a place like Haiti."

"Can you *blame* her?" Ethan countered in a knee-jerk reaction. This time, he admonished himself to listen more and talk less.

"Sure, we have the luxury of a choice," Noah answered. "People like Amy and myself always have a choice. But, of course, that's not something the children of Haiti have, is it?"

Ethan swallowed hard and bit down on his tongue as a reminder to slow down the conversation.

"Yes, that's a fair point," responded Ethan. "So then, what are you going to do?"

Noah continued to gaze downward, hypnotized by the steady rhythm of the waves. "I don't know," he finally answered. "I feel like this is one of those moments where you realize you've come to a fork in the road, and whatever path you choose will affect the remainder of your life."

Once again, Ethan found himself commiserating with his son's dilemma. And once again, he chose to submerge his predicament, at least for now.

"Yes, that's for sure," Ethan added, joining his son in studying the rising tide creeping towards their feet. "You're not just talking about a new job in a new city, are you? You're talking about potentially ending your marriage. Have you and Amy reached the point where your relationship might be terminal if you *didn't* move to Haiti? I don't mean to pry, but I noticed your potential partner in Port-au-Prince is a woman."

Noah turned to face his dad. "No, we haven't reached that point. And while my medical school buddy *is* single and, I'll confess, quite attractive, our relationship has always been platonic. Dad, as I said before, this is all on me." Noah glanced down, picked up a shell between his feet, and curiously examined it like a small boy. Finally, he added, "If I turned down this offer in Haiti and told Amy I was ready to start a family, we'd be just fine."

Ethan exhaled a conspicuous sigh of relief and hoped the twilight breeze blowing off the ocean had camouflaged it. For a moment, a gulf of silence divided Ethan from his son. Then, he pivoted to face Noah, and in the waning glow of the evening, they locked eyes.

"I've already said too much. Years ago, your Mom and I agreed that as you and Jenny grew older, we'd only offer advice when asked. Otherwise, we'd always be badgering you guys, like my dad constantly did with me."

"Okay," countered Noah, "*I'm asking*. What do you think I should do?"

Ethan shook his head. "You know I can't answer that. You're a grown man, and you're the one who'll have to live with this decision. Only *you* can make it."

Noah grinned. "You're not getting off the hook that easy. Let me rephrase the question, counselor. What would *you* do in my situation?"

Ethan glanced up at the afterglow on the horizon, glimmering like charcoals at the end of a barbecue. Haystack Rock and its neighboring stone columns were all backlit by a rose-tinted radiance that would soon give way to an inky but star-filled night. Except for the distant squawking of high-flying gulls, father and son shared another moment of quiet stillness.

Finally, Ethan turned toward Noah and replied, "When I was your age, I probably would've taken the job in Haiti."

"*Really?*" Noah exclaimed. "I'm shocked."

"Yeah," Ethan replied. "As a younger man, I also burned with ambition. So it would've been tough to turn down an offer like that."

"But?" Noah asked.

"But?" echoed Ethan.

"There's a 'but' coming, isn't there?"

Ethan sighed. "Okay, just remember, you asked." He cleared his throat. "*But*, knowing what I know now, it would have been a mistake."

"Why?" Noah asked with growing bewilderment.

"Because," responded Ethan, glancing at this son. "I understand something now that took a lifetime to figure out. As someone who's probably lived more than two-thirds of his life, I've come to realize that what matters most isn't work, career, or even the difference you make in the lives of others."

Ethan suddenly whirled to face his son, to look him squarely in the eye. "It's *family*, Noah. Nothing else in the world comes close. I can see the day coming soon when I'll reflect back on my life, and it won't be the clients I'll remember. Instead, it'll be you, it'll be your sister, and it'll be the memory of your mother."

Ethan had astonished himself. From where had this come? Only as the words exited his mouth did he realize how his values had shifted, almost imperceptibly, like the tectonic shift of the plates within the earth's crust. Was this advice about family aimed only at Noah?

Before his son could respond, Ethan felt a vibration from within his pocket. Out of habit, he reached down, slipped out his cell phone, and glanced at its screen. In the gathering darkness, the name stood out in its brilliance. It was Ellen. Ethan figured it must be approaching eleven o'clock in St. Louis on a Friday night. What could she possibly want? Something must be seriously wrong for her to disturb him at this time. Ethan held up a finger, indicating he needed to take the call.

"Hi, Ellen. Is everything alright?"

"Yes, Ethan, and I sincerely apologize if this is a bad time. But I know it's earlier where you are, so I figured you wouldn't be asleep."

Ethan scowled, thinking this was another call where Ellen sought his work-related advice. Of course, he was not asleep, but it was still a Friday night.

"No, it's fine," Ethan replied. "You didn't wake me. But I wouldn't think you'd be working right now, Ellen. It's pretty late on a Friday night."

"Actually," she responded, "I was about to go to sleep. I live a pretty dull life," she chuckled. Ethan could visualize Ellen reclining in bed with a book in her lap, an adorable pug snoring by her side, and a sleepy grin on her face.

"However," she added after a brief pause, "I just received a call from the city justice center. It was from an inmate trying to reach you, but somehow, he got my number. I normally don't answer my phone this late, but when I listened to his message, he sounded pretty desperate. So, I called him back."

"*Interesting*," Ethan reflected, "Did you get a hold of him?"

"Yes," Ellen answered. "It wasn't easy. I called the Justice Center, and they finally managed to locate him. When we spoke, he said the police had just arrested him for first-degree murder. When I suggested applying for a public defender, he said he'd much rather have you as his attorney. Then, I explained you were out of town and that I'd taken your place. He was adamant, though, that it *had* to be you. I think he knows you, Ethan. He *begged* me to contact you."

There was a momentary lapse while Ethan tried to think of who this man could be. His clients always faced white-collar charges. Who could possibly be facing murder one on a Friday night?

"Hmmm," Ethan pondered. "What's his name, Ellen?"

"Daryl," she answered. "Daryl Armstrong."

chapter
12

Ethan lay on his bed in the rear of the camper, gazing at a shadowy ceiling. Every time he closed his eyes, he could see the steely glare on the face of an eleven-year-old boy. It had been more than thirty years since Ethan last saw Daryl. The eleven-year-old boy would now be a man in his forties. Ethan had not heard a word from or about Daryl for over three decades. When he reflected on his life, Ethan took immense pride in his multiple roles—attorney, friend, husband, and especially father. But sending Daryl back to Social Services had *not* been his finest hour.

Noah immediately had questions after his Dad ended the phone conversation with Ellen the night before. Ethan was not eager to answer them, though, since he had never shared Daryl's story with either of his children. Moreover, he wanted to avoid the subject because he was embarrassed by his role in returning Daryl to Social Services.

Ethan had tried to steer the conversation back to the Port-a-Prince versus Portland issue, but his son made it clear he did not want to continue that discussion. Noah thanked his dad for the insightful advice, saying that Ethan had given him much to consider. For now, though, his son was "all talked out." And when Noah persisted in probing the phone conversation he had just overheard, Ethan brushed aside his questions by insisting that Daryl was simply a potential client who was in serious trouble. While this explanation was technically the truth, it nevertheless bothered Ethan that he had not told his son the whole story.

Somewhere around one a.m., Ethan scampered into the camper's bathroom to relieve himself. As he climbed back into bed, Noah's raspy voice suddenly sliced through the silence.

"I guess neither of us can sleep," he declared from across the camper. "We both know what's keeping me up. So, Dad, what's your dilemma?"

"Nothing," Ethan retorted. "I just needed to go to the bathroom. Getting up three or four times a night to pee is just part of growing old. You'll see one day."

"Oh, come on, Dad, who are you kidding? I've heard you tossing and turning since we turned the lights off almost two hours ago."

Ethan did not respond while he mulled over how to answer his son's question. For a moment, the only sound came through an open window where an owl hooted somewhere off in the darkness. Noah, however, was determined to outlast his father. So finally, Ethan reached over, turned on a lamp, and slumped back on a raised pillow. As their eyes adjusted to the light, each saw a grin splashed on the other's face. Since sleep had eluded them both, Ethan finally decided this would be as good a time as any to fill Noah in on the details behind Ellen's phone call.

It took about thirty minutes to review Daryl's background story. Except for an occasional murmur, often accompanied by a nod, Noah did not say a word. He just let his father talk, inwardly enjoying the reversal of roles. Ethan covered everything, including his reason for not being more candid earlier in the evening.

"So now," Ethan concluded, "Daryl's in *serious* trouble. He's sitting in a jail cell at the City Justice Center, charged with a double homicide. At a minimum, he's facing a mandatory life sentence."

"So," Noah asked solemnly, "What are you going to do?"

Ethan immediately responded with a knee-jerk response, "If Ellen agrees to take his case pro bono, I'll try to assist her from a distance."

Noah's quizzical expression took the place of a verbal response.

"*What?*" Ethan countered. "I came out here to spend time with you, Noah. It's been wonderful so far, but what's it been? 36 hours?"

Noah's smile bordered on becoming a condescending sneer. Ethan recalled seeing a similar expression on Sarah's face at moments like this.

Finally, he shook his head and raised his palms upward, silently inviting a counterargument.

"Okay," Noah finally retorted, "You once told me, Dad, there are two basic types of arguments: moral and pragmatic. So here's one of each for you."

Before continuing, Noah sat up, swung his legs over, and scooted to the edge of his bed. Even though he had chosen a path to medical school, Noah knew how to plead a case with his attorney father.

"Morally," Noah continued, "You *owe* it to Daryl to take his case. Who knows what kind of life he's led since returning to Social Services? It obviously was not what you and Mom would have given him. Dad, your two natural children grew up to be a teacher and a doctor. The one you could've adopted was just charged with murder."

Noah paused momentarily to let this thought marinate. Then, he followed it up with a question. "Dad, if you could go back thirty years, would you still send Daryl back? Because I got the impression a few minutes ago when you told me about him that you've regretted that decision ever since. You and Mom had the chance to make a meaningful difference in Daryl's life, and you chose to do otherwise. So here's an opportunity to return and possibly make it right."

Without realizing it, Ethan noticed he was silently nodding in agreement. Then, he abruptly shook his head to break the spell.

"I'll probably regret this," Ethan finally murmured, "But what's your pragmatic argument?"

Noah grinned. He could see his pitch was succeeding. Ever since his teenage years, Noah relished the challenge of engaging in these debates with his attorney father.

"I *think*," Noah announced in a Clarence Darrow voice, "Going back to take Daryl's case presents a classic win-win solution. Dad, you take the case and hopefully free Daryl. If you do, he wins. Even if the jury rules against him, you'll still have given him his best chance possible. Meanwhile, you shed the baggage you've been carrying for over three decades. And then, you'll win. As I said, it's a classic win-win."

For a moment, a stillness permeated the inside of the camper. Then Ethan drew in a deep breath, preparing his rebuttal. He knew from decades of litigation that sometimes, the best approach was to begin by conceding a little to his opposition.

"You're right, Noah. I've been carrying the guilt of sending Daryl back to the state for decades. And I have felt guilty, although I often managed not to think about it. Still, it's always been there." He paused, indicating that a transition was coming.

"However, guilt is a powerful motivator," he finally continued, "It can also be a double-edged sword. Noah, if I go rushing back to St. Louis, I'll later wrestle with the guilt of fleeing when I should've been here to support you at a major crossroads in your life."

"What do you mean?" Noah interrupted dubiously.

"Let's go back to last night," Ethan countered. "You were talking about an idea that could upend your marriage and, really, your whole life. Noah, you're *my son*. Whatever happens, I want to be a part of your decision-making process. Otherwise, there's a reasonable chance I'll live with a different source of guilt for the rest of my life." Then, almost as an afterthought, Ethan added, "What's more, I originally took this trip to reconcile my life with the loss of your mother. I *know* she'd want me to be here to support you right now."

Before his son could respond, Ethan realized his mistake. He instantly reminded himself, however, that the goal was to make the best decision, *not* to win a debate with his son.

"No disrespect intended, Dad," Ethan refuted, "But that's *bullshit*. You and I both know that given a choice between helping your physician son make a career decision and defending the man that Mom wanted to adopt to fight a murder charge, Mom would tell you to GO HOME."

Ethan quickly conceded the point with a smile and a friendly salute. But then, he thought of another argument.

"But why me, Noah? There're some excellent public defenders in St. Louis. I could probably pull some strings and get one of the best assigned to Daryl's case. Then, as you say, it could still be a win-win for all of us. I could continue my trip, spending more time with you, and Daryl would still get good legal representation."

"*But*," Noah answered, "Daryl insisted on having *you* as his lawyer."

"Yes, I guess so," responded Ethan, "But I'm not sure *why*. He had to work hard to track me down. It would have been much easier simply applying for a public defender." Then, after a pause, he added, "You know, those guys get a bad rap, primarily because they're so overworked. But most of the P.D.s in St. Louis are excellent trial lawyers."

"You said Daryl was pretty smart, right?" There was a gleam in Noah's eyes, the same one Ethan always saw whenever an idea suddenly came to his son. "For starters, he probably appreciates the seriousness of his trouble and simply wants the best lawyer available."

"And why would he think I'm the best lawyer?"

"Because he got to know you that summer, right?" Noah rolled out of bed, opened a kitchen cabinet, and pulled out one of the Hershey bars they had brought to make s'mores, another family tradition. He was steadily growing more animated.

"Yeah . . . , so?"

"So," Noah answered, "From the time he spent with you that summer, Daryl learned how smart you were. And now that you've got thirty years of experience, he figured you're one of the top lawyers in the area. And I'll bet you even told him about your plans to pursue criminal defense work. Am I right?"

Ethan nodded, waiting for the next question. Noah purposely hesitated. Without realizing it, Noah had switched to employing the cross-examination skills he had picked up from his father rather than formulating arguments as he had learned on the high school debate team.

"But," Noah finally pronounced, "That's not the *biggest* reason why Daryl tracked you down to be his lawyer, is it?"

"No? What's the biggest reason?"

"I can answer that in a single word," replied Noah. Then, after another pause, he announced, "*Guilt*."

Ethan's perplexed expression soon transformed into a broad grin. "I get it," he pronounced, "Daryl thinks I feel guilty about turning him back to Social Services thirty years ago. So naturally, I'd be highly motivated to take his case and win a favorable verdict."

"Well, don't you?" Noah asked. "Feel guilty, I mean."

Ethan lowered his gaze, momentarily studying the hands clasped in his lap. Finally, when he peered up, Noah could see the dampness in the corners of his father's eyes.

"Okay," Noah proclaimed as he snapped the candy bar in two and then strolled over to offer half to his father. "Here's what I think."

Ethan grasped the grooved milk chocolate and mindlessly took an ambitious bite. Then, finally, he nodded for his son to continue.

"I've had my entire life to build a solid, loving relationship with my father. And that's why, Dad, you don't need to stay in Oregon. You and I can talk, text, or FaceTime as much as necessary to help me make the best decision regarding my career and marriage situation. But you do not need to be here *in person.*"

Once again, Ethan found himself nodding in agreement. Building on this momentum, Noah continued.

"Dad, you need to go back to St. Louis. *Now.* And you need to win Daryl his freedom."

"Yes," Ethan responded with a furrowed brow, "But what if I don't win? From what Ellen's told me, this case doesn't have much going for it."

Noah sat down on the edge of his Dad's bed, chuckled, and patted his father on the shoulder. Then, finally, he responded, "I'm not the lawyer, Dad. You are. But I bet you'll find a way to win. And even if you don't, I'm confident you'll still give Daryl the best defense possible."

Observing his father's unease, Noah clenched his lips together and inhaled a deep breath through his nose. "Alright, let me ask you something, Dad. Intuitively, do you believe Daryl's guilty?"

Ethan shook his head. "I don't have any proof or evidence, at least not yet, but in my heart, no, I don't think that kid's capable of murder."

"Then do *your best* to get him off," responded Noah. "It's like you always told me: the most you can ever do is your best. If you do your best, you said, you'll always respect the man you see in the mirror."

At that moment, Ethan glanced toward a mirror on the camper's closet door. At first, the image peering back was almost laughable. It looked like Mr. Potato Head with dark bags beneath its eyes, wisps of ashen hair jetting in every direction, and old man ear lobes starting to grow unnaturally large. Then Ethan gazed into the eyes. Although reddened by fatigue, a low flame had ignited them as though each was reflecting a lit candle.

The corners of his mouth slowly turned upward. Ethan recognized this expression. He assumed this must be what Sarah saw that day in the grove when he suddenly realized what they needed to do to descend the mountain above Banff. Ethan understood there are only a few moments in a person's life when they genuinely admire their reflection in the mirror. This was one of those times. Ethan turned toward his son, clenched his lips together, and nodded.

"This may be tough," he finally proclaimed, "But we need to get some sleep. I've got over 2000 miles to drive and not a lot of time. They'll bring Daryl in front of a judge on Monday to officially charge him. I can probably get it pushed back a day, but I'd like to be standing next to him when that happens."

Noah arched his eyebrows above a broad grin. Although he had kept this to himself, he

was deeply concerned about his father. Jenny had sworn him to secrecy, but she had told him about their Dad's suicide attempt. Now, for the first time since his mother's ceremony at Creve Coeur Lake, Noah thought his Dad would be okay. At least for now, his father had a purpose, a mission.

Without uttering a word, Noah reached over and embraced his father. Neither could see the mirrored expression of the other. Both men had closed their eyes, and the same devoted smile stretched across their faces. Then, Noah stood, walked over to the lamp, turned off the switch, and quietly tip-toed back to his bed on the other side of the camper. By 2:30 a.m., father and son were both fast asleep.

Six hours later, Ethan and Noah were rounding the curves of Highway 26, snaking their way back to Beaverton. Whatever had initially motivated Ethan to embark on his meandering road trip out West had instantly dissipated. Sarah's death had been the impetus to start this journey. Now, the chance to defend the man who had triggered his wife's first maternal instincts was a compelling reason to end it.

PART II

chapter
13

Ethan knew it would take at least thirty hours to drive home, so there was no time to waste. When they pulled into Noah's driveway, Ethan came inside just long enough to grab some sandwiches and a few other snacks. Amy had an early shift, so the house was empty. Noah then walked his dad out to his SUV to see him off. Anticipating this moment, Ethan turned to face his son.

"First," Ethan pronounced, recalling words he had mentally prepared while driving back from Cannon Beach, "Our time was short, but I had a blast over the past couple of days. Thanks for taking time off to join me for this little venture."

"*Same*," Noah responded with a flash in his eyes.

"And I especially appreciate the talk last night," Ethan continued. "Noah, you've got a good head on your shoulders."

"Well, if I do," Noah replied, "I got it from you and Mom."

Ethan paused and looked away for a moment. He had carefully formulated his next words, but since he did not have written notes, he wanted to be sure they came out as planned.

"And I trust," Ethan finally asserted, "You'll use that good head to make the best decision regarding your future. Because whatever you decide about Haiti, you'll have to live with it for the rest of your life."

Now, it was Noah's turn to look away. He glanced downward for a moment and absently shuffled his feet.

"Yeah," he finally replied, "I've been giving that a lot of thought, especially what you said last night." Then, he smiled and added, "You know, I could tell during those moments of silence on this morning's drive that our brains were working overtime."

Ethan nodded and returned his son's smile. "So?" he responded, "Come to any decision?"

"No, not yet," Noah replied. "But soon. I'll keep you posted."

Ethan nodded again and, this time spread his arms out for the family bear hug. Father and son embraced one last time. Then, Ethan climbed into his vehicle, gave a final wave, and backed out of the driveway. It took almost an hour to navigate through Portland's unexpectedly snarled traffic, but by late morning, Ethan was cruising east on I-84. At one point, it dawned on him he would be following the Oregon Trail in reverse.

Over the next two days, Ethan drove eastward like a maniacal truck driver with a tight schedule to keep. He made rapid progress with the help of stale coffee at rest stops and a couple of Grisham books he paid extra for on his Audible account. This time, there were no imaginary conversations with his recently deceased wife or grave philosophical ruminations over the meaning of life. Instead, Ethan generally thought about his future when he allowed his mind to wander.

It was somewhere north of Salt Lake City that Ethan began to marvel at the possibilities. First, he noted that the question of ending his life prematurely was firmly settled. There was no way he would ever consider suicide again. Even the thought of his recent effort in the garage left him with a sense of shame. Now, the only question remaining was how he should ideally spend the remainder of his days. Ethan grew increasingly intrigued the more he pondered over this question.

Daryl Armstrong would be his focus in the short term. Beyond that case, though, contemplating Ethan's future legal career was like peering into a blackened tunnel. However, his professional life was a subject he would address on a different day. The more immediate question involved the people in his life. Ethan had never been a loner. With whom should he spend his time? How much energy should he devote to his grown children? And what about friends? Coming down the eastern slope of the Continental Divide, an idea struck Ethan with the force of an avalanche.

It was time to place some phone calls. Ethan pulled over at a rest stop east of Laramie, where he still had a signal, made himself a sandwich, and strolled over to an outdoor table for an impromptu picnic. While absent-mindedly chewing on his BLT, Ethan mentally assembled a list of four people to call. He then planned what he would say to each one of them.

The first was Jenny. Ethan wanted to assure his daughter that even though he would soon be home, she and Matt were welcome to remain with him as long as it took to find, purchase, and move into their ideal starter house. Next, he succinctly told her about Daryl, starting with the decision to take in a foster child thirty years ago and ending with his arrest Friday night. This explanation was necessary so Jenny could understand her dad's unexpected decision to return home suddenly. From start to finish, she proved characteristically empathetic, so this call proved the easiest to make.

Next, Ethan called Ellen. After informing her about his plans to return to St. Louis, he explained that he intended to take on Daryl as his sole client and that, otherwise, he wanted to maintain the status quo regarding her employment with the firm. She would continue to represent all his former clients, and Ethan would continue to be available on an as-needed basis. In the interim, he asked Ellen to contact Daryl and let him know he would be his attorney of record and that he would be dropping by for a meeting at the Justice Center on Monday afternoon.

Next, Ethan reached out to Keith at home. Since it was Saturday afternoon, there would be more time to explain his connection to Daryl and why Ethan felt compelled to take on this case. As expected, Keith empathetically understood and agreed with Ethan's plans regarding Ellen. He even offered his junior partner all the office space and resources he would need for the upcoming trial. Keith asserted that Daryl Armstrong would be one of the firm's primary pro bono cases.

Finally, Ethan prepared to call Tom. Reaching out to his old college roommate had been his recent inspiration on the road and the primary reason he pulled over to make his calls. Ethan wanted to build a stronger bond with Tom, not just for self-serving reasons. During his recent stop in Fort Scott, Ethan recognized Tom was wallowing in the mud. He was overweight, depressed, and drank too much. Despite what he might say to the contrary, Tom's future was bleak. Between his divorce, declining practice, and devoted attachment to a weathering town, Tom was waiting to die.

Ethan was pleased when his buddy answered after the first ring. When he announced that he would like to swing through the quiet town on his way home, Tom sounded like a father who had just learned his soldier son was returning home from the war. This time, though, Tom insisted that Ethan stay with him, not out in the campground. He zealously appreciated that Ethan was going out of his way to make this stop. On the other end of the call, Ethan was delighted by Tom's response but thought it best to wait and spring his proposal in person.

Shortly before 6:00 p.m. the following evening, after a fatiguing drive through the rolling prairies of Nebraska, Ethan pulled into the driveway of Tom's Victorian-style home. Located on the west side of town across from Gunn Park, the house was a redbrick, two-story cubicle with a wrap-around porch and a witch's hat turret. The structure was constructed in the late 19th Century and possessed a solid mass that looked like it could survive any Kansas tornado. As Ethan exited his SUV, he saw Tom standing on the porch, grinning broadly and holding a can of Budweiser high in the air.

"Hey buddy," Tom bellowed, "How was the drive?"

Ethan waved a response while yanking an overnight bag out of the backseat. He was thrilled to be spending the night in a less confining space.

"It was uneventful," replied Ethan while clambering up the porch steps. "That's the best you can hope for nowadays on the interstate highways." He exchanged a man hug with Tom, accepted a can of beer, and then plopped down on one of two wicker rocking chairs guarding the front porch. "How've you been?"

"Oh, the same old, same old, " Tom answered. He slowly descended into the other rocker, reached down into a small cooler, and jerked out another member of the six-pack. Tom effortlessly popped the lid and threw his head back to guzzle half the beer like a fraternity boy. Then, wiping his mouth with the back of a chubby wrist, he belched softly and asked, "How's your trip been overall?"

"*Great,*" Ethan replied. "It didn't last as long as planned, but it served its purpose." Ethan developed a steady cadence to his rocking as he admired the cloud sculptures dancing above the park across the street.

"How so?" Tom inquired.

Ethan took a swig of beer and turned to face his friend. "In two ways," he replied. "First, a hike in the Tetons convinced me there could still be life even after Sarah."

Tom nodded curiously but waited for his friend to continue.

"Second," Ethan replied after another swig of beer, "When I was in Oregon, Noah helped me realize there's an important task awaiting me back in St. Louis."

"Oh yeah? What's that?"

"*That,*" Ethan exclaimed, "Is a longer story. Why don't I tell you about it at dinner?"

"Alright," responded Tom. "I thought we might barbecue some burgers and dogs out back."

"Nah," Ethan replied, "I'd like to treat you to a nice meal tonight, you know, to thank you for playing host. So . . . , what's the best restaurant in town?"

All of a sudden, beer exploded up Tom's nose. When he finally caught his breath, he turned to face Ethan with a mischievous grin still painted across his face.

"Oh, you're serious." Then he added, "I guess it's a tossup between Crooners Lounge and Luther's BBQ. At least they're both open on Sunday nights."

"*Really?*" Ethan asked. "You think we can get reservations so late?"

"Let's go to Crooners," Tom asserted, ignoring his friend's sarcasm. "I'm in the mood for some of their pork chops."

An hour later, Tom parked his pickup on South Main in front of the restaurant. As they approached the entrance, Ethan observed that under the eatery's name were the words "STEAK – SEAFOOD – PASTA – CHICKEN."

The two old friends were seated next to a front window providing the perfect view of a deserted Main Street. Ethan glanced around and soon realized he had misjudged the restaurant. A dainty white cloth frosted each table, anchored by attractive centerpieces. The artwork on the red brick wall opposite the polished wooden bar was tasteful, adding a sense of coziness to the overall décor. Crooners was unexpectedly the ideal place to enjoy dinner with an old friend.

For the first couple of minutes, they studied the menu. Then, true to form, Tom asked for the pork chops. Ethan ordered the beef tenderloin tips well done. Next, they both agreed to share a decanter of wine. Finally, after ordering the food and uncorking the bottle, Tom raised a glass and suggested a toast.

"To *friendship*," he pronounced.

Ethan smiled, raised his glass, and clinked it with Tom's. "Very appropriate," he commented. Then, looking around, he added, "And I *like* this place."

"Glad you approve," Tom replied. "Now, tell me why you're suddenly heading back to St. Louis. I figured you to be on the road for months, so the fact you're already on your way home was a bit surprising."

Ethan nodded, but before he could respond, the waitress returned and dutifully lowered two weighty plates onto the table. "Can I get you anything else, gentlemen?"

Ethan glanced up and noted the waitress looked like one of the seniors who lived across the hall from James back in St. Louis. She was wafer thin and had to be pushing eighty. Ethan briefly pondered the circumstances leading a woman to take a job like this so late in life.

Tom looked up with a wide grin and responded. "No, Edith, everything looks great."

"Smells delicious, *too*," Ethan added with a somewhat exaggerated smile. He noted how Tom and Edith were familiar with each other. Once the waitress had parted, Ethan cut off a piece of tenderloin tip, scrutinized it, and then smiled when he did not see any pink. After placing it in a mouth already awash in saliva, Ethan closed his eyes and beamed.

"This is *truly* delicious," he proclaimed.

Tom grinned and then began to slice into his pork chops. For the next few minutes, the only sounds came from distant conversations and the two men chewing and swallowing. Their table had become a vegetarian's nightmare.

"Okay," Ethan finally stated after washing down a bite of beef with a sip of wine, "Remember that story I told you about Daryl, the foster kid Sarah and I took in a long time ago?"

Tom nodded, too busy gnawing into his chops to answer.

Ethan waved his steak knife like a conductor's baton to emphasize the next point. "Well, he's suddenly reemerged into my life. I just got a call from a fellow attorney in my firm, and she told me the cops arrested Daryl." Ethan placed his knife and fork on his plate, taking a little break. "I'm not sure why," he added, "But Daryl insists he wants me as his lawyer."

"*No* kidding," Tom replied, repeating Ethan's actions with the tableware. "Are you going to take the case?"

Ethan nodded. "Yes, that's why I cut my trip short."

"What's he charged with?" Tom inquired, grabbing his cutlery and preparing for round two with the pork chops.

"Homicide, first degree," Ethan hastily responded. "*Double* homicide. He's in a boatload of trouble."

"So . . . ," Tom replied. Ethan could hear the gears spinning inside his friend's head. "This is your chance to make things right?"

Ethan drew in a deep breath and nodded. Then, finally, he asserted, "Tom, I don't know most of the particulars, but I'm pretty sure about two things."

Tom lifted an eyebrow. "Yeah?"

"First," Ethan continued, "This'll be a mammoth undertaking. I've learned the evidence overwhelmingly favors the prosecution." Ethan picked up his utensils and prepared to carve up the rest of his tenderloin tips. "And second, even though no one can be a hundred percent sure, in my heart, Tom, I don't believe Daryl's guilty."

"As you know," Tom replied, "It doesn't matter what a defendant's lawyer personally thinks, but that said, why do you feel this way?"

"Because I *know* Daryl," responded Ethan. "There's just no way the kid who lived with us that summer is capable of such a brutal crime."

Tom looked away to conceal his misgivings. Then, finally, he asserted, "Ethan, you *only* knew this kid for one summer thirty years ago. And what was he at the time, eleven? Daryl's a fully grown man now approaching his mid-forties. He's probably a completely different person."

"I don't think so," Ethan replied patiently, "I got to know Daryl pretty well when we were hiking in the mountains. I spent enough time with him to get to know his true character. My instincts tell me, Tom, that he was a good kid then and a decent man now. What did Wordsworth say, 'The child is the father of the man?'"

Tom gazed at Ethan, studying the embers burning in his friend's eyes. Then, finally, he glanced down at his plate, empty except for a smattering of mashed potatoes. Tom gently placed his knife and fork down with finality and pushed the plate away.

"Okay, I get it," Tom pronounced, "You're pretty passionate about this kid. So now I understand why you're heading back to St. Louis."

Tom glanced at his plate and then sluggishly pivoted to stare into the empty darkness. Ethan followed his gaze, observing the shadows haunting the street. He wondered what his friend was thinking. On the exterior, Tom suddenly appeared catatonic. His countenance had altered as though the spirit of another suddenly lodged within his body. Ethan was on the verge of announcing his plans for his old roommate, but now, he thought it best to await Tom's return to the conversation. Finally, Tom turned and confronted Ethan with renewed vigor.

"Ethan," Tom announced ardently, "You'll probably think this is nuts, but I've got an idea."

"Yeah?" Ethan responded with mounting curiosity. He silently wondered if there was an overlap between Tom's proposal and the plan he was harboring.

"Why don't I join you?" Tom blurted out.

A smile burst across Ethan's face, but before he could answer, Tom continued.

"I could serve as your second chair, Ethan. I've lived within spitting distance of Missouri for years, so I got a license to practice over there. My experience with criminal law's minimal, but I have some. If nothing else, I could do a lot of the leg work. I could investigate possible leads that might produce evidence to support Daryl's defense. "

For a moment, the two men quietly grinned at each other. Then Ethan put aside his knife and fork, leaned back in his chair, and placed both hands behind his head. Finally, he broke the silence.

"Tom, if there was ever a time proving that great minds think alike." Ethan heartedly chuckled before continuing. "I was getting ready to propose the *same* idea to you."

Before Tom could respond, Ethan added almost in a whisper, "I couldn't pay much, though. And will you be able to put your life here on hold for an indeterminate time?"

Tom smiled. "What life? I still take on a client every now and then, but nothing is pressing right now. Ethan, I'm essentially retired and bored out of my mind. As for money, I just put in for social security. Plus, I've got some investments. It's enough."

"What about your family and friends?" Ethan inquired.

Again, Tom flashed a smile. "My parents are long gone, and my sister packed up and left for L.A. years ago after she got married. As for friends, I can usually make them anywhere."

Tom looked downward, pushed aside his plate, and then clasped his hands together like he was about to recite a prayer. "Look, Ethan, you remember the conversation we had a few weeks ago about Irena Sendler?"

Ethan nodded but remained silent.

"You recall how we agreed that the real heroes are the ones who try to make a difference in the lives of others?"

Again, Ethan nodded. Before he could reply, though, Tom continued, "Well, I'd like to do something like that. And at my age, there are probably only a few years left to give it a try. Who knows, if I can help Daryl, maybe this will snowball. You know what I mean?"

Ethan gazed intently at his friend. He recognized that he and Tom had taken different paths to reach the same destination. Yet, now in the early stages of retirement, both men still needed something meaningful in their lives. Ethan wanted to steer his life in a new direction. And Tom was wasting away here in Fort Scott. At the rate he was going, Tom would be dead of a heart attack within a few years.

On top of everything else, Ethan and Tom were friends, old friends. Working together on Daryl's case would not only fill a hole in their lives but also patch a bond that had gradually dissolved over the years. Ethan had also recently grasped that, at this stage, it was impossible to make a new "old" friend.

"Alright," Ethan declared, "Here's what I propose. We started as roommates long ago, so let's go back to the beginning. Even though Jenny and Matt have moved into my basement, I still have a spare bedroom upstairs. You can live there rent-free for as long as you want. And like roommates, we'll probably take most meals together, and I've actually become a decent cook. That's all I can offer, Tom, but I hope it's enough. Yes, I'd love to have your help."

Ethan observed the corners of Tom's mouth edge upward. Within a few seconds, Tom's face exploded into a full grin. Then, without saying a word, he reached for the half-empty bottle of wine, uncorked it, and flooded their two glasses. He then slid one glass back toward Ethan while hefting the other up for a toast.

"Ethan, that's *more* than enough." And for the second time that evening, the two men simultaneously raised their glasses and repeated the words, "To friendship."

chapter

14

Ethan navigated his camper out of Tom's driveway shortly after sunrise. It was Monday morning, and he had a busy day planned. Tom awoke just in time to make a pot of coffee and some buttered toast. Then, once Ethan departed, Tom stumbled back into bed. His alarm would not go off for a couple of hours. Tom had given himself the rest of the day to pack a few suitcases and then drive to St. Louis in time to meet Ethan for dinner.

Two and half hours later, as Ethan circled Osage Beach on State Highway 54, he called the clerk's office in downtown St. Louis. He began by patiently explaining he would be the attorney of record for Mr. Daryl Armstrong, who had been taken into custody Friday night. Since Ethan was more than two hours away and still needed to meet his client, he asked the clerk to postpone this morning's initial appearance for 24 hours. Ethan knew this was standard practice.

By mid-morning, Ethan was positioning the camper behind his house in Creve Coeur. Since the garage faced the rear of the lot, there was more than enough space in the back to stow his miniature house on wheels until he could decide its long-term fate. Since Ethan had not given much thought to his future beyond the upcoming trial, he wanted to keep the camper for the time being. Ethan knew Jenny and Matt would already be at work, so their cars were not in the way. From now on, though, they would have to park on the street.

Ethan took the rest of the morning to unpack and clear out a spare bedroom for Tom. Since four adults would be living in his home indefinitely, he also saw to it that everyone had clean sheets, towels, and whatever else they might need. Ethan also inspected the refrigerator and pantry to inventory the food situation. Next, he made a list of items to pick up at Schnuck's later in the day. Finally, Ethan finished unpacking, hastily changed into a suit, and then made himself a PB and J sandwich to eat in the car.

Thirty minutes later, Ethan pulled his SUV into an open spot inside the Justice Center garage. He glanced at his watch. It was only 2:30 in the afternoon, plenty of time to meet with Daryl, hear his side of the story, and then review their short and long-term plans. He glanced at his reflection in the rearview mirror and slightly adjusted the knot in his tie. Over the years, Ethan had spent more time in the St. Louis County courts than he did in the city, but this was still familiar terrain. Ethan realized his edginess had nothing to do with visiting an inmate in the City Justice Center, something he had done countless times in the past. Instead, he was nervous about meeting with this particular inmate.

As he approached the front entrance, Ethan glanced at the six-story edifice. It was a boxy building, fronted with concrete and glass, that, from the outside, could be mistaken for one of the many office buildings dotting the downtown landscape. Inside, though, it housed almost 900 inmates in the heart of one of the nation's most crime-ridden cities. Ethan recalled the recent riots where several inmates had escaped from their cells, shattered the front windows, set fires, and thrown debris down onto the street below.

Ethan speedily glided through the security hurdles, including undergoing a personal pat down. This procedure was required whenever an attorney wanted to meet a client privately rather than communicate through a plexiglass sheet. Once settled into the claustrophobic conference room, Ethan would ordinarily busy himself by reviewing files from other cases. But instead, today, he anxiously reread the police report from Daryl's arrest for the third time. The wait was interminable, but there was no escaping that it took time to locate, secure, and bring down a prisoner.

Finally, the door opened to reveal a gaunt figure swallowed up by an oversized jumpsuit. The brilliant orange color would mark any prisoner that might ever escape. An anonymous guard quickly unlocked the handcuffs behind the inmate's back and disappeared. Ethan and the inmate gaped at each other for a moment, diligently taking stock of how much the other had changed over the last thirty years. Ethan observed that Daryl's blond hair was long and greasy, his eyes were bloodshot, and his face was thin and rumpled like that of a much older man.

Daryl circled the wooden table like a puma stalking its prey. He never took his eyes off his new lawyer. As he sank into the chair opposite Ethan, a smile slowly cleaved his face. There was a sparkle of recognition in his eyes.

"You've gotten old," Daryl pronounced in a guttural voice.

Those three words shattered the ice. Ethan immediately grinned at the irony of Daryl voicing his own thoughts.

"It happens," Ethan replied wearily. "You're not exactly a kid anymore, either."

Ethan knew there was much to discuss, but he also understood the first few minutes with Daryl were critical. He needed to address their history in order to establish a workable level of trust. Without confidence in each other, the attorney-client relationship could be more of a liability than an asset. Ethan planned to refrain from taking the lead. Instead, he wanted Daryl to guide the conversation, at least at the outset. Therefore, Ethan folded his arms, sat back in his rigid wooden chair, and waited. Silence saturated the closet-sized room.

Finally, Daryl tilted his head back as though looking through reading glasses. "You ever think about me?"

The question caught Ethan off guard, but he quickly recovered. Under the circumstances, he did not want to play any games. Instead, Ethan wanted to be as honest and straightforward as possible.

"Yes," Ethan replied, "I do. Quite often."

"And . . . ," Daryl continued, "Do you ever feel bad?"

Ethan was pleasantly surprised by Daryl's candor. It was an uncomfortable conversation, but it was evident that Daryl was also trying to clear the air.

"About our decision to turn you back to Social Services?"

"Yes," Daryl replied, "Although, as I recall, it seemed like it was mostly *your* decision. I got the impression your wife wanted to keep me around. She was such a nice lady. By the way, how's she doing?"

Ethan twisted awkwardly in his chair and looked away. For a moment, silence again filled the vacuum. Then, seeing he had struck a nerve, Daryl's demeanor softened. He continued to employ a direct approach, though, keeping his words to a minimum. "Is she still alive?"

Ethan shook his head, slowly returning his gaze toward his new client.

"Oh, man," Daryl mumbled, "I'm sorry. When?"

"Just a month ago," Ethan answered dolefully. "Leukemia. It was fast." After a pause, he added, "God, I *miss* her, though. I think about Sarah constantly." Ethan was not sure why he included that last comment. He wanted to be direct with Daryl, but bearing his soul might be going a bit too far.

Daryl nodded woefully and then looked away. Ethan studied his profile and observed that while it probably had been a while since Daryl last shaved, his face was still more stubble than a beard. A downy mustache overlooked his upper lip, and some wayward hairs grew beneath his chin, but there were also hairless patches on his cheek. Daryl had showered but had ignored his facial grooming. This look would not matter much for an initial appearance, but he would have to undergo a complete makeover before appearing in front of a jury.

"You okay?" Ethan asked. He was surprised by how Daryl absorbed the news about his wife's passing. Then, when Daryl turned back to face his lawyer directly, Ethan observed a narrow wet streak beneath one eye.

"*Hey*," Ethan stated bewilderedly, "You only knew Sarah for a few months, and at the time, you were just eleven years old."

Daryl whisked away the moisture from his cheek with an index finger. "I know," he responded sympathetically. "But she had been the nicest of all the people I encountered in the foster care system. I still remember her like it was yesterday." Then he added, almost as an afterthought, "And I was also thinking about you. I've been where you are now, and I know what it's like to lose the love of your life."

Ethan's eyebrows climbed. "You were thinking about *me*? I thought you'd be pretty pissed off with me. As you just reminded me, I was the one who returned you to the state."

Daryl smiled, revealing the boy Ethan remembered. "Man, I don't hold a grudge. I'll admit I wanted to guilt you into being my lawyer, but

I understand what you did thirty years ago. After all, it's not like you're the only foster parents who bounced me back to the state when they'd had enough."

Ethan leaned forward, rested both forearms on the varnished table, and smiled sheepishly. "Well, I'm glad you're not holding a grudge, but I wouldn't blame you if you did. For what it's worth, that decision's haunted me ever since you left." After drawing in a deep breath and then exhaling, he added, "Before we get to last Friday night, why don't you catch me up a bit on what's been going on in your life since the last time we saw each other?"

Daryl clasped his hands together on top of the table and sighed. "You sure you want to hear all this? It's kind of a long story. Do you have the time?"

"Yes," Ethan answered, "I have the time. Since Sarah's funeral, I've taken a break from work. In fact, Daryl, you're currently my *only* client. And since I arranged to push back your appearance in front of the judge until tomorrow morning, we have the rest of the afternoon." Then, after a brief pause, Ethan added, "I always like to know my clients. It helps me mount a better defense. And besides, on a personal level, I'd like to hear your story."

"Alright," Daryl replied like a man about to leap off a high dive, "Here goes . . ."

There's not much to say about my teenage years. The state just passed me around from one foster family to another. Some were better, and some lasted longer, but I never connected with any of them. You and Sarah were the only people who seemed to care. You didn't just buy me food and clothes. Your wife took me all over, and I still think about that trip to Colorado. Those days hiking with you in the Rockies were among the happiest in my life. The other foster parents always saw to it that I had three meals a day, showered every night, and didn't skip school. Otherwise, they just collected a paycheck. For them, I was only a job.

I mostly stayed out of trouble. I got busted once for some weed, but otherwise, I kept my grades up at Ritenour High School and never got anything lower than a C. I ran cross country for a couple of years and even played on the school's chess team. I fell in love for the first time during my junior year, but that ended when she got accepted to Mizzou. Finally, in 2001, I walked across the stage to get my high school diploma.

My plans after graduation were to work for a year, save up some money, and then enroll in a community college. Therefore, within a week after graduation, I found a job waiting tables at Zia's, you know, that Italian restaurant up on the Hill? I made enough to move into an apartment near Tower Grove Park with some friends. That summer, I got around mostly on a bicycle but figured by winter, I'd have enough to buy a cheap used car.

Then, I'm sure you remember what happened on September 11th, right? I was glued to the TV the whole day. I called in sick that morning and stayed up late into the night talking to my buddies about what had happened. The whole thing made me sick, and I felt like we needed to do something.

I told my friends about this older history teacher back in high school who always spoke about his experiences in the Vietnam War. Mr. Costanza was his name. Most of the students thought his class was like watching paint dry since he talked so much, but I always liked him. Mr. Costanza let me eat lunch in his room and told me about the Tet Offensive and his secret missions into Cambodia. He said he'd enlisted and didn't wait for the military to draft him. Mr. Costanza told me that when his country went to war, right or wrong, he should go too. He said his dad had also enlisted right after the Japanese attacked Pearl Harbor. Mr. Costanza told me it was a personal decision, so he never blamed the hippies who burned their draft cards or fled to Canada.

I'm not sure I agree with him now, but I was just a kid at the time, and Mr. Costanza was one of the few teachers who ever took an interest in me. So when I watched those towers crumble into the streets, I thought about him. Do you know how certain teachers have that kind of influence? When I brought this up with my friends that night, they thought I was crazy. But the following day, I quit my job and enlisted in the army.

Now, I know what you're thinking. Something must have happened in Fallujah or maybe Kabul that messed me up when I returned home and then later pushed me to live out on the streets. But that's not the way it played out. I did serve in Afghanistan for a year and then did a couple of tours in Iraq. And believe me, I saw plenty of bloodshed and violence. But I was never injured, and everything seemed fine once I took off the uniform. Or so I thought.

As it turned out, I was wrong. There was one event I'd tried to ignore, but it later emerged like a ghost from the grave. I was in Haditha in the fall of 2005 when a convoy of Marines was hit by an IED, killing one of their lance corporals. The Marines then went crazy and butchered a group of Iraqi civilians. I didn't witness this firsthand, but I was part of the patrol that later came across the battlefield. Twenty-four bodies were lying about, all unarmed. Among them were men, women, seniors, and even children, including one infant. They'd all been shot multiple times at close range.

My outfit only stayed in the area for a few minutes since it wasn't safe. We called it in, though, and they later investigated the massacre. Afterward, I discovered that eight Marines faced charges, but only one was ever convicted, and that was just for dereliction of duty. I tried later to forget about that day, but one image stood out, and it has never left me. There was a baby, a little girl, I think, wrapped in a black shawl so you could only see her face. She looked like a porcelain doll. Her eyes were frozen like she was still staring at the Marine who'd blasted her with his M4 carbine.

For years, I tried to forget that image. It infiltrated my nightmares, but on the following mornings, I just reminded myself that terrible things happen during times of war. Besides, I didn't have anything to do with that bloodbath, so why should I feel guilty? But these kinds of things don't go away. They never do. Instead, they lie beneath the surface, like lava inside a dormant volcano. Keep this in mind, Ethan, because it'll come up again later in my story.

It took a while to realize it, but I was a different man once I got home. You know, tattooed biceps, an endless craving for beer, and a growing chip on my shoulder. Afghanistan was one thing, but as it turned out, the war in Iraq had nothing to do with the thousands of Americans who died on 9/11. So once I heard about how easily they'd convinced W to believe all that bullshit about weapons of mass destruction, I grew increasingly pissed. I'd made some good friends in the service, but not all were as lucky as I'd been. So why exactly did we go into that country? Five thousand Americans died in Iraq, and for what? Even worse, hundreds of thousands of Iraqi civilians also lost their lives.

Still, once I came home and resumed civilian life, I just wanted to move on. So, using my veteran's benefits, I enrolled in Maryville University and started taking computer programming classes. And that's when I met Holly. She was in their nursing school at the time. Within three years, we went from casual lunch conversations in the student center to getting married and having a baby girl.

Holly had dark brown eyes and jet-black hair. She was the most *beautiful* woman I'd ever seen. There were days when I looked at myself in the mirror and wondered how a shlub like me could end up with someone like her. It must've been pure luck, I guess. Anyhow, even though it's a cliché, Holly indeed became the one true love of my life. She was also my best friend. It got harder and harder to spend any free time with my buddies because, given a choice, I wanted to spend all of it with her.

Something else drew us together, though, besides hormones. We were both veterans. Holly said that with all the death she'd seen in the Middle East, she was ready for a new career where she could save lives rather than end them. I admired that about her. You know Ethan, she reminded me a lot of your wife. Just like Sarah, Holly was loving and compassionate and absolutely *adored* children.

Holly was a year ahead of me in school, so she got a job as a nurse at Barnes-Jewish Hospital while I was still finishing my final year at Maryville. Our baby was born in mid-November, and afterward, Holly took off for six weeks and then returned to work at the beginning of the new year. Since I was just starting a paid internship, we made plans to place the baby in the hospital's daycare center. That way, Holly could see her during breaks.

Since we chose to wait and be surprised about the baby's gender, we had not settled on a name until after she was born. Holly then insisted we name her Daisy. At first, I said no, since I wasn't crazy about naming our daughter after a flower, but then Holly explained that her Grandma

Daisy had always been there even when her parents weren't. After that, I soon got used to the name. Besides, when I first laid eyes on little Daisy, she even smelled like a flower.

My daughter was born with a head covered with blond, downy hair. It was *so* soft. I sometimes liked stroking it like she was a little puppy. Daisy's eyes sparkled, and when she smiled at me for the first time, I'm telling you, it melted my heart. From the stories I'd heard about other infants, it was super easy to care for Daisy. She slept through the night at three months, and everything else, like feedings and diaper changes, happened like clockwork.

Daisy was born in the fall of 2008. Holly and I agreed that once I graduated the following May and then found a permanent job, we'd save up for a down payment to buy a house, probably somewhere just outside the city. And then maybe we'd think about giving Daisy a little brother or sister. For the time being, though, we were still crammed into a small apartment up in Maryland Heights.

Over the following year or so, life continued to improve. Most of the time, I felt like I was floating in the clouds. After graduation, I found a job as an IT development specialist for a local car wash company. The pay was decent, and I liked the work. Holly managed to schedule fewer evening and weekend shifts so we could spend more time together. And after little Daisy learned to walk, she was soon running everywhere. I know every parent feels this way, but I thought she was the most adorable toddler in the world. Meanwhile, we socked away a lot of money and even started going to open houses on Sunday afternoons.

Now, Ethan, it's difficult to talk about this next part. I've always believed that everyone spends their lives like they're tip-toeing through a minefield. A small number will make it through without triggering a single blast. Others will step on the filament, but with some luck, they'll survive and manage to go on. Then there's the tragic few. They'll walk directly onto a landmine and will end up scarred forever. For them, life may go on, but it'll never be the same.

My world exploded on the night of March 5, 2010. It was a Monday, and I had just come home from work. The phone rang, and some nurse from the emergency room at Missouri Baptist called, saying my

wife and daughter had been in a car accident. She said the situation
was critical but wouldn't go into detail. To this day, I still don't know if
this was because the nurse didn't know their actual status or didn't want
to discuss it over the phone. Anyhow, she wanted me to come down
immediately.

It was still rush hour, and the traffic was even worse, thanks to the
unexpected snow that had just started to fall. I frantically drove south on
270, but the traffic was as frozen as the slush on my windshield. I must've
covered at least half the distance on the icy shoulders.

Holly was already in surgery when I first arrived. The doctors did
their best, but there had been too much internal bleeding, and she died
on the operating table. I never even got to say goodbye. And my little
Daisy? The EMTs later told me she had expired by the time they arrived
on the scene. Their only consolation was they believed she went fast and
didn't suffer. When I saw her tiny body, they had laid her out like Sleeping Beauty. There was no blood anywhere, not even a cut or a bruise. She
looked so peaceful. I later learned my daughter died of a broken neck.

The police report stated Holly was driving west on 64 and had just
squeezed past the traffic near the Galleria. Then, according to a witness,
some idiot in a BMW was texting and drifted toward Holly's little Civic.
Do you know Missouri is one of the few states where this is not against
the law? Anyhow, when my wife swerved to avoid a collision, she ran
into the teeth of an 18-wheeler. The idiot in the Beemer just kept going,
unaware of the chain reaction she'd started.

My whole life fell apart that night. Holly's family made the funeral
arrangements because I was a wreck and couldn't do a damned thing.
They decided on open caskets at the wake. I remember Holly looking
like an angel, but it was different with little Daisy. Her eyes were closed,
but in my mind, I kept seeing that baby girl in Haditha, the one with the
blank stare that looked like a porcelain doll.

I planned to take some time off from work after their funeral, but as
it turned out, I couldn't even climb out of bed. I just lay there, gazing up
at the ceiling. I must've been in a catatonic coma. When my cell phone
rang, I hurled it against the wall like a grenade, and it shattered into
a dozen pieces. Finally, when some people banged on the front door,

maybe friends or it might've been some of Holly's family, I tossed on some clothes and bolted out past them. I didn't bother with my wallet or the car keys. To this day, I still have no idea who was at the door. And I never returned to that apartment.

Later on, someone at the VA hospital told me there was a name for what I was going through. It's called delayed-onset PTSD. But, of course, I had no idea what was happening at the time. All I knew was the only way to survive was to avoid thinking about the past, which meant living strictly in the present. So I avoided the people I knew because they reminded me of things I didn't want to think about, and pretty soon, they must've forgotten about me as well.

For days, I wandered the streets like a zombie. Then, realizing there were shelters in the city, I somehow managed to move to a spot beneath a downtown overpass. Unfortunately, this is also when I began to drink. I quickly realized that if I downed enough to stay permanently blitzed, everything became muddled, and I wouldn't think about Holly and Daisy.

Meanwhile, of course, I stopped going to work, and I'm not sure what happened to my car or the possessions I left behind. There must be an infinite number of ways to end up homeless, and this was mine. The days soon became weeks, and then the weeks turned into months. I hardly have any memory from this time. When I look back now, it's like staring into a shadowy fog.

To survive, it soon became necessary to develop a daily routine. My new life consisted of wandering the streets during the day begging for money, using it to buy a little food and a lot of liquor, and then drinking away those hellish images every night. I'd do anything to stop thinking about my wife and daughter. But it wasn't just them. If I stayed sober too long, I'd see that little Iraqi girl too. Pretty soon, it all meshed together into the same bad dream.

It didn't take long to get used to my new life. I'd usually curl up beneath the overpass at night. If the weather were terrible, I'd move into a shelter, but it was hard to sleep on those cots when surrounded by so many other mental cases. Let's say I wasn't the only one whose midnight screams could wake the dead. Also, shelters had too many rules, especially about drinking.

After a while, I managed to get my hands on a tent. Besides giving some protection from the weather, it also reminded me of those days when we'd gone camping in Colorado. I'd put up the tent near a busy intersection and stay close enough to keep an eye on it during the day. I didn't have much, but I kept everything inside the tent, including a sleeping bag and some old clothes. I also learned to make a few friends, if you know what I mean, and sometimes, I'd share my home with one of them. That way, we could look out for each other.

Ethan, I was sharing my tent last Friday night with one of those friends, an older man named Burt. We had been buddies for a long time, although since neither of us liked to talk about the past, we didn't actually know much about each other. Also, Burt's elevator didn't climb up to the top floors, if you know what I mean. He was a good guy, but Burt wasn't all there. Nevertheless, he was a person you could count on in a pinch.

Shortly after we'd climbed into my tent and zipped ourselves up into the sleeping bags, we heard this loud commotion outside. I could tell it was two guys swearing, laughing, and making an unbearable racket. Then, suddenly, they began to shake our tent. Hard. When it finally stopped, I heard a noise that sounded like someone was pouring liquid onto the side of the tent. That's when I realized one of them was urinating on the canvas.

Burt must've come to the same conclusion, and he got angry. Suddenly, he unzipped his sleeping bag and reached up to undo the tent's flap. I told him to stop, but he wouldn't listen. For an older man, Burt could move pretty fast when provoked. Before I knew it, he climbed out of the tent to confront these guys. That's when I realized I could no longer remain inside the tent and cower.

Now, Ethan, before I go further, you need to know that everything I did from this point on was in self-defense. Unfortunately, though, it still wasn't enough to save Burt.

Ethan held up a hand like a crossing guard. He was overwhelmed and needed a little time to digest everything he had just heard. Daryl had been speaking almost non-stop for close to two hours. His background story was jaw-dropping, and now he was preparing to leap into his account of what had happened on Friday night. Ethan needed to slow Daryl down a little so that from this point on, he could record every relevant detail. While pulling out a mechanical pencil, Ethan asked a question, primarily out of curiosity but also to slacken Daryl's recitation.

"Daryl, it's been at least thirty years since we last saw each other. How did you manage to track me down?"

"You know, I was pretty tanked up last Friday night," answered Daryl. "But then again, I've been pretty smashed *every* night, so now, I guess, it takes a lot to knock me off my feet."

He paused for a moment, smirking at his increased tolerance for alcohol. Then, he continued, "So, I was still sober enough to befriend one of the guards, who was kind enough to help me out. He used his phone to look up your firm's number on the internet. That's what brought you here, right?"

Ethan nodded, smiled meekly, and then positioned his pencil to scribble notes onto his legal pad. Before he could answer verbally, Daryl added, "I've got to tell you, Ethan, this is the best I've felt in three days."

"Really?" Ethan inquired. Then, he recalled the symptoms of alcohol withdrawal syndrome he had encountered with previous clients. "Let me guess," Ethan continued, "Nausea? Trouble sleeping? The shakes?"

Daryl smiled knowingly. "What are you, Ethan? A doctor *and* a lawyer?"

"Nah," Ethan answered, returning Daryl's smile, "But I've dealt with clients suddenly deprived of alcohol once they're locked up." He glanced down at his blank legal pad and unclogged his throat. "Look, Daryl, before you get into what happened Friday night, let me first tell you what I already know."

He paused, and Daryl nodded for him to continue.

"First," Ethan announced, "I've read the report written by the arresting police officers. They claim you were standing over two bodies, literally holding the smoking gun. They also have a reliable witness, one of the victims." Ethan paused, glanced about, and then returned his gaze to meet Daryl's eyes. "And our side? As I understand it, all we have, for now at least, is your word of what happened."

A grimace swept across Daryl's face, but he remained silent. Then, after another pause, Ethan continued. "What's more, the press has already jumped on this story. We know shootings happen all the time in the big city, but in this case, the two victims were white college kids from the suburbs, and the accused is a homeless man with a serious drinking problem."

"So," Daryl interrupted, "What can we do?"

"For starters," replied Ethan, "You need to tell me everything that happened last Friday night. You just did an exceptional job summarizing your past thirty years. Now I need you to do it again. Fill me in on *every* detail from that night."

Daryl nodded but waited to see if Ethan had more to say. Sure enough, he did.

"Oh, and one other thing. Daryl, you're going to have *two* lawyers in your corner. I have an old friend that'll be joining us. He's even older than I am." Ethan flashed a grin as he mentioned Tom's involvement. "But don't worry, between the two of us, we've got over 80 years of experience. *And*, what's more, your case is our only case. So, I can't make any promises, but we'll figure out a sound defense between the three of us. "

Some of the wrinkles on Daryl's face began to dissolve, and a glimmer of light returned to his bloodshot eyes. It was instantaneous, like someone had just turned a switch. Then, as though he had just charged his battery, Daryl spoke continuously for the next hour and a half, at times becoming visibly animated. Ethan listened assiduously, nodded throughout, interrupted infrequently with questions, and took copious notes on his legal pad.

chapter
15

Ethan reclined on one of the Adirondack chairs overlooking a garden choked with weeds. The backyard had always been Sarah's domain; in the past, it had provided fresh, tasty vegetables to fill their dinner salads. Now, the lawn service's weedwhacker kept the wild plants in check, but otherwise, Ethan would soon have to decide what to do with this small plot of land. Glancing over the edge of his deck, he saw an eastern cottontail scamper out of the weeds, pursued by its amorous mate. Ethan smiled at the growing family dwelling in Sarah's garden.

The sun crept over the horizon, casting a luminous glow over the deck. Landscape photographers craved this kind of light, and there had been times when Ethan had set an early alarm just to enhance his photographs. He no longer had to set the alarm, though, since he now arose every morning with the sun. Sarah had always been the early riser in the family, but ever since her passing, he had unwittingly assumed her routine.

Ethan had built the deck years ago but rarely used it in the summertime. The afternoon sun would bake the composite boards, creating a steamy sauna, and the twilight mosquitoes chased everyone inside at night. Finally, Ethan realized the best time to sit on his deck was the early morning. The quiet serenity was soothing, the best way to launch a demanding day. Birds, squirrels, and rabbits were everywhere, but Ethan was the only human in sight.

The sudden opening of the sliding glass door abruptly shocked Ethan from his reverie. Out of the corner of his eye, he saw Jenny approach, wearing a white, textured robe and carrying two mugs of steamy coffee. After setting them down on an end table, she fell back onto another Adirondack chair, turned to her father, and beamed a broad smile.

"Just cream, no sugar, right?"

Ethan reached over, grasped the mug closest to him, lifted it to his mouth, and blew at the rising mist. Then he inhaled a lungful of the coffee's aroma and smiled.

"Yep," he replied. "This is perfect."

Jenny picked up the other mug and replicated her dad's routine. For a moment, father and daughter sat in silence. The only sound was the sipping and slurping of their coffee.

Jenny suddenly broke the stillness by stating, "I *really* like Tom."

"I do, too," Ethan agreed, "Although, like most old friendships, we've had our ups and downs over the years."

"You'd never know it from what I saw at dinner last night."

"What do you mean?" Ethan inquired.

Jenny cupped her tepid mug with both palms, seeking its warmth in the cool morning air. "There were times last night when you two shared a brain." Then, seeing her father nod faintly, she continued, "While discussing Daryl's case and a legal strategy to get him off, you were finishing each other's sentences."

"You know," Ethan responded, "This is one of the few times I actually believe my client's not guilty. And because of our history, I'd love to get Daryl off. But for the moment, this appears to be a mammoth undertaking. And seeing his alleged crime splayed across the front page of the *Post-Dispatch* doesn't help." Then, recalling the original reason for making this statement, Ethan added, "And I can *definitely* use Tom's help. He's got a good head for the law, and he's one of the most analytical people I know."

Jenny nodded and stared absentmindedly at the privacy hedges walling the backyard. Then, desiring to change the subject, Ethan asked, "Sweetheart, you know that you and Matt are welcome to stay here forever, right?"

A smile creased Jenny's face, although she continued to gaze straight ahead. "Is this where you politely give us an eviction notice?"

"*No*," Ethan replied uneasily, "Not at all. I just wondered if you guys had thought any more about buying your first home."

"I'm just kidding, " Jenny reacted. She looked over at her father with the shadow of a smile still on her face. "Actually, we've just signed with an agent and instructed her to search for a two-bedroom in the Kirkwood or Webster Groves School Districts."

Ethan glanced at his daughter with raised brows but stayed silent. He remembered last night, recalling how Jenny had declined the beer everyone else had enjoyed with their dinner.

"We've recently learned," she added, "There're affordable neighborhoods in places like Rock Hill and Shrewsbury that'll get us into one of those districts."

"School districts?" Ethan inquired soberly. "You have any news to share?"

A charming blush swept across her face. For a moment, Ethan reflected on the first time he had observed this when she was a little girl. "No, Dad." Then, after a brief pause, she smiled artfully and added, "At least, not yet. Although we've been trying."

"*Really?*" Ethan responded with widened eyes.

"Yeah, for a couple of months now."

Jenny stated this casually, as though she was discussing the weather. Ethan placed his nearly empty mug down on the table and turned to face his daughter squarely. Before he could say more, however, the sliding glass door thundered open, and Tom stumbled out wearing faded khaki shorts and an old KU T-shirt.

"*Wow*," Tom uttered, "So this is what sunrise looks like." After running fingers through his scruffy gray hair, he added, "Hmmm, frankly, I think it's overrated. You guys *really* feel the need to be out here so early?"

Ethan and Jenny exchanged "to be continued" glances and then looked up at Tom, who was yawning, oblivious to the conversation he had just interrupted. Jenny sprang up, stating she needed to get ready for work, but suddenly stopped, offering to fetch some coffee for Tom. After she went inside, Tom dropped solidly into the Adirondack chair Jenny had just vacated.

"I didn't interrupt anything, did I?" Tom asked inelegantly.

"Nah, it's alright," answered Ethan. "How'd you sleep?"

"Like a baby," Tom replied. "I only got up three times to pee, well under my usual average."

"Only three?" snickered Ethan. "Then, you've got me beat."

Jenny reemerged, handed Tom a mug of piping hot coffee, and then disappeared.

"That's a great kid you've got. You know that, right?"

Ethan smiled. "So I've been told."

"She and Matt will be around one day," Tom continued, "Pushing you in a wheelchair and checking to be sure they're changing your diapers." He sighed and peered down at the remnants of Sarah's garden. "I've got to tell you, Ethan, you're one *lucky* man. Although, I'll admit to being a little envious."

Ethan gazed at Tom, too flummoxed to reply. He was unsure which point to address first, the comment about his good fortune or the one about Tom's misfortune. Before Ethan could figure it out, Tom abruptly changed subjects.

"So," exclaimed Tom, "What's the plan for today?"

Ethan glanced at his watch. "Oh, *wow*, we need to get going," he responded. "I'd like to stop by the office before heading downtown for Daryl's initial appearance."

An hour later, Tom's dusty pickup swerved into a parking spot behind Ethan's law firm. The two men jumped out briskly and entered the front lobby. Ethan quickly exchanged pleasantries with a couple of secretaries before moving on toward Keith's office in the rear of the building. As they passed an open door, Ethan involuntarily slammed the brakes. He peered in, surveying what used to be his office. An unfamiliar Tiffany lamp illuminated the familiar desk. Behind sat a middle-aged woman who looked up blankly before flashing a broad grin.

"*Ethan,*" broadcasted Ellen. "It's good to see you again. When did you get back into town?"

After glancing at Tom, who was grinning at Ellen like a schoolboy, Ethan nodded for his friend to follow him into his old office.

"It's nice to see you as well, Ellen," Ethan responded. "I got in yesterday morning and then went downtown in the afternoon to meet with Daryl."

Ethan discreetly scanned the room. His landscape photos still adorned the walls in their original spots, but the family pictures on the desk were of strangers. Manila files were piled haphazardly on the cabinet behind the desk, and there was classical music wafting from a speaker buried somewhere in the back corner. When Ellen stood and reached across her desk to shake hands, Ethan observed she appeared slimmer and fitter than he had remembered. Her grip was also surprisingly firm for a woman who appeared to be in her mid-fifties.

"Oh, I'm sorry," Ethan declared, "Where's my manners?" He glanced back at Tom, who was gawking at Ellen like she was the ghost of Marilyn Monroe. Ethan smothered a smile and then pivoted around to face Ellen.

"Ellen, this is Tom Flaherty. Tom's an old friend from college. He currently practices law in Fort Scott, Kansas, but since he's agreed to work with me on Daryl's defense, I'm hoping he might decide to stay here for good."

Ellen extended her hand, but it hung limply for a moment. Then, finally, Tom snapped out of his trance, exploded into an exuberant smile, and vigorously began to shake Ellen's hand. Ethan started to explain how Ellen had taken over his caseload, but the effort was futile. Neither appeared to be listening. Ethan suddenly realized he had become invisible.

"So . . . ," Ethan continued, "I've got an idea. Let me head down the hall for a few minutes to confer with Keith. There's something I'd like to run by him, but it shouldn't take long. Meanwhile, why don't you two get acquainted? Ellen, maybe you can share what you know about Daryl's case with Tom."

Ellen glanced at Ethan, nodded faintly, and then turned her attention back toward his buddy. As Ethan turned to exit, he noticed Tom and Ellen were still gazing intently at each other as they simultaneously sank into padded office chairs.

Fifteen minutes later, Ethan returned to find that Tom had lugged his chair behind Ellen's desk, and the two were gaping at pictures on her phone. They were laughing together like childhood pals. Ethan studied them for a moment before Ellen finally glanced up and beamed.

"Oh, Ethan, I didn't see you standing there."

Tom peered up with a sparkle in his eyes. "Where've you been?" he asked. "I thought we had an appointment to keep downtown." Then, after a moment, he added, "And Ethan, why are you grinning like a Cheshire cat?"

Ethan wavered a moment to process the scene in front of him. Then, he heard Tom's question and finally thought of an answer. "Let's just say I had a good meeting with Keith," Ethan replied. "But for now, we need to get going."

Tom stood, turned to face Ellen, and smiled hardily. Ethan also caught him winking at her while they fervently shook hands again. Then, as Tom rounded her desk, Ethan observed Ellen discreetly hand him a folded note.

"Ethan," Ellen added as the two men turned to leave, "Please keep me updated on Daryl's case. Tom and I just shared some thoughts about a good strategy for his defense. I'd like to help out if I can. Would that be alright?"

Ethan glanced at his old friend, who was still glowing. Tom faintly nodded, sporting a drunken grin he could not wipe off his face even if he tried. Ethan raised his hand to his mouth, mostly to conceal a smile, and then spun back to face Ellen.

"Yeah, you bet," Ethan replied. "I know your plate's pretty full, but if you can squeeze in a little time for Daryl, we could certainly use the help. Also, in a case like this, three heads will certainly be better than two."

Ten minutes later, Tom navigated his Ford pickup eastward through the maze of traffic on I-64. The weather was flawless, without a cloud in sight, and Ethan knew the Gateway Arch would soon appear on the horizon. As a boy, he had made a game of spotting the parabolic structure whenever he ventured into the city. Then, as the family minivan approached downtown, he loved to watch it swell in size.

Ethan glanced at his friend, who, despite his best effort, could not wipe away the buoyant smile still splattered across his face.

"Alright," Ethan commented, "You've been grinning like a clown since we left Ellen's office. Care to explain? And what's with that note she passed you? I felt like we were back in middle school."

Tom glanced at his friend in the passenger seat and suddenly burst out laughing. "You caught that, huh?" Then he added with a snicker, "You know, Ethan, for the last several years in Fort Scott, I've been living like a hermit." His smile wilted as he sighed and turned his attention back to the road.

"So?" Ethan inquired, noting Tom had still not answered his question.

"Quid pro quo, counselor," Tom finally answered. "First, tell me first about your little meeting with Keith. Who, by the way, I was hoping to meet today."

"I don't mean to be so mysterious," Ethan replied, "But since we mostly just speculated about the future, I'd rather wait until we've had a chance to work out some details." Then, after a pause, Ethan added, "Besides, we decided to put it all on a back burner until after Daryl's trial. Now, tell me about Ellen."

"We had an instant connection," Tom responded. "I know she's divorced and at least ten years younger. But we agreed to meet later tonight for a drink. Then . . . , we'll just see what happens."

"You old hound," Ethan teased. "I'll bet ten to one her cell number is on that note."

Tom glanced in Ethan's direction. His smile and eyes all answered in the affirmative.

"Well," Ethan continued, "You'll need to lose that silly grin by the time we get into court. Otherwise, the judge will think something's wrong with you."

As Ethan and Tom entered the courtroom, they immediately spotted a trim, middle-aged woman bent over files scattered across the prosecution table. She was peering through reading glasses perched halfway down her aquiline nose. Seated next to her was a younger man with wispy, champagne-colored hair. He was probably her second chair, but he looked fresh out of law school.

"Damn," Ethan mumbled as they headed toward the defense table. "I *know* her. She's one of the circuit attorney's biggest guns."

Tom glanced at Ethan, beckoning him to say more.

"Her name is Michelle Jones," whispered Ethan, "And she devours young defense lawyers. Behind her back, most of her opponents refer to her as the Dragon Lady. So if they've assigned her to this case, the prosecution's playing for keeps." Then, after a pause, he added, "I guess this is the result of all the media coverage. Because, believe me, if there's one thing the St. Louis circuit attorney cares about, it's her public image."

Ethan glanced around and noticed the courtroom was slowly starting to fill. He had seldom seen this many people turn out for an initial appearance. Judging from the affluent, suburban aura born by some of the spectators, Ethan assumed they were family members or friends of the two victims. Several others looked like journalists. Either way, *his* cheering section appeared empty.

Ethan peered through a plate-glass window and observed the Arch standing guard a few blocks down Market Street. In the foreground, a large American flag danced in the breeze. For a moment, Ethan wished he was outside, strolling down the city's main drag, checking out sites like the sculpture parks and the Soldiers Memorial Military Museum. It had been a long time since Tom had been to St. Louis, and Ethan longed for the chance to be his tour guide.

Then, a slight commotion roused Ethan from his daydream. He looked up and noted that while the clerk and stenographer were already at their posts, the judge's seat was still vacant. Then, he observed Daryl emerging from a door behind the witness chair, still sporting his oversized, orange jumpsuit. They had cuffed his arms behind his back, and a bailiff had a firm hand locked on his bicep as he led Daryl toward an empty seat at their defense table. Ethan saw that his client had shaved, combed his hair, and spruced up his general appearance. And when Daryl spotted his legal team, a smile radiated across his face.

"*Hey*," voiced Ethan, "How're you holding up?" Daryl nodded, but before he could say more, Ethan continued, "Daryl, this is Tom Flaherty. He'll be serving as your other lawyer."

The bailiff removed the handcuffs but made it clear he would only be a few feet away. Daryl unthinkingly rubbed his wrists and then took the empty seat between his two attorneys. Before they could say more, the clerk stood and bellowed for all present to rise.

"The Court of the Twenty-Second Judicial Circuit, Criminal Division, is now in session, the honorable Judge Robert Larson presiding."

Ethan watched as a gray head atop a black robe slowly ambled toward the judge's bench. He knew from the rumor mill that Judge Larson was almost seventy and had a reputation for running a tight ship. Ethan and Tom exchanged uneasy glances. Finally, the judge fell into his cushy chair, picked up his gavel, gave it a single rap, and then instructed everyone to be seated.

Facing the judge, the clerk announced this was the initial appearance for Mr. Daryl Armstrong, who had been arrested the previous Friday night on two counts of first-degree murder. Silence pervaded the spacious chamber as the judge examined the documents on his desk. When he finally glanced up, Judge Larson scrutinized the prosecuting attorneys, cleared his throat, and nodded deliberately. He then swiveled toward Daryl and the attorneys who flanked him. When he finally spoke, his tone was surprisingly empathetic despite the gruffness in his voice.

"You understand," he began, speaking directly to the defendant, "This is just an initial appearance. It's your constitutional right to be brought into court shortly after your arrest so we can be sure to protect your other constitutional rights."

Glancing down at what appeared to be a checklist, Judge Larson continued. "Mr. Armstrong, when the police placed you under arrest, did they inform you that you had the right to remain silent?"

Daryl stood and nodded. "Yes, your honor," he mumbled.

"And did they inform you that anything you said could be used against you in a court of law?"

Daryl again replied affirmatively. The judge was reinforcing the same Miranda warnings the police had recited while slapping the cuffs on his wrists. This protocol undoubtedly was a safeguard designed to reduce the chances for a subsequent appeal should the defendant be found guilty.

"And finally, Mr. Armstrong, you understand that you have the right to an attorney?"

After Daryl replied "yes" for the third time, Ethan and Tom stood to introduce themselves. Michelle Jones and her underling then did the same. For some reason, this put a smile on the judge's face.

"So," the judge uttered, "Now that we've completed our introductions, what happens next?" Turning again to face the defendant as though engaging in a one-on-one conversation, the judge continued, "We cannot proceed further, Mr. Armstrong, until the prosecution secures an indictment from a grand jury. This step does *not* involve you or your attorneys. However, for now, I'll schedule a preliminary hearing to take place in 30 days. If the prosecution has secured an indictment by then, you'll have the chance to respond formally, and if you choose to plead not guilty, I'll schedule a date for your trial. If, for some reason, there's still no indictment after 30 days, I'll entertain a motion for a continuance from the prosecution. Is this clear, Mr. Armstrong?"

Daryl swallowed hard and then stated that it was. Ethan could tell his client was nervous, but he was nonetheless proud of how Daryl maintained a confident bearing, at least on the outside. The judge paused to scan the faces of the four attorneys in the room.

"Now, there's one more matter we need to address today."

Taking this as her cue, Michelle Jones rose from her chair. "You honor," she announced, "On the matter of bail, we request that it be denied. The defendant, as you know, is facing two counts of first-degree murder. Moreover, he has no known family in the St. Louis area, nor does he have a job. In fact, your honor, Mr. Armstrong doesn't even have an established address. He's the textbook definition of a flight risk."

Judge Larson turned toward the defense table, patiently awaiting the expected rebuttal. Ethan stood but, for the moment, remained silent. Finally, he drew a deep breath, clasped his hands together, and pivoted to face his client. A thought had rocketed up from a canyon deep inside his brain. Even Ethan was unaware of its existence until it suddenly materialized. Daryl looked up at his lawyer with a blank expression. Finally, Ethan turned back to face the judge.

"Your honor," Ethan finally announced, "I'm about to make a highly unusual request." Then, glancing at Tom, who appeared just as stunned as everyone else in the courtroom, Ethan continued. "I've known Mr. Armstrong for over thirty years and would gladly vouch for his character. Your honor, I will *guarantee* unequivocally that my client will be here in court whenever ordered."

Ethan paused and then looked down at Daryl. "In fact," he added, "I'm so certain of this belief, if you agree to a one million dollar bond, which is reasonable in a case like this, I'll put up the ten percent as required out of my own funds."

When Ethan, at last, looked up to face the judge, he observed skeptical indecision etched into the wrinkles of the judge's forehead. Ethan knew this was a highly unusual move and might even raise ethical concerns about his motives.

Judge Larson squinted at Ethan and then asked, "You mean to say, Mr. Marshall, that you're willing to put up a hundred thousand dollars of your *own* money?"

"Yes, your honor. You see, I've known this defendant since my wife and I served as his foster parents many years ago. What's more, once you release Mr. Armstrong from the state's custody, I intend to invite him to reside in my home in Creve Coeur."

"*Really?*" the judge asked incredulously. "For how long?"

"For as long as he needs," Ethan replied.

For a moment, a stillness saturated the courtroom. Ethan glanced around, noting first the open mouths at the prosecution table. Then he observed Tom, whose eyebrows had arched upward toward the ceiling. Finally, he looked down at his client. Daryl was gazing dreamily out of the window towards the flapping flag, with its undulating stars and stripes framed by the Gateway Arch. Ethan saw that his client's face was void of expression. Then, he observed a single golden droplet streaming down the side of his cheek.

chapter
16

Ethan and Tom darted from the courtroom as though they were escaping before the judge could change his mind. Judge Larson's decision to approve Daryl's bail had given them both a shot of adrenaline. Seeing a cluster of news reporters obstructing their path to the elevator, Tom raised his arms like an offensive lineman preparing to block for a running back. Ethan's instincts, however, having been honed by countless clients from the past, immediately understood the advantage of winning over the media. After all, Ethan could use the reporters to address the potential jury pool indirectly. He called out to Tom and then put on the brakes.

Ethan realized the public's knee-jerk reaction would be to sympathize with the victims, who were harmless college kids, and to villainize the boozy homeless man. As Daryl's defense lawyer, Ethan needed to reverse these images. So when the reporters zeroed in on his decision to not only post bail for his client but to invite him into his home, Ethan saw his opportunity. For the next ten minutes, he reviewed Daryl's background, including his foster case experiences, his military record, and the tragedy that had pushed his client onto the streets.

The coup de grace was Ethan's admission that he could have adopted Daryl thirty years ago. He explained to the reporters that if he had, Daryl would have grown up with all of the same advantages enjoyed by the two victims from the suburbs. By the end of the impromptu news conference, Ethan had most reporters eating out of his hands. He concluded by passing out cards with his contact information and inviting the journalists to schedule one-on-one interviews. The pitch was to tell the human interest story of a relationship between two men, the falsely accused homeless man and his lawyer, who was seeking absolution for the terrible injustice he had committed against his client decades earlier.

Once Ethan and Tom entered the parking garage, their next task was more straightforward. They needed to drive to the closest branch of Ethan's bank, pick up a certified check for one hundred thousand dollars, and then return to the justice center to secure Daryl's release. Over the next several months, Ethan and Tom would have to continue this legal war, and their chances for victory were still quite uncertain. But today's opening skirmish had been a triumph.

As Tom pulled his pickup truck out of the garage, he proposed they stop somewhere for a quick bite to eat. Ethan guessed his motivation was more than just hunger. He was starting to realize that Tom preferred a slower pace. In all likelihood, his friend wanted to tap the brakes, catch his breath, and process everything that had just occurred. However, Ethan countered that there would be plenty of time for food after they had secured Daryl's release. He wanted to obtain his client's freedom as swiftly as possible.

As Tom accelerated onto the entrance ramp heading west on I-64, he firmly clenched the steering wheel with both hands, exhaled a lung full of air, and slowly shook his head. Ethan could make out the quizzical smirk on the side of his face.

"What?" inquired Ethan. "What are you thinking?"

He knew Tom was stunned by what had just happened in the courtroom. Still, he put on a front, like forking over a hundred thousand dollars of his own money to bail out a client and then offering to take him into his home was all part of the daily routine of a St. Louis criminal defense attorney.

"I don't know where to begin," Tom mumbled. He diligently kept his eyes fixed on the road but continued to swivel his head back and forth. "First, do you have *that* kind of money just lying around?"

"Actually, yes," Ethan answered. "Sarah and I created an investment portfolio years ago. You know, for our retirement? A large bond recently matured, and I've been dragging my feet over where to invest the money. Meanwhile, it's just sitting in a savings account. I might as well put it to work securing Daryl's freedom."

"*Huh*," Tom replied. For the moment, he could not think of a better response. Then, after a moment, he added, "And you have enough faith in Daryl to *risk* all that money?"

"Honestly?" Ethan replied, peering out the window at the towering Ferris wheel that now guarded the front of Union Station, "I don't know. I *think* he's a good bet, but I'm not a hundred percent certain."

A quiet permeated the truck's cab. Tom knew Ethan had more to say but patiently waited for his friend to gather his thoughts. Then, a canary yellow Mustang roared by, ending the silence and rousing Ethan from his trance.

"Tom," Ethan stated in a resolute tone like he was starting a political speech, "There are several reasons behind my decision. One is the guilt I've been nurturing for the last thirty years. That wasn't just a tagline for the reporters. We should've provided Daryl with a good home; if we had, all of this could've been prevented. Sarah wanted to do just that, but I was too selfish."

Ethan paused. He observed Tom glancing into his mirrors before passing an ancient Cadillac driven by a fluff of silver hair. But his friend was simultaneously nodding, signaling for Ethan to continue.

"Another factor is what you and I discussed back in Fort Scott. You know, that conversation about unsung heroes? Just think how much better the world would be if everyone took a chance on someone else at some point in their lives. I think Daryl's recent difficulties have given me that opportunity."

"Alright," Tom responded. "I get it. As you know, it's also the main reason I'm here." He glanced at this friend, following Ethan's gaze towards the congested parking lot flanking the south side of the zoo.

"But while it's admirable to put up the money," Tom continued, "It's quite another to invite a homeless man you barely know into your house."

"Yes, I hadn't planned on that one," Ethan admitted. "And I'm already sharing my home with three other adults, none of whom I bothered to consult."

"Well, I can't speak for your daughter or son-in-law," responded Tom, "But I'm fine with this decision. What's more, you magnificently turned it into a publicity triumph." After a brief pause, Tom squinted his eyes and added, "However, I'm curious about one thing. I got the impression you didn't plan this. Am I right? And if so, what prompted you to do it?"

Ethan glanced at Tom and flashed an uneasy grin. "You're going to think I'm a bit crazy," he asserted, "But I suddenly got the idea from a little voice inside my head."

Tom instantly smiled. "*Really?* Did you recognize the voice?"

"Oh *yeah*," Ethan promptly responded. Then, after a brief pause, he added, "I've been hearing it for over forty years."

Tom grinned knowingly but remained silent while navigating his truck through the clogged streets of downtown Clayton. Because it was the seat for the heavily populated suburban county that encircled St. Louis on the Missouri side of the river and because it was an affluent city in its own right, Clayton's skyline was beginning to rival that of its older sister to the east. Its midday traffic was even more congested than the downtown they had just left. Tom, therefore, planned to circle the block while Ethan ran into the bank to acquire the check.

An hour and a half later, Tom and Ethan reenacted the same exit from the parking garage outside the City Justice Center. This time, however, Daryl diffidently climbed into the backseat to join them. He had shed his orange jumpsuit, naturally, but was now wearing his threadbare street clothes. Tom and Ethan exchanged distressed glances. Then, after Tom commented about the beautiful day outside, they simultaneously opened their windows despite the oppressive afternoon heat.

Ethan followed up on Tom's remark about the weather by suggesting they grab some fast food at the Chipotle drive-thru near St. Louis University. They could then have a "little picnic" in Turtle Park just south of the zoo. Tom immediately seconded the motion while their client remained passively silent.

Daryl did not say a word for the next twenty minutes while they loaded up on burritos and cokes and headed west into Dogtown. After parking on Oakland Avenue, Forest Park's southern boundary, Ethan led the way past a swarm of children scrambling over a massive Turtle sculpture to an empty picnic table shaded by an ancient oak tree. Then, after unwrapping the burritos and spearing the soda lids with their straws, Daryl surprised them both by launching their lunchtime conversation.

"So Ethan, I don't mean to sound ungrateful," he mumbled, "But you don't need to take me into your home."

"I'm delighted to have you," Ethan slurred while swallowing the first bite of his burrito. "It's no trouble."

Sitting beside Daryl, Tom glanced at him sideways while sipping his soda. He frowned, comprehending what might be the real purpose behind Daryl's statement.

"It's not just about *that*," Daryl countered. He paused, searching for the right words to continue.

"You'd prefer to live in your tent?" Tom inquired discreetly.

Daryl turned to face Tom and then swiveled back toward Ethan. His eyes enlarged, and he gulped a deep breath. Then, although he remained silent, Daryl finally began to nod.

"Well," Ethan responded indignantly, "*That's* not going to happen. When I told the judge you'd live with me, he assumed I'd take responsibility for you and guarantee your appearance in his court."

"You know," Daryl asserted with mounting confidence, "I was there, too. I never heard the judge say I *had* to live with you."

Ethan glared at Daryl. For a moment, an uncomfortable chill hovered over the picnic table. Tom's eyes darted back and forth between Ethan and Daryl while he slowly chewed a large bite of his burrito.

"You know," Ethan finally began, purposefully echoing Daryl's opening words, "I really put myself out for you back there. Defense lawyers don't make it a custom to bail out their clients and then offer to provide them with housing. What's more, I'm *not* a public defender. Those guys will never get rich, but at least they can count on a regular salary. In private practice, though, my clients *pay* me for my services. "

Tom twisted toward his old college roommate, eyeing him in disbelief. He could tell Ethan regretted the words before they had exited his mouth. Meanwhile, Daryl studied his uneaten burrito. Then, after a moment, he looked up and whispered, "Maybe this was a mistake." He pushed back from the picnic table and began to rise.

"Wait a moment," declared Tom. "Daryl, have a seat."

Daryl froze like a sculpture, momentarily mulling over what to do.

"*Please*," Tom added. "Just listen to what I've got to say."

As Daryl slowly dropped back onto the picnic table's bench, Tom turned to confront Ethan. "First of all," he continued, "Ethan, you need to *shut* up and stop being such an ass. Is this why you agreed to represent Daryl? To make *money*?"

Ethan was stunned, but after a moment, he began to shake his head deliberately. "No," he answered innocuously. "It isn't. And Daryl, I *am* sorry."

Tom then turned back to face their client. "And Daryl, you're right. There's nothing that requires you to move in with us."

Ethan then turned toward Tom like a wife shocked by what her husband had just said to their children. Before he could utter a word, though, Tom raised a hand in his direction while continuing to address Daryl.

"Ethan told me about your background, Daryl, including your military experience. And that means, of course, you've been through boot camp, right?"

Daryl nodded intently. He and Ethan were increasingly eager to hear where this was going.

"Well, I also served in the military," Tom continued. "A marine, in the years between college and law school."

"I forgot about that," Ethan remarked.

"And like you," Tom continued, ignoring Ethan's comment, "I also went through boot camp. So, this has given me an idea."

Tom looked around the table, purposely pausing. For a moment, the only sounds were the squeals of children climbing the turtle sculptures and the whizzing traffic on the nearby interstate. Then, noting he still had their undivided attention, Tom finally resumed.

"Daryl, you're used to living on the streets, but I've got to believe that deep inside, you know that's a dead end. The heat and the cold, the uncertain meals, the lack of medical and dental care, and the fear of dealing with cops and criminals - that's no life, my friend, and we both know it. You've been wasting your life."

Tom paused to sip his soda and then continued. "And on top of everything else, you're heavy into the booze, right? That'll kill you pretty soon, even if you survive everything else. And I know *that* from personal experience."

"You mean," Daryl inquired inquisitively, "You had a drinking problem too?"

"Not *had*," Tom replied, "I still *do*."

Ethan and Daryl turned toward each other and simultaneously raised their eyebrows. "So, Tom," Ethan asked, "What's your idea?"

"I propose," Tom responded, "That Daryl and I go through another boot camp. *Together*. We'll serve as each other's drill sergeants, and we'll keep each other away from any alcohol."

Tom paused again and glanced toward Ethan. He imperceptibly winked the eye not visible to Daryl. Ethan also thought he saw the hint of a smile on his old friend's face.

"But Daryl," Tom added gravely, "This means you'll have to move into Ethan's house, at least up through your trial. That way, you and I can become roommates. It's the only way this plan will work."

"Hmm," Daryl responded with a budding interest.

"Ah, don't worry, Daryl," continued Tom. "You'll still have your own room. And believe me, it'll beat the shit out of living in a tent. But my bedroom will be right across the hall. And that way, we can keep each other away from the booze. And Ethan," Tom continued while glancing toward his former roommate, "That means you'll have to get rid of all liquor in the house."

"You got it," Ethan exclaimed supportively.

"Also," Tom added while rotating back toward Daryl, "You and I will need to attend AA meetings. I did that years ago, and it *really* works. Unfortunately, I stopped going. I need to return, and partnering with you, my friend, should make it easier for both of us."

Daryl balled his fingers together on the table in front of him, drew in a deep breath, and then exhaled audibly. He studied the burrito in front of him for a moment and then, with tightened lips, began bobbing his head up and down slowly.

"Finally," Tom added, "There's one last point." Turning to confront his old buddy, he stated, "Ethan, you're going to need some investigators.

Right now, the prosecution has all the evidence, and all you've got is Daryl." Then, glancing toward their client, he added, "No offense."

"None taken," Daryl responded. And then, sensing where Tom was going, he turned toward Ethan and added, "And Tom's right. To convince a jury that I acted in self-defense, we'll need to find some proof to back it up."

Tom grinned like a car salesman who had just clinched the big deal. "So Ethan," Tom exclaimed, "Daryl and I should partner as your investigators. And we should start by holding a meeting as soon as possible to brainstorm all the leads we can pursue. Maybe we should also include that cute attorney I met in your office this morning. What was her name?"

Ethan snickered. "You know her name." Then rotating toward their new client, he added, "Daryl, you should know in advance your new roommate's a horny old man."

Silence reigned at the picnic table while the three men grinned like fraternity boys. Then, Ethan added, "In all seriousness, we *should* include Ellen in our meetings. Daryl, she's the attorney you spoke to Friday night. Ellen's the one who tracked me down so I could return to St. Louis. It'll be good to have her on our side."

Tom and Daryl both silently nodded their agreement. Then Daryl suddenly reached before him and attacked the untouched burrito like he had not eaten in a week. Ethan glanced toward his old roommate, and they simultaneously exchanged smiles. Ethan also hoped Tom could see the gratitude in his eyes.

Then, peering down at his watch, Ethan exhaled and spun to face Daryl. "So," he inquired, "Does this mean you're on board with Tom's idea?"

Daryl's cheeks were too inflated to speak, so he raucously smiled and nodded.

"Alright then," Ethan proclaimed, "Eat up quickly. We still have a lot to do."

Over the next couple of hours, Tom chauffeured Ethan and Daryl to several spots scattered around Creve Coeur. The first was Supercuts, where Daryl timidly emerged sporting a well-groomed haircut that took years off his appearance. The second stop was Kohl's down the street. There, Tom and Ethan helped their client select a new wardrobe consisting of various T-shirts, dress shirts, khaki slacks, blue jeans, cargo shorts, and an ample supply of undergarments. On their way out, Tom wisecracked about the treasure of Kohl's Cash Ethan had just earned.

The final stop was Dierbergs, where Ethan bought steaks to grill. While Tom visited the men's room, Ethan quickly called Ellen, inviting her to join them for dinner. An early cold front had just blown through Eastern Missouri, cleansing the air and lowering the temperature so it would be a perfect evening for a little celebratory feast out on the deck. Asking Ellen to join them would be a pleasant surprise for his friend. Besides, the plans Tom had made with Ellen to go out for drinks that night would now have to be modified.

Once they arrived home, everyone scattered in different directions. Tom went off to shower, dress, and prepare for his date. Daryl took his new clothes and moved them into the empty bedroom across from Tom's. Ethan headed into the kitchen to put away groceries and prepare dinner. Along the way, he observed the tan leather couch facing the fireplace. It had been a long day, and he could use a few minutes off his feet.

Ethan collapsed at one end of the sofa and robotically felt for the button on the side that would tilt him back and elevate his feet. Then, with eyes closed, he called for Alexa to broadcast music from the playlist he and Sarah had constructed years ago. Suddenly, he was bathed in the gentle, introspective melodies of *The Lark Ascending* by Vaughan Williams. Ethan swiftly unwound and almost fell asleep.

Then, Ethan unbolted his eyes with a slight startle and turned to confront the framed photograph next to him on the end table. Again, Sarah was smiling back at him, this time from the crest of Longs Peak. She was considerably younger and in top physical condition. Sarah and Ethan had just climbed one of the most formidable fourteen-thousand-foot mountains in the Colorado Rockies. It had been one of the most memorable days in their young lives.

"I know, *I know*," Ethan mumbled, speaking directly to Sarah's exuberant grin, a smile foreshadowing the lush life they had only begun to live. "I've still got a lot of work to do."

While reaching for the button to lower his feet, Ethan yanked out his cell phone from his pocket. He had not checked his email all day.

With his feet firmly planted on the dark, hardwood floor, Ethan opened his email and immediately spotted a fresh message from Noah. He was alarmed after reading the subject heading, "Looks like I'll need to brush up on my Haitian Creole."

Hi Dad,

First, I want to say how much I enjoyed your visit. The hiking along the coast brought back some delightful memories, and I also appreciated our late-night talks. Unfortunately, your time here was much too brief, but I understand why you cut it short. I hope you've gotten off to a good start with Daryl's defense.

On my end, unfortunately, there's been nothing but frustration. The more I talk to Amy about our future, the more it seems we're moving in opposite directions. She wants to start a family tomorrow, whereas I would prefer to wait a few more years. And while I would like to work where there's the greatest need for my medical skills, Amy's content to remain in Portland.

We keep going back and forth over these issues, creating unbearable stress. Finally, last night, I told Amy I'd decided to take the position in Haiti. I made it clear I wanted her to join me, but it's doubtful she will. So, Dad, the ball's now in her court. If she chooses to remain in Portland, we'll separate indefinitely. Neither of us has used the "d" word yet, but I can see it coming.

I keep vacillating back and forth between sadness over my marital situation and the exhilaration of getting a fresh start by opening a medical clinic in Port-au-Prince. Hopefully, we'll resolve this dilemma soon so I can start to sleep better at night. I'll keep you posted.

Love you,
Noah

Ethan reread Noah's email while slowly shaking his head. Then he dropped the cell phone into his lap and stared into space. What should he say to his son? The answer to Noah's predicament was crystal clear to

Ethan. He could see Noah's future as though he were peering into a crystal ball. Time would gradually polish the rough edges in his son's marriage, and the day would eventually come when Noah and Amy would fit together perfectly like a two-piece jigsaw puzzle. Moreover, Ethan could see the extraordinary children they would raise together. But, unfortunately, this foresight and acumen only came with age. Sharing this vision with Noah now was like loaning him glasses ground only to his unique prescription.

Ethan then remembered some advice his father had once given— sometimes, the best way to make a point is also the briefest. So Ethan picked up his phone and reopened his email. Then he replied to Noah's message, typing just ten simple words—"Compromise. In the end, it will all be worth it."

After sending the email, Ethan turned again to face the picture on the end table. The joyful smile on Sarah's face was frozen, but Ethan could still hear her voice. Then, a sudden idea inspired Ethan, flexing the corners of his mouth into a broad grin. It was a long shot, but maybe there was an elegant solution to Noah's crisis. And it had the potential to be a life-altering win-win resolution for everyone involved.

Ethan reopened his email and started typing a new message to his son. This time, it would be considerably longer.

chapter

17

Ethan glanced at the digital alarm clock for the fourth time in fifteen minutes. Over the past month, he had developed a new sleep regimen. Lights out by 11:00, plunge into a dreamless coma for a few hours, and then awaken, usually around three in the morning. After a brief trip to the bathroom, Ethan would quickly fall back asleep. He then experienced a dream, the same one that visited him almost every night.

It began with Sarah disrobing and slowly undressing him in their bedroom. She then lovingly planted moist kisses on his neck and upper chest. Next, Ethan stepped back to examine his wife. A soft light from behind accentuated the tiny hairs on her smooth skin while her lips parted into a sensual smile. Finally, Sarah would step forward and gently lean in for another kiss. Ethan closed his eyes in the dream, awaiting the feel of her soft lips. Then, when nothing happened, he would awaken to discover she had vanished. One moment, Sarah was joyfully seducing her husband; the next, she was gone.

At that point, Ethan always awoke. He was stretched out on his side, usually embracing Sarah's fresh pillow. Desiring to return to the dream, Ethan would then roll onto his back, close his eyes, and visualize bedroom images from their marriage. While this proved to be a pleasant way to start the day, the problem was that he was now wide awake, and it was only four in the morning.

For the next several minutes, Ethan would lay in bed, taking inventory of the essential affairs in his life. He realized the more he could distract himself with these day-to-day tasks, the less he would pine over his recently deceased wife. But, of course, this would not shield him in the middle of the night.

The preparations for Daryl's trial were always at the top of his mental checklist. Ethan had handled all courtroom appearances, including the recent preliminary hearing where the prosecution presented their formal charges, and he had entered a not-guilty plea based on self-defense. The actual trial was still months away, but Ethan was satisfied that, at this stage, he had done everything possible to get ready.

Tom and Daryl had taken on most of the leg work outside the court-room, working seamlessly together as a team. Their task was to search for exculpatory evidence, and a brainstorming session held weeks ago in Ellen's office had given them direction. Tom and Daryl would dig first into the record of the two "victims" to find anything that might damage their credibility. This task entailed multiple trips to Columbia to locate anything from the victims' college days they could use under cross-examination. Second, Tom and Daryl planned to thoroughly examine the crime scene in pursuit of witnesses, video footage, or anything else that might support their self-defense theory.

Beyond preparation for Daryl's trial, Ethan was also making signifi-cant progress on his long-term project. While Noah and Amy were still deciding about the level of their involvement, Ethan had begun seeking financial commitments and was on the verge of signing a long-term lease. He purposefully kept these developments under wraps since he did not want to distract the others from Daryl's upcoming trial. However, Ethan promised to provide more details about this project after the jury had handed down its verdict.

Next, Ethan did a mental checklist of the people in his life. Starting with Tom, Ethan acknowledged he had never seen his old roommate happier. Tom had befriended their client to the point where they were almost inseparable. In addition to their research preparing for the trial, they kept each other flawlessly sober and never missed an AA meeting.

What's more, Tom's crush on Ellen was blossoming into a full-scale romance. While his devotion towards Daryl could be a time-consuming impediment, Ellen professed she completely understood. Also, the fact that Tom was now sober made it easier for him to efficiently juggle his time between trial preparations, hanging out with Daryl, and courting Ellen.

Daryl's situation was a bit more volatile. Physically, he cleaned up nicely and had become an unequivocal teetotaler, but his past still stalked him like a shadow. There were a couple of times when loud moans or screams from down the hallway disrupted Ethan's early morning reflections. When he leaped up and dashed into the hallway, Ethan caught a glimpse of Tom entering Daryl's room. Later, Tom told him that nightmares still plagued Daryl's sleep, but he never went into specifics.

Then there were Jenny and Matt. They had recently signed a contract to purchase a small starter home in Rock Hill, a two-bedroom bungalow that would meet all their needs, at least for the near future. Since then, Ethan had barely seen his daughter. He knew she spent every spare moment planning the move, including making additional purchases to furnish their new home. Since it had been a while since their last private conversation, Ethan still had no idea when he might expect to become a grandpa.

Finally, Ethan thought about Noah and Amy. The email he had recently sent his son was long and filled with specific details. Moreover, Ethan knew it would further complicate the decision-making process between Noah and Amy, who were already struggling with communication issues. Noah quickly replied, but only with a brief message saying he had received Ethan's offer and that he and Amy would need time to mull it over.

Ethan usually imagined Sarah lying next to him when he conducted these thought sessions. For decades, he and his wife had engaged in their most prolific conversations while lying naked, side-by-side in bed, after a bout of vigorous love-making. Now, Ethan pretended that Sarah's legs were still intertwined with his as they discussed the people and events in his life.

Just as he was about to end his one-sided conversation with Sarah about the latest developments involving their children, Ethan realized the significance of today's date. Three months. It had been exactly three months since his wife had passed away. Suddenly, an epiphany struck.

Why was he still lying in bed? If Sarah were alive, she would be preparing to make her daily pilgrimage to Creve Coeur Lake. Maybe the best way to honor his wife would be to do the same.

Ethan jumped up, flicked on the bedside lamp, and proceeded into the bathroom to brush his teeth. Five minutes later, he scoured the floor of his closet to locate the best footwear for an early morning stroll at the lake. Ethan had never owned running shoes. The best he could find this morning was an old pair of sneakers. For now, they would have to do. Whether or not this became a daily ritual, Ethan made a mental note to purchase a comfortable pair of walking shoes.

A steely gray sky accented by streamers of high cirrus clouds began to replace the darkness as Ethan drove up Marine Avenue toward the park's entrance. As he descended the steep hill zigzagging into the Missouri River floodplain, an ashen vapor hovered over the lake's surface. His headlights pierced the fog, and when Ethan finally pulled into a parking spot near the waterfall, two white-tailed deer gaped at him over the hood of his car, frozen like sculptures. They vaporized into the mist as soon as he opened the car door.

Ethan tentatively approached a bench and gazed toward the shoreline where he had recently spread Sarah's ashes. He noted how the lake's surface gently undulated like it was alive and breathing. For a moment, Ethan scoured the desolate area, surveying the woods enclosing the falls and then scrutinizing the lake's far shore. He realized he was searching for signs of his wife. Finally, Ethan grinned embarrassingly, stood, and turned towards the asphalt path encircling the lake. Then it occurred to him that maybe he had a better chance of discovering her spirit on the trails where she had spent so many joyful mornings.

At first, Ethan focused on his pace. He thought Sarah would probably chuckle if she caught him leisurely sauntering around the lake. She had always preached that his movement should be vigorous enough to elevate his heartbeat but not so fast that he could not carry on a conversation. Ethan thought about jogging but then remembered Sarah's admonition about running. When you run, she said, your body leaves the planet with every step, and when it comes crashing back to Earth, it can cause irreparable harm to aged bones, muscles, and ligaments. So instead, Sarah preferred a brisk walk, an exercise she claimed had been favored by presidents like Theodore Roosevelt and Harry Truman.

As he developed a rhythm, Ethan sought topics to occupy his mind. At first, he turned to pragmatic and mundane thoughts. Was he up to date paying the bills? Was there enough food in the household to feed all the adults who had taken up residence beneath his roof? When was the last time he had done laundry? So many of the daily chores he had shared with Sarah now fell entirely on his shoulders. Jenny and Matt made a conscious effort to help out, but Tom and Daryl sometimes acted like they were living in a hotel with maid service.

On the west side of the lake, near the recently installed soccer fields, Ethan caught a glimpse of the sun as it peeked above the wooded hills guarding the park's eastern flank. Filtered through the city's smoggy haze, the upper crescent of the sun bounced its rays off the lake's glassy surface, creating long shadows that crisscrossed the path in front of him. As he approached a densely wooded area, Ethan realized a smile had creased his face. He had been too busy for decades to join Sarah on her early morning hikes. This thought would forever rank near the top of his list of regrets.

Once enveloped by the trees and brush, Ethan experienced a moment of déjà vu. This stretch of the trail evoked the recent memory of driving through the mountains of Wyoming, holding a conversation with Sarah inside his mind. It had spontaneously occurred then; why not now?

"Sarah, are you there?" Ethan asked aloud. "It's been a while since we last spoke, so I thought this might be a good time."

For a moment, the only sound he heard was a gentle breeze whistling through the leaves in the upper limbs of the oak and hickory trees. Then, to his left, a brilliant red Cardinal fluttered out of a honeysuckle bush, and shortly afterward, a ground squirrel noisily rustled through a pile of dead leaves. Ethan tried again.

"Sarah?" After a brief pause, Ethan added, "Well, I'm just going to start talking and hope you'll respond." Ethan cleared his throat and glanced around to be sure he was alone.

"Not long ago," Ethan continued deliberately, "I tried suicide. But, of course, you know this already. I either wanted to join you, or if that wasn't possible, I figured it was time to end my journey. I didn't see much point in going on if the best times of my life were behind me."

Suddenly, Ethan heard Sarah's comforting voice as though she was walking next to him. He knew this was pure fantasy, but since no one was in sight, he felt at ease conversing with the memory of his wife. Others might think he was insane, but since Ethan had the woods to himself, he saw no harm in engaging in a soothing, if not therapeutic, activity.

"I know," Sarah responded. "But I also know you changed your mind back in the Tetons." Then, pausing momentarily, she added, "And I'm *so* glad you did."

"But since then," Ethan stated, "I'm still searching for reasons to go on."

"What about Daryl?" Sarah inquired.

"Daryl's indeed come back into my life," Ethan answered, "And his crisis has given me a chance to make up for a terrible mistake. But while his case keeps me busy during the day, it doesn't do much to get me through the night."

"Then what is it you need?"

"*You*," Ethan replied unequivocally. "I need you, Sarah."

"And your life was complete when I was alive?"

"At the time, I never gave it much thought," Ethan responded, "We were always *so* busy. I never even considered what held our lives together."

"And now?" Sarah inquired.

"And now," Ethan answered, "I roll over at night to reach for you, and all I get is your empty pillow. I miss you, Sarah." Then, he added, "You see, we take it all for granted. We just assume everything that makes life worth living will always be there. But then I lost you."

Ethan began to slow his pace. First, he unthinkingly wiped away the moisture beneath his eyes with the back of his hand. Then, finally, Ethan swallowed hard and continued.

"Sarah, I never thought about how big a role you'd played in our lives until after you were gone. You were the keystone upon which everything else rested. Remove the keystone, and the arch collapses, right? Of course, the other pieces still exist, but they lie scattered like the debris after a tornado."

For the moment, Sarah remained silent as though she was thinking of a reply. However, since a runner was about to interrupt the morning's stillness, the momentary break in conversation came at an auspicious time. The runner dashed by with the grace of an antelope. He was young, and his fluid movements appeared effortless. Ethan assumed he was a gifted high school kid ambitiously training for his cross-country team. Once he had passed, Sarah finally ended the silence.

"Ethan, you've done well filling in some of the holes in your life. I applaud not only your efforts to assist Daryl but your long-term plans as well. It appears you're trying harder and harder to make a difference in the lives of others."

"But I'm still not sure it's enough," Ethan countered. "Sarah, I'm 65 years old. My career's about over; the kids are grown, and now you're gone."

Then, after another pause where Ethan glanced around to confirm he was alone, he added, "You know, I recently read that 107 billion people have lived on this planet, both past and present. None of them, of course, not a single one, lived forever. And I don't believe that after they died, their souls entered heaven, hell, or any other place. So we're all born, we live, and then we die, and except for the few names that live on in the history books, we soon disappear from memory."

"*Wow*," replied Sarah, "When did you become so joyful in the morning?"

Ethan smiled. He briefly wondered whether the sarcasm had come from within his mind or elsewhere. Sarah then continued, this time in a more serious vein.

"Ethan, since the void in your life is most apparent at night, I think I know what's missing."

"*No*," Ethan countered so loudly he glanced around to see if anyone else was within earshot. "If you're suggesting," he added, almost in a whisper, "That the solution is for me to find another love interest, then you don't know me nearly as well as you thought."

"Well, that's always an option," Sarah responded, "And I'm fully on-board if you could find someone who makes you happy."

Ethan shook his head back and forth and then quickened his pace. Fortunately, Sarah's following comment instantly settled him down.

"However, that's *not* what I was about to suggest."

Ethan stopped dead in his tracks. Glancing around, he checked the path in both directions. Beams of sunlight filtered through the upper branches, helping to illuminate the empty stretches of asphalt.

"Go on, Sarah," Ethan finally proclaimed. "You've got my undivided attention."

"Ethan," she responded with passion, "You carry within every cell of your body the genetic material of the generations from your past. Those ancestors are all gone, and we've admittedly forgotten most of their names, but they still live on within you, don't they?"

"Hmm," Ethan countered, "I see where you're going with this. But you and I procreated a long time ago. So our genes already live on within Noah and Jenny."

"Yes," Sarah agreed, "But it won't end with them, will it?"

Ethan did not answer, recognizing the rhetorical nature of the question. Instead, he nodded and patiently waited for Sarah to continue.

"Ethan, if you peer hard enough into the dark tunnel, you'll see a distant light. Do you know what that light is?"

Without waiting for an answer, Sarah continued. "It's the coming of your grandchildren. And just like with Daryl, you can make a huge difference in *their* lives. And I'm not just talking about the genes you'll pass down. Ethan, you can also be immortalized by spending *time* with those children. If you choose, you can help mold their values and their character. It's true that many years from now, you'll be gone. But, you can still live on through your children, grandchildren, and all future generations."

Ethan could hear Sarah pause to draw in a breath. Then, finally, she added, "And in your situation, it's even more imperative. I wish we could share this responsibility, but you'll have to go it alone when it comes to grandparenting."

Ethan slowly began to walk up the trail. He knew Sarah's points were compelling, but something was still missing.

"Alright," Ethan mumbled, "I get it. I'm an essential link in a genetic chain reaching for generations. And I can visualize a future where family, friends, and co-workers potentially surround me. But, there's still no Sarah, no head matriarch who can serve as the keystone for the arch."

"But that's where you're *wrong*," Sarah countered. "There may not be a head matriarch, as you say, but that's all the more reason why the family will need you. So, Ethan, you *must* become the head patriarch. This is a vitally important role; you're the only one who can fill it. As for the nights, yes, some of them could be long, and you might be a bit lonely, at least for a little while. But you'll find the inner strength to survive. And when you do, you'll be the keystone which holds up the arch."

Ethan nodded but did not say a word. Then, he unknowingly began to accelerate his pace. After a brief interlude, Sarah finally continued.

"Ethan, you need to live a long, *long* time. Helping Daryl is just a start, and then, you can go on to make a positive difference in the lives of others. And do whatever it takes to be happy, my love. Marry again if you wish. But more than anything, you should leave a lasting imprint on the generations to come. I will never get this chance, so you must do it for both of us."

Ethan suddenly stopped again. From where was this coming? He looked up and down the grainy tarmac path and deep into the woods on both sides. Then, suddenly, two deer ambled onto the trail thirty feet ahead and turned to face him. Were these the same two he had seen earlier?

For a moment, Ethan stood motionless, engaging in a staring contest. Then, he looked down at his watch and realized time was running out. Ethan still needed to drive home, shower, and prepare for a full day. Before starting up again, though, he quickly peered over his shoulder. Then, seeing no one in sight, Ethan decided he needed to wrap up his early morning session with his wife.

"Is it really you, Sarah?" Ethan inquired out loud. "Am I actually speaking to my wife? Or is it your ghost or spirit? Maybe I'm just tapping my memory of you to imagine what you'd say. Or is all this just coming from somewhere deep in my subconscious?"

Ethan resumed his staring match with the deer. Then, as though he was speaking directly to the stag and the doe, who had yet to budge, Ethan slightly shook his head and continued.

"But, you know, I don't think it matters. It's still *damn* good advice, and you've given me much to consider. Thank you, my love."

Until now, the deer had listened to Ethan's conversation without a twitch. Then, suddenly, they turned and scampered up the path. Ethan glanced at his watch again and sighed.

"Ah *hell*," Ethan mumbled, "A little jogging won't kill me."

He began to run behind the two deer, but they soon vanished. It was less than two miles to complete the loop around the lake, and Ethan managed to jog the entire way. When he finally stopped, he bent over with both hands on his thighs, searching for a breath. Ethan never saw his white-tailed friends again, but as he approached the parking lot, he noticed it was half-full. Several people were unstrapping bicycles from their vehicles while others were preparing to begin their expeditions on foot. The area around Creve Coeur Falls was awakening for another autumn day, as it had been doing for generations.

Fifteen minutes later, Ethan was back home. He soundlessly tiptoed towards his bedroom shower. As he passed the hall bathroom, Ethan noticed the door was closed, but a loud retching noise came from the other side. His first thought was that Tom or Daryl had fallen off the wagon and was now paying a heavy price. Then the door suddenly opened, and he came face to face with his daughter.

"Are you alright?" Ethan asked without hesitation.

Jenny looked up and smiled. She then motioned for him to follow her into the den. Ethan observed something that looked like a white stick in her hand. The house was quiet, and Ethan assumed Matt had already left for work since he kept earlier hours. Once they entered the large living area, Jenny plopped onto the voluminous leather couch and patted the space beside her. Ethan slowly sat down, self-conscious of the sour smell he had developed from his morning workout.

When he looked at his daughter, the morning light spilling through the sliding glass door brightened her face. Her hair was piled a little higher on one side, pushed up by her pillow from the night before. Jenny's face was pallid, but there was a glow in both cheeks. Ethan reached up and wiped away what looked like a crumb beneath her bottom lip. He realized it was a little piece of vomit when he held it up to the light. He stared at it for a moment. Maybe it was the father within him, but Ethan did not find it repellant and wiped it on his shirt sleeve.

"Yes," Jenny proclaimed, "It's puke." A smile erupted across her face. "Vomit, Dad, it's *vomit*." Her smile morphed into an animated cackle. Jenny had just thrown up and was laughing about it out loud. Then Ethan noticed a tear streaking down her cheek. Finally, she lifted the white stick for her father to examine. Ethan took the plastic rod in his hand and held it up to the light. He could make out a pale blue line on a gray oval window.

"*Positive*," Jenny exclaimed. "Dad, it's positive!"

She lunged forward and wrapped both arms around her father's neck. Neither said a word. Ethan sat frozen like a statue, resting his hands in his lap. He was paralyzed into a daze. Ethan peered over his daughter's shoulder at the dazzling streaks of sunshine streaming in from the deck. Floating dust particles danced in these spotlights as though celebrating the news. Ethan momentarily closed his eyes and could instantly see Sarah's radiant smile.

Suddenly, his eyes sprung open. Ethan reached up to grab his daughter and hugged her tightly like she had just won the lottery. He was no longer concerned about his body odor any more than he fretted over Jenny's pieces of puke. Then, Ethan closed his eyes tight again and began to echo his daughter's boisterous laughter.

chapter
18

Ethan opened one eye, blurrily peered at the clock beside his bed, and groaned. 4:26 a.m. This ungodly time had become the starting point of every day throughout the gray winter months—comatose sleep for five or six hours, followed by stress-induced insomnia. Ethan noticed that the closer it came to the start of the trial, the less he slept. Win or lose, the conclusion of Daryl's legal troubles would hopefully mean additional sleep. For the time being, though, Ethan no longer resisted the inevitable. He clicked the Tiffany lamp on his nightstand and climbed out of bed.

Ethan peaked between the horizontal blinds of his bedroom window and saw nothing but white blanketing the back lawn. He could make out at least two inches of pristine snow in the moonlight. This was a bit of a surprise since spring had already officially begun. For a moment, he wrestled with logging his morning miles on the treadmill downstairs in the basement. Ordinarily, he despised the monotony of walking in one place without changing scenery, but it might be tolerable if he chose an interesting Netflix film.

Then he thought about Sarah's routine. She had loved walking in the snow. As long as it was not too deep, Sarah would lace up her hiking boots and head for the wooded area south of Creve Coeur Lake. She loved crunching the flakes beneath her feet and inhaling the fresh, crystalline air. Sarah said she would encounter few people at the park on those days, and when she returned home, rosy cheeks always bookended her beaming smile. Ethan threw on some long underwear and prepared for the short ride to the park.

The drive was surprisingly easy. On this late March day, the pavement was still warm enough to melt the snow, so it only stuck to the grass and tree limbs. Within minutes, Ethan was tramping through the snowy woods, listening to a recently compiled classical music playlist. He hoped that selections by composers like Gustav Holst, Claude Debussy, and Aaron Copeland would match the scenery and help him to relax at the outset of a stressful day.

Occasionally, a clump of sticky, damp snow would tumble to the ground. One landed squarely on Ethan's left shoulder. By this point, though, he did not notice. Ethan was oblivious to his surroundings since his mind had drifted to a courtroom twenty miles away. He quickly gave up falling into a sleep-like trance and, instead, decided to replay everything leading up to the start of the fourth day of Daryl's trial.

Michelle Jones had contacted Ethan months ago about a plea deal. Rejecting it was a no-brainer. In return for a guilty plea, she only offered to remove capital punishment from the table, leaving Daryl with a mandatory life sentence. Ethan and Daryl quickly brushed that option aside and continued their trial preparations. In addition, they had recently acquired some information that offered a glimmer of hope.

Tom and Daryl had spent weeks beating the bushes at Mizzou and around the surrounding town of Columbia. Finally, they uncovered evidence that might help discredit the state's most important witness. But since they had yet to locate a convincing defense witness who could support their self-defense theory, Ethan and Daryl knew the odds were still against them. Their only consolation in rejecting the plea deal was that juries in the city were usually adverse to handing out the death penalty, so there was probably nothing to lose.

Selecting a jury had taken up most of the trial's first day. Ethan and Tom's goal during the voir dire had been to diversify the jury panel as much as possible, figuring it would increase the odds of a split decision. After all, a hung jury was preferable to a guilty verdict. Ordinarily, the racial composition of a jury was a significant factor in city trials. However, since this case involved a white defendant and one of the victims was

black, Ethan focused on other factors, such as age, gender, and occupa-
tion. While he was not fully happy with the outcome, Ethan acknowledged it could have been worse.

The second day of the trial began with opening statements. Michelle Jones led off with a haughty oration asserting this to be "an open
and shut case." When the police had arrested Daryl, as she pointed
out, he was "literally holding the smoking gun." In addition, she promised that the surviving victim was highly credible and his testimony
would persuasively convince them that Daryl Armstrong was guilty. To
Ethan, Michelle Jones' came across as arrogant, but he figured this was
intentional. She probably wanted to communicate that her witnesses
and evidence were so compelling that this trial would be a waste of
everyone's time.

Ethan's opening was shorter, aimed primarily at clouding the prosecution's case. Lawyers generally know that juries are the most attentive
at the beginning and end of a trial. Still, since Ethan's self-defense case
was admittedly weak, he wanted to employ a different approach. Ethan
wanted to raise several questions, many of which he knew the prosecution would fail to answer by the end of the trial. For example, why were
two college kids poking around a homeless campsite long after the conclusion of a Cardinals baseball game? What was the source of the gun
that shot the three victims? And what about a motive? Why would Daryl
want to shoot anyone? Ethan also continually stressed the fundamental
precept that Daryl Armstrong, like any defendant, was innocent until
proven guilty. The prosecution's duty was to prove otherwise, and they
had to do this *beyond a reasonable doubt.*

Throughout the afternoon and the following day, Michelle Jones paraded a series of witnesses to prove "her open and shut case." Her experts
asserted that the same gun had fired the bullets found in the bodies of
the three victims, and these bullets had been the cause of death for Burt
Bennett and Frank Abalone. The arresting police officers testified that
this was the gun they found in Daryl Armstrong's possession when they
arrived at the scene and placed him under arrest. They then produced a
written statement signed by the defendant acknowledging that he had
killed Frank Abalone and wounded his friend, Charles Graham.

During Ethan's cross-examination, however, the police officers conceded that Daryl had steadfastly claimed his actions were motivated by self-defense from the start. Ethan then instructed both police officers to read a lengthy excerpt from Daryl's statement. He respectfully requested that they speak with clarity, precision, and at a high volume. At the risk of overkill, Ethan wanted the jury to hear Daryl's words multiple times, understanding the value of repetition. The prosecution had objected to the second reading. Still, Ethan convinced Judge Larson to allow it because he wanted to probe how each officer had interpreted Daryl's words.

According to what Daryl told the police, on the night of the shooting, he and Burt Bennett, another homeless man, had already crawled into their sleeping bags when they heard a loud commotion outside the tent they had erected beneath the I-44 overpass. Over Daryl's whispered objections, Burt climbed out of his sleeping bag, unzipped the flap, and exited the tent, curious to discover the source of the noise.

Daryl peeked through the tent's flaps and saw two young white men approaching Burt. At first, they made jokes and laughed at his friend, an older African American who slurred his words and could be challenging to understand. The situation, however, soon escalated into physical harassment. Finally, when one of them, later known as Frank Abalone, pulled out a revolver, Daryl opened his pocket knife, slit the rear canvas of the tent, and quietly slipped out.

According to Daryl's written statement, after seeing Frank fire two shots at Burt, one at his head and the other in his torso, Daryl lunged at him from behind, knocking the revolver out of his hand. All three men, Daryl, Frank, and Charles, leaped for the gun lying on the pavement. Daryl reached it first. He then stood, aimed, and fired a single shot at Frank's head, killing him instantly. When Charles stepped toward him, he shot him as well, grazing him in the arm. Charles then turned and fled.

Once the arresting police officers concluded reading from Daryl's statement, Ethan had each one of them acknowledge they had arrived on the scene too late to witness the actual shootings for themselves. They also never found any other witnesses beyond Charles Graham, the one wounded victim, nor could they locate any security cameras beneath the overpass. Finally, Ethan wrapped up his cross-examination by getting both officers to admit that Daryl's account of the facts was at least "possible."

On the afternoon of the trial's third day, Michelle Jones called her most crucial witness to the stand. Charles Graham was the keystone to her arch, the one eyewitness to the entire crime. Graham would have to be credible and convincing to win a conviction. Since Daryl had provided an entirely different version of what happened that night, Charles Graham would have to persuade the jury that the defendant was the one who was lying and that his account of the facts was the truth. But, of course, the prosecution was banking on the likelihood that the jury was more likely to believe a college kid from Mizzou who had grown up in the middle-class suburbs than an alcoholic homeless man with a sketchy background.

Michelle Jones' star witness surpassed even her expectations. Ethan admitted it was an Oscar-worthy performance, especially after he saw moist eyes on some of the jurors' faces as Charles described how much he missed Frank, his childhood friend. With his blond curls and a doe-eyed expression, Charles Graham gazed convincingly at the panel and told an enthralling story.

Michelle Jones also did a masterful job of questioning her witness. If this were a play, she would have been the director standing in the wings while the spotlight shone on her star. Despite Ethan's objections about their relevance, Charles told some nostalgic tales about growing up with his best friend, Frank, in the idyllic neighborhood surrounding the area near Six Flags St. Louis. He then related their plans to attend the University of Missouri together after graduating from Eureka High School.

As they were preparing to begin their final year of college at Mizzou, the two friends decided to attend one last Cardinals game at Busch Stadium. Therefore, in the late afternoon of Wednesday, August 3, 2022, according to Charles, or Chuck as he was better known to his friends, they drove Frank's 2014 BMW downtown and parked it in a paid lot on South 8th Street beneath the I-64 overpass. Admitting they downed several Budweiser's apiece throughout the evening, Charles acknowledged this may have contributed to their disorientation after the game.

Therefore, according to the witness, when searching for their car, they mistakenly stumbled upon a different lot located on South 4th Street just west of the I-44 overpass. Here, they observed an altercation between two men in the rear of the lot. According to Charles, Frank approached the two men. Although unsure, he believed his friend wanted to defuse the conflict since "Frank had always been a habitual do-gooder." When Frank failed to heed his friend's warning to turn back, Charles hesitantly followed from behind. According to the witness, the two men were pathetically wrestling around on the ground, but they looked relatively harmless.

Charles then testified that one of the men, who later turned out to be Daryl Armstrong, suddenly produced a .38 Special Revolver and aimed it at the other man, Burt Bennett, an African American. The confrontation occurred in front of a beaten-up camping tent erected beneath the overpass on the peripheral edge of the parking lot. Just as Frank neared the scene of the altercation, Charles saw Daryl fire two shots at Burt, one at his head and the other in his torso. Then, seeing Frank approach, Daryl pivoted and fired a single shot into Frank's head, instantly killing him.

Charles claimed he was momentarily stunned. Then Daryl fired one shot at him, grazing his left arm. Charles grabbed the arm, saw blood oozing through his fingers, and turned to flee the crime scene. He then stumbled across Gratiot Street and managed to run a block to the Dive STL, a country and western bar. From there, he called 911 and waited for the police and an ambulance. At this point, Michelle Jones asserted she had no further questions. Then Judge Larson adjourned the trial for the day, announcing that Ethan could begin his cross-examination of the witness the following morning.

As Ethan hiked the final mile of his loop around Creve Coeur Lake, he thought about how the jury had perceived Charles' testimony the day before. No matter how much he "coached" Daryl, his client could never match that performance. As a result, Ethan was uncertain if he should put Daryl on the stand, although his client insisted he wanted a chance to tell his side of the story.

For months, the local media had been amplifying the plight of Charles and Frank, the two innocent college kids who had stumbled into the lair of a vicious homeless man. Throughout the city, the unhoused were ubiquitous, begging on every street corner. It had reached the point where, to most people in St. Louis, the unhoused were either perceived as annoying or had become entirely invisible.

What was more, Daryl's self-defense story simply did not ring true. Would the jury give credence to an account that two college kids had brought an unlicensed gun downtown, seeking to harass the unhoused after a baseball game and then killing one of them? Since Busch Stadium's metal detectors would have prevented the boys from sneaking a gun into the game, they would have needed to return to their car before commencing their hunt for the homeless. Ethan could not visualize any scenario where even a single jury member would buy this version of the facts.

Ethan did have an ace up his sleeve, though, and it would get played when the trial resumed this morning. He imagined several variations of how best to use it during his cross-examination of Charles Graham. The kid was savvy, though, and would be difficult to trap. What is more, Charles already knew what was coming. By law, the prosecution and defense had to exchange a list of their potential witnesses. Indeed, when Michelle Jones reviewed the defense's list, she had most certainly talked over these names with her star witness. Charles, therefore, had ample time to develop a credible strategy to counter Ethan's questions.

Since Tom and Daryl had uncovered these witnesses in Columbia and were familiar with their potential testimony, Ethan wanted to preview his cross-examination questions with them before the trial resumed. Therefore, as he was about to drive home, he texted Ellen, asking her to join them for an early morning breakfast. An hour later, as they poured syrup on their pancakes and coffee into their mugs, Ethan role-played a cross-examination with Tom filling in for Charles Graham. They all agreed it went well. But, of course, the problem with cross-examinations is that no matter how much you rehearse, you can never anticipate how the actual witness will respond to your questions in court.

Two hours later, Ethan stood before his nemesis. Charles was wearing the same navy blue corduroy sports jacket from the day before, although now, he sported a powder blue shirt instead of the lackluster white, and his tie was striped in multiple colors rather than a solid maroon. A confident demeanor had also replaced the dour expression he displayed throughout yesterday's direct examination.

"Good morning, Mr. Graham. My name is Ethan Marshall, and I'm one of the defense lawyers."

When Ethan paused, Charles cocked his head slightly, unable to conceal a sneer while waiting for the first question.

"Let me begin by expressing my sympathy for the loss of your friend." Then, glancing toward the jury, Ethan added, "Of course, what we're doing now is trying to learn the truth about *why* your friend died."

Without waiting any longer for a question, Charles impatiently responded. "I explained all that yesterday. You heard it. I know because I saw you sitting beside the man who killed my friend."

As he spoke, Charles pointed toward Daryl with a scowl on his face that blended anguish and outrage. Ethan barely managed to keep his eyes from rolling up to the ceiling.

"Yes," Ethan quipped, "The defendant has already acknowledged he fired the gun that killed your friend. The question, however, is *why*. That's what I'd like to explore now."

Charles returned his glare toward Ethan, leaned back in the witness chair, and dramatically folded his arms. He remained quiet, defiantly awaiting the next question.

"Let's return to high school, Mr. Graham," continued Ethan. "You and Frank Abalone both attended Eureka High School, correct?"

"*Objection*," Michelle Jones interrupted, "Relevance?"

Without uttering a word, the judge pivoted his gaze towards Ethan, plainly wanting an explanation to justify his question.

"The prosecution," Ethan countered, "Asked about their high school experiences yesterday and thereby opened the door to this line of questioning. What's more, your honor, if you allow me a few more questions, I'll reveal the origins of the state of mind behind Mr. Graham and Mr. Abalone's actions on the night of the shooting."

Judge Larson sat back in his padded leather chair, nodded slightly, and momentarily glanced downward. An inquisitive expression had unfolded on his face upon hearing Ethan's intent to reveal something about the motive behind the boys' actions that night. Then, finally, he peered up and responded.

"I'll allow it; the objection is overruled."

Ethan tightened his lips to conceal a smile and then swiveled back to face the witness.

"Would you like me to repeat the question?" Ethan inquired.

"No," Charles answered. "I remember your question." His tone was that of a sulky child responding to a patronizing adult. "Yes, we both graduated from Eureka High School almost four years ago."

"And Eureka High School is located in the far western suburbs, at least 25 miles from downtown St. Louis, correct?"

"I don't know the exact distance," Charles replied, "But, yeah, it's out there in the suburbs. So?"

"So," Ethan continued after glancing at the jury, "Is it safe to say that growing up in the distant suburbs, you and Mr. Abalone seldom interacted with the unhoused?"

Charles began to smirk, but after glancing at the prosecutor, he sat up straighter, and his grin faded.

"No," the witness answered, "There weren't many homeless people in Eureka, but I saw quite a few whenever we'd head into the city for a Cardinals game. Sometimes, they'd approach, usually panhandling for money, but I'd politely shake my head and keep walking."

"Yes," Ethan agreeably added, "The unhoused do like to beg from the fans coming downtown for the Cardinals games at Busch Stadium, don't they? Did you ever give them anything?"

"No, I didn't," answered Charles. "I was told they'd probably spend the money on liquor or drugs. Also, if they really can't find work, assuming they've even been looking, some churches or charities will help them. They shouldn't bug the sports fans coming downtown to catch a game."

Charles glanced around the courtroom, pleased with the little speech he had just given. Once again, a subtle shake of the prosecutor's head wiped away his smirk.

"And, on a field trip downtown," Ethan continued, "When the senior class from Eureka was attending a Cardinals day game, some of your fellow students have reported that you and Mr. Abalone were approached by a homeless person asking for money, correct?"

"*Objection*, hearsay."

Before Judge Larson could respond, Ethan offered to rephrase his question.

"Mr. Graham, isn't it true that on a field trip downtown, while walking toward the stadium, you and Mr. Abalone shoved a homeless person requesting money? In fact, you pushed him so hard he fell to the ground, didn't he?"

"We may have accidentally bumped into someone in the crowd," Charles sneered, "But we would *never* deliberately push anyone, homeless or not. In fact, on the night of his death, Frank was trying to help someone he saw sleeping on the streets."

Ethan glared at him and waited. Then, finally, he strolled back toward the defense table, where Tom handed him a sheet of paper. Ethan glanced at it and then looked up at the defendant.

"Mr. Graham, isn't it true that on the night of September 22nd, 2021, you, Mr. Abalone, and a group of friends went trolling for homeless people on the streets of downtown Columbia?"

As Charles glanced toward the prosecution table, out of the corner of his eye, Ethan observed Michelle Jones' eyes enlarge and her mouth open into a circular zero.

"No, not at all," Charles responded. "We were simply out with a small group of pledges from our fraternity that night. It was part of what you might call their hazing. Frank and I told them they had to approach some homeless people and ask them for money."

"I see," replied Ethan sarcastically. "That's a funny twist. Begging from the homeless rather than the other way around. Is that it?"

"It was just a harmless prank," Charles responded. "No one got hurt."

"No one got *hurt*?" Ethan glanced down at the piece of paper in his hand. "Isn't it true that some of your pledges punched the homeless people they encountered and then took some of their possessions?"

Charles glanced down and began to fidget with his hands. Then, for the second time, he wriggled in his seat. Finally, as though he suddenly remembered his lines from the play, Charles glanced up and confidently proclaimed, "Some of the pledges may have gotten a little carried away, but if they did, Frank and I never saw it. If we had, we would have put a stop to it. *Immediately*."

"Hmm," Ethan responded. "The two of you never encouraged these assaults? Never joined in?"

"No," Charles resolutely answered. "*Not* at all."

Once again, Ethan glanced down at the sheet of paper. He paused like a fisherman waiting to set the hook before yanking up his rod.

"Mr. Graham," Ethan deliberately stated, "Do you know two people in Columbia named Latisha Brown and Henry Hubbard?"

"Yeah, I know *of* them," answered Charles. "They work at this dive called the Show Me Bar. Henry's a bartender there, and Latisha's a waitress."

Ethan gazed at the witness like a father, patiently waiting for his child to tell the truth. Finally, the witness responded with what sounded like a rehearsed explanation.

"Look, Mr. Marshall, I know you've spoken to Latisha and Henry." Charles hesitated as though he was searching for the following line. "Go ahead and put them on the stand if you want. But they couldn't possibly see what was going on that night. They would've been inside the bar, and our pledges were outside. Moreover, it was late, completely dark, and the street lighting in that area was almost nonexistent." Then, as though delivering the play's final line, Charles twisted toward the jury and added, "Frank and I were *never* involved in what you're talking about, Mr. Marshall, and Latisha and Henry would not be able to say otherwise."

"Hmm," Ethan purred again. The wrinkles in his forehead reflected extreme skepticism. "We'll have to see." Ethan paused, deliberately heightening the courtroom drama. "Let's move on, Mr. Graham. Do you know Orville Henderson, a student at the University of Missouri?"

Orville Henderson was another name on the defense list of potential witnesses. Ethan stared at Frank Graham wide-eyed, waiting for another one of his prepared rebuttals. Meanwhile, Charles shook his head while a slight grin streaked across his face. Then, finally, he sat up and returned Ethan's gaze.

"Okay, I'll give you credit, Mr. Marshall; you've done your homework. Yes, I *know* Orville Henderson. He was one of our pledges that night."

"Thank you, Mr. Graham; we *have* done our homework. Now, do you *still* want to insist that you and Frank were nowhere to be found when the pledges beat up an unhoused man that night in Columbia?"

"Let me guess," Charles countered, "You got Orville to say otherwise? Well, again, Mr. Marshall, feel free to put him on the stand. I only saw him briefly at the start of the evening and didn't see him again until the following day. But let me just say again, for the record, that Frank and I had *nothing* to do with what may have happened to any homeless people that night."

Then, after briefly pausing to glance at Michelle Jones, he added, "And if Orville says otherwise, he'll be lying. You see, Mr. Marshall, I was the one who black-balled Orville from entering the fraternity. He always seemed pretty disingenuous when it came to accepting our patriotic values. He also got upset when I started dating a coed who had just broken up with him. So Orville may have his reasons to tell you a different story, but that doesn't mean he's telling you the truth. "

Ethan nodded, smiled faintly, and pointed at the witness as though saluting the cleverness of his response. Then, while briefly turning his back to Charles Graham and inadvertently glancing toward the crowd behind the prosecution table, Ethan observed a bald, middle-aged man glaring straight at him. Ethan would be lying in a pool of blood if the man's eyes could fire bullets. But, instead, the man, who Ethan presumed was the father of one of the two Mizzou boys, subtly raised a finger to his throat and drew it across in a slashing manner.

Ethan froze. He knew this trial had stirred up an emotional whirlwind, and this was not the first time he had encountered anger from a family member his defendant had victimized. However, this man was different. His expression was not just livid; it was overtly threatening. Ethan turned around, but not before making a mental note to discuss a heightened level of security with his family and entourage. Unfortunately, the judge was studying some documents and did not see the man's threat. Charles did, however, because he was grinning condescendingly.

To Ethan, it appeared that the prosecution's key witness had thrown down the gauntlet, almost daring him to call any of those witnesses to the stand. Knowing their limitations, Ethan had primarily been bluffing when he mentioned the names of Latisha Brown, Henry Hubbard, and Orville Henderson. Charles appeared to know this. Ethan wanted to plant seeds that might lead the jury to question Charles' credibility and, with some luck, maybe rattle his nerves. Now, it was difficult to ascertain just how successful he had been.

Charles Graham continued to smirk while patiently waiting for the cross-examination to continue. Finally, he filled his lungs, sat back in the witness chair, and shrugged, secure that his word was sounder than anyone Ethan might call to the stand. Then, before Ethan could continue, Charles inquired with a disdainful sneer, "So, Mr. Marshall, does this mean we're done?"

Ethan clenched his lips and inhaled deeply through his nose while casually stepping back toward the defense table. He turned and gently set down his sheet of paper. Ethan would no longer need notes. For the rest of his cross-examination, he planned to navigate Charles through every step that led to the shooting outside Busch Stadium on August 3rd. Ethan knew the details intimately, as though he had personally experienced them.

The roadmap for the next two hours was simple. Ethan planned to employ a series of leading questions that would steer Charles Graham through an entirely different story from the one he had told the day before. Of course, the witness would avidly deny anything pointing towards self-defense, but Ethan knew that, at the minimum, he might sow several more seeds of doubt.

Ethan looked up at the witness, anxiously awaiting a response to his question, and grinned. "Oh *no*, Mr. Graham," he announced with a sparkle in his eye, "We're not even close to being done."

chapter
19

Ethan glanced around the table in Blueberry Hill. At this time of night, college kids from Washington University typically packed this celebrated eatery in the heart of the Delmar Loop. Since it was spring break, however, Ethan, Tom, Daryl, and Ellen had a section of the sprawling restaurant to themselves. Ethan had chosen a table next to a floor-to-ceiling picture window so he could keep an eye on the heavy foot traffic outside on the Street. Occasionally, a couple strolling by would halt to read the text below one of the five-pointed stars that made up the St. Louis Walk of Fame. The more than 150 stars sprinkled over six blocks honored an eclectic mix of St. Louisans, ranging from Ulysses Grant and Charles Lindbergh to Maya Angelou and Tina Turner.

The foursome began by sharing a plate of toasted ravioli, but since the trial would resume first thing in the morning, they chose to wash down their appetizer with bottles of Fitz's root beer rather than a pitcher of Budweiser. Afterward, Ethan ordered and devoured his usual plate of chicken wings doused in BBQ sauce. Ordinarily, the mood around the table should have been breezy, especially after the points Ethan had scored that afternoon against the prosecution's most critical witness. Tonight, though, a dour feeling hung over the table like a dark cloud.

There was a consensus that today's cross-examination would not be enough. Even if Daryl took the stand, they needed additional evidence or testimony to corroborate his self-defense story. Originally, Ethan had hoped to connect the unlicensed gun used in the shooting to the two frat boys from the suburbs. However, laws recently enacted by the buffoons in Jefferson City had made it cartoonishly simple for anyone to acquire a firearm. Therefore, guns like the one Daryl had wrestled from Frank Abalone were practically available on every street corner. Ethan grimaced at the thought that an unhinged eighteen-year-old in Missouri would be denied a beer in a place like Blueberry Hill but would have no problem purchasing any kind of gun legally.

Their only hope would be to find another eyewitness who could match the credibility of Charles Graham. Since the shooting had taken place less than a block from the Dive STL, a bar that should have been teaming with people after a Cardinals' game, Tom and Daryl had spent many hours interviewing several of the bar's employees and patrons. But, with the prosecution's case all but over, time was running out.

"Hey, buddy?" Tom rumbled. He snapped his fingers before Ethan's face like a hypnotist trying to rouse a subject. "Earth to Ethan?"

Ethan had been gazing out the window. He was lost in his thoughts, appearing almost catatonic. Somehow, his thought process about locating an eyewitness had morphed into reminiscing over the many times he had spent with Sarah in this restaurant. Ethan shook his head, trying to stir himself out of the trance.

"I'm sorry," he finally replied, "What did you say?"

Tom grinned sympathetically. "Long day, huh?" He continued without waiting for a response, "I said Ellen would give me a lift home. We'll probably stop by her place for a little while, but I should be home by 11:00." He glanced toward Ellen, who nodded with a faintly uncomfortable smile.

"Yeah, sure," Ethan answered. He could not help but chuckle a little at Ellen's flushed cheeks.

"You'll get Daryl home?" Tom added. His bore an expression like a concerned parent.

Ethan turned toward Daryl and nodded. "Of course." After a pause, he added, "Although we're not in a rush, right?" Daryl nodded with a mouth full of food while he scraped the bottom of his chili bowl.

As Tom stood and prepared to help Ellen out of her chair, he turned to face Ethan.

"So," he pronounced, "The plan tomorrow is to put Daryl on the stand?"

"I still don't know," Ethan replied. "We'll discuss it some more tonight. It may be a last-minute decision."

"Alright, sounds good," Tom replied with a yawn. "I'll see you guys in the morning." He then spun around and trailed Ellen out of the restaurant.

Once they were gone from sight, Ethan turned to face Daryl. He could not help but grin at the diligence his client employed to get every last bean onto his spoon.

"They do make good chili here," Ethan laughed. "It's okay with me if you want to lick the bowl."

Daryl froze. As he gently lowered his spoon to the table, Ethan noticed Daryl did not return his smile. Instead, his client lowered his eyes and frowned.

"I'm sorry," Ethan murmured. "I was just kidding."

"That's alright," answered Daryl. "It's just hard to break some old habits."

Ethan's brow furrowed. Then, throwing caution to the wind, he inquired, "Daryl, can I ask you a question?"

Daryl looked up, nodded, and reclined back in his wooden chair.

"You were unhoused for years, right? What was that like?"

Daryl glanced away and turned to face the window. Outside, he saw the frigid wind bend a small tree beneath the street lamp like a bow about to sling an arrow. Ethan could see him bite down on his lower lip.

"I'm sorry," Ethan finally uttered after not hearing a response. "It was inappropriate, and you certainly don't need to answer."

Daryl turned to face Ethan. "So then, why'd you ask?" Then, after a brief pause, he added, "Am I still a pet project? You know, to get over your guilt from the past?"

"*No*, not at all," Ethan hastily answered. "That's not why I asked." For a moment, the two men gazed questionably at each other. Daryl patiently waited while Ethan searched for the right words to continue.

Finally, Ethan responded, "It's just, I remember that day in the park when you said you'd prefer not to move into my house. I didn't know then if this was just stubborn pride or if you . . ."

Daryl abruptly interrupted, "If I what?" Liked living on the streets?"

"Well," Ethan replied with a slight shrug. "I thought maybe you had grown attached to your freedom."

Daryl looked away again, focusing on a scene across the street. Next to the statue of Chuck Berry, a shadowy figure was digging through a waste can. Then, finally, he turned back toward Ethan.

"*Freedom?*" Daryl inquired. "Freedom to do what?"

Ethan inhaled deeply. He then leaned forward, placed both hands on the table, and clasped his fingers together. Ethan had been looking for the chance to build a sturdier rapport with Daryl, but now he deeply regretted asking the question.

"Look, Daryl," he stated solemnly, "There's another reason I brought up the question about your life on the streets."

Ethan maneuvered his chair closer to the table, placed one elbow squarely in front of his plate of greasy chicken bones, and then cradled his chin in the palm of his hand. He studied his client momentarily as if deciding how much to share. Then, looking directly at Daryl, Ethan finally continued.

"I've been giving some thought lately to a special project after the trial, and assuming we can keep you out of prison, there might be a vital role for you to play. Your experience of surviving on the streets of St. Louis for years could make you a valued asset to this program."

"So you're looking to serve the needs of the unhoused?" Daryl inquired. The chip on his shoulder had instantly vanished.

Ethan nodded and then leaned back in his chair. "I've probably said too much. This project doesn't have wings yet, and there's no point in getting people's hopes up."

"Alright," Daryl said, "Yeah, I'm interested in *any* plan that will help the unhoused. But before I answer your question, Ethan, you should know there's nothing good about being homeless. *Freedom?* Yeah, you're *free* from holding down a job, paying bills, or raising kids, but that's not the kind of freedom anyone should want."

Ethan nodded, leaned back, and clasped his hands behind his neck, waiting to hear more.

"For starters," continued Daryl, "You constantly feel rootless. You're exposed twenty-four hours a day, seven days a week. It's like you're the only naked person in a room filled with people wearing clothes."

Daryl glanced towards the window and sighed with a bit of relief when he saw the person scouring the trashcan had moved on. Then, he pivoted back toward Ethan and continued.

"The whole neighborhood soon knows your business, but no one cares. The human vultures quickly pick over your stuff and steal whatever's not guarded. You spend all your time looking for a way to get a hot meal or searching for a seat where someone won't tell you to move on. In between, you're always seeking somewhere to take care of your bathroom needs or a warm place to sleep. There's no safe way to secure your belongings. Even getting a glass of water can be a challenge. And man, *nobody* wants you around."

Daryl used a crumbled napkin to wipe away droplets that had gathered above his upper lip. Ethan remained frozen. Then, getting a second wind, Daryl continued.

"You walk everywhere, regardless of the weather. Transportation's not free; even if you can beg enough to ride a bus or the Metrolink, no one wants to sit next to you. Laundromats aren't free either, and in all likelihood, it's probably been a long time since you've had a shower. If you decide to go into a shelter, you share a shower and a toilet with 15 or 20 other people. There's *no* privacy. The shelters are dirty, dangerous places with rigid rules and schedules. And it's hard to fall asleep when surrounded by mothers with their children, people with mental and physical illnesses, and a wide range of criminals."

Ethan was shocked by Daryl's eloquence. He had forgotten that his client had lived two lives, the first where he had earned a college degree and had been a husband and father before tragedy jettisoned him into his second life. It had taken some effort to get Daryl started, but now the words flowed like a mountain stream.

"The longer you're homeless," Daryl continued, "The more you lose your self-identity. It's demoralizing and depressing. You no longer have a foundation in your life. It becomes harder to focus. Constant problems chip away at your self-esteem, and you start to disintegrate on the inside. You become scared, frustrated, angry, bitter, and distrustful. You're always tired and overwhelmed. Even the smallest tasks become big chores as the depression saps your energy. The stress clouds your judgment. Pretty soon, you grab at anything that looks like an opportunity, but you never seem to get anywhere."

Daryl paused and looked away again. This time, his eyes had grown a bit glassy. Finally, he swiveled back to face Ethan and continued.

"Every homeless person is different. Many sleepwalk through the experience because of mental health issues or an addiction. In my case, though, I never became completely oblivious to my circumstances. There might've been a few days when I even felt like a sociologist doing an undercover study, but most of the time, I was usually smashed, and I frequently spent entire days sleeping off a hangover. And let me tell you, nothing is satisfying or redeeming about begging for money from complete strangers."

Daryl hesitated. Ethan could see that describing his years on the streets was a humbling experience. Maybe it was time to wrap things up.

"I understand what you're telling me, Daryl. You speak quite well and with powerful conviction. But you don't need to go on any further."

Daryl nodded with a contented countenance. He looked drained but, at the same time, a bit relieved. Then he added, "Of course, there's still one point I never addressed."

Ethan looked puzzled but remained silent.

"*No*, Ethan," Daryl exclaimed with a tone of finality, "I absolutely would *never* want to return to the streets. If that is what it means to be free, you can keep your freedom. So Ethan, what I said that day in the park? That was simply foolish pride."

Silence permeated the room as Daryl abruptly stopped talking. For a moment, the two men gazed at each other. Then, finally, Ethan shook his head and uttered a single word - "*Wow.*"

"You know, Ethan," Daryl finally resumed, "In a country as wealthy as the United States, housing should be a right, not a privilege."

Seeing an opportunity to amplify his friend's words, Ethan added, "And I imagine it's even worse for the unhoused in St. Louis."

"Yeah," Daryl agreed, "Mainly due to our high rates of crime. And we've become the murder capital of the nation."

"Yes, that's what I was thinking," Ethan retorted, "I know in your case, you're the one charged with a double homicide, but more often than not, it's the unhoused who are the victims. They're just out there on the front lines without any protection from the bad guys. That must bring on a constant state of fear."

After pausing to reflect momentarily, Ethan added, "And there's something else ironically unique about St. Louis. In a city with thousands living on the streets, there's actually more than enough housing."

"*Really*?" Daryl asked incredulously.

"Yeah, over the last 70 years, this city lost almost two-thirds of its population. We went from over 850,000 people to less than 300,000. As a result, parts of the city, especially on the north side, resemble a sprawling ghost town. The city currently has as many as 33,000 empty lots and buildings. Daryl, one in five properties in St. Louis is vacant."

"*Hmm*," Daryl moaned. "All that property is boarded up, but it's off-limits to the souls living on the streets?"

Ethan nodded while simultaneously lifting his eyebrows. "Yes, that's the exact situation. And what's more, if a homeless man were to sneak into one of those empty houses, the cops would arrest him for breaking and entering."

Ethan and Daryl shared a moment of silence as they shook their heads in disgust. Then, finally, Daryl smiled and stated, "Well, at least I won't be unhoused anymore."

"No?"

Daryl shook his head. Then, he joked with a grin, "I'll have permanent housing provided by the Missouri Department of Corrections."

"Not funny," replied Ethan. "You haven't been convicted yet."

"Yeah, but it's not looking good, is it?" Then, after a pause, Daryl inquired, "Are you planning to put any of those people we found in Columbia up on the stand?"

"Probably not," Ethan responded, shaking his head. "We might gain a little from the jury hearing their stories, but like Charles Graham pointed out today, there are serious limits to what they actually know. This will all come out under cross-examination. Besides," added Ethan, almost as an afterthought, "None of them are eyewitnesses who can support your self-defense argument."

"What about putting me on the stand?" Daryl inquired. "I can be pretty persuasive."

"Yes, I just witnessed that," Ethan laughed. Then, he grew a bit more solemn.

"We'll probably have to put you up there since we don't have anyone else. However, the same problem recurs. I'm afraid that whatever we gain from your direct will be mitigated during cross-examination."

Daryl frowned. Seeing that, Ethan added, "We'll rehearse your cross-exam at breakfast tomorrow morning. I'm sure you'll do fine."

"Any other ideas?" Daryl asked despairingly. He leaned back in the stiff wooden chair and slumped with his arms folded, like a child who had just discovered a Christmas stocking filled with nothing but school supplies.

"I'm afraid not," Ethan answered.

The two men sat quietly, each gazing in a different direction. Then, while Ethan fixated on the dark street outside, Daryl studied the bar in the adjourning room. Despite his drinking problems, Daryl had spent little time inside bars, and when he did, it was with Tom scouring for potential witnesses. But now, Daryl observed that, unlike the Dive STL, the sun's bright rays were not filtering into the bar inside Blueberry Hill, creating an entirely different ambiance.

"Holy *shit*," Daryl suddenly exclaimed. The abrupt outburst almost knocked Ethan off his chair.

There was an intense sparkle in both of Daryl's eyes. "Man, we were *so* stupid."

"Yeah?" Ethan asked after he caught his breath. "How so?"

"You know how Tom and I went to that place, the Dive STL, at least half a dozen times looking for potential witnesses?"

Ethan nodded.

"Oh man, we're *so* stupid," Daryl repeated.

"What?" Ethan asked with growing agitation.

"We always visited the Dive during the day. We never went there *at night*."

Ethan froze. Then, he bolted up from his chair and began fishing for his wallet. Ethan fumbled around, looking for the check the waiter had left earlier. When he found it, Ethan spun around, looking for the waiter, who was nowhere in sight.

"Ah, hell," he grumbled, "I'll just leave cash."

He pulled out several twenties from his billfold, threw them on top of the check, grabbed his coat from the back of the chair, and pivoted to face Daryl.

"Let's *go*," he exclaimed. Then, turning toward the exit, he added over his shoulder, "It's a long shot, Daryl. A 'Hail Mary.' But the shootings occurred at night, so maybe the night is when we'll find our savior witness."

Five minutes later, as his Subaru cruised down Delmar Boulevard, Ethan pondered his recent conversation about St. Louis. He envisioned the standard map of the city. This street, running east and west, was known as the Delmar Divide and was a line separating St. Louis into two distinct worlds. This boundary was unofficial, of course. Delmar Boulevard was simply a thoroughfare that ran from University City on the western edges of St. Louis to the city's midtown region. This boulevard was nothing exceptional, but local natives understood its significance.

With only a few exceptions, everything to the south of Delmar was a vibrant city. There were strip malls, universities, restaurants, and playgrounds. And there were uniquely distinct neighborhoods. The Central West End, the Hill, Lafayette Square, Dogtown, Cherokee Street, and Soulard were among the better known, but there was also DeBaliviere Place, Dutchtown, Shaw, and Clifton Heights. Forest Park was one of the most beautiful municipal parks in the nation, enfolding an art museum, a science center, a history museum, an outdoor opera house, and, of course, the world-famous Zoo. This area in and around Forest Park once simultaneously hosted a world's fair and the Olympic Games.

North of Delmar, on the other hand, was an urban wasteland. Empty lots overgrown with weeds encircled boarded-up homes abandoned for decades. Virtually everyone on the north side was African American, and most lived below the nation's poverty line. Schools, parks, and playgrounds also dotted the North Side, but they were all infected with the social distress associated with extreme poverty—gangs, crime, and indiscriminate shootings.

Most people who grew up in the sprawling suburbs outside the city, including Ethan, never ventured into the territory north of the Delmar Divide. One could drive up I-64 to attend Cardinals or Blues games, bring the kids to the zoo, or visit the Arch east of downtown. Only the hopelessly lost ever ventured north of Delmar. As he contemplated this feature of his beloved city, Ethan shook his head with despair. And he instantly noticed how his surroundings perked up the moment he turned south onto Skinker Boulevard.

Ethan observed the picturesque streetlights lining the western fringe of Forest Park. On the other side of the street, he noted the Medieval castle guarding Washington University's entrance. Ethan knew the roads in this area. Grand mansions dating back to the Gilded Age lined these thoroughfares, stretching from the Central West End in the east to the well-heeled inner suburb of Clayton to the west. This expanse was one of the most beautiful urban areas anywhere in the country.

As Ethan neared the entranceway to I-64, he suddenly noticed his passenger had twisted in his seat to confront him directly.

"Yes?" Ethan pronounced with a smile parting his lips. "Something on your mind?"

Without hesitation, Daryl answered. "You know, Ethan, as far as I'm concerned, you're off the hook. You've been off the hook for a long time."

"What do you mean?" Ethan asked while glancing into the side mirror to merge onto the highway.

"What I said back at the restaurant," answered Daryl. "You know, about you trying to get past your guilt."

Ethan glanced to his right and then returned his eyes to the road. Traffic at this hour was light, but it was always best to keep your guard up whenever approaching downtown.

"You've already done so much for me," continued Daryl. "First, you agreed to take my case. Then you put up your own money to bail me out of jail. Finally, you took me into your home. I mean, how can I ever thank you?" During the pause that followed, Ethan could hear Daryl inhale deeply. "Ethan, *man*, you've more than made up for that decision not to adopt me."

Even inside the dim shadows of his car, Ethan could make out Daryl's ivory teeth encased within his wide-open smile. There was also genuine gratitude shining in his eyes.

"Have I?" Ethan inquired. He paused to gather his thoughts. "I don't see it that way. This isn't just about me performing some penance for my past. You know, the way Catholics do after they go to confession. This is about me getting a second chance to do it right."

Ethan glanced over and observed Daryl narrow his eyes bewilderedly while lifting a hand to his chin. "What do you mean?"

"Okay," Ethan responded, "Let's say I could step into a time machine and return to that day when Sarah informed me that you were looking for a permanent home. And let's say this time, I agreed to the adoption. Daryl, if we had adopted you back then, that would've made you my oldest son today."

Ethan glanced to his right, and in the glare produced by the head-lights of oncoming cars, he could make out a sheen beginning to build around his passenger's eyes.

"Yeah," Daryl replied hoarsely, "I suppose it would."

"You'd have a younger brother and sister," continued Ethan, "And we would've raised all three of you the same. What's more, since you would've grown up in Creve Coeur, Daryl, it's a safe bet most of your life would be completely different today. You never would've been homeless and certainly would not be on trial now for murder."

Ethan noticed how Daryl turned away briefly to glance out the passenger window. He could hear Daryl's breathing, but otherwise, the car had grown quiet. Then, Daryl swiveled back in his seat, and Ethan observed how a frown had replaced his previous smile. It was like Daryl had suddenly put on a different mask in a Greek play.

"Well," Daryl stoically proclaimed, "As they say, you can't change the past."

"*No?*" Ethan replied.

Daryl's long face began to melt. "What do you mean?"

As Ethan slowed to exit at the 6ᵗʰ Street ramp, he glanced over at his passenger and beamed.

"Daryl, there's something I want to share with you. I'd planned to have this conversation after the trial, but since it's come up now, I guess this is as good a time as any."

Not hearing a response, Ethan continued. "Listen, I've already run this by Noah and Jenny, and they're both on board. Daryl, if you agree, I'd like to adopt you legally. It isn't too late. The law allows for the adoption of an adult."

"But *why?*" Daryl inquired.

"Because," Ethan answered, "I want you to know that regardless of what happens in this trial, my commitment to you will continue for as long as I'm alive."

As Ethan pulled into the parking lot next to the Dive STL, he shut off the engine and turned to face Daryl squarely.

"If you agree, Daryl, you'll legally become my son. And for as long as I live, I'll be your dad. This even applies to the instructions in my will."

Daryl bit down gently on his lower lip. Ethan noticed this was his habit whenever he was at a loss for words.

"And this might sound a bit crazy," Ethan admitted with a grin, "But over the past year, I've found a way to consult with Sarah. And I want you to know, Daryl, she was *delighted* with this decision."

Inside the SUV's dim cab, Ethan observed a glistening spot trickling down Daryl's cheek, leaving behind a streak like a trail left by a snail. For a moment, the two men exchanged solicitous glances. Then, finally, Ethan reached over and lightly placed a hand on Daryl's shoulder.

"You see, Daryl, I can't change the past. But I can still do a lot to make things right in the future."

For another moment, silence imbued the inside of the SUV. A street lamp illuminated Daryl's face enough to reveal the moisture surrounding his eyes.

"However," Ethan finally exclaimed, "You won't be able to join us for Thanksgiving dinners from a prison cell. So, let's get out of here and see if we can't complete that Hail Mary pass."

Without waiting for a response, Ethan flung open the car door, climbed out, and approached the bar's front entrance. Daryl swiftly caught up and passed Ethan, darting ahead to open the front door.

Holding the heavy entryway open for Ethan like a formal doorman, Daryl exclaimed, "After you." Then, with a twinkle in his eye and an impish smile, he added, "Dad."

For the next two hours, Ethan and Daryl questioned every bartender, cook, and server they could find. The lights were dim, and the music was loud, but since this was a weeknight before the start of the baseball season, there were only a few patrons gathered around the bar. The high stools around each of the raised tables were mostly empty. The only movement around the outer perimeter of the room came from mounted televisions broadcasting the requisite sports stations.

Ethan began each interrogation by asking if the person had been working the night of the shooting. If they had, Daryl politely inquired if they had seen anything that night or if they knew anyone else who might have. In each case, they came up empty. Ethan then ended the conversation by leaving his card and requesting to please call if anything came to them later. Most of the bar's employees were friendly and polite, but none gave any reason for hope.

The most sympathetic was a bartender in his forties named Jim. This bartender reminded Ethan of Sam Malone, the bar owner in the 1980s television show *Cheers*. Jim promised to keep his ear to the ground and even agreed to take a small stack of Ethan's cards to circulate among his steadiest customers. Jim also gave him the impression that for the clientele who lived nearby, the Dive STL was indeed the place "where everybody knows your name."

Ethan and Daryl wrapped up their dialogue with Jim shortly after eleven o'clock and prepared to leave. Discouragement had visibly etched itself across their faces. As Ethan and Daryl stood and strode toward the front door, they failed to notice an older gentleman on the other side of the bar who had been nursing a large flask of beer while casually listening to their conversation.

chapter

20

Ethan looked up from his legal pad and smiled at his witness. Daryl had delivered a stellar performance. He answered Ethan's questions earnestly and clearly, surpassing all the rehearsals they had run through earlier that morning.

Ethan began the direct examination by asking Daryl to describe the circumstances that had led him down the path to homelessness. Before inquiring about his military experience, Ethan made it a point to "thank him for his service." Next, while Daryl vividly explained the story of Holly and Daisy's tragic car accident, Ethan observed moisture around the eyes of some of the jurors, men and women. Finally, Ethan deftly led the defendant through his version of what had happened the night of the shooting. Daryl laid out the details of his self-defense narrative like a seasoned storyteller.

The direct examination lasted all morning. When the Judge finally recessed the court for lunch, Daryl approached the defense table with a weathered grin. He was visibly proud of his performance, but mentally, Daryl was exhausted. Ethan had purposefully timed the direct to end so his witness would have the lunch break to catch his breath. Tom, Ellen, and Ethan took turns patting Daryl on the back and then led him to a nearby conference room. Lunch would consist of deli sandwiches Ethan had purchased and packed the night before. He wanted to spend the next hour and a half delicately balancing the time between rest for his client and a last-minute rehearsal for the upcoming cross-examination.

At that moment, Ethan was starting to feel cautiously optimistic. After all, there had only been two eyewitnesses to the shooting, and one of them was his client, who had just provided a convincing scenario to support a not-guilty verdict. Charles Graham was the other, and he also told a believable story. Moreover, both men managed to elicit sympathy from the jury at different times. Still, Ethan had damaged some of Charles' credibility during his cross-examination. Now, it would be Daryl's turn. How would his client cope with the hurricane-force winds he would soon encounter? Above all else, Michelle Jones had built a reputation for her lethal cross-examination skills.

When the court reconvened after lunch, Daryl guardedly approached the witness stand like it was the electric chair. Ethan observed how his client inhaled deeply while firmly clenching his lips together. As Michelle Jones looked over her notes, Daryl glanced at the defense table. He looked like a six-year-old boarding the school bus for the first time.

Michelle Jones stood, cleared her throat, and addressed the Judge.

"You honor, may it please the court," she began.

The Judge nodded for her to proceed. Meanwhile, Ethan smiled to reassure Daryl and then darted his eyes toward the jury to redirect his client's attention in their direction. During lunch, Ethan had repeatedly reminded Daryl that the jurors were the only people in the room that mattered. Therefore, he should ignore the prosecutor as much as possible and maintain eye contact with the people sitting in the jury box. They are the ones who hold your fate in their hands.

"So . . . , Mr. Daryl Armstrong," the dragon lady intoned, "You remember that you're under oath, correct? And you understand what that means?"

"Objection!" Ethan immediately pronounced. "Compound question."

The Judge looked down at Ethan with disbelief scrawled across his face. Technically, the prosecutor had asked a second question before the witness had answered the first, but this was an absurdly picky disruption. Ethan knew the Judge would overrule his objection but wanted to buy Daryl a few extra seconds. The confidence Daryl had been exuding all morning appeared to have vaporized, so hopefully, this brief pause would enable him to regain his mojo. Besides, the wording and tone of the prosecutor's opening salvo had been condescending.

"Overruled," Judge Larson quickly shot back without hesitation. He had seen these lawyer tricks throughout his long career.

"Yes," Daryl replied with rising buoyancy. "I understand that I've sworn to tell the truth. That's what I've been doing from the start."

For a moment, Daryl returned the prosecutor's scowl. Then, remembering his coaching, he pivoted back toward the jury.

Michelle Jones smiled and then continued. "Mr. Armstrong, I'd also like to thank you for your service." Then, after a deliberate pause, she added pleasantly, "But I'd like to ask you a few questions about that service. Alright?"

Daryl nodded but did not bother with a verbal response.

"I understand that during your time in Iraq, you stumbled across the bodies of many civilians in Haditha. Is that correct?"

"It is," Daryl responded. Ethan noticed his facial muscles begin to tighten.

"Did you play any role in the killing of those civilians?"

For a moment, Daryl looked like he might leap from his chair and strangle the dragon lady. But, instead, he paused, swallowed hard, and coolly answered her question.

"I never saw the massacre. I simply came across the bodies afterward. So, *no*, I had nothing to do with killing those civilians."

"I see," Michelle Jones responded. After a pause, she added, "However, is it safe to say, Mr. Armstrong, that you returned from the Middle East mentally disturbed by what you had seen over there?"

"Objection!" Ethan bellowed. "The witness is hardly qualified to answer that question."

"Sustained," the Judge responded.

"Alright, fair enough," Michelle Jones replied. "But maybe the witness can answer *this* question. Mr. Armstrong, did you return from your military service with training in the use of sidearms?"

"Yes," answered Daryl, "We carried M4 rifles into long-range settings but used a sidearm in close combat."

"*But*," Michelle Jones retorted, "You were comfortable using your .38 Special on the night of the shootings, weren't you?"

"It wasn't *my* .38 Special," Daryl replied. "As I've already explained, the gun belonged to Frank Abalone. I simply disarmed him and then used it in self-defense."

"Right . . . ," replied the prosecutor, spinning to face the jury. She then snickered and rolled her eyes like they were all sharing a little secret.

The verbal jousting between Michelle Jones and the defendant continued for the next two hours. The lead prosecutor challenged Daryl over every detail concerning his self-defense narrative. She also probed his checkered background and the flaws in his credibility. The prosecuting attorney did her best to paint a picture of the defendant as a dangerous and volatile threat to society. After a deft nod of sympathy for the tragic loss of the defendant's wife and daughter, Michelle Jones emphasized this still did not justify the taking of two innocent lives.

As the cross-examination continued, Daryl appeared to grow stronger. He countered every question like a skillful boxer determined not to get trapped in the corner of the ring. The harshest blows came when the prosecuting attorney questioned Daryl about his alcoholism. He took the punches by admitting to his drinking problem. He then explained, however, that he drank to sedate himself, to avoid, at least temporarily, the horrific memory of the accident that wiped out his family. Daryl unequivocally asserted that while the alcohol tended to make him sad, it never left him angry.

Throughout the cross-examination, Ethan studied the jurors' faces. When Daryl painstakingly explained why he drank, some jurors empathetically furrowed their brows. Clearly, at least a few did not view the defendant as an out-of-control, drunken murderer. Instead, they understood why he had turned to alcohol. Ethan reminded himself that not every jury member had to take Daryl's side. But as long as at least one juror persisted in reasonably doubting his guilt, Michelle Jones would never get the unanimity required for a guilty verdict.

Like every defense lawyer, Ethan had struggled over the decision to put his client on the stand. The Fifth Amendment allowed a person to remain silent in their trial, but once they waived this right, a defendant became fair game and would have to answer all questions posed by the prosecution. They could no longer "plead the Fifth." Ethan began to smile inside as his opponent's cross-examination slowly ran out of steam and neared its end. It might still be close, but his confidence was rising that the jury would either find Daryl not guilty or, at the very least, fail to reach a verdict.

Ethan could visualize the discussion that would soon take place in the jury room. At least some jurors would acknowledge there was a good chance Daryl was guilty. But beyond a reasonable doubt? It was his word against that of Charles Graham. Both had made compelling points, just as both had their shortcomings. In the end, though, Daryl appeared just as sympathetic as the prosecution's primary witness. Charles was a college kid, a frat boy, who had lost a close friend that night. On the other hand, Daryl was a combat veteran whose life had suddenly been shattered in a single heartbeat by a careless driver. So why should the jury be more inclined to take Charles' word over Daryl's?

The worst nightmare for any defense lawyer in this situation was the unknown. So far, Ethan had anticipated every line of questioning pursued by Michelle Jones. He had raised similar questions during their mock rehearsals, and Daryl's performance on the witness stand had been Oscar-worthy. Survive this firestorm from the dragon lady for a few more minutes, and then Ethan was confident he could deliver a closing state- ment that would keep his client from ever going to prison. They were about to enter the final round of the boxing match, and anything short of a prosecution knockout should lead to a defense victory.

"So, Mr. Armstrong, I have just one more avenue to explore." Mi- chelle Jones dramatically paused before continuing.

"Last April, isn't it true you were living in a community of tent en- campments along the banks of the River Des Peres on the city's south side?" Michelle Jones glanced down at her notes to confirm the location. "Let's see," she continued, "I believe it was near the intersection of River Des Peres Boulevard and Gravois Avenue."

Ethan observed the Adam's apple in Daryl's neck begin to quiver. His eyes enlarged, his lips tightened, and his fingers visibly clenched the side arms of the witness chair. Daryl turned toward Ethan with raised eyebrows. He looked like a man staring directly at a streaking locomotive about to leave nothing behind but a large bloodstain on the tracks. This line of questioning had come out of nowhere. Where was Michelle Jones going?

Finally, Daryl replied. "Yes," he uttered. "That sounds correct."

"And at that time," she continued without hesitation, "You shared your tent with a Mr. Burt Bennett, correct?"

"Yes," Daryl replied. "So?"

"This would be the same Burt Bennett you gunned down on the night of August 3rd?"

"As I've stated on multiple occasions," Daryl replied exasperatedly, "I did *not* shoot Burt. Frank Abalone killed him."

"Yes, I know," replied the dragon lady. "That's *your* version of the facts."

"It's the *truth*," Daryl retorted.

"The truth?" responded Michelle Jones. "Okay, let's get to the truth about last April. Isn't it true you were involved in a *violent* scuffle with your roommate, Burt Bennett?"

"What?" Daryl asked. He turned his palms upward to accentuate his confusion.

"You punched Burt, didn't you?" the prosecutor accused. "He was an elderly man who didn't have a chance, did he? And you knocked him flat on his rear."

"I, ah, . . ." While Daryl struggled to answer, the prosecuting attorney continued. Finally, she had the witness up against the ropes and wanted to score a knockout.

"Then, while you were standing over Mr. Bennett, you yelled down at him, didn't you? In fact, you called him a 'dirty N-word,' didn't you?"

"I don't recall any of this," Daryl replied feebly.

"Then," Michelle Jones stated as though she was delivering the final blow, "You threatened to *kill* Mr. Bennett, didn't you? You hollered for everyone to hear that you'd shoot him right there on the spot if you had had a gun."

"No . . . , I don't remember any of that," Daryl mumbled. He shook his head and then looked puzzled at the defense table.

Struggling to regain his composure, he added, "It's true, Burt could be a messy roommate, and we had had a few minor quarrels. But I *never* threatened to kill him. I never threatened to kill anyone."

"How do you know?" Michelle Jones inquired. "You were drinking so heavily at the time you probably wouldn't remember, would you?"

"No," Daryl responded while vigorously shaking his head. "There's no way I could ever have said such a thing, no matter how much I'd been drinking."

"No? No way?" echoed the dragon lady's words. "Mr. Armstrong, do you know a man named Sammy Bordeaux?"

Daryl shook his head but remained silent.

"Because he knows *you*. And he was there that night to witness this little incident."

"*Your honor*," Ethan interrupted thunderously, "Permission to approach?"

When Judge Larson nodded, he and Michelle Jones escorted each other up to the magistrate's desk. Once close enough to place his hands on the edge of the counter, Ethan looked up and whispered, "Your honor, I've never heard of Sammy Bordeaux. He was not on the list of witnesses submitted by the prosecution."

"That's true," admitted Michelle Jones. "That's because we only learned about Mr. Bordeaux last night. The police recently arrested him for robbing a liquor store. In discussions with his defense attorney, Mr. Bordeaux shared this story about the defendant's threats against Burt Bennett. He had heard about this case in the news and indicated a willingness to testify against Mr. Armstrong."

Turning towards Ethan, Michelle Jones interjected, "If the defense prefers, we'll move right now to endorse this witness. You could then call a half-day recess for the defense to conduct its deposition." Then, after a pause, she added, "Your honor, Mr. Bordeaux has vital information that will prove motive in this case. Therefore, you should allow him to testify."

Ethan was flabbergasted. Finally, he responded, "Judge, this is simply one of those times when the prosecution has cut a deal with a jailhouse snitch. I'm sure this Sammy Bordeaux would say *anything* to save his skin."

"Actually, your honor," responded Michelle Jones, "I had hoped it wouldn't be necessary to call this witness. And I still won't," she continued, "Provided Mr. Armstrong here will own up to the threats he made against Burt Bennett."

When Ethan unintentionally glanced toward Daryl, who likely had overheard the prosecutor's offer, he observed his client subtly nod his approval. Meanwhile, Judge Larson briefly glanced down and sighed. His ruling right now was a potential game-changer in the trial. Finally, he swiveled to confront the two impatient faces before him.

"For now," he pronounced, "Let's finish this cross-examination. Then, if the prosecution still wants to call this individual as a witness, I'll entertain their motion to endorse him at that time."

The dragon lady turned towards her adversary and smiled. Ethan shook his head in disgust and then trekked back to his seat. Once she had resumed her position in front of the jury, Michelle Jones folded her arms and repeated the question.

"Mr. Armstrong, do you know a man named Sammy Bordeaux?" Then she added, "Remember, you're under oath. You've already told this court you understand what that means."

By now, Daryl had had the time to gather his thoughts. He had searched his memory and recalled something Sarah had told him many years ago. Back on that day at Creve Coeur Park, when Daryl had wandered into the water to cool off, she had asked whether he had deliberately jumped into the lake. Daryl was about to lie and say he had fallen in by accident. Before he could, however, Sarah told him to tell the truth. "*Always* tell the truth," she preached, "And be prepared to accept the consequences. You might not like the immediate results, but you'll always respect the person you see in the mirror."

"I didn't personally know Sammy Bordeaux," Daryl finally answered, "But I knew of him. And *yes*, he lived in one of those tents in our encampment last year."

Daryl glanced at Ethan but did not wait for a visual cue. Instead, he returned his attention to the prosecutor and added, "Look, Mrs. Jones, I don't remember making those threats against Burt. But back in those days, there's a *lot* I don't remember."

For a moment, silence ruled the courtroom. Daryl looked down while everyone else focused their attention on him. Michelle Jones milked the moment for as long as she could and finally, in the tone of a compassionate mother, asked, "So, Mr. Armstrong, is it at least *possible* you threatened to kill Burt Bennett?"

Daryl looked up to face Michelle Jones squarely. They briefly locked eyes. Then he nodded and, in a whisper, said, "Yes, it's possible. I don't remember doing this, but as I said before, there's a lot I don't remember."

"You don't remember?" Michelle Jones echoed. "Because you were under the influence of alcohol?"

Daryl meekly nodded his agreement.

"And weren't you still under the influence of alcohol on the night of the shootings?"

"Yeah," Daryl answered in a whisper.

"I'm sorry, Mr. Armstrong. Can you repeat your response?"

"*Yes*," Daryl replied, growing visibly agitated.

"*So*," the prosecuting attorney stated decisively, "If it's *possible* you threatened to kill Burt Bennett one year ago while under the influence of alcohol, isn't it just as likely that you repeated this threat less than a year later?"

Daryl hesitated. He looked down at his hands tightly clenched in his lap, forgetting the importance of eye contact. Then, finally, he glanced up at the dragon lady and responded.

"Yeah, it's possible."

"Except *this* time," Michelle Jones proclaimed while gazing at the jury, "You didn't just *make* the threat, did you?"

Before Daryl could answer or Ethan object, Michelle Jones pronounced, "No further questions."

Daryl turned toward his lawyer, wearing the expression of a man who had just fallen overboard and was desperately seeking a life jacket. Ethan briefly considered redirecting his client but could not think of anything to ask that would repair the damage. Once Daryl had stepped out of the witness box, the Judge asked the defense if they had any further witnesses to call. Ethan resignedly said no, that the defense rested. Michelle Jones, evidently satisfied with Daryl's recent admission on the stand, also stated that she had no further witnesses to call.

Judge Larson then reviewed his tentative plans for the following day. First, he wanted to briefly meet with the attorneys on both sides to go over his jury instructions. Then, when the court reconvened, the Judge requested that both sides be ready to give their closing statements. Finally, after the lunch break, the Judge planned to deliver his instructions, and then the jury could have the rest of the afternoon to begin their deliberations.

Twenty minutes later, the courtroom was almost empty. After Tom escorted Ellen out of the courtroom, Ethan and Daryl were the only ones left. They both slumped in their chairs behind the defense table, gazing parallel lines toward the empty witness stand. Simultaneously, they both sighed, exhaling loudly. At a different time, this probably would have elicited smiles, maybe even laughter. However, with the wind completely taken from their sails, both remained visibly shell-shocked.

Ethan and Daryl had plunged so deeply into the doldrums they failed to notice when the door swung open behind them. A man with snow-white hair and a face wrinkled like a prune quietly approached from behind. His age was difficult to determine. He could have been in his eighties, although in this case, he was only 63. He had lived a hard life.

"Mr. Marshall?" he uttered, looking down at a business card in his palm. "Ethan Marshall?"

Ethan and Daryl simultaneously awoke from their stupor and swiveled around to confront the voice.

chapter
21

Ethan walked down Market Street with an extra bounce in his step. He consciously slowed his pace to match that of the two men on his left and right. Bumper-to-bumper rush-hour traffic still choked this main artery in downtown St. Louis. Still, only a few pedestrians were on the sidewalk, and most were walking in the opposite direction. Once the threesome turned right onto 10th Street, the walkway was completely empty.

Ethan turned up the collar of his overcoat to shield himself from the frigid gusts blowing from behind. The narrow street acted like a funnel, accelerating the wind speed. There was still a glimmering in the western sky, but it would soon retreat before the advancing nightfall. The chilly conditions, though, were the last thing on Ethan's mind. Instead, he was replaying the brief conversation that had just occurred back in the courtroom. After meeting Owen Stevenson in person and hearing why he had tracked them down in the Circuit Courts, Ethan suggested they continue this vitally important conversation over dinner.

Daryl, the most familiar with the streets of downtown St. Louis, had suggested grabbing a bite to eat at a pub called the Wheelhouse. For years, he said, one of their cooks had frequently provided him with leftover food. Daryl said it would be gratifying to eat one of their meals inside for once and then be able to leave behind a generous tip. Ethan quickly glanced over their menu on his cell phone and then made a reservation for three. The description of their blackened chicken sandwich had cinched the deal.

Since the Blues hockey team was off on an extended road trip, the restaurant was relatively empty. The three men hung their coats and were seated at a quiet booth near a corner window. A few minutes later, an alluring young waitress with dark hair and even darker eyes introduced herself and took their order for a pitcher of Fitz's root beer. Since Daryl and Tom had begun attending A.A. meetings, no one thought to order alcohol anymore. Ethan smiled at the irony of the name "Hope" on the waitress' nametag. He also observed that Daryl's cheeks were strikingly red in her presence.

Silence hovered within the booth for a minute while the threesome studied their menus. When Hope returned with their pitcher and three empty glasses, she took an order for one blackened chicken sandwich and two Wheelhouse burgers. Ethan noticed how she gazed intently at Daryl when he wavered back and forth over what to order. His bashful, aw-shucks manner appeared to cast a spell over Hope. She giggled like a schoolgirl at his silly jokes, barely noticing the other two men at the table. Ethan had spent ample time with Daryl over the last several months, but this was the first time he had seen his soon-to-be adopted son so cheerful.

After Hope left to put in the food order, Ethan pulled out his cell phone and set it to record the conversation. He also produced a pen and prepared to jot down bullet-point notes on a napkin. Then he looked up to face Owen, seated directly across the table. Beneath a mop of white hair and surrounded by a topo map of wrinkles were two of the bluest eyes Ethan had ever seen. They sparkled like a pair of polished aquamarine stones.

"So, Owen," Ethan began, "I'd like to take you through your story just like I'll do in court. Will that be alright?"

"Sure, sounds like a good plan," he replied. The rapid speed with which he spoke hinted at his edginess. Ethan deliberately paused to refill Owen's glass of root beer. He wanted to calm his potential witness as much as possible.

"Alright," Ethan continued, "Let's start with some personal background. Tell me a little about yourself. Start with your age, marital status, current address, place of employment; you know, the usual stuff."

"Alright." Owen paused to sip his soda, primly wiped his upper lip with a cloth napkin, and then inhaled deeply. "I'm 63 years old. My address is 1531 South 8th Street, apartment 211. It's an apartment complex just north of the Soulard Market. Ah . . . , let's see, what else? I've never been married." After another pause to gather his thoughts, he added, "As for employment, that's a bit tricky. I do part-time maintenance work around my apartment complex to cover the rent. Otherwise, I mostly live off disability payments. Pretty soon, I'll also be able to collect a small pension."

"Disability?" Ethan inquired quizzically.

"Yes," responded Owen tentatively. "You know, some mental health issues. Mostly depression."

Ethan glanced at Daryl but remained silent. He wanted to allow his potential witness to share more when he was ready. Owen leaned back in his chair, slurped another sip of root beer, and peered wearily through the large picture window out to the street. For a moment, he appeared captivated by something out in the darkness. Finally, Owen glanced back at Ethan as though there had never been a pause in the conversation.

"You see, I was a high school math teacher in the St. Louis Public Schools for many years. I got my degree from UMSL, but because my mother, who's now deceased, was in a wheelchair, I had to live at home to care for her. So during those years, I only went out to attend class or to work as a part-time waiter."

Ethan noticed how Daryl leaned forward, listening raptly to every word. He was laser-focused on Owen's narrative. Observing Daryl's increased receptiveness, Owen twisted to face him more directly.

"I was an only child," continued Owen, "And I was always pretty introverted by nature. So I seldom dated through high school or college, and by the time I got my first teaching job, I'd come to accept that I'd always be a bachelor."

Ethan flashed a sympathetic smile. He was pleased by how his witness was steadily opening up and wanted this to continue.

"Roosevelt High School, where I taught, became my whole life," Owen intoned. "After my mother passed away, I gradually joined a circle of friends amongst the teaching staff. We'd go out to happy hour every

Friday to blow off steam. And as a hobby, I started to play chess. Pretty soon, I spent most of my weekends playing in local tournaments. So, needless to say, I was overjoyed when they opened that new club in the Central West End. Did you know this city has recently emerged as the nation's chess capital?"

An embarrassing grin crept across Owen's face. "I know . . . ," he uttered, "You could look up the word geek in the dictionary and find my picture next to the definition." Then, after a brief pause, he added sheepishly, "But I was happy, you know? It's all relative. Compared to some, my life may have seemed pretty dull, but I was living the high life compared to what was soon coming."

Ethan and Daryl exchanged glances and simultaneously arched their eyebrows. "So what happened?" Daryl inquired.

"It was all *so* stupid," Owen uttered. "I was climbing the front steps of school on a snowy morning and slipped on a patch of ice. I fell. *Hard.* I remember looking around to see if anyone had noticed. The pain hadn't registered yet, so I was actually more concerned about people laughing. There was no one around, though. It was way too early. But when I tried to stand, the pain in my back was excruciating."

Once again, Owen paused to gather his thoughts while Ethan and Daryl patiently waited for him to continue.

"That one slip and fall," Owen finally continued, "Changed my life, and *not* for the better. I never spent the night in the hospital, but the pain became chronic. It was like someone was torturing me twenty-four hours a day. I tried to learn to live with it, but it never let up, even after countless visits to doctors and chiropractors. The school gave me time off with pay, probably out of fear I'd file a lawsuit or something. But I didn't want to stay home. So, I had to do *something.*"

Ethan observed how Owen's piercingly blue eyes began to turn glassy. Minus the wrinkles, he had the eyes of Paul Newman. Before Owen could continue, Daryl cut him off.

"It was Percodan, wasn't it?"

Owen was stunned. He looked up at Daryl like he had just seen a ghost. "How'd you know?"

"Let's just say I've been around," Daryl answered.

"Well," Owen continued, "Then you must know that stuff is incredibly addictive. When my doctors refused to write more prescriptions, I started writing them myself. I was desperate. Pretty soon, I got arrested. Fortunately, the prosecution was sympathetic. I agreed to spend time in a rehab facility in return for a guilty plea. Of course, I also had to surrender my teaching license."

Owen glanced around as if others were eavesdropping. Then he continued. "After that, I bounced around from one menial job to another. Thanks to my back, keeping any jobs involving physical labor was hard. But as I said earlier, I've managed to get by on disability payments."

As Owen took another timeout to polish off his root beer, Ethan and Daryl exchanged apprehensive glances. Their potential savior witness was obviously intelligent, but Owen was the textbook definition of an unfulfilled life. Ethan and Daryl subtly nodded in sympathy toward the fragile man seated across the table. Finally, Owen continued his narrative.

"My social life, what there was of it, also changed since I no longer saw my teaching buddies every day. I tried to return to playing chess, but my game *seriously* declined. Chess had always been a source of frustration, but now, it had become intolerable. So, I started spending more time in neighborhood bars to get out of my apartment. Beer soon took the place of Percodan. Some might call me an alcoholic today, but in my defense, I usually avoid getting drunk. And recently, the Dive has become my favorite watering hole."

At the mention of the Dive, Ethan and Daryl snapped to attention. They understood everything Owen had been saying up to this point was intended to lay a foundation for whatever he may have seen outside the Dive on the night of the shooting. Ethan and Daryl slid to the edge of their wooden chairs, eagerly anticipating what was coming next.

Before Owen could say more, Hope appeared with a cart bearing three heavy plates. A fog of silence settled over the table. Ethan smiled compassionately at Owen while Hope reached across to set down their dinners. When Daryl looked up and said thank you, Hope rewarded him with a wink and a smile. Once she stepped away, Ethan turned back to confront Daryl.

"I'll minimize much of this during his direct exam," he pronounced. "It's a compelling story, but it won't do us much good on the witness stand." Then, pivoting back toward his savior witness, Ethan added, "Let's get to the part that *could* do us some good. Owen, you mentioned that you liked hanging out at the Dive. I assume you were there on the night of the shooting?"

"Yes," he responded with a loud sigh, "I was there." Owen appeared noticeably happy to change the conversation's direction. "I've made a few friends at the Dive, and I especially like Jim, the bartender. I make it a point to hang out there whenever he's working."

"Okay, Owen, so let's talk about the night of the shootings. When did you first observe something out of the ordinary?"

"Well," answered Owen, "It wasn't until I walked out of the Dive to head home. It'd been a quiet evening, and my other buddies had already left."

"How much did you drink that evening?" Ethan interrupted.

"Only a couple of beers," responded Owen. "I've told Jim about my dependency background, so he knows when to cut me off."

"So," Daryl eagerly interjected, "What did you see when you left the Dive?"

"I'd only taken a few steps before hearing this loud commotion coming from the other side of an empty parking lot. So, out of curiosity, I angled in that direction to get a better view."

"It was pretty dark," Ethan asserted. "How well could you see?"

"There was a security light on one side of the parking lot. It was enough for me to make out three figures standing in front of what looked like a tent."

"Can you describe them? What were they doing?" Ethan inquired.

"Two of them were white, and it looked like they were friends," Owen answered. "They were taunting the third person, who I think was African-American."

"Could you hear what they were saying?" asked Daryl.

"Not everything. But, it appeared that the African American man, the victim, was homeless because I heard them saying how he should get a job and stop harassing people on the streets. Oh, and I also heard them call the poor guy a . . ."

"The N-word?" Ethan guessed, finishing Owen's sentence.

"Yeah, I guess that's the best way to say it nowadays, isn't it?"

"So, *then* what happened," Daryl asked impatiently.

"They started to shove the African-American gentleman. I think he was older because he mostly wobbled around and couldn't defend himself. But I could tell he was getting agitated. Finally, when the older guy took a step toward his abusers, one of them pulled something out of his jacket. I couldn't make out what it was, but suddenly, it flashed twice. At the same time, I heard what sounded like shots. At that point, I could see the African-American crumble to the pavement in front of the tent."

"And what were you doing while all this was going on?" Ethan interrupted.

"I just stood there in shock," replied Owen. His eyes grew larger, constricting the wrinkles on his forehead. "You know, it was like watching a car crash in slow motion. I couldn't look away even if I tried. And since it was dark, it seemed safe to observe since I was mostly hidden in the shadows."

"So," Daryl probed excitedly, "What happened next?"

"Suddenly, a fourth figure emerged from the shadows. I couldn't see this person clearly, but he was younger and appeared to be white. It looked like he was wearing jeans and a white tee shirt. This guy lunged at the shooter and knocked the gun out of his hand. There was a scramble, and the guy in the white tee shirt must've come up with the gun because when he stood, he fired it at one of the original two. After the first one went down, the guy with the gun shot at the second. He appeared wounded but could still turn around and run away."

There was a sudden pause in the conversation. Ethan glanced down at the table and noticed their food was largely untouched. When he peered up at Daryl, there was a look of unbridled joy on his face. Finally, when Ethan returned his gaze to Owen, he observed their savior witness pointing straight at Daryl and grinning.

"*Holy* cow," Owen exclaimed. "I'm *so* dumb. That was *you*, wasn't it?" His eyes were glued to Daryl. "*You* were the guy who shot those two creeps."

Daryl looked at Ethan and smiled exuberantly. Then he turned back to confront Owen. "So, you recognize me?"

"Well, not exactly," answered Owen. "It was pretty dark, and you must've been at least fifty yards away. Damn, this whole time, I just assumed you were another lawyer. But you're the *defendant*, aren't you? Hmmm. That should've been obvious, but I don't always see the obvious."

"So, Owen," Ethan interrupted, "What did you do when you saw the second bully turn to flee?"

"Initially, I froze," Own replied. "He was coming straight at me, and I was afraid the guy with the gun would chase him. So, after a few seconds, I ducked back into the Dive. Then, when I realized they might follow me inside, I headed straight for the men's room and hid in a stall."

Owen paused when he saw the smirks on their faces. "I know," he stated with a smile, "I'm like the Cowardly Lion bursting through the window in *The Wizard of Oz*. But, honestly, I wasn't just afraid of the gun."

"No?" Daryl inquired as he finally took a bite from his Wheelhouse burger.

Owen sighed and looked down at his lap. For a moment, the only sound came from the slurping of Daryl's soda as he washed down the first bite of hamburger. Then, finally, Owen peered up with embarrassment.

"Honestly," he proclaimed, "I just didn't want to get involved." He looked from Ethan to Daryl, searching for validation. "I knew shots had been fired, and three men had been hit. I knew if I emerged from the bathroom, they'd ask what I'd seen, and the next thing you know, I'd have to be a witness in a trial where I'd end up pissing someone off. So, . . ."

"So," Daryl exclaimed scornfully, "You hid in the bathroom until it was safe enough to slip out without being noticed." Indignation had replaced Daryl's grin.

"I'm afraid so," Owen responded timidly. "Look, I'm not proud of my actions that night. But after my previous run-in with the law, I didn't want to go anywhere near cops or courts."

"I get it," Ethan pronounced understandably. He glanced over at Daryl and slightly lifted his eyebrows. The unspoken message was to chill, not to scare off this witness.

"So," Daryl queried more calmly, "Why did you change your mind?"

"Yes," Ethan added, "Why did you come to find us today in the courtroom?"

Owen gazed at Ethan and then Daryl with his cerulean blue eyes. A smile parted the wrinkles around his mouth.

"It was because of what you guys said," he finally answered. "You must not have noticed me last night at the Dive, but I saw both of you. I'd been talking to Jim when you first came in. So when he walked over to the other side of the bar to speak with you, I laid low, nursed my final beer of the night, and listened to your conversation."

Ethan glanced at Daryl and inquired, "Did you notice Owen last night?"

When Daryl shook his head, Owen grinned. "Well, that's the story of my life. I'm like the fly that blends into the wallpaper. However, that talent to remain invisible sometimes can come in handy."

Twisting back toward Owen, Ethan asked, "What did you hear us say that convinced you to change your mind?"

"There were several things," Owen answered thoughtfully. He glanced toward Ethan and continued. "First, when I heard you tell Jim your version of the shooting, I realized it was identical to what I'd seen. Understanding it *was* self-defense, I realized it would be a cruel injustice if your client spent the rest of his life in a state pen just because I was too cowardly to come forward."

Ethan nodded and waited for Owen to continue.

"Second, I saw the look on your face when Ethan was talking to Jim." Owen pivoted to confront Daryl. "As I said, I thought you were a lawyer, too, since I assumed the defendant was locked up in jail. Nevertheless, you have a kind face, and you appeared to have strong feelings about this trial. When you think about it, it's easier to care less about others when those others remain anonymous. But when you put a face to their story, it takes on greater urgency. Seeing the expressions on your faces last night made it a lot harder to block you out of my mind."

Ethan nodded approvingly. "Anything else?"

Owen turned back to face him, and once again, the wrinkles around his mouth expanded into a broad grin.

"Yes, Mr. Marshall, there is one other thing." He paused to collect his thoughts. "I heard what you said to Jim last night about your client. I didn't understand everything, but it sounded like you've taken a special interest in this young man. You didn't sound like the typical lawyer who is only in it for the money. I heard you say that your client was, and I quote, 'like a son to you, that you'd do anything to keep him out of prison.'"

Ethan gazed toward Daryl and smiled. Then he turned back toward Owen and reached across the table to pat his hand.

"Well, my friend," Ethan pronounced, "Whatever the reasons, I'm glad you found us."

Sensing he could finally take a break from speaking, Owen nodded, reached for his lukewarm Wheelhouse burger, and took a giant bite. Hope suddenly reappeared to ask about the food. She had probably noticed how much of it had gone uneaten. Ethan observed that she unobtrusively placed a light hand on Daryl's shoulder while she spoke.

Hope's interruption gave all three men a chance to dive into their plates, finally making her smile. After she departed, silence engulfed the table, giving Ethan time to clarify his thoughts. Finally, after a couple of minutes, he put down the remnants of his sandwich, finished chewing, and clapped his hands together like he was about to make an announcement.

"So," he declared, "This is what I think we should do." Then, directly confronting the face across the table, he asked, "Owen, can you meet us in the same courtroom tomorrow morning at nine o'clock sharp?"

Owen's mouth was full, but he vigorously nodded.

"Good!" stated Ethan. "Then what I'll do before the jury returns is to make a motion to endorse you as a witness."

Daryl crammed the final piece of Wheelhouse burger into his mouth, wiped around his lips with a napkin, and tilted forward with mounting interest.

"This will enrage the prosecutor," continued Ethan, "She'll argue you came out of nowhere at the last moment and that I had already rested our case."

"Shouldn't you argue this up at the bench?" Daryl inquired, "Or even privately in the judge's chambers?" The food still in his mouth partially muffled his words.

"Not initially," answered Ethan. "I want my motion to be on the record. That way, if the judge denies the motion, the written transcript will support our appeal."

"I see," Daryl said, nodding. "So, what do you think about our chances now? I mean, if Owen gets to testify, it'll win our case, won't it?"

"To be honest," Ethan replied, "I'm not sure Owen will get to testify. Judges tend to be leery of witnesses who appear at the last moment. Judge Larson will want to know *why* Owen didn't come forward sooner. After I explain Owen's change of heart, and more importantly, if I can convince him that your whole life hinges on this decision, he'll hopefully grant our motion. If he does, then *yes*, our chances will greatly improve."

Silence returned to the booth momentarily while all three men considered Ethan's final words. Then Hope reappeared with the check, which Ethan automatically grabbed. As she turned to leave, Daryl climbed out of the booth, saying he needed to use the men's room. Ethan then spun back to face Owen.

"Would you like to walk back with us to the courthouse? My car's in a nearby garage, and I'd happily give you a lift home."

"I don't mind walking," Owen responded.

"Nonsense," replied Ethan. "It's dark outside, and it's cold."

"The walk back to your car will be almost as far as my walk home," Owen replied.

Ethan nodded in agreement and, without saying a word, yanked out his cell phone, tapped the screen a few times, and then glanced up.

"Sir," he stated, "Your ride home will be here in three and a half minutes." When Owen stared back quizzically, Ethan added, "Uber. I just ordered you a ride home. Come on. I'll join you outside to wait. We'll be looking for a gray Toyota Camry."

Owen shook his head and grinned as he stood and grabbed his coat. "I've heard of Uber but never used one. Will I need to pay for the ride when I get home?"

"No, of course not," answered Ethan. "It's on me. It's the least I can do."

Ethan threw cash on the table, slid on his overcoat, and followed Owen toward the front door. Along the way, he observed Daryl chatting with Hope. Ethan managed to make eye contact and pointed toward the exit. Daryl nodded and held up a finger, indicating he would join them in a minute.

Outside, the chilly breeze was invigorating. Ethan felt lighter, as though a weighty burden had just been lifted from his shoulders. He glanced at his phone and smiled as he saw headlights rounding the corner. "Here comes your ride," Ethan uttered.

As the Camry pulled to the curb, Ethan reached over to shake Owen's hand vigorously.

"My friend," he pronounced. "You did the right thing coming forward. The world would be a much better place if everyone did what you just did."

Owen smiled but remained silent. Finally, he pulled the car door open, but before climbing in, he looked back and asserted, "Don't you worry, Ethan, I'll be there tomorrow at 9:00. Sharp! And thank you for dinner."

Ethan nodded. Owen climbed into the backseat, and Ethan shut the door behind him. As the Camry pulled away, Ethan looked up to see Daryl standing beside him.

"Get her number?" Ethan inquired.

"You bet," answered Daryl with a beaming smile.

Ethan glanced at the man he soon intended to adopt and, for a moment, thought he was actually glowing as though he was radioactive.

"You know, Ethan, it's been *so* many years since a woman smiled at me, and I actually felt like smiling back." Then, after a brief pause, he asked, "Think her name's just a coincidence?" Then, without waiting for a reply, he added, "I think it's a good omen."

chapter
22

Ethan anxiously paced the hallway outside the courtroom. He glanced at his watch for the fourth time in five minutes. It now read 9:01. Owen was officially late.

"You need to relax," Daryl proclaimed optimistically. "He'll be here soon enough."

Daryl was now comfortably slouching on a wooden bench.

"You're not even a little concerned?" Ethan inquired.

"The man said he'd be here. Besides, I have a good feeling about Owen. I don't believe he'd go to all the trouble of tracking us down just to bail when we needed him the most."

Before Ethan could respond, a bell chimed, indicating the elevator door was about to open. Daryl and Ethan spun around just in time to see Owen cautiously step out, leaving a crowd behind. When he spotted them, a smile burst across Owen's face. He removed the tattered newsboy cap from his head and strode with a hand extended to greet his new friends.

"Sorry guys," he exclaimed apologetically, "I would've been here sooner, but I got off on the wrong floor, and the elevator took forever to return."

"That's quite alright," Ethan replied. "But we need to go in right now."

Ethan placed a hand on the small of Owen's back to guide him into the courtroom. He instructed his witness to take a seat behind the defense table. Then, Ethan and Daryl took their usual seats in front of

Owen. They exchanged nervous glances while simultaneously exhaling. The bailiff called the court into session a minute later and asked everyone to stand while Judge Larson entered the courtroom.

The Judge marched in from the rear, fell into his plush leather chair, and scanned the room. First, he noted, to his satisfaction, that the jury box was empty. After all, Judge Larson had instructed the bailiff to keep the panel out while he reviewed his instructions for the jury. Next, he gazed at the two tables before him, mentally taking roll to confirm that the defendant and all the attorneys were present. Finally, he grabbed his gavel and banged it a bit too hard on his desk.

Ethan responded to the sharp crack like a starting pistol going off. He immediately jumped out of his seat and announced he wanted to make a motion. Judge Larson chuckled a bit at the defense lawyer's curious enthusiasm so early in the morning.

"Go ahead, counselor," the Judge intoned. "I'm all ears."

"Your honor," Ethan exclaimed, "It's now *our* turn to make a motion to endorse a witness." He glanced back at Owen to be sure his new buddy had not fled. "I know it's late in the trial, your honor, and that this is highly unusual, but an eye witness to the crime came forward last night, and this morning, we'd like to move to endorse him as a defense witness."

For a brief moment, silence ruled the courtroom. Then, as though Ethan had aroused a sleeping dragon, Michelle Jones barked, "We *object,* your honor!"

Every head in the room turned instantly in her direction.

"This is not just highly unusual. This is completely outrageous." After a brief pause to catch her breath, the prosecutor continued, "Less than 24 hours ago, the defense rested. *Rested,* your honor. Now, they suddenly have an eyewitness?"

Ethan interrupted, "You *honor . . .*"

Before he could say more, the Judge banged his gavel three times. He then calmly laid it on his desk and lifted both hands as though surrendering. He wanted the gesture to calm both sides and restore order. It worked.

"Mr. Marshall," Judge Larson inquired coolly, "Is your new witness present in court?"

Ethan turned partially and gestured toward Owen. "He's right here, your honor. This is Mr. Owen Stevenson. I just met him myself for the first time last night. Your honor, he has quite a story to tell."

"Your *honor*," the dragon lady countered, "This is most dubious. I've never even heard of *Mr.* Owen Stevenson. I don't know anything about this witness. If Mr. Marshall's allowed to pull a witness out of his hat after he's rested his case, that'll become a slippery slope leading to even more magic acts."

Ethan had purposefully saved his most persuasive argument for this very moment. He inhaled a deep breath.

"Your honor," he stated evenly, "Under most circumstances, Mrs. Jones' arguments should win the day. Regrettably, however, these are *not* most circumstances."

Ethan observed that Judge Larson was gazing intently at him. He had clasped his fingers together, and his lips were locked tightly into a firm grimace. Then, the shadow of a smile crept across the Judge's face. Judge Larson contemplatively raised one hand to his chin to conceal his rising interest in the legal drama unfolding before him.

"A man's life is in jeopardy," Ethan continued. "If Mr. Stevenson is not allowed to testify, there's an excellent chance that an innocent man will spend the rest of his life in prison. In addition, your honor, there are valid reasons why Mr. Stevenson waited until now to come forward. If you allow him to testify, he can explain all this."

Michelle Jones opened her mouth to respond, but the Judge again raised his palms to cut her off. He then swiveled his chair toward the window to stare at the fluttering American flag. Ethan unknowingly leaned toward Daryl and placed a hand on his shoulder. He sucked in a deep breath to await the most critical moment of the trial. Judge Larson continued to gaze off into space as though lost in a trance. Then, a smile slowly creased his face, and he returned to the courtroom.

"Here's what we'll do," the Judge finally declared. "Today is Wednesday. I'd like this trial to go to the jury by Friday morning so that, hopefully, we can have a verdict before the weekend." The Judge paused, almost as if trying to build up the anticipation on both sides.

"Mr. Marshall," he continued at last, "I'm going to *grant* your motion."

The air rushed out of Ethan's lungs like a pair of balloons deflating. Then, the Judge turned to face the defense table squarely.

"Since your witness is present this morning, I'll provide you with a conference room so Mrs. Jones can conduct a deposition and prepare for her cross-examination."

Twisting to face the prosecutor, he added, "I know this is short notice, Mrs. Jones, but I'll grant you the entire day to complete your task. Tomorrow morning, we'll hear from this witness. After that, we'll do the closing statements in the afternoon and then send this case to the jury."

Glancing up to address the entire courtroom, the Judge concluded, "I know this will pose a hardship, especially on the jury. However, despite the adage that 'justice delayed is justice denied,' I've always believed that 'justice rushed is justice crushed.' One more day will not make much difference in the grand scope of a man's life."

Judge Larson leaned back in his plush chair, folded his arms, and smiled satisfactorily at the wisdom of his ruling. Then, he reached forward, picked up his gavel, and slammed it to reinforce his decision. When the buzz throughout the room finally subsided, Judge Larson asked the attorneys on both sides to join him in chambers to briefly review the details of Owen's deposition. Next, the Judge turned toward the bailiff, requesting that he release the jury for the day with his apologies. Finally, he adjourned the court, stood up, and exited through the room's rear door.

A commotion exploded as several conversations concurrently ignited throughout the courtroom. Without hesitation, Ethan spun around and huddled with Daryl, Tom, and Owen.

"Let's keep this in perspective," Ethan whispered. "We still have a long way to go." Then, turning towards his new star witness, he continued, "Owen, you're going to face a lethal grilling from Mrs. Jones, first in today's deposition and then in tomorrow's cross-examination."

He glanced at the prosecution table and locked eyes with the dragon lady. If her scowl could transform into a laser beam, he and his little assemblage would instantly vaporize into a mound of ashes.

"Don't worry," Owen whispered, "I'm up to it."

Ethan turned back to face his witness. Owen's crystal blue eyes, encircled by furrows and wrinkles, unveiled a steely resolve.

"I know what I saw that night," he continued. "Your client's *not* guilty. He was simply defending himself from a couple of bullies, and there's *no* way the state should punish him for a crime he didn't commit. It would be a mockery of justice, and I'm more determined than ever to keep that from happening."

Ethan nodded as the corners of his mouth turned upward. Whatever concerns he had harbored just minutes earlier while awaiting his witness to arrive had dissipated entirely. Now, his confidence in Owen was rising by the minute. After reassuringly patting his new star witness on the shoulder, Ethan turned back toward the defense table, reached into his leather case, pulled out a legal pad, and handed it over to his partner.

"Since we're pressed for time, Tom, why don't you and Daryl polish these questions for Owen's direct while I sit through his deposition?"

"Sure," responded Tom, "We'll just do it right here."

Hearing Michelle Jones clear her throat, Ethan glanced towards the prosecution table, nodded, and then turned to follow her into the judge's chambers.

"This shouldn't take long," he uttered over his shoulder. "Meanwhile, Owen, you stay here until we need you."

Twenty minutes later, Ethan reemerged from the judge's chamber. He was beaming like a teenager who had purchased a six-pack for the first time with his fake ID.

"Man, she's pissed," he pronounced excitedly. "The more I talked about Owen, the more enraged she became. Until now, the prosecution must've thought they had this case in the bag. Now, they're afraid that if Owen lives up to his billing, their case will crumble like a house of cards. Let's face it; we now have two credible eyewitnesses to their one. That should create more than enough reasonable doubt."

Daryl, Tom, and Owen were enthralled, like high school kids on the last day of school. Try as he might, Ethan could not repress his mounting confidence. For a moment, silence held sway as the group processed his words. Then, finally, Ethan glanced at his watch and gently nudged Owen toward the back of the courtroom.

"Let's get going, my friend," Ethan uttered. "It's show time."

Daryl and Tom watched them depart. As the door swished behind them, Tom pointed toward a chair at the defense table and nodded for Daryl to sit. Then, he unexpectedly let out a chuckle.

"I don't mean to add pressure," Tom murmured, "But there goes your *entire* future."

Daryl arched his eyebrows, exhaled loudly, and slowly shook his head. He then glanced at the legal pad laden with Owen's direct examination questions. Daryl motioned for Tom to join him, and then, for the next three hours, they went over every word. Since Daryl had heard Owen's story the night before, he assumed the witness' role in rehearsing the lively exchange planned for the following day. The goal was to develop a slate of questions that would form the basis of a natural conversation while always keeping the spotlight on Owen.

During the start of their lunch break at a nearby sports pub in Ball-park Village, next to Busch Stadium, Tom received a text from Ethan. For a long moment, he studied the screen of his cell phone. Daryl waited patiently, pausing his assault on another bowl of chili. Finally, he could not wait any longer.

"Well?" he inquired. "Is it from Ethan? How'd it go?"

Tom glanced up from the phone and then cocked his head in bewilderment.

"I *think* it went well," he finally answered.

"Why do you say that?" Daryl asked anxiously.

Pointing at the screen of his phone, Tom answered, "Because it says right here that 'It went well.'"

A smile brightened Daryl's face. "You *schmuck*. Why didn't you say that from the start? What else did Ethan say?"

"Not much," answered Tom. He dipped a toasted ravioli into a small bowl of marina sauce, bathed it thoroughly, and then crammed the entire piece of stuffed pasta into his mouth. Daryl had to wait at least thirty seconds before Tom could resume. When he finally did, Tom's first words were, "Man, I *love* this stuff. Toasted ravioli alone should earn St. Louis a place in the international foodies hall-of-fame."

Daryl rolled his eyes but could not stifle a smile. Then he pressed, "Are you going to answer my question?"

"What question?" Tom inquired while reddening a white napkin with the sauce spilling from his mouth.

"What *else* did Ethan say?"

"Oh, *that* question," Tom replied. "Just that we're to meet him for an early dinner tonight. Five o'clock, at J. Gilbert's next to the West County Shopping Center."

"What?" Daryl asked quizzically. "Any idea why?"

"No," responded Tom. "I just know it's a pricy place where Ethan likes to go for special occasions. He recommended it to me when I was looking for a place to take Ellen for her birthday. Their steak was one of the most tender I've ever eaten. "

"*Huh?*" Daryl replied. "Man, stop with the food descriptions. Is that all you care about? Tell me what you think this dinner means regarding the *trial.*"

"Look, buddy, I gave up drinking. So, *yeah*, food has taken on a new meaning for me. Is that alright with you?"

Daryl leaned back in his chair and grinned. He had learned that if you waited long enough, Tom would always get back to the original subject. Eventually.

"Okay, as I see it," Tom finally rejoined, "There are two possibilities. One, tonight's dinner is a celebration. At the very least, Ethan must think that Owen will bowl them over when the trial resumes tomorrow. Of course, the second possibility is that Ethan wants your last meal as a free man to be as memorable as possible."

"Did I mention you're a *real* shmuck?" Daryl responded.

After their leisurely lunch, Tom drove Daryl back to Ethan's house. Tom had recently moved out to take up residence in Ellen's condo. However, Daryl wanted to shower and change into more comfortable clothes for dinner. The trek south on I-270 during the early stages of rush hour was mainly stop-and-go, but they still managed to arrive at the restaurant with a few minutes to spare. As Tom and Daryl approached the hostess' podium, Ethan flagged them down from a nearby table parked next to a gas fireplace. He and Owen were basking in the warmth of the dancing flames and nursing a bottle of wine that was already more than half empty.

"Hey guys," Ethan gushed, "Come on over and join us."

Remembering Tom and Daryl's recently pledged sobriety, Ethan casually lowered the bottle of wine to the floor. He then pointed toward two empty chairs directly across the table and beckoned them to sit. Tom and Daryl shed their coats, draped them over the backs of their chairs, and sat down, sporting eager expressions. The four men faced each other briefly beneath a cloak of silence. Each waited for one of the others to break the ice.

"Well?" Daryl finally queried. "How'd it go?"

"As I said in my earlier text to Tom," Ethan replied, "It went well. But as you see from the empty chairs at this table, we're still waiting for three more people. So . . . , since you've already waited this long, I hope you don't mind being patient a little longer. That way, I only have to tell this story one time."

"Okay, fair enough," Tom proclaimed. "But who else are we waiting for?"

Before Ethan could respond, he peered over Tom's shoulder, grinned cheerfully, and then stood up and waved. "*Ellen*," he called. "Over here."

Tom's face immediately brightened. He strolled around the table and greeted Ellen with a warm hug. Then Tom directed her to an empty chair next to him. He helped Ellen remove her beige overcoat and held her chair as she sat.

"Tom, to partially answer your question, I wanted Ellen to join us. I figured you wouldn't mind."

Ethan smiled and winked at his friend. Meanwhile, Ellen introduced herself to Owen, although she already knew who he was and why he held a prominent spot at this table.

Tom glanced at Ellen, and they exchanged knowing smiles. Then, after a few more pleasantries, Tom gestured toward the remaining two empty seats at the table. Instead of responding, Ethan rocketed up again to welcome two more people who had just entered the restaurant.

"Jenny. Matt. Over *here*!"

Jenny waddled towards the table while forcing a grin across her reddened face. Ethan carefully embraced his daughter, mindful of her bulging belly. Jenny looked like her water could break at any moment. Matt helped remove his wife's maroon peacoat, draped it over the back of her chair and then assisted as she judiciously descended into her seat. Once everyone was finally situated, Ethan introduced Owen to his final two guests. The mood brightened even more when Ethan referred to him as "our man of the hour."

Boundless anticipation loomed over the table. It was early, so the restaurant was still relatively empty. Ethan scanned around the circle, taking in the expression on everyone's face. Framed by sinuous wrinkles, Owen's grin bespoke the satisfaction of someone who already knew the expectant news. The fireplace glow behind him created an aura reflecting his current stature within this small band. Jenny was still radiant but struggled to catch her breath. Matt, her dutiful husband, gaped at her with genuine regard. Then there were Tom and Ellen. They had become a serious couple, always holding hands, speaking in whispers, and finishing each other's sentences. Finally, there was Daryl, who tried to appear nonchalant but, with more on the line than anyone else, was the most eager to hear what Ethan had to say.

Ethan cleared his throat, but before he could speak, a middle-aged waiter in a white collared shirt accessorized by a black bow tie and a gold vest glided up to the table. He introduced himself as Ken, provided menus to the latecomers, and then spent the next minute reviewing the night's specials. The circle of diners respectfully smiled and nodded, patiently waiting to give their drink orders. Meanwhile, Ethan observed how Daryl's left leg began to vibrate nervously.

Noting that everyone already had a full glass of ice water, Ethan recognized that any more delay would be needlessly cruel. So, as soon as Ken departed to retrieve a tray of soda and iced tea, Ethan raised his glass of water dripping with condensation.

"I'd like to offer a toast," Ethan boomed loud enough to drown out the side conversations around the table. "First, to Owen, our hero who courageously came forward last night to exonerate Mr. Daryl Armstrong."

Everyone clinked their glasses of iced water but kept them raised while waiting anxiously for the second item on Ethan's list.

"Second, to Mr. Daryl Armstrong, who will permanently remain a free man as of this moment."

The circle of diners was so collectively shocked they neglected to clink their dripping glasses. A hush fell over the table. The only sound was Frank Sinatra crooning *My Way* in the background over the restaurant's sound system. It was Daryl who finally broke the silence.

"Are you *kidding* me?" he queried. Then, after his face erupted into a broad grin, he reworded the question at an even higher volume. "Are you *serious*?"

"Does this mean the trial's over?" Tom added.

Ethan, who still had his glass partially raised, broke into a broad grin and fervently nodded. For a moment, he was unable to speak. Finally, like floodwaters breaking through a dam, Ethan gushed, "*Yes*, the trial's over."

"Did Michelle Jones drop the charges?" Ellen inquired in a surprisingly calm tone.

"Yes," Ethan immediately answered. "To make a long story short, Owen came through with flying colors. This man was credible and *amazingly* persuasive. Once his deposition was over, the prosecuting team retreated into the hallway for a short break. When they returned, the dragon lady announced she'd be dropping *all* charges."

Applause spontaneously exploded around the table. Ethan rose, soon followed by everyone else. Three men sitting at the bar across the room suddenly turned toward the uproar, and one raised his beer in salute. Behind them, Ethan could see the image of Michelle Jones on a television monitor. Everyone took turns hugging Daryl. Ellen handed him a cloth napkin for his watery eyes. Then, the diners offered hugs and handshakes to Owen, who modestly grinned, enjoying his moment in the spotlight.

After a few minutes, the commotion gradually subsided, and the small crowd sat down to give their dinner orders to Ken. Once the waiter departed, Tom turned to Ethan with a question.

"This may be asking the obvious, Ethan, but why do you think Michelle Jones dropped the charges so close to the end of the trial?"

Quiet descended over the table as everyone eagerly awaited Ethan's response. Even the bar patrons, who must have been eavesdropping, grew silent. Ethan glanced around and smiled, enjoying his opportunity to spout an opinion everyone appeared anxious to hear. Finally, Ethan responded as though he was about to begin a story for a circle of children.

"Outside the courthouse, the press was waiting with an ambush. I purposefully kept Owen inside since he'd already said he didn't want the media attention. And knowing there's probably some crazies out there who'll never accept that a couple of West County college kids could be the villains in this story, I don't blame him."

Ethan paused while quietly acknowledging Owen's appreciative smile. Then he continued without skipping a beat.

"I explained that a reliable eyewitness had come forward to support Daryl's self-defense position and that no one would ever have been hurt if those kids from Eureka had not decided to go hunting the homeless after the ballgame. Before I could answer any more questions, though, Michelle Jones stepped into the spotlight. So I retreated, figuring it was best not to piss her off."

"What did *she* have to say?" Jenny asked resentfully. Hearing the dragon lady had shoved her dad out of the limelight triggered Jenny's soon-to-be-emerging maternal instincts.

"She had the audacity to hint that it was *her* staff who'd uncovered Owen and thereby prevented a last-minute travesty of justice. Michelle Jones then suggested they'd be looking into bringing charges against Charles Graham."

"*Man,*" Tom interrupted. "She's unbelievable."

"Unbelievably savvy," Ethan countered. "With all the publicity swirling around this case, she knew the damage it would do to her reputation when the jury handed down a not-guilty verdict. So instead, she turned it around to make herself out to be Daryl's savior."

"That's alright," responded Matt, chiming in for the first time. "We all know the truth. Besides, the important thing is that Daryl will remain a free man."

"Here, *here,*" Ethan replied, offering up his glass of diet coke for another toast.

"Around this table, good things are happening to good people." Then, lifting his glass even higher, Ethan added, "May this continue."

The tinkling of their glasses sounded like the pealing of bells. Ethan scanned around the table one more time. First, he saw the exhilaration blazing in Daryl's eyes. Then he noted Owen was beaming at Daryl like a proud grandpa. Jenny and Matt were also grinning, and then Ethan observed that Jenny had Matt's hand pressed snuggly to her swollen abdomen to feel his future daughter's kick. Finally, he noticed Tom grinning at Ellen. Ethan watched him lean over to whisper something to her. Ellen immediately nodded, smiled, and then retrieved something from her purse. Like a magician, she slipped the object palmed in one hand over the other.

"Hey folks," Tom abruptly announced, "We've got one more piece of good news."

He patiently waited until he had made eye contact with everyone seated around the table. Then his shoulders rose as he inhaled a deep breath. Tom slowly pivoted toward Ellen, and the corners of his mouth lifted into a crescent. Ellen's eyes glazed over with moisture.

"While you guys were out meeting with Owen last night," Tom solemnly pronounced, "I was with this young woman. We've also made a life-altering decision."

Tom then lifted Ellen's hand to reveal a solitaire ring. The diamond sparkled luminously, reflecting the fire burning next to their table.

PART III

chapter
23

Ethan strode into the East Terminal of Lambert Airport. He wanted to surprise Noah and Amy, who were expecting to be picked up downstairs in the arrivals section. So Ethan parked in the short-term lot, hiked into the main terminal, and positioned himself outside the security area where Noah and Amy would have to pass on their way to pick up their baggage. As a silly joke, he scribbled their names on a cardboard sign and held it up as though meeting a couple of celebrities for the first time.

Ethan studiously examined each face in the parade of weary travelers. Southwest Airlines now occupied almost every gate in the East Terminal. Since American Airlines had swallowed TWA and moved its hub out of the city, Southwest had emerged as the largest air carrier in St. Louis. So Noah and Amy had purposefully booked an early Southwest morning flight since it was one of the few from Portland that was nonstop.

Suddenly, Ethan observed a face that stood out in the crowd. He instantly recognized Noah's trademark grin, flashing snowy-white teeth. Above his smile, unfortunately, was a pair of wearily reddened eyes. Ethan scanned around but saw no sign of Amy. Then, spotting his Dad, Noah broke from the pack about to U-turn down the escalator, held out his arms, and warmly embraced his father. Stepping back, he noticed the cardboard sign bearing his name. Noah's playful smile resurfaced while he slowly shook his head.

"Classic *dad* humor," he snickered.

"Guilty as charged," Ethan confessed. "I couldn't help it." Then, after a brief pause where he glanced around again, he inquired, "Where's your lovely wife?"

"She got called into work at the last minute," Noah answered. "Some kind of emergency. No need to worry, though. Amy was able to rebook another flight. I'll pick her up later this evening."

Ethan stepped back to examine his son. Noah looked leaner and fitter than ever, except for the shadowy crescents beneath his eyes. His visage was like many young men who go west and adopt a healthier lifestyle built around snowboarding, a wholesome diet, and backpacking in the mountains. Knowing he would be going straight to a meeting in downtown Clayton, Noah was already clean-shaven and wearing a button-down shirt that he would soon adorn with a sports jacket and a silk tie.

"You're looking *good*," Ethan exclaimed. "Life in Oregon seems to suit you. Are you sure you're ready to give it up?"

"I'll miss the West Coast," Noah sighed, "But there're more important considerations."

He swallowed hard and looked away. For a moment, Noah appeared hypnotized by the gliding beltway of the escalator. Then he peered up and looked directly at his father.

"I've taken your advice, Dad. *Compromise.* That's what you said, right? St. Louis isn't Oregon; it certainly isn't Haiti, where I could make the biggest difference. But your idea for this city's homeless population is potentially ground-breaking, and I'd like to be a part of it."

Noah paused while a smile spread across his face. Then he added, "Even more important, I think it'll save my marriage. Amy's about ninety percent onboard, and hopefully, she'll be a hundred percent after this weekend."

Ethan nodded and grinned but remained silent. Then, he reached up to Noah's shoulder to guide him toward the escalator.

"Let's go down to get your luggage," he directed.

"I didn't check any," Noah responded. "I'm wearing my nicer clothes. The rest are in this backpack." He turned partially to reveal the rucksack draped over his shoulder.

"Some things will never change," Ethan joked.

Father and son turned away from the escalator, exited the building, and trekked outside to Ethan's parked car. Once they reached the SUV, Noah pulled out his carefully packed coat and tie and then flung his pack with the rest of his clothes into the rear. They cruised down the inner belt five minutes later toward the county seat's crowning skyscrapers. One of those high-rise buildings was the corporate headquarters for Readiness Rent-A-Car.

Ethan had finally managed to secure an appointment with the Readiness Holdings Foundation. In preparation, he had done his homework. Ethan knew this philanthropic arm of the corporation, one of the nation's largest car rental agencies, had already committed more than half a billion dollars to nonprofits. Usually, they preferred to fund them first on the local level and then take them nationally, depending on how much of a difference they made.

Now that Daryl's trial was behind him, Ethan had more time to focus on this potentially life-altering undertaking. He had loosely orchestrated a presentation that included speaking roles for Tom, Daryl, Noah, and even Owen. Ethan, however, would be the presentation's primary conductor.

As they climbed out of the SUV, Ethan received a text from Tom saying that he, Daryl, and Owen were already waiting in the building's lower lobby. After the five men quickly exchanged salutations and introductions, they headed for the nearest elevator.

"You don't think our group's too large?" Tom casually asked once the elevator doors were sealed behind them.

"Maybe," responded Ethan, "But since each of us has a specific role to play in our little enterprise, I thought it best if we each personally explained that role. By the end, they'll appreciate why we included so many people."

"How specific should we get?" Owen inquired. As the team's newest member, he also felt the most out of place.

"They already have plenty of details in the written proposal," replied Ethan. "When it's your turn to speak, just share a few words about what you'll be doing. Two to three minutes should be fine."

The elevator door whooshed open before anyone else could raise a question. For a moment, Ethan regretted not spending more time rehearsing their performance. He had convinced himself, however, that natural and spontaneous was better than slick and polished. In the end, Readiness would hopefully approve the funding because of the merits of their endeavor. So, it probably would not make a big difference if one of Ethan's group stumbled over his words. Besides, he wanted each team member to start taking personal ownership of their specific contribution.

A receptionist ushered them into a conference room, beckoned them to sit in the posh leather chairs encircling an oval table, and offered them coffee and bottles of water. Each member of the team politely declined. Once the receptionist was gone and the troupe comfortably settled, Noah glanced around and whispered, "Judging from the furnishings in this room alone, I'd say Readiness should be more than ready to fund our request."

Daryl nodded and responded, "This is a different universe from where I once lived."

Tom turned toward Ethan and nervously asked, "Do we have a backup plan in case they turn us down?"

"There's a lot of corporate money out there," Ethan answered, "But no, I haven't sent out any other proposals. Not yet, at least. I just haven't had the time."

Ethan glanced around at the concerned faces. Then he added, "Remember, my law firm has already agreed to stake us with enough money to provide basic legal and medical services for at least two years. As you know, I've already purchased a three-story house on Cole Street just west of where the Rams used to play, and we got it for next to nothing. Once upon a time, it was a beautiful, Victorian-style home, but now it's in a rundown area, and, as you might expect, it's been a bit neglected. Until we get corporate sponsorship, though, there'll still be enough money to pay for the site and to employ a skeletal team of legal and medical professionals."

"When you say *team*," Noah asked, "Who're we talking about?"

Ethan leaned back in his chair, sank into its soft leather embrace, and swiveled around to face his son. He briefly caught a stunning view of

Shaw Park in the distance through the floor-to-ceiling window. The sun's rays glittered through the droplets spiraling above the imposing fountain that reigned over a handsomely landscaped pond.

"Good question," Ethan answered. "As you know, I've already spoken to each of you about your individual roles. But I thought the *team* would consist of the following: Noah, you and Amy would make up the medical crew while Tom and I provided legal services. Daryl will head up a volunteer outreach team and be responsible for security. Finally, Owen will handle the facility's maintenance."

Ethan glanced around the table again and noted the relief on their faces. Then, to buoy the team's spirits even more, he added, "Of course, with additional corporate money, we'll be able to spruce up our house a bit more, hire some additional staff, and possibly even provide more services. There's enough space surrounding our site that if the grant's big enough, we might even consider creating a village of about two dozen tiny homes to house some of our clients, at least temporarily."

Ethan paused and observed the appreciative smiles that had replaced the earlier expressions of relief. Then, almost as an afterthought, he added, "Oh, I almost forgot, corporate money or not, we'll also need to hire a reliable receptionist."

"I have a thought on who could fill that position," Daryl interjected with a coy smile.

Ethan chuckled. "Hope? Is she interested?" After a pause, he added, "Of course, it's a bit of a gamble. You haven't known each other for long, and things might get a bit uncomfortable if you two don't work out."

"It *won't* be a problem," Daryl responded assuredly.

"And we're calling this new non-profit 'GUS'?" Noah asked sardonically. "That sounds like the name of one of the clients we'll be servicing. So remind me again, what does GUS stand for?"

Ethan smiled uneasily. "It stands for Gateway Unhoused Services, but I'm open to suggestions. For now, it's just a working name."

Before anyone else could say more, the receptionist popped his head into the room and apologetically announced a delay. He explained that a three-person panel typically hears the larger requests and that a traffic jam on I-70 had delayed one of its members. He asked if this would be a problem with anyone's schedule. After Ethan instantly responded that it would not, the receptionist again offered beverages. This time, Tom and Ethan requested coffee while the others agreed to bottles of water.

"This may work to our advantage," Tom proffered after the receptionist exited the room. "They may be more generous after keeping us waiting."

"It can't hurt," Ethan responded. "Besides, it's given us a chance to review details I should've covered earlier."

"I wish GUS had been around earlier," Daryl moaned. "It would've made my life a lot easier."

Ethan paused to gather his thoughts. During the interlude, Daryl sighed deeply, and Noah looked over at his adopted brother. The two exchanged glances and then smiled. Noah finally broke the silence.

"So, I assume this three-story building you've purchased has room for us to grow?"

"Indeed it does," Ethan replied. "And if we can secure the additional funding from Readiness, our first priority should be to expand the medical program, particularly in terms of vision and dental services."

"That sounds good," Noah agreed, "But as I see it, we should also use some of that extra money to hire well-qualified social workers and employment counselors."

"What about providing meals?" Owen inquired innocuously. "That seems like it should be one of our highest priorities."

"You're absolutely right," answered Ethan. "Fortunately, a Catholic Center a block away has done a wonderful job feeding the unhoused since the 1980s. So . . . , dealing with our clients' hunger is one of the few areas that's not a concern. And frankly," he added ruefully, "The little kitchen in our Victorian is not set up to feed a crowd regularly."

Daryl noisily cleared his throat. He sucked in a deep breath and then deliberately scanned around the table. Seeing that Daryl had something on his mind, the others leaned back in their lavish, over-stuffed chairs and patiently waited for him to speak. Finally, Daryl began to summarize their shared vision.

"If GUS had existed when I was out on the streets, at the very least, I could've had a place to go for basic medical and legal services. And if fully funded, I could've had my teeth checked, my eyes examined, and been provided with a small private place of my own. Moreover, a social worker could have steered me away from the booze, and an employment counselor could have steered me toward a meaningful job. That's about it, right? Because if this comes to pass, I know plenty of people still living on the streets who could significantly benefit from GUS."

Silence once again filtered into the conference room. Each man seated around the semi-circular end of the table exchanged knowing glances and smiles. In the center of the five men, Ethen leaned back in his chair, clasped his fingers behind his head, and grinned like a proud father.

Finally, he stated, "I guess that's our presentation. We just need to repeat this when the panel arrives."

Suddenly, the door opened, and three people marched into the room. The first was an older gentleman with white hair and rimless glasses, who sat at the other end of the table after making cursory apologies and introductions. Two executives, a young white man and an older African-American woman, flanked him on each side. The man in the middle, who introduced himself as Mr. Harvey Nathan, said all three had carefully read the entire GUS proposal from start to finish. Therefore, he requested that the presentation follow a more relaxed Q and A format. Ethan could not have been more delighted.

Lively dialogue consumed the next two hours. The eight individuals appeared to share one vision from start to finish. In the past, the three corporate tycoons might have tacked in a more traditional direction, fearful of being associated with the negative image of the homeless begging on the streets. However, to Ethan's surprise, the times must have changed. Whether it came from a desire to improve their corporate image, genuine altruism, or a combination of these, the minds of the Readiness executives were wide open to playing a significant role in meeting the basic needs of the unhoused.

There was uniform agreement in the epicenter of this corporate affluence that homelessness was endemic in the St. Louis community. GUS, or whatever they named the nonprofit, could be a model for treating this national malady. By the end of their session, Mr. Nathan walked around the room and vigorously shook the hand of each presenter. He assured

Ethan that the GUS proposal would receive thorough and *immediate* attention. Then, he shocked the presenters by stating that Readiness would make their decision within *one* week.

When Ethan appeared visibly stunned by this announcement, Mr. Nathan pronounced homelessness was like a rampant fire. Every delay means more lives irretrievably lost. Families living on the streets of the St. Louis area were a problem needing an immediate fix. Then he singled out Daryl for praise. During the informal presentation, Daryl had eloquently told his story. Mr. Nathan was in awe of how a man who had been homeless for so many years could so abruptly turn his life around with the personal assistance of others. How many others might benefit from a similar approach if it could work so effectively for Daryl Armstrong?

This final comment may have revealed more than intended. But, on the other hand, maybe Mr. Nathan did not care. He effusively liked the GUS proposal, and hopefully, he was one of those rare straight-shooters who did not see a reason to conceal his poker hand. As the five presenters left the conference room, they quietly exchanged energized grins. Once the elevator doors closed behind them, they exploded into cheers and high-fives heard by the panel upstairs.

Down in the lobby, the five huddled briefly to set a date and time for their next meeting. They scheduled it to occur in exactly one week when, hopefully, they would have heard an answer from Readiness about the grant. No one wanted to jinx the upcoming decision, but it was impossible to conceal their shared optimism. If a generous donation came their way, they would quickly have to make several major staffing decisions. There was also vigorous agreement that the meeting should occur inside their Victorian bungalow on Cole Street since they were all anxious to tour their new digs.

Noah was visibly exhausted. As a result, Ethan turned down the offers for lunch and, instead, drove his son home. A half-hour later, Ethan and Noah pulled into the garage, guarding the front of the house. Ethan glanced over at Noah and observed the same nostalgic expression he saw whenever his son returned to the home where he had grown up. Until venturing off to college, this was the only place Noah and Jenny had ever lived, and Ethan liked to believe it mainly harbored good memories for his children.

When they piled out of the SUV, Ethan pressed the button, closing the garage door. Noah glanced around and teasingly asked, "Dad, did you ever think about buying an all-electric vehicle?"

Ethan, who was used to his son's droll humor, immediately understood why the garage had provoked this question.

"You're a funny man, Noah." He glanced around the garage's interior and stated, "You don't need to worry about *that* again. I give you my word." Then, after a brief pause, he added, "And yes, I *am* thinking about going all electric."

Ethan escorted Noah and his small rucksack through the kitchen and into the more spacious family room. Noah glided down the steps into the finished part of the basement without stopping. During his teenage years, his bedroom had been down here where the only windows lined the upper part of one wall. Since the curtains were especially dark, this space, which had become a guest room, was still the best place in the house to take a daytime nap. Within minutes, Ethan could hear buzzing sounds coming from downstairs. Glancing down the gloomy steps, Ethan imagined he was peering into a cave occupied by a hibernating bear.

As Ethan collapsed into his recliner, his cell phone buzzed. He was astonished to hear Mr. Nathan's animated voice on the other end. The Readiness executive did not waste time with pleasantries. Instead, he joyfully informed Ethan that Readiness had already decided to fully fund the GUS nonprofit venture for the next five years. The overall grant even surpassed the amount requested. Ethan knew the presentation had gone well, but still, he was astonished they would approve such a large grant so fast.

Ethan was torn. He eagerly wanted to share the news, but Noah was already sound asleep downstairs, and while he could call Tom or Daryl or Jenny, ideally, he preferred to share such delightful information in person. So, once again, Ethan texted invitations to all the interested parties for a celebratory dinner that night at J. Gilbert's. It would be hours before the party could begin, but Ethan would relish the anticipation that would slowly build throughout the rest of the afternoon.

Sleep was out of the question, so instead, Ethan kicked off his shoes, touched the button to recline as far as possible, and threw his hands behind his head. He closed his eyes for a bit of rest while a broad grin settled across his face.

"Congratulations, my love," Sarah declared.

Ethan's eyelids flashed open. He lifted his head and methodically scanned the room. The tick, tick, tick of the clock's pendulum on the fireplace mantel produced the only sound, and Ethan quickly realized he was utterly alone. Then he understood. Ethan's lips parted into a slight smile as he lay his head back down, reclosed his eyes, and resumed his previous position. Then, in a low voice, Ethan continued the conversation.

"Well, it was a group effort," Ethan replied modestly. "Besides, we got the good news so quickly because they understood the scope of the problem."

"I admire your humility," Sarah countered, "Nevertheless, I'm still proud of you. GUS will make a huge difference in this area. What a legacy it'll leave." Then, after a pause, she added something Ethan did not expect.

"The grant will enable you to hire others to help staff your new non-profit, correct?" Without waiting for a reply, Sarah continued. "Ethan, you've earned the right to work part-time at your age. This grant, my love, has bought you the greatest luxury a man in your position could want."

"More *time?*" Ethan uttered, a bit mystified. "What would I do with the extra time?"

He waited for a response, but none was forthcoming. Finally, Ethan recognized this silence. As a teacher, Sarah had always understood the value of "wait time," the brief quiet moment between the teacher's question and the students' first answer. This was when the real thinking took place.

Ethan's eyes popped open like a couple of jack-in-the-boxes. Finally, he understood what Sarah was telling him. Before he could respond, though, a ding chimed from inside his pocket. Ethan pulled out his cell phone and read the text from his son-in-law. A broad grin creased his face as he scrutinized the screen.

"Oh *my*," he exclaimed. Ethan swiftly flattened the recliner and leaped to his feet. He found a legal pad in his briefcase and scribbled a note to his son.

"Noah, your sister's at St. Luke's having her baby. I'll take an Uber to the hospital to join her and Matt. You can use my car to pick Amy up at the airport and then come join us." While tearing off the page to leave on the kitchen table, Ethan added, "What a day, huh?"

While waiting for the Uber, Ethan sent an apologetic text to the crowd he had just invited for dinner, suggesting they postpone their celebration for 48 hours. He then explained that Readiness had already responded with a generous grant offer and that he would provide further details when he saw everyone at J. Gilbert's. In the interim, Ethan explained, he was headed to the hospital to greet his new granddaughter.

Ethan was staking out his territory in the maternity waiting room thirty minutes later. He chose a few chairs in a corner far from the television screen filled with silent news programming. Except for the TV, the area was serene, with powder blue walls, a large, panoramic painting of aspen trees flaming in fall colors, and tasteful light fixtures dangling from the ceiling. Matt soon appeared, promising to return with updates at least every hour.

Ethan caught up on email for the next two hours, read a little, and then finally played Scrabble on his phone. When Noah arrived, he affirmed that Amy's plane would not touch down until 10:30. Ethan was delighted to have his son's company, though, and treated him to a surprisingly tasty dinner in the hospital cafeteria. After returning to continue their vigil in the waiting room, they spent the rest of the evening drawing up tentative plans for the Readiness grant money. Ethan joyfully noted that his son increasingly spoke as though he planned to play an integral role in this new project.

Since this was Jenny's first baby, everyone knew there was a good chance the infant would probably not be in a rush to enter the world. Matt explained that Jenny's cervix was dilating in ultra-slow motion. Shortly before the ten o'clock news, Noah disappeared for an hour and returned with Amy, who insisted she was too excited to head home to sleep. Besides, to her, it was still two hours earlier. Ethan observed with a slight grin how Amy meticulously absorbed every aspect of the birthing experience.

As the evening wore on, a steady stream of toxic coffee from a coin-operated machine kept the threesome from nodding off. Matt dutifully appeared each hour and, at midnight, explained that the OBGYN had just administered something called Pitocin to induce labor. In addition to the caffeine, the Readiness news provided plenty of fuel to sustain the conversation between Ethan, Noah, and Amy. For hours, they dissected the plans for GUS and how the new non-profit would dramatically impact their lives.

Somewhere after six in the morning, Noah asked whether they should grab a quick bite of breakfast down in the cafeteria. As he considered the question, Ethan observed the pale pink light starting to illuminate the shadowy room. He never noticed the large picture window throughout the evening, but now it was impossible to ignore. Then Ethan witnessed the sliver of a fiery arc ascending on the eastern horizon. Today's sunrise would be spectacular.

"Hey *guys*," someone whispered.

The familiar voice came from behind. Ethan turned to see his son-in-law draped in blue-green scrubs with a mask hanging beneath his chin. Wrinkles were lying across his forehead, and stubble had darkened his hollow cheeks. In between, though, were glassy eyes shining with radiance, and underneath, a wide grin extended across his face.

"Guys," repeated Matt, "The baby was just born. She weighs seven pounds, six ounces and is 20 inches long. Mother and daughter are both doing fine." Then, after a brief pause, Matt turned to face Ethan directly and added, "Before everyone goes in to see them, however, Jenny requested a few minutes alone with Grandpa."

In Ethan's exhausted euphoria, it took a few seconds to register that *he* was Grandpa. Then Matt extended a hand and placed it on Ethan's shoulder to guide his father-in-law down the hallway leading to Jenny's labor room. Both men remained silent for the few seconds it took to coast through the empty corridor. This was one of those rare times when no words could accurately reflect their feelings. Finally, when they arrived at the open doorway, Matt, the taller of the two, peered over his father-in-law's shoulder from behind, smiled at his wife, and nodded to acknowledge their covert plan. When Ethan glanced over his shoulder, Matt had vanished.

"Come on in," Jenny whispered, "Come in and meet your granddaughter."

For a moment, Ethan could not move. He knew a silly grin was draped across his face, and despite his best effort, he could not alter the expression. Ethan was also speechless. His eyes were fixed on the little bundle wrapped in a rose-colored blanket. Ethan could not even blink. Nor could his granddaughter, who was staring right back with round green eyes the size of two pennies. Her cheeks were a reddish pink like someone had applied blush to them. And on top of her head was a mop of buttery hair.

Ethan carefully scrutinized his granddaughter. When he observed her hair, he almost blurted out she looked a little like Harpo Marx but quickly realized that Jenny might not appreciate his humor at that moment. Then he zeroed in on his granddaughter's face. Its oval shape, combined with a pug nose and circular eyes, looked vaguely familiar. Then it hit him.

"She looks just like your mother," Ethan finally managed to murmur. He was doing his best to hold it together, to not burst out into a rainstorm of tears. "Not the hair so much, but I see it in her face." Then, after a brief pause, he announced, "She's the spitting image of your Mom."

The corners of Jenny's mouth curved upward, and her eyes turned watery. Now, it was her turn to be speechless. Jenny waved a hand to beckon her father to come closer, and as Ethan drifted toward the hospital bed, she offered the little bundle up to her dad. Then, acting like they were handling a flask of nitroglycerin, father and daughter cautiously made the exchange. For a moment, Ethan was transfixed as he gazed down at the waiflike face staring back up at him.

"Dad," Jenny finally intoned, "I'd like you to meet someone special. This is my daughter. *Your* granddaughter. Her name is Sarah."

chapter

24

Ethan gazed off hypnotically into the distance. He was propped up on his elbow, laying sideways on a blanket spread broadly across the coppery sand. Directly beneath him, the gentle April winds rustled the delicate curls of his 13-month-old granddaughter. She was sound asleep, lost in the enigmatic dreams of a toddler taking her afternoon nap. Little Sarah lay on her back, occasionally wiggling and extending her plump arms.

When Ethan heard on the news that the day's spring conditions would be ideal and wildflowers would be bursting with color, he immediately prepared a picnic lunch, packed Sarah's diaper bag, and crammed her stroller into the crowded rear of his SUV. He then spent the morning steering her through the woods and pushing her back and forth in the playground's bucket swing. Sarah had been walking for a few months and relished waddling around on the playground's rubbery surface. Naturally, therefore, now that she had eaten her lunch, his granddaughter was thoroughly exhausted.

A steady drone came from behind, the perfect white noise to blanket a baby's siesta. Heavy rains the day before had turned Creve Coeur Falls into a torrent. The patter of water slapping the boulders, accompanied by the swishing of the nearby stream racing toward the lake, drowned all other sounds, including the banter of the occasional pedestrians on the nearby bike path. For the most part, Ethan was alone with his thoughts.

He looked up to admire the scenery across the lake. An emerald green had recently invaded the trees lining the opposite shore, heralding the coming of spring. White and pink specks dotted the dogwood branches scattered along the horizon. A red-tailed hawk hovered over the forest canopy, where many of the higher limbs were still barren from the blistery winds of winter. Ethan noted how the hawk rode the warm breeze, remaining aloft without flapping its wings. The sun's rays illuminated the pastoral scene but would suddenly vanish with the passing of a feathery cloud. It reminded Ethan of when little Sarah would repeatedly pull the on-and-off chain of a lamp switch, something she loved to do back in Ethan's den.

He looked down at his granddaughter to study her sublime features. Sarah's chest see-sawed up and down, her breathing as steady as a clock. Ethan gently brushed aside a few strands of hair dancing across her forehead to enjoy a better view. In his mind, he could see the youthful face of his wife, whose ashes lay beneath the lapping waves just a few yards away. Even the baby's rapidly emerging personality reminded Ethan of her namesake. She could be ferociously stubborn but, at the same time, gentle and loving. Like her grandmother, little Sarah possessed unlimited energy and passion. She was spunky, full of fire.

For now, though, Little Sarah was out cold. Ethan had been waiting a long time for this day. Unfortunately, his numerous responsibilities getting GUS off the ground, combined with the increasing amount of time he was spending with his granddaughter, had kept Ethan from finding the chance to engage in a lengthy dialogue with Sarah. There had been brief conversations in the shower or while driving, but these could never last more than a few minutes. Ethan desired to bring his wife up to speed on everything that had occurred over the last several months. Plus, he missed hearing her voice. For decades, chatting with Sarah over the dinner table had frequently been the highlight of Ethan's day.

For a long time now, Ethan had been craving the first balmy day of spring. He longed to lie on a blanket near where he had spread Sarah's ashes and engage in an unhurried conversation with his deceased wife. To accomplish this goal, Ethan planned to exhaust the little demon all morning so she would take an unusually long nap in the afternoon. As he examined the small body asleep next to him, Ethan was satisfied that his plan had worked to perfection.

Ethan shut his eyes and immediately called to his wife as though participating in a seance. Then, after a moment, he saw her face. Since Ethan's fantasies involved intermingling his memories of Sarah, he always chose the image of how she appeared just prior to the onset of the illness. Her smile was timeless, though, and even on her worst days, there had been a sparkle in her eyes. Today, Sarah was more stunning than ever.

"Ah, Sarah," Ethan intoned, "It's been almost two years since we spread your ashes in this lake. But I still think about you every *single* day."

Ethan did not wait long before hearing a response.

"You're looking good, my love. You look happy. Fulfilled might be a better word. "

Sarah's voice sounded the same. Even though it had been a while since they last spoke, these internal conversations had become as natural as breathing. Ethan did not like to think about the metaphysical nature of the experience. Was he chatting with his wife's apparition? More likely, he was entertaining a fantasy within his imagination. It did not matter.

"Do I?" replied Ethan. "If so, a big reason for my happiness is lying right beside me."

Ethan lay flat on his back and clasped his hands behind his head. To the outside world, he appeared to be napping next to his slumbering granddaughter. Inside, though, he was conversing with his beloved.

"I see that," Sarah responded with adoration. "Ethan, she is *so* beautiful."

"And yet, she's a big reason I haven't had more time for our conversations."

Inside his mind, Ethan winked at his wife and flashed her a roguish grin. "However, this morning, I spent hours tiring the little bugger out so she'd take a long nap after lunch. That way, we could have more time to catch up on everything that's been going on lately."

"*Smart,*" Sarah exclaimed. "Still, we'd better get started. Toddlers' naps can be totally unpredictable."

"Okay, for starters," answered Ethan, "I need to share some bad news." Without waiting for a response, Ethan pressed on. "My darling, your father recently passed away. We got the call from Brookdale a few

weeks ago. They said James passed quietly in his sleep. As per his instructions, we had him buried next to your mother. It was a nice little
ceremony. Most of his friends are long gone, but there was a good family
turnout. Both of your kids had charming stories to share about James.
And as you might guess, I repeated the anecdote about when James used
the Heimlich Maneuver to save my life. ”

From the sallow expression on his wife's face, Ethan could tell Sarah
did not already know about her father. Once again, he could not dis-
cern whether this was real or how he would imagine her response. In his
mind, Ethan saw his wife raise a hand over her mouth, but she remained
silent. Ethan elected to continue.

"Ever since your passing, I've stopped by at least once a week to see
James. So have your children. We purposefully visited him separately so
he could see a different family member practically every other day. Of
course, he never responded. Nonetheless, we dropped by faithfully until
the end. Each of us regularly participated in a one-way conversation.
We'd give him updates on the latest news on the off chance that maybe
he understood some of what we were saying."

Sarah quietly nodded as tears streamed down both cheeks. She continued to cover her mouth, but her moist eyes reflected gratitude.

"I don't know how this works," Ethan whispered, "But maybe at
some point, you'll be able to reunite with your dad." Then, after a pause,
he added, "For what it's worth, James lived a long time, and up until the
last few years, it was a fulfilling life. When his time came, Sarah, he went
peacefully in his sleep."

Sarah lowered her hand enough for her husband to see a faint smile.
"That's good to hear, my love. And I appreciate everything you and the
kids did for him." Then, after a pause, she added, "From what I remember about his years in Brookdale, Dad's Alzheimer's had reached the point
where his final passing may've been for the best."

"I didn't want to sound insensitive," Ethan echoed, "But I was thinking the same thing. I always admired James's journey, but it might've
been better had it ended sooner."

Ethan appeared to be asleep outwardly, but he could still visualize his
wife inside his mind. Sarah reticently nodded in agreement but seemed

to stare off into the distance. Ethan thought he understood the reason behind her glum expression.

"I'm sorry, my love," Ethan murmured. Then he added, "Sarah, I'll just say it - *unlike* your dad, your journey ended way too early."

Ethan reached up to wipe away the moisture gathering in the corners of his eyes. He kept them tightly sealed, afraid that if he opened them, the magic would end, and Sarah would suddenly vanish.

"You're right," Sarah replied, "My journey *did* end too early. And I'll admit it; I feel cheated. I'll never take any more road trips into the mountains. I'll never be able to spend time with our children. I'll never be able to make a difference working with the unhoused. And I'll never be able to hug that little bundle of joy lying right next to you."

Ethan was dumbfounded. He instantly felt a wave of melancholy sweep over him. Sarah's reaction was not just the result of an unintended faux pas in his choice of words; this was a more deep-seated acrimony. Was Sarah envious? Resentful? She had just cited four experiences that had recently enriched *his* life. Ethan was at a loss for words. Before he could speak, though, Sarah mollified her bitterness.

"I'm sorry, Ethan. I didn't mean to sound so harsh."

"No, no," Ethan interrupted, "You have *every* right to be angry."

"No, I *don't*," Sarah countered. "But I notice that you keep referring to life as a 'journey.' I don't remember hearing you using this metaphor before. Where's it coming from?"

A wisp of a smile crossed Ethan's face at the thought of the bearded giant in the mountains. What did he say that day? Ethan studied his wife's expectant face a bit longer before finally replying.

"There was a wise man I met in the Tetons not long ago who strenuously maintained that life's a *journey*. More and more, Sarah, I've come to believe it's true. His name was John Cassidy, and he did not believe in God or an afterlife. Instead, he emphasized that one should live every day to its fullest. John said we get just one chance, and there shouldn't be any regrets when one nears the end. That way, when lying on your deathbed one day, you can look back at your journey and smile."

"No disrespect to your mountain friend, Ethan, but that sounds like a homespun philosophy you can probably find in the self-help section of any bookstore."

"Well, that's probably *true*," Ethan agreed, "But I've given the matter a lot of thought, and there's something appealing about this existential perspective. I mean, think about it, Sarah. There's zero consciousness before you're born, and when life ends, you go back to . . ."

"*Careful*," Sarah interrupted.

Silence ensued as Ethan and his deceased wife shared an awkward moment. What should he say? Ethan was far from convinced that Sarah's spirit had lived on beyond her death. She resided only in his imagination, right? Yet, here she was, fully engaging in their conversation. Finally, it was Sarah who broke the tension with a playful grin.

"Oh, come on, Ethan, I'm only joking. We both know that I only live on within the memory of those I've left behind. So, go ahead and finish telling me about this guru in the Tetons."

Ethan breathed a sigh of relief. "Well, assuming people don't exist before conception or after they die, and I believe this to be true since there's no evidence to the contrary, the only thing that truly matters is what one does in between. How one navigates through their journey."

"Alright," Sarah agreed, "That sounds like a good map to follow, provided you also create a moral compass to guide you on your journey. But let's play out your buddy's metaphor a little further. Yes, life's a journey, and yes, you should always live it to its fullest. But, sometimes . . ."

Sarah hesitated. Ethan cocked his head in puzzlement but patiently waited for his wife to resume.

"But," Sarah finally continued, "Sometimes, regrettably, there are limits to one's free will. And these limits don't allow for the unexpected twists and turns you might encounter on your journey."

"Like cancer," Ethan emphatically pronounced.

"Yes, like cancer," Sarah repeated. "But I didn't mention your road trip or our granddaughter to make you feel bad. On the contrary, Ethan, I brought them up to remind you that you should *not* take these things for granted. Instead, you should arise each morning feeling thankful for everything good in your life."

For a moment, a stillness reigned inside Ethan's head. The sun continued its hide-and-seek game behind the clouds, a warm breeze blew steadily from across the lake, and little Sarah carried on her nap beside her Papa. Inside Ethan's head, however, he swiftly tried to sort through what his wife had just said. Sarah was unquestionably correct. John Cassidy had preached that one should live life to its fullest, but now, Sarah reinforced this position by reminding Ethan to cherish what he already had. Finally, it was Sarah who broke the silence.

"Now, my love, tell me about *your* journey. I know you almost ended it two years ago. Unfortunately, while grieving for me, you came close to concluding your journey far too soon. Thank goodness Jenny and Matt returned in time to prevent that."

"Yes," Ethan pronounced, "I agree. Whole-heartedly." After a brief pause, he added, "I'm not sure how, but don't you already know everything that's happened to me over the past two years?"

"Mostly," answered Sarah with a snicker. "But I'd still like to hear it again."

"Alright," Ethan responded. "Let's see, where should I start? Do you know about GUS?"

"The mechanic who used to maintain our cars?"

As Ethan chuckled inside his mind, a smile unknowingly spread across his face. He shook his head even though he knew Sarah was teasing.

"No, I'm talking about the nonprofit we created last year to provide services for the homeless. They're now increasingly referred to as the unhoused. GUS stands for Gateway Unhoused Services. We planned to come up with a better name, but this one stuck. We then secured a multi-million dollar grant, so GUS can now provide a wide range of services, including legal, medical, dental, psychological, and occupational. It also maintains a village of tiny homes to serve as temporary housing for anyone living on the streets."

"I like the name," Sarah replied. "It's simple and easy to remember."

"And it's doing quite well," Ethan added. "Your son and daughter-in-law staff the medical clinic that's performing miracles. Although, we need to get them some help."

"Yes," Sarah responded, "I'd imagine they're flooded with patients."

"That's part of it, but there's *another* reason."

Ethan knew there was a time limit with his granddaughter lying next to him, and there was still much to cover. If he wanted to get through his checklist to update Sarah fully, he would need a find ways to segue from one topic to another more efficiently.

"Oh my *goodness*," Sarah interrupted. "Amy's pregnant?"

"I see your radar's still in good working order," Ethan uttered. "Yes, Amy's due in early August. And this one's going to be a boy!" After a brief pause, he added, "For now, though, we still need to work out the details of their maternity and paternity leave."

"Oh, *Ethan*," Sarah exclaimed, "I could care less about those details. Why didn't you tell me this from the start? That's *so* exciting. Little Sarah's going to have a cousin?" Then, after a pause, she added, "And we're going to have our first grandson."

Ethan blindly reached over until his hand brushed against the top of little Sarah's head. He softly patted her hair to confirm the toddler was still beside him. Then, like pressing a button, Papa's touch triggered some movement. Little Sarah rolled onto her side, flung one fleshy arm over Ethan's torso, and maneuvered closer to her grandfather. With his eyes closed, Ethan automatically extended his arm to stroke his granddaughter's hair like a lovable puppy. His eyes remained shut, but a smile creased his face.

"And pretty soon," Ethan announced, "We may have *more* than two grandchildren. I hear Jenny and Matt are working on giving this one a little brother or sister."

"Ah, Ethan . . . ," Sarah purred. The beaming smile draped across her face was enough to complete her sentence.

"And ours is not the only family that's growing," Ethan exclaimed.

Sarah's eyes widened as she silently waited for her husband to continue.

"For starters, I attended a wedding last weekend," Ethan proclaimed. "Actually, I was *in* the wedding."

"Who got married?"

"Tom," answered Ethan. "He married Ellen, the attorney who took my place at the firm."

"I don't know, Ellen," Sarah replied. "Do you like her?"

"Yes, I *really* do," answered Ethan unequivocally. "She's a bit younger than Tom, but they're an ideal match. Of course, they've only been together for about a year, but if you saw them, you'd think they were one of those old couples who'd been blissfully married for decades."

"I see," Sarah confirmed, waiting for Ethan to resume.

"Keith originally hired Ellen to take my clients while I traveled out west. As it turned out, she did a terrific job. Recently, Ellen made partner, and the scuttlebutt is that if Keith ever retires, which is hard to imagine, Ellen will take over the firm."

"And you were in their wedding?" Sarah inquired. "Did Tom ask you to be his best man? I know that's something you'd like."

"No," Ethan replied. "Since Ellen's parents are both deceased, they asked me to walk her down the aisle, you know, to give her away."

Sarah covered her mouth to stifle her laughter. Then, finally, she lowered her hand and unabashedly cackled. Ethan flashed an embarrassed smile but remained quiet.

"That's *sweet*, Ethan. I figured you'd only play that role when we walked Jenny down the aisle. Besides," she added, "I thought you were going to tell me you got the online credentials to perform their ceremony." A smile reappeared on her face.

"No," Ethan replied, "Owen volunteered for that duty."

"Owen?" asked Sarah. "*Who's* Owen? And why is this starting to sound like Abbott and Costello's *Who's On First* routine?"

Ethan grinned at the connection Sarah had just made. "On the St. Louis team, we have Who's on first, What's on second, I Don't Know on third . . ." The hilarious confusion generated by these nicknames in the iconic comedy skit caused Sarah and Ethan to laugh many times throughout their marriage.

"Owen also works for GUS," Ethan continued. "He's responsible for the building where we all work. Since it's an aging structure, he's slowly remodeling the place. It's a huge undertaking. You should see it, Sarah. You'd be impressed by what he's done."

"I see," Sarah affirmed, "But Owen must be more than just a GUS employee if Tom and Ellen wanted him to perform their wedding ceremony."

"Oh *yeah*," Ethan proclaimed, "I forgot to tell you about Owen. He was the man who came forward during the darkest hours of Daryl's trial.

As it turned out, Owen saw everything that happened the night of Daryl's arrest, but like many people who witnessed a serious felony, Owen was afraid to come forward. When he finally did, though, his deposition was so convincing the prosecutor dropped all the charges. She didn't want to lose, so she pulled the case before it could ever go before the jury."

Sarah arched her eyebrows upward. "Hmmm," she exclaimed. "That's quite impressive. It sounds like he came through as Daryl's last-minute hero. So I assume you like Owen?"

"Yes, I *do* like him," Ethan replied fervently. "He cut things a bit close with his timing, but when it was all over, Owen proved to be the star of the trial. Since then, we've learned he's lived a rather sad and lonely life. However, Owen has truly blossomed since joining our little family."

"Okay," Sarah stated, "So let's go back to the wedding. You walked Ellen down the aisle, and Owen performed the ceremony. So, *who* was Tom's best man?"

"Daryl," Ethan answered with a hint of filial pride.

"*Daryl?* I knew you'd agreed to defend Daryl to make up for the past. Is there more I don't know?"

"Yes," replied Ethan, "There's a *whole* lot more."

Ethan paused momentarily. He was relishing this lively banter with his deceased wife. It was probably just a fantasy, and some might fear Ethan was losing his grip on reality. But did it matter? For now, it reminded him of the countless conversations he had shared with Sarah for over forty years. What harm would it do if Ethan continued conversing with her memory? He picked up right where he had left off.

"Tom originally moved to St. Louis to help with Daryl's defense. Once he did, the two of them hit it off right away. Tom treated Daryl like he was the kid's protective older brother. They were roomies in our house for a while, and each supported the other when they decided to give up drinking."

"Alright," Sarah responded curiously, "I get it. So that explains why Tom would choose Daryl as the best man in his wedding. But what about *your* relationship with Daryl? Where does that currently stand?"

Ethan sighed. Immediately afterward, he could hear his grand-daughter, curled up in the crux of his arm, do the same. Ethan again wondered if Sarah knew what he was about to say. If not, this would be momentous news.

"I recently adopted Daryl. You'd wanted that decades ago, and I should've listened to you back then. Well, as they say, better late than never."

Sarah's eyes doubled in size, and then a panoramic smile swept across her face.

"Ethan, that's wonderful news. *Good* for you!"

"There's nothing to it, really," Ethan asserted modestly. "Daryl's a likable kid, and he's quickly ingrained himself within our family. I was also proud of how fast Jenny and Noah welcomed him as their brother."

"I'm not surprised," Sarah commented.

"And," Ethan added, "It looks like the family's still growing."

"Is someone *else* pregnant?" Sarah asked incredulously.

"No," Ethan quickly responded, "But someone else will soon be getting married."

He paused to build suspense, something he enjoyed doing throughout their marriage. "It's Daryl," he finally blurted. "During his trial, Daryl met Hope, a young waitress at a downtown restaurant. Since this was when Owen had just come forward, Daryl thought her name was so fitting. I believe it was love at first sight for both of them. They've been joined at the hip ever since."

"Do you like *her*?" Sarah inquired.

"Yes, *very* much," Ethan instantly answered. "She's a sweet girl, and she's got bigger ambitions with her life than waiting tables. We recently hired Hope as the receptionist down at GUS, and since Daryl has several responsibilities of his own at the nonprofit, they get to work together every day. Watching them reminds me of us forty years ago.

Ethan paused to gather his thoughts. Then, he added, "For Daryl, this is the first time he's been in love since losing his wife in a tragic car accident. You know, that's what altered his journey's path toward alcoholism and homelessness, right?"

Sarah sighed, ignoring her husband's question. Then, she followed up with one of her own. "So Hope makes Daryl happy?"

"I've never seen him happier," Ethan answered. "Daryl's in a good place right now, Sarah. During the day, he plays a vital role at GUS, reaching out to the same people with whom he once shared the streets. At night, Daryl's taking graduate classes at UMSL. He's currently working on a master's degree in social work. And Daryl spends every free moment of his limited time with Hope. And get this: at the rehearsal dinner the night before Tom's wedding, Daryl ended his best man's toast by getting down on one knee and proposing to Hope. It brought tears to almost everyone's eyes."

"*Wow*," exclaimed Sarah. "I would've thought that might upstage Tom and Ellen a bit since it was their rehearsal dinner."

"Normally, *yes*," Ethan countered, "But Daryl had already cleared his plan with Tom and Ellen. Moreover, after Hope had accepted the proposal and was already flaunting her ring, Daryl turned toward Tom and asked if he would be *his* best man. As I said, they've become like brothers."

Ethan could see the gears spinning inside Sarah's head for a moment. She shook her head in disbelief while a grin spread across her face. Finally, she peered squarely at her husband.

"So let me see if I've got this straight," Sarah pronounced, "You're now at the center of an expanding circle of family and close friends. There's Jenny and Matt, who are currently working on having their second child. There's Noah and Amy, who recently moved back to St. Louis and will soon have their first baby. There's Daryl, whom you've adopted as our third child and who recently became engaged to Hope. There's Tom and Ellen, close friends and coworkers, who recently married each other. And then there's someone named Owen, who also recently joined the circle. Is that about it? Because I've got to tell you, Ethan, remembering who's on first was much easier."

"Yes," replied Ethan with admiration. "You got it!"

"And most of these people," Sarah added, "Work with a nonprofit that provides vital services for the unhoused. Something called GUS."

"Not *all* of them," Ethan countered. "Ellen helps out at times, but she still works primarily in my old firm. And Jenny and Matt, of course, still have their same old jobs."

"You've always been such a stickler for details," Sarah joked. Then, after a pause, she added, "Still, Ethan, I'm *so* proud of you. Considering you almost gave up two years ago, that's quite a rebound."

Ethan almost opened his eyes. He knew this might end the magic, like unplugging a TV during the critical moment of a film. Still, what was going on here? Was he using Sarah's memory to stroke his ego? Or had he uncorked a wormhole into the afterlife to somehow converse with his actual wife? He softly rubbed his granddaughter's forehead while pondering this question.

Finally, he settled on an answer that made sense. When Sarah was alive, she generously praised people for doing the right thing. This practice came as second nature to someone who spent a career teaching adolescents. Sarah would even do this at times with Ethan, which was why he often told people that his wife brought out the best in him. So, after forty years of marriage, he figured he knew his wife well enough to accurately conjure up the words she would say inside his head. Of course, Ethan would never be sure if this explanation was accurate, but it would have to do for now.

"Thank you, Sarah," Ethan finally murmured. "Whether that's something you said or just the words I'd imagine you'd say, I'm still grateful to hear them." Ethan paused briefly before continuing. "Sarah, I've loved you every moment since our first date in Breckenridge Hills. And that'll *never* change. So much of that comes out of respect. I have more respect for you than anyone I've ever known. That's why your praise means so much."

"Oh, *go* on," Sarah proclaimed in the exaggerated tone she frequently used whenever Ethan complimented her.

Quiet then ensued while Ethan and Sarah gazed at each other with the same starry eyes that always highlighted their most loving moments. Meanwhile, Ethan could feel a slight movement on his side. He knew this was the dance his granddaughter performed shortly before waking from her nap. Finally, Sarah broke the silence.

"And what about *you*, my love? Are you as happy as the rest of the clan?"

Ethan inhaled deeply. The commotion on his side temporarily lessened, giving him a reprieve to wrap up his internal conversation.

"Sarah, I suppose I'm as happy as a widower can be. Loving family members and friends surround me, and you're right; I shouldn't take any of them for granted. But talking to you right now is still the highlight of my life."

"And will this be enough? Can I feel confident you'll live a full life? That your journey is far from over?"

Ethan nodded. He could feel his head move up and down on the blanket.

"You know Ethan," Sarah added, "I don't expect you to spend the rest of your life alone. So it's fine if you'd like to remarry. I want you to be *happy*, my love."

Ethan reached up to wipe away a tear gliding down his face. This time, he could feel his head vigorously shaking back and forth. Finally, he responded.

"I don't intend all my friends to be men, but I'm still not ready to enter the dating pool. And I'll certainly never get married again. As far as I'm concerned, Sarah, you were the one true love of my life. There'll never be another."

Ethan suddenly felt a little arm press the side of his torso. Then he heard the faint voice in his ear—"Papa?"

A smile wrinkled Ethan's face. He knew the time had come to open his eyes and awaken. He momentarily recalled when Noah or Jenny, as toddlers, would burst into the room, forcing him to end a telephone conversation prematurely. How often did he tell the person on the other end that he'd have to call them back later?

"Sarah, my love, I'm going to have to go. But I'll be back, and we can continue this on another day." Then, almost as an afterthought, he added, "Oh, one other thing I neglected to tell you. I've taken your advice, Sarah, about how to spend my time. I recently arranged to only work at GUS two days a week. We've hired another full-time attorney to partner with Tom, and an unlimited number of law school students want to help out as volunteers."

"*Really*," responded Sarah. "Then what will you do when you're not working downtown?"

The answer to Sarah's question was lying right beside him. Ethan suddenly opened his eyes and found himself staring into the mischievous green eyes of his granddaughter.

About the Author

Joe Regenbogen taught high school history for 40 years. He began in the Ninth Ward of New Orleans in 1979, where two years later, he was named runner-up for New Orleans teacher-of-the-year. After moving to St. Louis in 1984, he continued to teach for the Parkway School District in the western suburbs of St. Louis. In the final years of his teaching career, Joe taught in a unique program for the exceptionally gifted, where his students ended their eighth-grade year by taking the AP exam in American History.

As Joe approached his retirement from teaching, he took up writing as a second career. To date, he has published five books. The first two, *Questioning History* and *Relearning History* were intended to deepen his students' understanding of the past beyond the classroom. Joe's third book, *The Boys of Brookdale*, told the stories of World War Two veterans who all lived their final years in the same senior living facility where Joe's father resided. His next book, *Making a Difference*, recounted the story of Irl Solomon and his 38-year teaching career in East St. Louis, Illinois, one of the most challenging school districts in the nation. Joe's most recent book, *Longs Peak*, is a novel.

Joe currently lives with Dana, his wife of 44 years, in the same home where they raised their two children, both of whom became attorneys. At present, Joe continues to travel and write. Joe and Dana also provide full-time daycare for Ava and Delaney, their two granddaughters.

www.ingramcontent.com/pod-product-compliance
Lightning Source LLC
Chambersburg PA
CBHW030358020726
47493CB00003B/864